THE SALT ROADS

Also by Nalo Hopkinson
Brown Girl in the Ring
Midnight Robber
Skin Folk

Edited by Nalo Hopkinson
Mojo: Conjure Stories
Whispers from the Cotton Tree Root: Caribbean Fabulist Fiction

THE SALT ROADS

NALO HOPKINSON

WARNER BOOKS

An AOL Time Warner Company

Copyright © 2003 by Nalo Hopkinson

Excerpts from the poem "The Balcony" are reprinted from *The Poems and Prose Poems of Charles Baudelaire*, ed. James Huneker. New York: Brentano's, 1919.

Excerpts from the letters of Charles Baudelaire and Apollonie Sabatier adapted from *The Letters of Baudelaire*, translated by Arthur Symons. New York: Albert & Charles Boni, 1927.

Translation of "Le Serpent qui danse" (The Snake That Dances) by Patrick Barnard, © 2003, Canada. Used with permission of the translator.

Warner Books, Inc., 1271 Avenue of the Americas, New York, NY 10020

Visit our Web site at www.twbookmark.com

 An AOL Time Warner Company

Printed in the United States of America

First Printing: November 2003
10   9   8   7   6   5   4   3   2   1

Library of Congress Cataloging-in-Publication Data

Hopkinson, Nalo.
    The salt roads / Nalo Hopkinson.
      p. cm.
    ISBN 0-446-53302-5
     1. Women—Caribbean Area—Fiction.   2. Mary, of Egypt, Saint—Fiction.   3. Spirit possession—Fiction.   4. Caribbean Area—Fiction.   5. Duval, Jeanne—Fiction.   6. Time travel—Fiction.   7. Prostitutes—Fiction.   8. Goddesses—Fiction.   9. France—Fiction.   10. Egypt—Fiction.   I. Title

PR9199.3.H5927S25 2003
813'.54—dc21

2003048580

BEAT . . . ,

It went in white, but it will come out a mulatto in a few months' time, yes?"

I was right; the oven of Georgine's belly was swelling up nice with the white man's loaf it was cooking to brown. I cackled at my own joke like the old woman I was becoming, stretched my neck a little to ease its soreness. A deep breath brought me salt-smelling air, blowing up from the cliffs at the foot of the plantation. Good to get away for a few minutes from stooping over sugar cane. Sixteen hours each day they had us working to bring the sugar in, and old Cuba the driveress would still push the first gang to pluck weeds sometimes into the deep of the night.

Georgine just stared at me in fear, never mind it was she had brought herself to me by her own will. Then she whispered, "No, Auntie, not just mulatto. I'm griffonne, my mother was sacatra. The baby will be marabou."

Eh. I ignored her, poked again at her belly, at her lolling on the flour bags that made my bed on the floor of my hut; she got to plant her behind in a softer bed nowadays—even had a mattress, I bet. I wondered if the ticks didn't bite her when she put her head on Mister Pierre's straw-stuffed pillows.

I knew Georgine's type. Made her road by lying down. Lie down with dog, get up with fleas, they say. Silly wench, with her caramel skin. Acting the lady because she worked in the great house, washing white people's stained sheets till her fingers cracked and bled from the soap.

Free-coloured Philomise had been making eyes at her; well-off brown man with his own coffee plantation and plenty slaves to work it, but no, our master didn't want a coloured to have her. Gave her instead to that yeasty-smelling carpenter imported to San Domingue—him from some backwards village in the ass end of France. And Georgine was puffing herself up now she had a white man, never mind he didn't have two coins to rub together.

True, she had cause maybe to be happy. Pierre was looking after her well. She might get two-three free children out of it too, and if she gave him enough boys, her Pierre might release her from slavery finally. When she was old.

But now she needed tending, and now that that flat-behind raw dough boy they called the plantation surgeon was too shy to even lay his hands on her belly to feel the baby, who did she come to? She didn't trust him. She wasn't an entire fool. Instead, she had found her high-coloured self to my hut.

And her carpenter had come with her too. Got time off from mending the wain carts as they burst under the weight of the cane they were carrying to the factory. Waiting outside, he was; screwing his hat into shreds between his big paws. Frightened I would poison his Georgine, his goods. All the backra round these parts were frightened of poison nowadays. Black people's poison was showing up in the food and bad ouanga in their beds. But Mister Pierre was more frightened to see woman's business. So outside he stayed, saying it was more decent.

Eh. What decent could mean to we with black blood? Who ever feared for my decency?

Niger woman spoiled fine as any lady. She'd best watch herself. Slightest thing she did that mispleased that backra man, he'd pack her off, out of his little house.

I went to turn up the hem of Georgine's dress. She gasped, flinched. I sighed. "Can't examine you with all this cloth in the way."

She considered, set her mouth firmly. "Proceed, then."

Proceed. Stupid wench. Pampered pet parrot, talking with backra's tongue.

I touched her dress again. A soft cotton hand-me-down from some backra's wife, and dyed a yellow pale like ripe guavas. The fabric caught on the calluses of my hands. I ruched it up around her waist, exposed her smooth legs, her pouting belly, her bouboun lips covered in black crinkly hair. She was even paler where the sun didn't touch her. Bleached negress.

Oh, but she was thin! Meager like the chickens scratching in the yard outside. "Eh," I muttered, on purpose as though my patient wasn't there, "would think the hair on the little bòbòt would be pale like the skin."

Georgine gave a small sound, made to push the dress back down with her hands, stopped. Good.

The clean salt scent of Georgine's body came up in my nose, mixed with sweet rosewater. Me, I smelled of sweat. Her thigh under my fingers was velvet smooth like my baby's, long lost. My body was dry wood after years of work; the brand that had got infected and nearly killed me tunnelled a ropy knot on my thigh. Her yellow dress reflected the sun back in its own eye. My one frock was a colourless calico cut from a flour sack, washed a thousand times, that Tipingee had darned for me over and over again, for my hands were impatient with needles, unless it was to sew up a wound. Georgine's skin was steamed milk with a splash of high mountain coffee. Me, the colour of dirt in the canefields.

I poked and prodded at Georgine's belly while she tried not to squirm. I took my time, in no hurry to get back to the fields. My back was thanking me for having a rest. "When did you get pregnant?"

"I don't know, Auntie," she said in a small voice. Know-nothing girl child.

"When did your courses stop?" I asked, trying another way to get the answer from her.

"Stop? They only started"— she was frowning, looking up into the ceiling while she did her figuring—"ten months ago. My first blood. Then I bled three times, three months, then pretty soon I started puking a lot, then I realised the bleeding had stopped. I thought it was going away and I was glad, for I didn't like the pain and the blood. I felt like the whole thing was only fatiguing me. When the bleeding came every month, I didn't have the strength to lift the washing down to the river. Marthe beat me one day, told me I was too lazy. So I was glad when the bleeding stopped, yes? It's Marie-Claire who told me I was pregnant." Her face got red and she smiled, glancing down. "For Pierre."

Seven months, maybe more. But the child under my hands was too small for a seven-month baby. "How are you feeling?"

"I'm tired all the time, matant. Even more than when I used to get my courses."

I went and looked under her eyelids. Her colour was poor. Her blood was thin. "You and Pierre are eating good?"

"Yes, matant! I'm keeping a nice garden Sundays when I have the day off. I'm growing cassava and pumpkin, plenty pumpkin. Pierre says I don't have to take none of it to market, for Master's paying him a wage we can both live on, if we're careful. Pierre says—"

"Pierre says, Marie-Claire says. I'm asking about you, not about them."

She looked chastened. "Yes, matant. What should I do, then?"

Back in my home, back in the kingdom of Dahomey, every Allada girl child and woman would know what to do if a woman wasn't strong enough to carry her baby. Eat foods to strengthen the blood. "You have beets in your garden?"

"No, matant. I should grow some?"

"Yes. I wish if you could get liver too."

"I get meat sometimes."

Eh. Maybe she thought her Pierre was a fine hunter as well as all his other talents? "How do you mean, meat?"

"Sometimes Pierre gets meat left over after the great house is finished eating dinner."

"Don't eat that meat!"

She jumped, startled to hear me speak so strong.

5

"No, child," I said, "I don't mean nothing by it. Just that white people don't know about food. Plenty times their meat is spoiled and they're still eating it."

"Oh. It tastes nice, though. Boeuf au jus with red wine sauce."

Little bit of girl was making airs that she got to eat great house food. "You can't stay weak and tired like this and have a baby."

"Oh," she said fearfully. "I'm going to die?"

Pride made me speak to her as I did to other women. "You've ever seen an African live more than ten years once he set foot on this island?"

Georgine shook her head no. Too right. Sickness and torture killed most of us on the journey across the bitter water, then the backra worked the rest of us to death when we got here. Plenty more were coming on the ships to replace us.

"Well, I've been here twelve years. Was apprentice to my mid-wife mother before I came. That's why they made me doctress. Don't you worry. I've taken dozens of babies on this island live from their mothers' wombs and put them in their mothers' arms."

She smiled. So I didn't tell her how many of those mothers had died of fever soon afterwards. Didn't tell how many of the babies had got the lockjaw, never breathed again. Didn't talk of my little dead one, so many years ago. Returned beneath the water to the spirits before his ninth night, so he had never really existed. No name for him. Except in my head. He was so beautiful, I called him Ehioze, *"none can envy you."* Should have been Amadi, *"might die at birth."*

Back in my home, we cared for women when they were breeding, gave them the best foods. They rested for days afterwards with their babies, getting to know them. Here I must help starving women squatting in sugar cane whose children were fighting their way free of their wombs. Afterwards, I strapped their children to their backs and if they were lucky, they got a day's rest in the slave hospital before they had to get their black behinds back to work.

A footfall came outside the window. A small face looked in on us, grinning. Then a shout came from outside: Georgine's owner man. Georgine screamed, "Who is it?" and shoved her clothing down over her thighs.

"Just one of the little boys," I told her, loud so the carpenter would hear. "Get dressed." O Lasirèn, let him not beat the child.

I stepped outside. It was Ti-Bois, all of his skinny six-year-old soul case quivering with excitement. "Sorry, Mister Pierre," I mumbled at the carpenter. He grunted, nodded, his eyes searching within my hut for Georgine. Ti-Bois had gotten off light this time.

I hissed at Ti-Bois, "Why did you push your face in my window? Little door-peep. If you make the backra man vexed, you and me both could get whipped. Maybe we should call you Ti Malice, hein?"

His face twitched a frightened, apologetic smile. "Sorry, matant, sorry Auntie Mer. It's the book-keeper who sent me. You must come quick; Hopping John stepped on a centipede in the sugar cane and it bit him. He's in the mill house, no time to take him to the slave hospital. Quick, Auntie; come!" He turned on his heel, running back for the canefields. I shouted for him to wait for me, then said to the carpenter: "Mister Pierre, Georgine's coming out now."

He was frowning. He really looked fretful for his Georgine. "How is her health?"

She was living; Hopping John might be dying. "She will be well, Mister Pierre. I already told her what she needs to do."

His face cleared a little. "Good. You're to be with her when her time comes, at our house."

"How . . . ?"

"Your master gave permission."

"Yes, Mister Pierre. I will send her out to you now." I dashed back into my room. "Someone's sick," I told Georgine. "I have to go and help."

"But—"

"You must grow beets and eat them, make yourself strong for the birth. And get ginger root and make a poultice, put it down there every night, on the opening to your bouboun."

She got a scandalised look. I didn't have time for that. "Not strong enough to burn, mind. It will make the skin supple so the baby will pass through without tearing it. And tell your carpenter not to touch you until after you wean."

She gasped. "So long?"

"So long. Or your milk will be weak and your child won't thrive."

Georgine looked down at her big belly like she was just now thinking of all that it signified.

"Your baby is coming in two months, not more. When your birth time comes, I'm to be there with you, Master says. I have to go now." I ran through the door, leaving her questions on her lips. Maybe they would let Tipingee come with me to Georgine's birth.

Lasirèn, pray you a quick death for Hopping John. Pray you no more of this life for him. Even though no gods answer black people's prayers here in this place.

Halfway to the mill house, I had to pass under the big kenèp tree. I just had time to hear a rustling in the leaves, when a body jumped down out of it in front of me. It landed on its two feet, then overbalanced, but only had one hand to put to the ground to steady itself. Makandal. Come all the way from Limbé to make mischief.

"Salaam aleikum, matant," he greeted me. *Peace be upon you.*

I didn't give him back his blessing. "Get out my way," I panted. "Someone's sick."

He straightened, cradling the long-healed stump of his right arm in his left hand. After his accident, he wouldn't take food from the same pot with us any more. He was a Muslim, and they count the left hand unclean.

Makandal stood tall. Grinned at me. "Tales flow from Hopping John mouth the way shit flows from a duck's behind," he said around a kenèp fruit in his mouth. "Always talking my business. Nayga-run-to-backra sometimes is in such a hurry to tell tales, he doesn't look where he's walking. Steps on something nasty. Gets piqué." He jabbed with a fingertip, a thorn biting into flesh. He put a fake sadness on his face. "It's a bad way to sicken, matant."

"It's you made Hopping John ill!" Not a centipede, but a piquette in the fields; a piece of sharpened bamboo the brute had jammed into the ground, smeared with his poison on the tip.

His smile brightened like the day. "I told the piquette to catch whoever was talking my business. Looks like I aimed it true." He spat out the pale ball of the kenèp seed. "Where's Marie-Claire?" he asked. "In the kitchen, you think? I have a new herb for her to flavour your master's food with."

I skinned up my face to think of him sticking that left hand he used to wipe his ass with into the cook pot. All the Ginen thought Makandal was so powerful, that he was our saviour. Me, I didn't trust him. I made to shove past him. "Get out my way and go!" Runaway. Thief. Hiding in the bush and making off with the yams the Ginen must grow to feed themselves and their children. Calling himself "maroon."

"I'm gone, matant Mer."

And just like that, he disappeared. Turned to air? No. There he was, a manmzèl now, doing its dragonfly dance level with my nose. So like Makandal, playing games when I was about serious business. The manmzèl landed on my hand, its wings flicking like when you whip your back skirt hem to contempt somebody. It was missing half a front leg.

"Get away, or I feed you salt!" I told him. Fleur had told me that Makandal's mother back in Africa had been djinn; a demon from the North, the desert lands. Me, I thought I knew how he strengthened the djinn half of him. Every man jack of us as we got off the slave ships, the white god's priests used sea water to make the magic cross on our foreheads and bind us with salt to this land. Maybe not Makandal. Never chained with white man's obeah, never fed the salt of the bitter soil of this new world to tie his earthly body down to it, never ate the salt fish and the filthy haram, the salt pork that was the only meat the Ginen got. A miracle. But he was still too much of this world to be able to fly back home. No, he was going to stay here and make mischief instead.

I went to clap the nasty fly dead like the vermin it was, but it scooted away, wings buzzing that tune: "Wine is white blood, San Domingo; we going to drink white blood, San Domingo . . ."

A black wave of retribution was set to crash over Saint Domingue, and its crest was François Makandal.

I ran to tend Hopping John.

Sometimes Mer seemed to Tipingee like the hands of Papa God himself. "People talk but do nothing," the Ginen people said. "Papa God doesn't talk, but he does plenty." Mer, her words remained in her head, but her actions went out into the world. There was healing in her hands. Release.

Standing on the factory floor with sugar cane leaves pricking her calves, Tipingee watched for Mer to come and see to Hopping John. A cockroach waddled out from under some leaves. It was longer than her thumb, fat and drunk on rotting cane. It spread mahogany-brown wings and flew towards the mill.

"Pardon, Tipingee." It was Jacques and Oreste, bringing in cane from the wain carts and feeding it into the crushers. Tipingee moved out of their way.

The sugar stench was making her head pound today. The whole six months of crop time, she could never get that heavy sugar smell out of her nose, or the stupid lowing of the oxen pulling the wains, or the hammering, hammering, hammering of the wainwrights and carpenters mending the carts and the troughs the cane juice flowed along. Everything was always breaking, everybody was always working. No free time to go and sit by the clean, peaceful wash of the salt sea and pray to Aziri near her waters.

The book-keeper, overseer of the fields, had made them carry John inside here. Then he'd sent everyone but Tipingee back to work. "Stupid, dumb black," he'd said to her as he stared in horror at John's leg, the flesh of John's heel swollen and discoloured. "Why'd he go and step on that thing?" He'd bent, groaning, to lace his boots tighter. Thick leather. It came up to his calves. Hopping John was in bare feet. "Tipingee, you stay here until matant comes, then you get right back to work, hear?"

"Yes, sir."

He started walking out, stopped in the doorway. Looked back at John. Bit his lip. John had been making him laugh just before the centipede stung, telling him the story about the screech owl who went a-courting. The book-keeper shook his head, jumped onto a cart that was heading back to the fields that were being cut.

Tipingee watched until the book-keeper was well gone before she went to kneel by John. Handsome, he was. Strong and tall with dark, smooth skin. Vain, too; she could smell the coconut oil he had used to make his hair gleam. "John? Hopping John?"

No answer. John was curled up into a ball, breathing in little sips. Not good. Mer had taught Tipingee to look out for that. Nothing to do till she got here, though.

For all that he was good-looking, John's breath was bad, like boiled rice that had gone rotten. From eating poorly, most of the slaves lost their teeth, one by one.

Oreste came to Tipingee with a stick of cane, hiding it in front of him so no one would see. He could get punished for helping himself to his master's produce. Last month the book-keeper had caught Babette chewing on some cane to refresh herself while she cut, and he had put her all night in the stocks with cane juice smeared over her naked body. Mosquitoes and ants had driven her nearly mad before he loosed her and Mer could tend to her swollen shut eyes and the itchy raised bites that covered her.

Oreste peeled back the hard rind from the cane with his knife and gave Tipingee the stick to chew. She smiled him thanks, set about gnawing the sweet juice out of the tough white fibres. He smiled back, tucked his knife away. He went and touched Hopping John on the shoulder. Hopping John never moved. "He's going to be all right?" Oreste asked.

"Don't know. Mer's coming."

The overseer shouted at Oreste, so he got back to loading the crushers. Before the overseer could see, Tipingee tossed the gnawed cane trash onto the floor and kicked leaves over it. She looked through the door that led deeper into the factory. The heavy odour of hot syrup from the big copper boilers climbed up inside her nose. Over by the boilers, Martinique dipped her thumb and forefinger into the smallest copper, testing the teache inside to see if it was thick enough. She was skilled at it, was training Hector. No chatter in the factory this time. Everyone was waiting to see if Hopping John would live.

Tipingee peered outside again. There she came. Ti-Bois was dragging her by the hand, like he didn't realise she was getting old. Sometimes Tipingee forgot too; could only remember Mer's strong hands, her eyes deep, the muscles of her thighs as she scissored her legs around Tipingee's waist. Mer always been there for her: shipmates; sisters before Tipingee's blood came; wives to each other after, even when they had had husbands.

Tipingee stepped out the door. "Honour, matant!" she called out over the racket of the sugar-making. "Hopping John's in here!"

"Respect!" Mer cried, returning Tipingee's greeting. In a sudden trough of silence, Tipingee heard when John pushed out one quiet breath.

All of the Ginen on Sacré Coeur plantation were grateful to have Mer as their doctress. Belle Espoir further down the way had only Jean Rigaud; the young, timid white man whose job it was to treat the Ginen on both Belle Espoir and Sacré Coeur when they sickened. People died faster on Belle Espoir; after six years of labour, maybe eight. Living twelve years in this land—the time it had taken for Mer to lose a child and a husband—meant that Mer had earned her place among the Ginen as one of the elders. So if she and Tipingee wanted to play madivinèz with each other like some young girls did while they were waiting for marriage, well, plenty of the Ginen felt life was too brief to fret about that. So long as Tipingee was doing her duty by her husband, most people swallowed their bile and left them be. Tipingee esteemed her Patrice for that, how he had never tried to take the joy of Mer from her. Another man would have beat her. Patrice had gotten to know that her love was bigger for having so many to love: him; her child Marie-Claire; Mer. She thought about Patrice often; hoped he was happy on his grand marronage, run away from the plantation and left her more than a year now. She missed his laugh and the feel in their bed of his strong hand on her hip. She missed dancing the kalenda too with her sweet light-footed man, but she hoped he was still free.

Mer came in, took one look at John, shooed Ti-Bois back off to the field to pick up cane trash. He whined he wanted to stay, but she got that voice. Tipingee knew that voice well. You never thought but to obey it. She'd seen the book-keeper himself hop quick sometimes when Mer used that voice. So off went Ti-Bois.

Mer looked around. People could see them, so she just touched Tipingee on her shoulder, quick and then gone. "Tipingee, soul." That warm touch would stay with Tipingee till evening, when she could see her Mer again, run her hands under Mer's dress, feel the smooth hard of her flesh.

Mer knelt by John, called his name, put her cheek to his mouth to feel his breathing. His lids were slack. Tipingee could see crescent moons of his eyeballs, peeking out. Not good.

Mer touched John's cheek and his eyes fluttered, opened. He grasped Mer's wrist, tried to lift his head. Mer helped. Tipingee could see John's lips moving, but she couldn't hear over the racket. What was he saying?

He stopped talking, but didn't close his mouth. His stare stayed planted over Mer's shoulder. Mer lowered him back down, put a gentle hand on his chest. She stayed so a little while, then looked over at Tipingee, grinning a smile sharp enough to cut. "Gone," she hissed. A tear oozed down her cheek; another. "Gods be praised, Tipingee! Another one has escaped."

"Mer! He's dead!" Mer always had that strange way of talking about death that made Tipingee's stomach heavy; about how it was their living souls flying back home to Guinea Land and freedom. About how it was good to leave life and flee away from this place where the colourless dead tormented them daily.

Mer straightened Hopping John's shirt, touched his face. "I didn't even have to ask him if he wanted to slip away," she said. She dashed at her eyes with her hand heel.

Healing hands, sickened spirit. Mer, whom Tipingee loved like life, hated this living. How not to? Many days Tipingee hated it too.

Tipingee looked over at the Ginen working the rollers and boilers, shook her head no, Hopping John's not here any more. Even from where she was standing she could see some faces tighten at that head shake. The gang boss had his whip, so no one dared to stop working, but one of the men began a song, a gentle one about resting when evening came. The raggedy voices filled the air along with the sweet cane juice smell.

Tipingee went back to the fields with Mer to tell the book-keeper the news. Hopping John's woman Belle would be working there in the fields too, waiting to know.

PARIS, 1842

A tiny pulse from Lisette's thigh beat under my ear: stroke, stroke, stroke. I contemplated the thick red bush of her jigger, so close to my face. I breathed her scent in deep. "You smell . . ." I said.

"I smell of cunt," she laughed, making my head shake as her body shaked. "And spit, and that honey dust you wear. And I have your face powder all over my skin." She raised up on one elbow. I hung on to her uppermost thigh for purchase. Oh, so warm, so fair, her skin! She said nothing, just reached a hand to me. I felt a tug along my scalp. She was stroking the length of my hair, spread out so all along her legs. "Beautiful," she breathed. "My beautiful Jeanne."

"Mm." I burrowed my head in closer and tunnelled my tongue into her gully hole. Lisette giggled, then sighed, my girl, and opened her knees wider. The salty liquor of her spread in my mouth. I lapped and snuffled, held her thighs tight as she wriggled and moaned. Pretty soon she was bucking on my face, calling out and cursing me sweet. All sweaty, she was, and she had her thighs clamped to my ears so that my hearing was muffled. My hair was caught beneath her. It pulled, but I cared nothing for that. I reached behind her and squeezed her bumcheeks, used them to pull her closer. She wailed and shoved herself at me, until to breathe at all I had to breathe in her juice. And she pitched and galloped like runaway horses, but I held her, held her down and sucked her button in, twirled my tongue around it. Then even her swears stopped, for she could manage words no longer, and only panted and moaned. The roar she gave at the

15

end seemed to come from the pit of her, to bellow up through her sopping cunny.

She collapsed back onto the bed and released my head. She was sobbing; gasping for breath. I wriggled up beside her and held her until she was still again. I licked my lips, sucking salt. I ran my hands through her cornsilk hair, blew on the wet place where it was plastered to her shoulder. She shivered. "Ah, damn," she said, all soft. She kissed me. Our tongues played warm against each other. She broke from the kiss and grinned at me as if it was she, not me, who was the cat that had ate the cream. "So good," was all she murmured. Then, louder: "Let me up. I need to piss."

"Go to, then," I told her. I lay and admired the smooth white moons of her bum as she climbed out of the bed. Bourgoyne was away on business, so the theatre was closed. All of us girls were free for a time. In the corridors and from the rooms beyond this one, I could hear the voices of the others, high and happy with their temporary liberty. Feet scurried and there was men's laughter, too. Lise and me had scarce been out of bed for two days now. The plates of half-eaten food on the dresser and floor were getting a bit strong, and the reek of the hashish we were smoking filled my brain.

Lisette reached under the bed, pulled out the chamber pot, squatted over it. "What do you want to do now?" she asked.

"Bring you back to bed," I told her. She giggled.

The tinkle of her piss against the pot made my bladder cramp to be emptied too. And the ache in my belly was starting back. I reached between my legs and brought my fingers away stained with red. "Fuck," I said. "Time to change the bung. You done there, Lisette?"

"Yes." She flicked the last few drops off with her fingers and wiped them on her thigh. I climbed down off the bed. She moved aside so that I could use the pot. I knelt over it, reached up inside myself and took hold of the plug of wadded-up bandages.

It was so soaked with blood that it came out as smooth as you please. My womb heaved with it and a gush of blood dripped out into the chamber pot. I dropped the plug in too, to be washed later. "Chérie, fetch me another, would you?" I asked Lisette. "In my purse, on the dresser."

She brought it back for me and sat, watching me insert it. "I could never do that," she said. "I like the rags better."

"The rags smell and I can feel them wadded between my legs. I don't like none of it. Why must women have courses?"

She frowned. "Because we have babies, I guess. I don't know how it works."

"I don't have babies. I won't. So why do I need this nuisance every month?"

Lisette was combing her fingers through her hair and twisting it into a plait. She reached for the hookah by the bedside and pulled on it merrily. The pleasant bubbling noise grew and bounced between my ears. I inhaled the pungent air and suddenly came all over dizzy. I grabbed on to the side of the bed. My fingers left a red smear on the sheets. Lise took her mouth off the pipe and coughed a racking hashish cough. Face red, she said, "You don't want babies? Ever?"

"Never. Stillborn baby nearly killed my mother."

"I do. I want them. A girl and a boy." She edged herself to sit at the side of the bed, an eager look on her face. "I know how to tell who will get them on me, too. Shall we try it?"

I pulled myself up to sit beside her. Dried my cunny off with an edge of the sheet. Soon time to send those sheets out for washing. I took the hookah from her and sucked its dreams into my lungs. I could hear my heart pounding in my ears. "You want to see who your true love will be?" I said, amused some, and piqued some, too. "You're sure?"

She pouted, sighed. "Well, there's nothing else to do. It's hours before we meet the men at the café."

"Huh. I could keep you occupied, but maybe you tire of my

sport." Suddenly I was sad and dull, with that dark mood that hashish can bring on.

Lise scuttled her bum close to me and hugged me tight.

I turned my face away, but, devil that she was, she only took the opportunity to nibble on my ear. "We'll do it again and once more again before the night even falls, sweet," she said. I giggled at the tickle of her breath in my hair. "But I like to play at other games, too."

She always knew how to make my heart light. I kissed her. "So we shall, then. And how will you scry for your true love?"

She reached for the wine bottle on the night table and held it up to the light. There were a few sips left. "Not enough," she said, then tipped the bottle to her lips and drank down what little there was. She rested the bottle in the bed, and looked around her, frowning. "We need water," she said to me. Then she smiled. Holding her plaits out of the way, she leaned over the bed and came up, triumphant and red-faced, with the chamber pot. "We can use this."

"What?" I looked with her into the chamber pot, at the orange liquid that swirled there, stirred by the unfolding plug; her piss and mine, my blood. "And what shall we do with it?"

"Oh, it's easy." She put the chamber pot down amongst the sheets. "Hold it, make sure it doesn't spill." She clambered carefully out of bed and turned down the lamp wick. "Not too dark," she said. "Can you still see the liquid in the pot?"

I chuckled. "Yes, my pagan girl."

As she came back into bed, Lise told me, "Claudette showed me how to do this. Here, put the chamber pot between us."

I did as she said, and now we were both sitting cross-legged with the piss and blood between us. A faint, heavy smell, acrid, wafted up from the pot. Red swirled in tendrils inside yellow piss.

Lise reached for the hookah, grinned, and sucked on it until even in the shadowy room I could see the tips of her ears get red.

She coughed and handed the hookah to me. "Suck the smoke in deep," she said. "It will sharpen your sight into the otherworld."

I giggled, and Lisette slapped my knee, sharply.

"Jeanne! You must be serious."

So I bit on my lips until the urge to smile had passed some. "Very well, I am sombre as a prelate." I sucked from the hookah. The warmth of the drug spread all through my body, bringing blissful ease to my cramping belly. I felt I was floating. Here in the warm dark with my Lise, no one to bother us, anything felt possible. "What do we do now?" I asked her. My voice could have been coming from the ceiling, I felt transported so far away.

She took the hookah from me and put it back on the night table. She kissed my fingers, then said: "Hold my hands."

I did. Her hot, soft little palms felt nice in mine.

"Now we have the water in the chamber pot sealed in a magic circle," she said.

I was giggling again before I knew I would do it. "This is so silly, Lise!"

She squeezed my hands in hers, not hard. "No, it is not. You simply must decide that it is not."

The seriousness in her voice made me sombre again. "All right. And then?"

"While we are scrying, do not break the circle of our hands. Whatever you do, we must keep hold of each other."

Suddenly I was apprehensive. "Else what?" I asked her.

"Else the vision will dissipate, and I won't see my true love!" she said. "Do you wish to scry for yours after me?"

I thought of my new beau Charles; of his high, pale forehead and petulant mouth, of his scribblings and his moods; his raptures and his miseries both. Truly, he filled me with wonder, that man. Made me want to know what magic there was in all those words he worshipped, that they should bring him to such extremes of feeling. "I think I have done as best as I may," I told her.

"So you have," she replied. "You've found yourself a fine one." Her eyes were pink from the hashish, as though she'd been weeping.

"Oh, Lise, his family has land! He says he will take me travelling sometime! I have never been away from France."

She smiled, happy for me. "He treats you well. Me, I have no rich gentleman yet to buy me gowns."

"You will, beautiful one. Shall we do this thing now?"

"Yes. No, don't leave go of my hands! Remember to hold on." Her fingers held mine tight. "Look into the liquid in the pot, and let your mind wander, but keep one idea always before you; that you wish to see with me a vision of my true love."

"And he'll appear in the pot? He'll get his feet wet."

"Silly Jeanne. A vision of him will appear, as though we were looking in through a window."

"Very well." This scrying business had a flavour about it of my grandmaman's juju, her African magic. Cleanse the floors with the morning's first urine, always keep a silver coin in a bag around your neck, with some sweet herbs in it. Harmless. I relaxed and did as Lise asked. I took a pull on the hookah, let the hashish fill my brain, open it wide.

Hot; it was so hot in that room. I breathed out smoke. It flowed from my nostrils, seemed to swirl in the piss pot, floating on its bloody waters. I stared into the pot and waited.

When there was money, Grandmaman would sometimes buy live chickens in the market for us to eat. She would cut their clucking throats on our back stoop, let the blood fall there. For the spirits to drink, she said. Fresh blood was life, she said. But she said the blood from a woman's time was stale, not fresh. What had we just put in that pot, Lise and I?

The smoke in the pot writhed and wound about the blood and piss.

Something began to form. Should I have been frightened? Not when sweet hashish filled me even to the tips of my fingers.

I could feel a pulse ticking in Lise's warm thumbs. The smoke in the pot began to drift away, and something, an image, was moving in the orange liquid. Lise gasped, her hands clutching tightly to mine. Me, I felt only a lazy, sly curiosity. *Yes, show us this perfect man,* I thought at the spirits swirling in the foetid pot, *this man who will love my sweet Lise as though she were the frailest doll, the purest virgin.*

Eh. There in the still liquid, as in a mirror. A black man. Dark as coal, as mud. "What is it?" asked Lise, then "oh," said Lise; a little, sad cry.

Is this what she will come to? Making black babies? I whispered, "Hush, sweet. Don't jerk, or you may disturb the image. Maybe there's more to see."

I knew faces like his. My grandmaman's skin was like that, and she had that flat, wide nose. He stood in a simple, empty room. Not a chair in it, not a lamp. He was poor, then. He wore plain clothing, a working man's baggy trousers and heavy shirt with a stained apron knotted around his spare middle. I felt a wash of shame for my Lise. Her hope, her true love, was an ugly black butcher. And poor.

The liquid in the chamber pot splashed, making the image shimmer. Lise and I kept ourselves even more still until it was becalmed.

The man was holding a hat of some kind. I thought it was a hat. Hard to tell, for he had twisted it into a mere screw of fabric between his loutish hands. He looked nervous, as well he might. Was that his house? Whose, then? Had he a right to be there? Perhaps he was a thief?

He turned at some sound we couldn't hear. He gazed off to my left. What he saw there made his face brighten as though angels had come to bid him enter heaven. Joy transformed him. They knew him in that house, then. Even thought it well to see him.

His lips moved; a greeting, perhaps. He reached out to someone. A hand reached back towards him; a woman's hand, in . . .

was that a pink sleeve? Difficult to tell in the yellow-orange piss water. The hand placed itself firmly in the centre of his chest and pushed. He stumbled back some little bit. Oh. The woman wanted him to leave. A lovers' quarrel? Had he vexed my Lise?

His face got sorrowful, dignified. His shoulders dropped. He nodded, smoothed his poor hat out, jammed it onto his head, and turned away.

The woman—Lise, I wager—was moving into the circle of the chamber pot. I could see more of her arm, the jut of a firm breast. I leaned forward. Soon I would see her face. Was my Lisette old? Was she still beautiful?

"Oh!" the real Lise exclaimed again. She picked up the pot, and before I could stop her, before I could see, she threw it across the room. It hit the wall with a tinny clang, spraying its mess everywhere. The bloody plug fetched up against the wall. "It's not true!" She wailed. "It's not!" She clutched my hand in one of hers, and ground the heel of her other hand into her eyes. She sobbed.

I gathered her into my arms. "Hush, Lise," I said, gently. "Hush. Let me hold you." I rocked and rocked her as she wept storms.

"He was so foul, Lemer!" She wept. "Black as the devil!"

I said nothing, only thought of the soft creases of my grand-mother's face. Once Grandmaman had given me molasses in a plate, and when I ran my fingers through it, it had left lines like those around her eyes and mouth. Sweet lines.

"And that apron!" lamented Lise.

I felt near to swooning from the hashish, and I was the more dizzy from the way I was rocking her, but I tried to think how to comfort her. "Maybe it was a mistake," I said.

"No," she cried, sobbing harder. "I am to be wedded to a black, and toil all my days killing pigs, and have nigger babies."

Something, something was working in me, making me think thoughts I don't think. "Well then, my beauty," I told her, "they will look like me."

At once she grew still in my arms. She was silent some little while. Then: "Yes," she said. "Yes, so they will." She turned her tear-tracked face to me and smiled, too wide. "My beautiful Lemer." She pulled out of my arms, scrubbed her face dry with a corner of the sheet. "And really, this is not a day to be gloomy," she said. "We are meeting our gentlemen at the café, after all!"

Gently, I pulled a lock of her long, fair hair through two of my fingers. Like silk. "You won't sulk any more?"

She giggled, too loud. "How foolish of me! No, no more. It's just that I'm tired. Let me nap a while?"

Even as I was nodding, she was lying back against the bed, pulling the covers over herself. She was asleep very quickly. I covered her bare shoulder. She didn't like drafts. I put my head out the door and shouted for someone to bring us some water. I went and sat on the bed, just regarding Lise's face as she slept.

If I had looked for my own love in that pot, I knew I would only have seen Lise, but she and I weren't rich women, to make of our tribadism a secret marriage.

A few minutes later, there was a quiet tap at the door. I opened it to see Maryvonne who danced in the chorus, holding a jug of water. To look at her always reminded me of home, of all the brown and black and teak-coloured faces of we who lived near the docks in Nantes. She smiled at me and held out the jug in her lovely plump arms. "You and Lise are liking your furlough?" she asked in the French of the Nantais coloureds.

I know my smile back was rueful. "Perhaps too much," I said. "We are become dull and womanish." I took the jug and closed the door again. I found a discarded chemise and used it to clean the stained wall.

This week I shall send some things for Maman. The emeralds, perhaps, that Charles gave me. He's so distractable, he won't notice if I'm no longer wearing them. Maman could get good money for them. Buy herself some new shoes, and some of the good brandy for Grandmaman. Grandmaman thinks it eases her coughing. It makes her sleep, at least.

Charles has been talking of setting me up in an apartment here in Paris. I scarce dared to hope that he would. Oh, how I would love him if he took me off the stage and away from Monsieur Bourgoyne!

The wall was clean again. I put my used bung back in the chamber pot, to be washed later. I put the pot back under the bed.

It was full dark. I turned the lamp up. We would have to leave soon.

The brightening of the lamp woke Lise. She yawned and stretched. I sat beside her. She just looked up at me, her waking eyes blank. Not enough of her in her eyes. Almost like she didn't know me. I said, "You mustn't let the vision frighten you, love."

She frowned. "Vision?"

Little prickly points rose on my arms. "Yes, the vision in the chamber pot. The man."

She giggled and patted my thigh. "Oh, my Lemer. Such sharp eyes, to see a man. Was he a gentleman?"

"You saw him, too," I whispered.

She only shrugged. She sat up and kissed my cheek. "I saw hashish smoke, dancing in front of my eyes. Shall we dress for dinner now?"

She had really forgotten. She heaved herself out of the bed and went and sat at the mirror. When I was little, Grandmaman used to tell me that people only see what they see. Used to vex me, for it made no sense. Children like for their adults to speak plain, to help us make the world come clear. But I understood Grandmaman now.

I had seen a vision of my Lise in that piss pot, and in her blank gaze at me now. She would leave me soon, to find her own gentleman. And me, I would cleave to Charles.

After the mountains, still more mountains. You aren't there yet, Georgine." I mopped her face with the damp cloth. "Soon you'll have to push again for Auntie Mer." I handed the cloth and water bowl to Tipingee to replace with fresh.

Georgine looked at me, wiry hair wild where it had slipped from her scarf, sweat in beads down her face and throat, eyes rolling like the goat's when it sees the knife coming down. So young she was.

"I'm tired, matant," complained Georgine.

"You think that little bit of tiredness is anything?" Tipingee smirked. "You will feel more fatigue in the weeks to come. Feeding the baby, changing the baby, and doing all your same washerwoman's work for the great house."

It was all true. Tipingee knew. Six babies she had pushed out; two dead, three sold away from her as soon as they had weaned. Fifteen-year-old Marie-Claire was the only one left, and she worked as cook's helper in the great house. Used to steal us the crisp salty fat off the roasts from time to time. Me and Tipingee would lick it off each other's fingers. Marie-Claire wasn't bringing us plenty now though, because she was sneaking slow poison into the backra's food. Makandal's poison. Salt hid the taste of Makandal's herbs. All I argued with Tipingee, she was teaching the child to do this thing.

A big contraction took Georgine. "Push, Georgine!" I laid hands on her belly, guiding the baby to turn. It was coming early. Jean Rigaud was supposed to have been here with us, for only white men could practise medicine by law. But he was back in the slave hospital, treating a man with yaws. Good. He would only be in the way.

Georgine held my arm, squeezed so till it hurt. Her cheeks blew out big, her face turned red, but almost no sound came from her. She spread her knees apart and bore down. The baby shifted a little, not enough.

Good, strong girl, Georgine. I didn't think she would be. And silent too, like a grown woman should be. Like me back home, on the day they cut away my vulva to make me an adult. She's just a whore, though. Opening her legs for the white man. Coloured man's not good enough for her.

Georgine was looking at me like I had spit in her food. Tonnerre. I was mumbling the words out loud. Talking to myself. No matter. She knew how all of us felt about her. But I pushed my lips shut against each other.

Georgine's contraction faded. She lay back. "He's a good man, Pierre," she said to me in a begging voice.

Tipingee rolled her eyes, sucked air between her teeth. "And where he is now when you need help?" She jerked her head towards the closed door. "Hiding. Playing door-peep."

A shadow outside, man-sized, shifted against the shutters. I warned Tipingee with a look. She well knew the carpenter was there, knew he wouldn't come in and interfere with women's business. Tipingee's mouth always ran away with her. The whipping scars on her back went deep from it.

Tipingee scowled, went on talking: "Best you pray to Aziri, have some water near you; man can't make your labour flow smooth like the river." Tipi was Akan, but on the ship, as we learned each other's speech, I would tell her stories of the power of Aziri, how she wouldn't let us drown. Tipi had adopted Aziri to herself.

Georgine pursed her mouth like she'd sucked green limes. "I'm a Christian woman. I could tell Master you still pray to demons. He'd do for you."

Time to stop this talk. I said, "Tipingee has a silly head sometimes, listens to too much old time stories."

Tipingee glared at me. Worry about that later. I told Georgine, "She just wants to use everything she knows to make your baby come easy."

Outrage flared behind Tipingee's eyes. Georgine closed her own. She was tired. She gave a weak whisper: "Best she pray with me to Holy Mother Mary, then. Pray for my baby. Pray for all our souls."

Tipingee glared at me, but she closed her eyes to make the Christian god's prayer. She and Georgine began to Hail Mary, full of grace, Tipingee's voice sullen, only aping the words, really.

Georgine's womb thrashed again around the baby. I could feel the ripple. This time she did make a little noise.

"Push, Georgine!" I guided the baby with my hands, muttering in Ewe for Lasirèn, for Aziri, to help me turn its head into Georgine's birth canal. Georgine grunted and strained, knees wide, no use for modesty now.

"Philomise is not the good man you think he is," she panted, "free-coloured Philomise, he."

"Hold my hands," Tipingee told her. Biscuit fingers grasped chocolate ones, squeezed hard. "Do your labour. Now's not the time to run your mouth."

"Is she well?" the carpenter sang out from the yard, his voice anxious.

"She's well, yes, Master Pierre," I told him. "You could fetch a clean sheet for her. And some pillows. And if you have any old blanket, soft cotton, tear it into strips to swaddle the baby."

His footsteps left running. I knew he had nothing like that in this hut of his. That should keep him away for a while, let us work.

"Philomise, he would taunt me," Georgine hissed, her womb heaving. "Ah, Mother Mary, please let this be over!"

"Sh, sh," said Tipingee.

Another contraction. A muffled shriek from Georgine. "He would visit our master. He would come into the kitchen when no one was there, touch my . . . tell me he would have me, buy me away and make me always his. Matant, please, please, sweet Jesus it hurts, please pull it out of me."

I pressed on her belly again. Slow like molasses, the child began to move. A few more pushes and the baby was crowning. Georgine grunted, bore down hard on trembling thighs, squeezed the baby out of her like a turd. It flopped into Tipingee's arms, the glistening rope of birth cord still joining it to its mother. A flood of bloody mucus spilled out of Georgine's womb after it.

A woman had died chained to me on the slave ship. Blood and liquid shit had been gushing from her anus for days before. In that narrow space we had lain together for weeks, but I never knew her name, couldn't understand her language. Was too sick myself to know she'd died. Was Tipingee, a little girl then, who had shouted and shouted till the sailors came and cut the dead woman away from me. The mess between Georgine's legs put me in mind of that death. It always did now, when I helped women birth. Back home, birth had been a thing of joy.

Tipingee held up the baby for Georgine to see. No, more like a fat maggot than a turd. Her marabou baby. Georgine's chest was heaving from her labour. She raised her head and looked at her child. She screamed.

Mister Pierre came running, slammed the door open. "Sly bloody niggers, what are you doing to her!" His eyes opened big and his nose too as he took in the scene: Tipingee clutching the worm child tied to its mother; me, my arms around Georgine, supporting her back; his Georgine, fouled skirts laid back, legs wide apart, velvet thighs covered in blood and her own shit, pushed out of her body by the baby's passing. The smell of woman's insides and blood and excrement was all through the room. "Gods . . ." Mister Pierre muttered.

The baby hadn't moved yet. I needed to get to it. It's Georgine who spoke first. "Pierre, these women are only tending to me."

I looked Mister Pierre calmly in the face. Yes, I could see he realised that we weren't doing anything to his Georgine, that birthing was the only thing happening here. I rushed and took the baby from Tipingee. Held it upside down and stroked its back to start its lungs. Tipingee found my knife and cut its navel string.

"Pierre," said Georgine, "I need soft cloths and more water. You could find things like that for me, please?" Her speech slipped always between poor coloured girl and the lady she wanted to be. Her eyes sidled over to the baby.

"They're outside. But Georgine . . ." Mister Pierre said. The child lay still in my arms. A boy.

"Please get them, Pierre?"

He still didn't move, his eyes gaping at the swamp of her crotch. His face was glazed, he was swaying on his feet. I put my ear to the child's chest. Silence. Its head flopped back. Its navel string hung from its belly, dripped a thin blood.

"Pierre, please . . . ?"

His eyes lifted to her face, searched it out like it was his life he saw in her features. "I'll get them," he whispered. He went outside.

"Mer," Tipingee said, "the baby's not breathing?"

I put the child on the bed. Rubbed and pressed on the little chest. I'd delivered plenty light-skin babies before. Backra men were always pushing their business into Ginen women. But I never had delivered one that so favoured a backra. Skin the blue-white of breast milk, with fine colourless hair. Its head was long like a mango, squeezed as it went through Georgine's body. "Pale like gruel," Georgine said, low. I glanced at her face and saw the surprise there. What colour did she think it would be? Isn't that what she had wanted, a cream-coloured child?

The baby was still blue, no breath going in. I wiped mucus off the face, put my mouth over the tiny mouth and nose and breathed in gently. Chest expanded, contracted. I blew nine more times. Its heart never beat once. I had to admit it; Georgine's baby wasn't living. I raised my eyes to Georgine's. "The birth was too much for it," I said. Georgine put shocked hands to her mouth.

A soul gone beneath the waters? Should I care that this milky child would have been in bondage too, unless its father had choosed to set it free?

Fear fluttered over Georgine's face. She clutched at her belly. "More pain, matant Mer! Is there another one inside me?"

Likely no. "Hush. It's just the afterbirth. It will come out soon." I gave the dead child to Tipingee and went to Georgine's side. A few more groaning contractions and she delivered the piece of liver-looking thing. Still holding the baby in the crook of one arm, Tipingee wrapped the placenta in a piece of flour bag, put it in the calabash I'd brought. Strong science, a placenta.

Georgine never moved to cover herself, just stared at the baby. "Dead?" she said softly. I nodded. "After all this, dead? And looking more like Pierre than me?"

Mister Pierre burst back in, his face tight, his arms full up of swaddling. "Here."

Me and Tipingee took it from him. He went back out, returned with a cook pot steaming from the hot water inside. Georgine was sobbing, at the end of her strength. She lay back and we cleaned her. She was torn. "Tipingee, bring me the aloe," I said. Pulp of the aloe plant, mixed with honey. It would sting, but some of that on the cut would help her heal faster.

Mister Pierre was finally looking at the baby's body. "A boy? Why aren't you two lackwits seeing to my child?"

There had been women's voices in this room all these long hours. Mister Pierre's booming was like sudden thunder during a soft rain.

"He's stillborn, sir," I told him. Mama, he was going to blame it on Tipingee and me?

He flinched like somebody had boxed him. "Tonnerre." He looked at the little body, the little free soul. Composed himself.

Stroked the baby's tiny arm with a finger. His voice was rough when it came out, but all he said was, "Nine months before you can breed me another, Georgine. I need a son to work with me."

Georgine opened red-shot eyes on him, her face a mask. "I'm sorry, Pierre. We will make another one soon."

"Mister Pierre," Tipingee piped up. "Georgine must rest a little bit now. We must leave her to sleep."

"Um, ah, of course, of course. You two see to her, then you can be on your way." He scowled at the baby. Picked up the cradle that had been waiting to receive it. Good work, that cradle. Mister Pierre must have spent plenty time on it. He left. I saw the look of him as he passed me; the look of a man who had just lost a son.

Tears were making a crisscross down Georgine's cheeks. "Don't leave me with Pierre tonight," she begged. "He doesn't know how to look after me. Hands always too rough. Don't leave me with the dead baby."

Tipingee's eyes made four with mine. Wasn't for us to say whether we could stay or go.

The baby, Georgine said; not *my* baby. Wasn't a baby anyway, with no life and no name. So they had told me about my child. Must be true. I didn't have no child, and Georgine didn't have none neither.

Tipingee finished cleaning Georgine up, put the aloe where her flesh was frayed. Georgine said nothing to us, just made like she was sleeping, though she winced some at the touch of the aloe. A hammering was coming from outside. I helped Tipingee to tidy up the room.

A knock came on the door. Strange that Mister Pierre would ask leave of three black women to enter his own house. "Come," Georgine called out. I mouthed the same word quiet in my own mouth, imagined myself like Georgine, in a fancy dress with no rips, lying in a good strong bed; a plain bed but with no splinters, calling out "enter" like I had the choice to say "yea" or "nay." I made Mer in my head beckon with one hand, felt my own arm

31

twitch, so strong I was imagining it. No use. I couldn't make my head sit on the Georgine body in my mind. Back home, I would wrap my body in fine indigo, lie on a soft bed. Nobody was so rude either, to bang on your house with their hands. They stood respectful near the entrance and called for your attention.

Mister Pierre came in. The cradle was in his arms. The rockers were gone and he had made a lid: the cradle had become a coffin for his child. He gave it to Tipingee. "Two carts are broken at the factory and it's slowing the work down," he said to Georgine. "I'm sent for to go and mend them."

A dirt-poor white man, he. Even he couldn't keep our master's work waiting.

"It's all right," Georgine told him from behind closed eyes. She knew how things were. It was still crop time. Even with the sun long gone down, the work went on. "Maybe they will feed you in the big house."

I didn't look at Tipingee this time. The great house kitchen, where Tipingee's Marie-Claire was putting Makandal's poison in the food.

"Mister Pierre?" Tipingee said. He looked to where she was standing, like if he was surprised to find anybody there.

"Yes?"

"Georgine's still bleeding a little."

"She's good, strong stock," he said. "She will mend."

I hope the great house gave him plenty of the roast.

Mister Pierre told us, "You two stay and make sure the bleeding has stopped before you go back to the cane. And bury the child's body."

And he was out the door again.

"Yes, Sir," Tipingee called after his back, looking sideways to me. This task would take us until the cane-cutting had stopped. No cane leaf razor cuts for us tonight.

Just the three of us and the little dead boy, his soul fled to the world beneath the water before ever he had breathed on land.

With her owner gone, Georgine let the salt water run freely from her eyes. "After all that, no son," she moaned.

"Your master will get another one on you soon," Tipingee told her. Condolence or threat? Never knew with my Tipingee.

I picked up the cold little cream-coloured body. He was pretty. But we don't make plenty fuss over a child born dead. "Where do you want it buried?" I asked Georgine.

Georgine looked on me with her red weeping eyes. Her face got a determined look. "By the river," she said. "Where my mother drowned. They will be company for each other."

Tipingee kissed her teeth in derision. "And who you think is going out all that way in this dark night, and how are we going to know the right place?"

"Go on back to the fields then, with your black self. I will take my child there on my own."

Tipingee spat on the floor and just looked at her, calm. "Take him, then," she said. "Let me see you stand up and take him."

Georgine glared at her. I looked on this fair-skin, soft-hand house girl, still fainting from her labour. Probably she saw the doubt in my face too, for she set her mouth hard, smoothed down her stained skirts, fought herself to her feet. She took two strong steps to me, for all that I saw she was biting her lips with pain. She reached out her hands. "Give him to me. I will take him."

Eh. The slattern girl had some true backbone. She had proved it plenty times already tonight. I gave her dead child into her arms, watched her shape them to receive him for the first and last time. Looking at his little body, her crying started up again, but she said nothing, just sucked her tears back into her nose. "Matant, you will come with me to carry the coffin? I will carry the shovel."

"I will come."

Tipingee swore. "Both of you have not an ounce of sense in your heads. No, Mer, I will carry the coffin. Wait there and I'll get the damned shovel."

Georgine just sighed, settled her baby in her arms, and sat on the bed, looking into the child's face, waiting for us to be ready.

Georgine walked tall all the way, though she hissed sometimes when she would stumble on a rock. Not one time did she ask me for help.

Saint Domingue, that merciless place, was a beautiful country. The night breeze was cool on the face. Fireflies like little stars flashed all around us. Once we got a little way from the sugar houses, the smell of cooking syrup wasn't so strong. We passed under the bay tree, breathed in the spiced scent of bay leaves that we mashed under our feet. I was carrying the shovel and a torch, Tipingee balancing the little wooden coffin on her head. Hope we got back before Mister Pierre came home to find his shovel and his woman missing. He had folded a soft cotton sheet into the coffin, to lay his child to rest on. Moths came and threw themselves at the guttering torch flame. Once a big one, blue. Nearly so big as my hand. I cursed, almost dropped the torch. The moth flicked its wings as it flew away. Did it have all its feet? Why was this Makandal plaguing me so?

We went around the slave quarters. Didn't want nobody to see us. Headed for the trickling sound of the river. Mosquitoes were bad this time of year, singing in our ears and biting, but Georgine wouldn't even self brush them from her face. She saved all her attention for the body in her arms. Whispered to it while she walked. I wondered what she was telling it. Then she said: "Matant, the baby would have gotten browner? If he lived?"

"Maybe so. If you had let him run too much in the sun."

"No. I would have made him wear a hat every time he went out. Wouldn't want him to get black. Only . . ."

"Hmm?"

"If he had got a little bit of brown to him, not too much, maybe he would see me in his face that way, know who's his mother."

"You will have another one, Georgine."

Tipingee just sucked her teeth for impatience.

We passed the big mango tree, and the tamarind, and the rock high so like a man. Makandal said that rock fell down from the sky, was blessèd. He said an old Indian man told him so, that the Indian man's people knew that rock from before the Spanish and the French came to this place.

The river sound was louder in our ears, and the mosquitoes were whining constantly. More of them were here near the water. Georgine was staring into the darkness, looking for something. "Matant, bring the light over here? Ah. No, come down this way."

We were in mud now, squirming cool between our toes. Could see flashes of fast-running river water gleaming like fishes.

"Look, the place here," Georgine said, softly. "It's here they dragged my mother from the water."

Tipingee peered into the water, looked around at the weedy banks where there was a mapou tree growing and Spanish moss climbing over it. "River's too deep here so to enter it. What your mother was doing in fast-running water?"

"She was upstream." Georgine jooked her chin in the direction. "Washing Master Simenon's white linen shirts. I was pounding out the dirt from the collars and spreading the shirts on the rocks to bleach for her. His favourite shirt got away from her in the water. She knew she had to get it back, or get beat, so she went in after it. But she slipped. The water carried her away before anybody could reach her. It's here so this tree root finally caught her dress and held her, but she'd already drowned long time. Dig here for me, Tipingee?"

Tipingee put down the wooden box. I gave her the shovel. "I will hold the torch so you can see," I said.

"The ground's too wet here," Tipi said. "The body will just come back up."

"Wedge it under the roots of the mapou," Georgine told her.

Tipingee sighed and got to digging. I held up the torch, held

Georgine who suddenly had collapsed against my side. Probably the fatigue. She needed some time to recover from doing labour. I put my arm around the little thin body of this girl a third my thirty-something years, holding her dead baby to tiny breasts just starting to bud. The mosquitoes sang and bit, sang and bit, and the river chuckled to see it so.

"She wasn't the mother who bore me," Georgine muttered. "But it was she who looked after me when they brought me to this plantation, when they bought me from further down the Cap and took me here. I don't remember my real mother. I was little little, barely walking. They gave me to her, to Calliope, for her to look after me. Her courses had come for the first time that same year, she told me. But she tended to me, made sure I got food to eat, taught me how to scrub and mend clothes, made me sugar bag dresses to wear. She held me at nights when I was bawling for Mama. I don't remember that Mama I was bawling for, but I remember Calliope."

Tipingee had nothing to say. She only grunted with each strike the shovel striked in the mud. But she started to sing, *"Koliko, Piè Jan o! Si ou capab' ou pito volé, enhé,"* keeping time with her shovelling.

Ay Lasirèn, what a night.

Tipingee dug and chanted: *"Koliko, Piè Jan o! Si ou capab' ou pito volé, enhé." (Colico, Pierre Jean, oh! If you could, you would fly, eh-heh!)*

Georgine muttered: "I saw Calliope drown . . ."

River Mumma, I thought, **why do we suffer so?**

"Koliko, Piè Jan o, se regretan sa, ou pa genyen zèl!" (Oh Pierre Jean, what a pity you don't have wings!)

"I saw the water take her . . ."

Lasirèn, take this child.

"Pierre Jean, if you could, you would fly away from here!"

"Calliope, look after my baby, please."

Take him back to Ginen with you.

"What a pity, Pierre Jean, you don't have wings!"

"Child is cold in my arms like a side of ham."

Come and take us, take us all.

"Fly away!"

Tipingee dug up a last clot of earth, threw it onto the bank. She looked to me, and what I saw in her eyes made me shiver. Was a lost soul looking back. She opened her mouth, and it's a baby's cry that came out.

"Tipingee?"

Georgine made the same cry. From her eyes, the same emptiness watched out at me, not seeing. And then something took me. A big, empty knowledge swallowed me, bigger than the sea, and in more turmoil. My own self shrank to nothing inside it and for a while, I didn't know myself, didn't know, couldn't understand.

Then I was back. My body mine again. Mosquitoes sitting on my arms, feasting. I slapped them away. Tipingee and Georgine were still standing before me, looking empty, swaying. "Tipingee?" I whimpered.

"What?"

She was back behind her eyes again.

"What happened, Tipingee?" I asked.

"What happened when?"

I stared at the two of them. Georgine looked like Georgine again, her face stiff with sorrow. Tipingee was leaning on the shovel, waiting. I knew them.

Eh. I must have been only tired, me.

I jammed the torch into the ground, held the little coffin open for Georgine. We *don't* fuss over a baby born dead. She kissed her baby, stroked his forehead. Put him in the box and closed the lid. Took the box from me. Let it slip from her arms into the hole. It splashed into the river water that was filling the hole from below. With her foot, Tipi shoved it under a thick root of the mapou tree. We covered it up. Then took Georgine back to her bed. I didn't point out to Tipingee the mongoose that followed us all the way back from Pierre's hut to the fields; it went at a limping run, for it only had three legs.

We had thought our task would take long, but when we got to the fields, the gangs were still in the cane. Tipi and I worked in the fields until it was time to stop.

We had done a common thing. Common. We had buried a dead child. Nothing strange about that. But that bigness I had felt back there by the river, swallowing me whole . . . ?

BREAK/

I'm born from song and prayer. A small life, never begun, lends me its unused vitality. I'm born from mourning and sorrow and three women's tearful voices. I'm born from countless journeys chained tight in the bellies of ships. Born from hope vibrant and hope destroyed. Born of bitter experience. Born of wishing for better. I'm born.

It's when my body hits the water, cold flow welling up in a crash to engulf me, that I begin to become. I'm sinking down in silver-blue wetness bigger than a universe. I open my mouth to scream, but get cold water inside. Drowning!

BEAT!

A branding sear of heat crazes my thigh. As the pain bites, I learn the words: brand, sear, heat, thigh. I scream again, swallowing salt. Iron holds me, I can't control my direction. I roll about, caught in a myriad memories of dark shipspace, slotted in berths too narrow to let me move far. My chains hold me tied to something—no, someone. I'm too hot then too wet, being tossed and tossed and awash in nausea. Something in me cramps, again. It hurts. Bloody stinking fluxes leak from holes I hadn't known I had. I vomit up the salt sea.

Time does not flow for me. Not for me the progression in a straight line from earliest to latest. Time eddies. I am now then, now there, sometimes simultaneously.

Sounds, those are sounds, from another place. I have heard them before, or am hearing them now, or will hear them later. Three sounds: Song. Prayer. Scream. From a riverbank, from the throats of black women. The ululated notes vibrate the chains that tie me to the ship. I thrash my arms in response, learning that they are arms the second I move them. The iron links of the chains break. Freed, I push out in front of me with my fingers. Those things kicking behind me are my legs. I pump them harder. Begin to rise, rise up through blue water. No, I am not drowning. I do not seem to be a breathing creature, to be drowning. I rise faster and faster till I am flying. The water heats from the speed of my passing—heats but does me no harm—boils to mist until it isn't any longer liquid, but clouds I am flying through. How do I know them as clouds?

ONE-

How do I know anything? How is it that my arms stretched out in front of me are so pale? How do I even know they should be brown like rich riverbank mud, as they were when I was many goddesses with many worshippers, ruling in lands on the other side of a great, salty ocean? I used to be many, but now we are one, all squeezed together, many necks in one coffle.

DROP

I fly.

What is that infant cry that never was in my head, and is, and never will be; what those three cane-rowed braids of loss, prayer, and bitterness? Sometimes active, sometimes passive, in small things, in large. A fractured melody, a plaited seedscale song of sorrow. Whose voices? Ah, I know whose, knew whose. I see them now/then, inhabit them briefly before I tumble away again. Do I have a voice? I open my mouth to try to sing the three-twist chant I can hear, and tears I didn't know before this were called tears roll in a runnelled crisscross down the thing that is my face and past my . . . lips? to drip salt onto my tongue.

At the binding taste of salt, I begin to fall once more.

Tossed helpless through the fog of the sky, going where I don't know. I land.

I am here. In someone's soul case. And though I beat and hammer on its ribs, I am caught. I can no longer see everywhere and everywhen, but only in straight lines, in one direction; to dissolution.

BLUES

PARIS, 1842

Bitter," his friends called me. I didn't pay them no mind. Most of them were only vexed that I wouldn't raise my skirts for them, those stingy men of money, counting every sou. *He* was generous. Lise was right; he treated me well.

Except this morning. He'd cancelled our regular Sunday morning assignation, so he and his hoity-toity mama could have petit déjeuner in the fancy Paris hotel she was staying in while she'd come to visit him. Yesterday evening when he and I had been at the café together, he'd scarcely acknowledged me, so nervous he was, anticipating his mother's arrival. And so I was alone today. Wouldn't do for him to introduce me to her. Just not done, to insult your mama with the presence of your mistress.

But I knew how to fix them. I knew where they were taking breakfast.

"Do you wish your boots now, Prosper?" asked Margot sullenly, using the nickname given me by the other girls. She yawned and rubbed at her eyes.

"Don't be an idiot," I told her. "Go and get my gown first."

She glared at me and slouched off. She couldn't complain, and she knew it. When I couldn't find Lisette in her room, I had panicked and woken Margot up to help me make my toilette. The younger dancers had to do what the more senior ones told them.

How nervous I was! My heart was fluttering like something frightened had flown in there and was trying to get out. But I wanted to see this formidable maman who had her fist so tight around the strings of Charles's purse. Lisette would help me do it, would meet me there at the restaurant, just two friends taking Sunday breakfast. Let Charles pretend that he did not know us; I didn't care.

But where was Lise? Probably she had spent the night in the apartments of the new gentleman who was courting her. Probably it was only that. Hoped she'd remember to meet me.

Would Charles be too displeased? Or would he think it great sport? He must remain sympathetic towards me. Now that I had known what it was to want for nothing, I couldn't sing at the Théàtre Porte-Saint-Antoine any more. Couldn't face pasty manager Bourgoyne grinning at me any more, pushing his hand sly between my legs while I waited to go on stage, while I remained quiet instead of spitting in his eye, for fear I would spoil my face paint. He liked to hide in the wings and fondle me again when I came off stage, salty with sweat; liked to shove his hand down there, hard, pull it away, smell the salt damp on me. I couldn't do it any more. And I had sent word for Maman to come, that she could live with me in the apartment that my lover would provide. She had left off whoring, was packing to join me in Paris. Charles was our only hope.

"Prosper?" called Margot, her voice muffled from among my gowns in the closet. "Jeanne?"

"What is it?" I kept smoothing chalk onto my cheeks.

"Which dress shall I bring you?"

I sighed. "Never mind that yet. Come and help me find my honey powder." I put down the chalk, dusted my hands, set about looking for the powder. It was nowhere on the dressing table. Grunting like a great lazy pig, Margot got down on her hands and knees and looked under the table. It wasn't there either. I set her to searching about the room, ignored the banging and scraping noises she made while she did it. I rouged my cheeks.

Where the devil could that honey dust have gotten to? Charles said it came from India. It had a sweet smell. He liked me to brush it on my bosom. Sometimes he did it for me, so that he could lick it off. At least his hands were dry when he touched my breast. He always smelled like soap, not like stale tobacco and bad rum. Not like Bourgoyne. Charles, he treated me like a lady. Waited gentlemanly after the performances while I scraped off the rouge and changed into something pretty. I think his mama might like me, if she got to know me. If I had pale skin like Lise. If I could fly to the moon and crow like the cock when I got there.

Margot was back under my dresser, still looking for the powder. I nudged her with my toe. "Never mind." Silly chit. I wager it was she who took my honey dust to try and make her stinking body sweeter. "Come and help me do my hair."

She came yawning and rubbing her eyes, took her sweet time to stand up, too, stood over me too close. "Yes, Prosper."

Her body was nearly touching mine. I opened my nosehole to breathe her in. Honey smell? Or salt sweat? Couldn't tell. "Never mind. Don't come near me. Go and get my day dresses. They're on the left hand side of the closet."

She brought them out. She held out the lavender one with its pale green sleeves and black ribbons. I put it against my body, looked in the mirror. Too vulgar, though I know Charles liked the way it showed off my bosom. So out of that dress, into the powder blue, the one with the blouse that was pale yellow and olive. No, too fussy; more better for evening. A dress like that would only inform Charles's mama that here was a showgirl, come to breakfast in a fine hotel. I wore that blue gown too often anyway; time Charles bought me a new wardrobe.

The terra-cotta made me look like a child. Its rose jacket with its brown fur trim brought out the darkness of my skin too much. Gods, I wish my mama had fucked a thousand more white sailors if it would have made me less brown!

I bade the slow girl fetch me the creamy pale yellow dress, though she was rolling her eyes at how I couldn't decide. Insolent missy. I wanted Charles to get me my own maid, but one with a sweet temper. And darker than me. He liked me dark, he said. Liked my spirit. Said hot country women always had more fire. I was born here in France, though, like my mama before me. I needed to send her some money for the trip to Paris. Hoped Charles would be generous with that.

When Lise and me are in the restaurant, I must try to remember to speak proper. I wished I had come younger into the company of gentlefolk, to learn their talk sooner.

I looked in the mirror, and I jumped. Were those my eyes looking back at me? Looked like someone else's. Frightened, I was so frightened today. My heart was dashing itself against my chest, beating me-out, me-out.

Margot shifted on one foot, still holding the yellow dress. I regarded it. It was nice. Champagne bodice with violet cuffs and bretelles. It showed how my waist was slim, and it moved gracefully with me when I walked. Maybe Charles's mama would spy me entering, would lean over and whisper to her son, "Who is that sweet young woman, dear? She's clearly of fine breeding." Huh. Maybe the salt would disappear from the sea, too.

"What hour is it?" I asked Margot.

"Just after half ten, Jeanne," she replied. "The bell tolled minutes ago."

"I'm late! I was to meet Lise at ten!" Oh God, Lise would leave if I wasn't there, and I'd have to sit there all alone, with Charles glaring at me! I struggled into my pantalettes, almost tripped over the lace ruffles with which they were hemmed. "My hair's still not done, and my shoes! Hurry, then, don't just stare at me so! Help me with my shoes!" *Move, silly wench!*

"Which ones, Prosper?"

I sucked my teeth with impatience and pointed out the pumps to her. She went to get them and brought them back, muttering, "I'll just come and fix your hair." But I ignored her. I sat at the vanity mirror and started undoing my plait. I was used to doing my own hair to go on stage anyway. Margot with her lanky tresses wouldn't know what to do with mine. I fiddled and fiddled with the damned hair. It was tying itself in knots today, strong as chains.

She put the shoes near me. I stuffed my feet into them. She straightened and picked up the comb just as I shook my hair loose. Undone, the tresses sprung out, a cloudy mass of wiry black. Her eyes got big. She put the comb back down. I ignored her, set to twisting and coiling and pinning. Charles's mother would shudder, were she ever to see my hair unbound like this and flinging itself about my shoulders and waist.

Hair done. Now more packets of powdered chalk for my face, neck, and hands; yes, I looked more like a lady now. Then the hoopskirt around my waist, binding it to a proper slimness. Margot helped me into my corset, laced it up the back. She pulled it damnably tight, the hussy. But it made my breasts thrust further, the way that Charles liked, so I endured it. She slipped the dress over my head carefully, so as not to muss my hair or face, but of course, a few of the curls came loose, so back I went to twisting and pinning. Gods, the time, the time was fleeting!

A few more minutes and I was finally ready. I grabbed my cloak and ran out of my room, down the echoing stairs, and out of the concert hall. I hurried as fast as I might onto the street. I was gasping a little for breath in the tight clothing. My heart beat even harder. So strange and unsettled I was feeling, not myself. I bustled past the street urchins on the roadside, just waking from where they'd wrapped their bodies around each other in the Paris mud and settled down to sleep. I stepped around horse shit and a gaunt, spotted bitch dog, her dugs hanging, nosing at garbage. Not many folk out yet this morning. Oh. There was a carriage free. I had some money from Charles. I was going to spend it on breakfast, but if I didn't get there soon, would be no breakfast with Lise for me. The driver stared at me as I approached, his eyes measuring my bosom, going slack with hunger when they marked my brown skin. I nodded at him. "Hôtel Saint-Michel, if you please. And quickly."

And for all that he had enjoyed filling up his eyes with me, the salaud never even got down to help me up. He just waited, looking, while I struggled into his flea-bitten carriage.

But he got me to the hotel quickly enough. His massive paw was sweaty when I dropped the coin into it, and his gaze fixed on my chest. I didn't tip him. Kept some of the money back for a sweet croissant and some coffee. I pulled myself up tall and swept into the hotel. The concierge made to block my path. He knew that some of his guests would never brook having to dine in the same room as an Ethiope. But I said, haughty as I might, "I am to meet my fiancé and his mother for breakfast. They are in the dining room, come before me." A lie, but he stood aside. Oh, my saints, I prayed that Lise would arrive soon.

I got closer to the dining room. I could smell meat and fresh bread. It made my belly grumble. My feet were heavy as blocks of wood as I approached the door. My hands were icy. My heart banging, banging. A waiter balancing a laden silver tray on one hand swept on ahead of me. He held open the door, and turned to bow at me, smiling. His cheeks were as pink as though they'd been rouged, and his blond hair dark with the macassar oil he'd used to slick it back. "Mademoiselle," he said, so respectful. There are some such as he. His graciousness lent me courage. I gave him a brief smile back. Time to play out this game I had begun. I stitched my brightest smile across my face and stepped with my foreign-feeling self into the room.

And there they were. Monsieur Charles Baudelaire and his mama the dame Aupick were at the table closest to the door. Charles saw me, gasped, and stood. He'd blanched utterly. Looked pale as the dead in his dandy's black. His mother turned to see what had made him act so. A bland, plump woman, scowling.

Everyone in the restaurant was looking. My waiter friend was placing butter and croissants at Charles's table. Charles sat back down, tried to compose himself. I slowed to a more graceful walk. I breezed right by Charles and his mother. Only then did

I see Lise, waving and smiling at me from a place right beside Charles's. Mischievous chit had arranged her seating so that Charles and I would have to look at each other the whole time. But she hadn't forgotten me. I went cold with relief, so grateful I was to see her there. I went to her.

"I knew you would be late, Jeanne," she said cheerfully.

"And you? When did you arrive?" The waiter was behind me, pushing my chair in for me.

"Oh, about five minutes ago." She giggled. "I was late too."

Then came a voice from Charles's table: "Pass me the butter please, chéri." It was Charles's maman.

"Here it is, Mother."

"Thank you, son. Are the blackberries sweet this year?"

"Yes, Mother."

"They only bear briefly, but their taste is strong. An almost vulgar tartness to blackberries, wouldn't you say?"

"They're sweet this year."

"You must be careful, though. If you eat too much of the blackberry, you might spoil your taste for the more genteel fruit."

"Yes, Mother."

"And they make such a dreadful dark stain, don't you think?"

"Yes, Mother."

"Soil your fingers with them, and you'd think that black mark will never come out."

"I'm sure I wouldn't know, Mother."

"Oh," said Lise, a little too loud, "you must try the cheese, my dear. They get only the finest here."

But I scarce heard her, for Charles was rising to his feet again, wiping his hands on his napkin. "Excuse me for a little minute, please, Mother," he said. And then I could barely hear myself think for the beating in my chest as Charles came over to me, grinning big and reaching eager biscuit-pale hands to hold my caramel ones, not so much darker than Lise's after all. Charles, he said, "Jeanne! My darling Lemer. What a pleasure to see you here."

SISTER

Blind, linear, I quiet inside the ginger-coloured woman's body. Words are new to me. They come to me as barrages of sensation that were her own, and are now mine. I know what she wants, sitting longing at the table with her hands in yours, though I do not yet know what her longing signifies. I sense from Jeanne the feelings that make her eyes burn. She longs to hear certain words from you, Charles. She aches for you to say something so: "Maman, this woman over here, she listens to me; sits still for hours staring into my eyes while I speak, opens her ears wide so that I may fill them with my hopes, my fears, my raw, new poems." She wishes for you to say, "She makes herself beautiful for me. Does not that gown suit her wonderfully well?" You never say them, and through my dim newborn's eyes, even I can see that you never will.

The ginger-coloured woman's tears bring me meaning in their salt. I learn quickly. Your mother would name her monstrous it seems, not beautiful. Your mother would think the ginger woman's pale brown skin too near the colour of dirt. Is that so bad, then? "Dirt" seems to be a kind of food. Food brings life, a yearning to move forward. Is my wanting to break free "life," then? Is it bad to be dirt and give life? Your mama would be mortified to know that any gentleman can have the pleasure of the ginger woman's voice on the stage, the sight of her beauty, perhaps even in a private assignation, if he can afford it.

I do not want to understand what all that is, do not want to care. I want to fly free again. But the ginger-coloured woman floods me with words, with meaning, and with something more powerful. Now I know them as emotions. Unwilling, I take it all in as the sea-sponge sucks in salt. Some more words: Do you remember unpinning the careful rolls and coils of her hair, Charles? How surprised you were to find it soft, like unspun wool? How you thrust your hands through it and brought it to your nose? She remembers that she did not wince, though you tugged dreadfully. She remembers how deeply you inhaled, how you breathed as you might the needful air the scents of that place—the Indies?—from her hair; remainders of things that had lived once; cinnamon and nutmeg and oil of cacao. Sweet perfumes, her mind tells me; not bitter. She wishes she could bind you to her with that hair; you and your money. "Money" seems to also be a kind of food, and the woman wants for it often. Goes hungry for lack of it. Has slept in cold open spaces for want of it. I feel in her body the memory of cold, of hunger. Those are bitter things. Your sweet "money" can soothe them. She does not want to be bitter. She has had to suffer touches that some-times hurt to this soul case that is our body. Men like you give her this food called money if she will allow them to do the things that are sometimes sweet, but sometimes hurt her. For yourself, you try not to hurt her, and often will feed her. For this, for this sweet thing that you do, she has agreed to be by your side. She wants to hear from you that you will honour that contract.

I learn more words. I sense what is in the woman's heart. You do not speak to your mother of her sweetness. You do not tell her how you sigh, "Douce, douce," singing her sweet-ness in the night as the wet warmth of her tongue laves the musk from your thighs.

The ginger woman longs to scandalise you and your mother both. She thinks how one does not speak to one's mother of these things that lovers do in the shameful dark. Dark I understand now, but not shame yet. She thinks whether she might speak out loud of the shameful things anyway. She imagines telling you and your proper mother how she prepares to greet you for your assignations, of the hours she spends dressing her hair and body, of the honey powder she keeps in a jar on her night table. You told her that it is brought in ships from the perfumed hives of India, as her grandmother was brought from Africa's belly and sold as a creature for the pleasure of gentlemen, whatever those are. Too many ideas I don't understand. But this money thing, this exchange of food for sweetness, that begins to make sense. You pay for her honey powder. It makes her nose itch, but it is to delight you that she wears it, dusts it over the dusky, smooth flesh of her breasts until her nipples stand forth proudly. And when you arrive in her room with your moist, longing eyes, are not those nipples ready to meet your hand or mouth? Are they not dark and sweet between your lips as those blackberries your mother fed you?

As you kissed the black woman's hand, you whispered in her ear, "Isn't it delicious? Maman thinks you are a whore," and this ginger soul case that held me quivered in shame. The ginger woman thinks *Yes, I am a whore and the daughter of a whore and a whore's whore's daughter.* "Whore" I do not understand yet, but I understand from her that her and her kin are your spices, your honey scent; she knows that you and your class have made them so. Wherefore then is she bitter? Do you find her so bitter then, Charles? What do you say, O man of words?

You whisper in my captor's ear, "She has given me some money, Jeanne. You will have your apartment!"

And ginger woman Jeanne is glad, but I do not, do not understand all the things that make her so, that make her rejoice or weep. I find I do want to know. So I still my waves of battering to get free. Perhaps in silence I can learn more, find a way to return to my all-seeing world.

SOUL

Swip! Crack of the overseer's whip tore into my back. I shouted out, jerked. The book-keeper yelled, "Mer, stop lollygagging there!" People cutting cane in front of me sped up little faster, so the next whip lash wouldn't be on their backs.

I chewed on my lips, to distract from the bite of the whip cut. Chopped down three more cane stalks, threw them to one side. Checked the ground. No, no poisoned piquette stake there. I advanced little more, cut some more cane, looked again. I was behind. Me, who was usually out in front.

Check the ground. Advance little bit. Cut.

Was hotter than a cooking fire today. The crackling sound all around could have been people stepping on cane leaves, could have been the fires of the blazing sun. Something was running down my back inside my dress. Was maybe sweat, maybe blood. Likely both. My back was burning, burning. I stayed bent over the cane, didn't dare raise up. Seasoned twelve years ago to stay bent that way whole day if I must, crouched over cane.

Shouts rose from over yonder, where one of the oxen was lazy to pull his wain cart to the factory. No wonder; they'd filled it almost to bursting with cane. Whip was landing on the ox's back like on mine. He had scars too. Off he staggered, slowly.

Check the ground. Advance little bit. Cut. Check. Advance. Cut.

No piquette yet. He must have hidden the one that killed Hopping John somewhere in this field. He, Makandal. Been seeing him slinking around and I know he's up to something.

But all I looked, I couldn't find another piquette with its sharp load of poison.

Book-keeper popped me with the whip two more times

before I finally caught up to the rest. Tipingee would have to rub my back good with aloe tonight.

Oreste spared me a quick glance, chopping all the while. "You're well, matant?" he asked, felling four cane stalks with one blow. He had only a breechclout to cover him from the cutting edges of the cane leaves. His skin was tough. His face was springing water, fat beads of it running down his chest and legs. I could smell the hot sun sweat on him, on me. And the sugar reek of cane.

"Well as I might be." Check. Advance. Chop. "Watch your feet today."

"Hmm?"

"Ouanga." *Bad science.* "Might be a piquette. Someone is up to tricks." I knew it was Makandal, but I didn't say. The other Ginen loved him too well, and the passion in him to see them free. I didn't want to bring anyone's wrath down upon me.

I shoved aside a pile of cane trash with my machète, making centipedes and grasshoppers wriggle and jump out. I think they had all their legs. Hard to see, so fast they moved.

Fear wrinkled Oreste's brow. "Matant, you can't make a gros arrête to guard us from the piquettes?"

"We should tell Makandal!" hissed Belle from the row ahead of us. Hopping John's woman once; no man's woman now. I watched the muscles in her backside heave under the sackcloth dress as she cut cane and threw it to the side. A piece of cane trash was stuck to the sweat laving her solid arms. She spit onto the ground. "He would help us. Makandal is going to be the saviour of the Ginen, going kick out all the grands blans, give us our own land to work!" She said it soft, so the book-keeper wouldn't hear. Last week Milo who brings the wood for the great house stoves was resting in the kitchen, spouting Makandal this, Makandal that, Makandal going to chase off all the plantation owners and make people like Milo rich as the whites. Our owner,

Master Léonard Simenon, got a bad bellyache after lunch that day, and Marie-Claire and the other women of the kitchen were whipped for spoiling the food. Two days Master stayed sick, spewing from mouth above and gut below. And every day he wasn't well, it was more beating for the kitchen slaves. Every night Tipingee wept as she spread aloe on the welts on Marie-Claire's back and behind. It had to stop. One of the kitchen slaves must have carried Simenon word about Milo's threats; Marie-Claire swore it wasn't her. On the third day, Master was better, though Marie-Claire said he was grey and sweating and only calling for wine, more red wine. That afternoon, he made us all to gather round and watch. Milo he made to be tied to stakes in the ground to scream out his life while Master Simenon peeled the skin from his twitching body with a knife. Peeled away all the skin, leaving the white fat glistening, quivering. "You want to be white?" the master shouted over Milo's howling as he cut his ears off. I had heard about this blanching of black people before. Mama, please you make me dead before I ever see it again. Three hours it took Milo's spirit to flee his body, back to Guinée.

Let Belle think Makandal will free us. It's so Tipingee thinks too, filling her child's head with stories of revolution. I pondered if to tell Belle it was Makandal killed her man. But no. We survive in this place by keeping our own counsel. I bent to pick up the cane I had just cut. Felt my cut back split open, start running blood again. Ignored it.

Check the ground. Advance. Cut. Wipe the sweat from my face. Check the ground. Advance. Cut.

And so it went the rest of the day. Was well into the night before the book-keeper allowed the second gang to go home. When I straightened up, first time in hours since the midday meal, the bones in my back creaked and complained. I remembered I wouldn't see Tipingee tonight. She was on first gang, helping the younger ones and the new, unseasoned slaves with their trash gathering.

I made to stretch my aching arms above my head, but my dress pulled where dried blood was sticking it to my back. Sweat was rank on me, dried salt prickling my skin. Blood unclean on me. I was dropping down with fatigue, my belly griping from hunger, but I wanted so badly to wash. Curfew soon, I was supposed to be in bed, but any of us with the brains the gods gave us knew how to catch a few hours for ourselves.

I walked the half-hour to my hut, got my fishing line and my tinder box, the one Marie-Claire had stolen for me from the kitchen. Hiked down to the beach in the dark. Sea water would wash me clean, and gods willing, I would catch some fish for my supper.

Path down to the beach was so rocky, my efforts to climb it opened up the slice on my back again. I didn't pay it no mind, just listened to the rush and wash of the waves whispering; just smelled the sea air. Should have bathed after fishing, not before, so my smell in the water wouldn't scare away my supper, but I couldn't wait no more. Put my tinder box down in the sand and walked right into the warm sea, dress and all. Ai, it stung, the salt water. Burning cut on my back, tiny burning nicks on my arms from cane leaves. But the sweat and the dirt washed away.

When my dress wasn't sticking to me no more, I pulled it over my head and threw it up on a rock to dry. I would pass by the river on my way home and wash it clean of salt. I ducked my head briefly beneath the waters, scrubbed at my itching scalp. My hair was all thick and matty-matty. Weeks now Tipingee and I hadn't had any time together to plait each other's hair. Lasirèn? Bondye who the Muslims call Allah, the god over all? All you gods, why did you bring the Ginen to this?

No. Couldn't think on that, else I would just let my head sink below this water and never rise again. Then who would treat the people when they sicken? Plantation doctor white man didn't know the herbs, the prayers. If I denied to help my people, then my spirit wouldn't fly home.

I waded out of the water. Night air made my skin pimple and chill. Today when the sun was high, all I had wanted was to be cool. Now I shivered until I was dry and warm again. Fetched my line from the shore. Climbed up on the rock where my one dress was drying. Mama, see how my muscles tremble from bending all day over the cane. Baited my hook with sea roach barnacles I dug out of the rock. All the fish loved those. I stood on the slippery rock, my toes gripping to hold me, and threw the hook into the swelling sea. If Mami willed it, I'd make a good catch. A fin fin, or a sad woz.

Glittering stars in a peaceful sky. The moon-face of Ezili floating above the waters. Mama, what a beautiful land this was.

Something pulled on my line. I looked down, saw my own reflection dancing beneath the waters, in the glowing path of moonlight.

And I realised it's not my own face I was seeing, for this woman was young, smooth; she was fat and well-fed. The bush of her hair tumbled about her round, brown, beautiful face in plaits and dreadknots, tied with twists of seaweed. Her two breasts swung full and heavy like breadfruit swaying on the branch. The fish tail waving lazy behind her instead of legs was longer than I'm tall. Light danced and trembled on it as it swept the water, holding her steady. *Lasirèn! Lasirèn!*

My two knees thudded down onto the rock. I never felt the pain of it. I let go my fishing line one time. "Wai, Lasirèn," I prayed, "beg you take me away!" *Oh, you Powers, to be gone from here!*

I stretched my arms to my water mother. Up out of the waves she reared, till I could see the rolls of her belly like mountains. She was laughing! Her breasts and belly bouncing. The hand she reached to me had my fishing line in it, with a big red snapper jerking on the hook. "Take your dinner, daughter." Voice like rushing waves.

Salt tears sprang from my eyes, I could feel them. "I don't

want it! I want to come with you, Mama!" I'm a big woman, but like any child, I cried for my mother to pull me into her arms, to rock me on the swell of her breast.

Her face got serious. "Mer, for all you have my name, if you jump into the sea right now, I will throw you right back."

I couldn't breathe for sobbing, for choking with my sobs. "Why?"

And Lasirèn, this lwa, this Power of all the waters, she frowned. She made to speak, stopped. Then she said, quiet, "I don't exactly know, daughter."

"What?"

She pressed her lips together, then forced the words out: "Something is not right. You must fix it."

"What do you mean?"

She didn't answer. Sucked her teeth, exasperated. Then she threw the fish up on the rock, sank back down into the sea. Her black shadow moved away from me, fast.

"How am I to help you?" I shouted to her.

Up her head came again, a few yards away. My heart rose with it, from the joy of just seeing her. "The sea roads," she said. "They're drying up."

"The sea is drying up?" I looked out over the massive, heaving water.

"Not this sea! Stupid child!" Her tail slapped, sent up a fountain, exploding and drenching me. "The sea in the minds of my Ginen. The sea roads, the salt roads. And the sweet ones, too; the rivers. Can't follow them to their sources any more. I land up in the same foul, stagnant swamp every time. You must fix it, Mer."

Fix it. Fix the problem a great Power of Africa has. If she can't fix it, who is me to try? Despair wanted to swallow me up again.

Little more time, yards and yards out into the deepness of the water, the lady breached. She'd grown. Fear leaped in my chest, to see the size and strength of her, big so like a house. She twisted in the air, dove down. Slapped her tail again at me, spraying me one more time in wet salt as she submerged. The last tip of the moon dropped below the waters. Then nothing. She was gone. Gone before I had the chance to ask her the thing that ate at me every day; why did the gods bring us to this? I was afraid to even think it to myself, but I was angry. I was angry at the gods! Me, one small woman! But the anger was not just for myself. All the Ginen. All the people sick and dead on the ships, and the ones sick and dead on this soil. What are gods for, then, if they let things like this to happen to their people?

I wouldn't think it any more. Mama said I must help. Maybe the gods had a plan?

My catch was barely twitching by now. Plenty meat on its bones for my supper. I threw my dress over my shoulder, climbed down careful with my fish, for it was full dark now. Mama, thank you for sea breeze to keep the mosquitoes away. I waded to the beach, thinking. *The sea in the minds of the Ginen,* she had said. What sea? I gathered driftwood, found a place between some rocks, where the fire couldn't be seen. I piled up the driftwood and set it alight. What sea? I went down back to the firm, wet sand where the shallow waves were breaking over my ankles. With my knife I scaled and gutted my fish right there, threw his entrails into the water. What sea? I rubbed him with salt water to season him, took him back, jooked a stick of drift-wood through him, and roasted him on my fire. And all the time I was cooking, all the while the smell of food was making my mouth water and my belly rumble, all I could think is, what sea? And how was I one woman going to help a great African Power?

A scuff of sand flew into my fire, making it pop blue stars. I looked up. A man shape was blocking out the moon from my view.

"Salaam aleikum, matant."

So. Finally he had caught up with me. I kept tearing with my teeth into the hot, salty fish. Wasn't going to make him know he had startled me. "Honour, Makandal," I said between bites. He had to give me the greeting, or scorn his elder.

He sucked air between his teeth in irritation, came around the fire to where I could see him. "Respect, matant."

"Nice night."

"Not too plenty mosquitoes."

"Hmm."

"Not like the night you three women buried Georgine's still-born."

Oh, such a sly brute! He was there when we did that, yes. I knew it. But all I would say was, "Hmm." I picked at my fish, tried to enjoy it. Bad-minded man, always making mischief, spreading doubt and fear. He was quiet some little while, just watching me. Then:

"Why do you hate me, matant?"

I ate fish. "You cause trouble, you and your big ideas. Make people take risks for your dreams. If Marie-Claire gets caught, it's she will feel Simenon's knife, not you. Then Tipingee would mourn, and me. Why do you stir the Ginen up so?"

"Are you so happy with your life, then, matant?"

"I stick to my work. I do what I'm told. Each day I live is another day I can help my people."

"Help them do what they're told. Ease their dying from over-work or starvation. Help them learn to be good slaves."

My dinner tasted like sand in my mouth. I didn't answer him. He said: "You were talking to somebody out on the rock."

"I was fishing for my dinner, and look, see it here so." I *would* relish my meal. I sucked tender flesh, spat fish bones at his feet.

Makandal stepped back, but not far enough. He was still standing too near. He said, "Somebody was in the water, talking to you."

"A porpoise, swimming in close to the beach. Must be my torchlight that attracted it. It went away back."

"They talk to you!" He crouched down in front of me. Normally he looked stern, proud. But now his face surprised me. It held sorrow. Loss. He was not angry. "The lwas, matant; they talk to you?"

67

Such a pleading in his voice. I'd never seen him so. Makandal has hurts too. Mama, help me not to forget that. I opened my mouth to tell him the beautiful thing that had happened to me. I felt the joy lighting my features. Opened my mouth to share with him the fearsome glory of Lasirèn, to share with him what she had told me, to ask him what he thought: "I . . ."

. . . and I remembered Hopping John's grey face as he was dying on that factory floor, remembered his cracked lips whispering to me, "I 'fraid centipedes, matant. 'Fraid them too bad."

I swallowed back the words I was going to say to the killer Makandal. "Was a porpoise," I told him.

He cried out, swiped more sand into the fire with his good hand. Blue stars crackled, spat. "Why they don't speak to *me!* I pray, I fast, I feed them, feed them; so many goats I feed them." He glared all around him, spread his arms, pleading: "Why this old woman and not me!"

And right that minute, I knew why. "Makandal," I said quiet-quiet, like to a fractious child.

He looked to me, all that hurt-little-boy still showing on his face. Red, his eyes were, and wet. So. That night I learned that Makandal can cry. "Makandal, you eat salt, or you eat fresh?"

He reared back, sullen now. "What stupidness is that, Mer?"

But he knew. "Just answer," I said to him.

It's so the stories go that the Ginen tell. If you find a beautiful fairmaid swimming in the river, her fish tail flashing; if you follow her down into her water home with her, she will make the water like air so you can breathe. But then she'll ask you, playful, *You eat salt, or you eat fresh?* And if you say salt, she will let you go back home, but if you say fresh . . .

"It's my business," he said. Pouted. Looked at the ground.

If you only eat unsalted food, fresh food, we believe you make Lasirèn vexed, for salt is the creatures of the sea, and good for the Ginen to eat, but fresh—fresh is the flesh of Lasirèn, and if you eat that, it's pride. You're trying to make yourself as one of

the lwas. Makandal never eats salt. He, a living man, giving himself powers like a lwa. That's why he couldn't hear the voice of
the lwas.

"I think you know good and well why they won't talk to you,"
I told him.

"But it's them I'm serving . . ."

"Oh, yes?" I said it firmly, to cover my own doubts. Maybe
there are many ways to serve the spirits?

"Yes, matant!" He opened his one hand to me, pleading. It's
not me he needed to plead to. "I'm doing this work for the lwas;
freeing the Ginen of this plague of whites so we can be like we
were before! They must understand, don't they, matant?"

Makandal *cries!* Tears were flowing like river water down his
face now. I saw how he was full of sorrow. But I must know my
own mind. I told myself he was just an own-way, murderous
man who thought if the Powers didn't act in a way that made
sense to him, well then he must make himself one of them and
do the job he wanted them to do. Yes, he thought he knew best.
That couldn't be right.

I stood up. Threw the bones of Lasirèn's gift towards the water
with thanks for my meal. A wave caught the bones and pulled
them off the sand, back to their home. And so I knew she
accepted my prayer.

A sniff came from Makandal. He was still weeping, looking to
me for answers. I wondered what it was like for him, turning
himself into a Power, no salt. The sweat of his body, the piss, and
the jism; I wondered did they taste sweet. "Those tears," I said,
"salt, or fresh?"

He flung himself to his feet, muscles popping out on his arms
and chest. I was an elder, I would not back down. He glared at
me. Hooked my dress with his staff; my one garment that was
lying on the sand to dry. Flipped it into the fire, he. Then stalked
off into the darkness.

For a while the fire flared brighter, trying to eat my frock, but the cloth was too wet. I snatched my dress back out again. By the light of the fire I watched at Makandal climbing the steep ascent back up to the plantation.

Eh. Children will throw tantrums. I pulled the damp frock on. It stuck to my skin, and it had a burned place. I would beg Marie-Claire to get me some more flour bags from the kitchen.

Was time for me to go too. Didn't want the overseer to look in my hut and see me missing. I pulled a half-burnt branch out of the fire. It would be my torch to go back with. I took another branch and spread the coals around with it to put them out.

Something was gleaming from the pile of dying coals; something the firelight ran over like liquid. I flicked it out onto the sand. It was glowing, red, too hot to touch. I fetched salt water in my mouth from the sea, spat on it. It hissed, grew dark. Fetched more water, did it again. Then I waited little bit, squatted over the thing, touched it with a fingertip. Still warm, but not hot any more. I picked it up, looked at it good by my torchlight. Glass. A lump of glass, shaped like a whale. I smiled. All that sand Makandal had kicked into my fire. Thank you, Mama. I folded my hand tight around her sign.

Climbed the hill, me, to Tipingee's arms. I'd be cutting cane again tomorrow as the sun rises. And all the time I was walking, I was thinking, how I must help a Power?

THROWING

PARIS, 1842

The delicate china cup clipped Charles's ear as I flung it past him to smash against the wall. His cry of pain mingled with the crash of breaking china. His hands flew up, too late, to protect his head. The cane in his right hand knocked one of his precious paintings askew on the wall. Hands to his ear, a look of horror on his face, he glanced to the painting, then to me. I smiled, pointed behind him at the havoc I'd wrought. "*That* for your jowly, pompous mama!" I said. Even a day after encountering that woman, the thought of her still made me want to spit.

Streaks of milky coffee trickled down the beautiful red wallpaper. The stain would never come out. He'd have to replace it. Good.

"You hurt me!" Charles cried, still cradling his wounded ear.

Gods. I can't act this way with Charles. Can't afford to. I needs must coddle him now, mustn't let my anger rule me so. I gave a little "oh" of contrition, a hand to my mouth. Let him see the regret on my face. I rushed to his side. "Oh my dear, my Charles, I'm so sorry. Here, let me see."

I clucked and tutted at him, exclaiming the while about my unruly temper. I remembered to keep my body inclined low, to shrink myself smaller than he. He was sensitive about my greater height.

He allowed himself to be fussed over. "Truly, Jeanne," he said sternly, "there are times when you go too far." He straightened the sleeves of that ridiculous frock-coat, smoothed down his lapels.

"Yes, I do, I do." Truly, he looked like a crow in that stern black. "Dear Charles, you are so kind, to bear up under my fits and tantrums." I blew gently on his reddening ear. He shivered. That always got his blood to rising. For good measure, I leaned over and licked the length of the ear. It was greasy, salty with sweat.

He gasped, giggled. "Jeanne!"

He's not the least bit scandalised at my ways, but he likes us to pretend that he might be. I could see the fabric of his trousers tenting. I laved his ear again with my warm, wet tongue, directed a warm breath into its very centre. He squirmed, stepped away from me. Not for long. I could see the little smirk on his face. He turned, took me by both shoulders. "My maman is a good woman," he proclaimed, gently. He shook one leg a little, trying to set his cockstand more comfortably in his trousers, I'd wager.

"And I am a mere entertainer, I suppose." I wasn't in the mood for this game.

His look became more serious. "Sweet Lemer, understand me," he pleaded. "Maman will allow much from me, her only son, but I cannot overstep her morals and manners too far. Recollect, her husband controls my inheritance."

Could I forget? Money had us both in thrall. "Oh, Charles, it's all so dreary. He controls your mama, your mama controls you . . ."

"She loves me. She wishes well for me."

". . . And you control me." I pouted, crossed my arms huffily over my bosom, well aware that the action made my titties swell. I saw Charles noticing. His little pointer stiffened to attention again. Oh, these proper gentlemen; how little it takes to excite them!

His desire heated my blood too. Sometimes it happened that way. Really he was a good man, my Charles, if overtimid with his mama. I cast my eyes down prettily, pretended shyness. He loved that. He swept me up in his arms, let his cane fall—oh, theatric man!—and began planting kisses and kisses and kisses on my face.

"Jeanne," he breathed, "how I want you."

His damp attentions were smearing my face powder. I giggled to see it dusting his lips, brushed it off him with my fingers. He took the fingers into his warm, wet mouth. Low, I murmured to him, "How do you want me, Charles?"

He groaned.

"Do you wish to throw me on the day bed, tilt my petticoats over my head?"

"Ah, you slattern, you gutter-tramp."

The wild strangeness I'd been feeling since yesterday flared inside me. I opened to it, let it feed my heat. "Do you wish to climb aboard me, straddle my waist, slip your cremorne into my mouth?"

He was unfastening my frock as quickly as he might, wrestling me towards the day bed as he did. He trapped my wrists in his two hands, stretched them above me so that my breasts strained to rise free from their corsetting. The nipples dragged against the fabric, arousing me further. I stumbled backwards. In his haste, Charles stepped on my hem. I heard fabric tear. I laughed, let myself fall onto the bed. He *would* buy me another frock after all. I swung my skirts into the air, spread my knees for him, so he might gaze on my purple, swollen coynte through the open crotch of my frilly pantalettes. He sighed, fell on me, mouthing me eagerly through the pantalettes.

For a time, my body responded to his as eagerly, and I was glad. But as ever, he nibbled too hard in some places, not hard enough in others. My bohemian Charles thrilled to think that he was doing such a debauched thing, but for the life of him, he couldn't seem to learn to do it well. I lay back and thought on other, softer, more skillful mouths.

Tipingee stood a minute to enjoy the sight of Mer laughing, laughing as she watched Oreste and Belle dancing the kalenda, twitching their shoulders at each other, making eyes. Mer didn't laugh much. This one day each year, when the blans were feasting the birth of their god, they let the Ginen celebrate, let them have some little joy. A few times today she and Mer had hid behind the cabins and Mer had smiled for her; put her lips in between Tipingee's and chortled sweet pleasure into them. The taste of Mer's mouth had danced in Tipingee's like the kalenda. The Christmas sun was hot, the music nice, and the smell of the sweet potatoes that Papa Kofi was roasting in the fire nearby was making Tipingee's belly rumble.

Ti-Bois and his sister Ti-Marie came struggling up from the beach, each of them bearing two green water coconuts the men must have chopped down. The little ones put down the coconuts and began imitating Belle and Oreste, jigging about and laughing, till Hector shooed them back to get more coconuts.

"Tipingee!" Oreste cried out. Belle had gotten tired, was fanning herself, coming to sit by her and Mer. This day, Belle was turned out in petticoats, and a fancy gown of bleached calico. That Georgine could turn a flour bag into a wonder, oui. Belle looked like a queen.

"Tipingee, you forgot how to dance?" Oreste said.

"Ouf," huffed Belle, planting her behind on a rock. "He wore me out. Go and dance with him, Tipingee?"

"Yes, Tipingee, go," Mer said to her, touching her shoulder lightly, so lightly. Oreste was dancing a little pattern towards Tipingee, moving his head in time to Hector's playing of the menuet. Georgine and Pierre were both clapping in time. It was strange to see a backra here. The Ginen were watching themselves, cautious with him around. But he didn't belong at the great house either this day; only the rich ones were invited there. Pierre was a man without two sous to rub together, and Georgine was his only family in Saint Domingue.

Tipingee marked how Georgine's belly was big like a watermelon again. She would soon have another porridge-coloured baby to replace the one she'd lost.

Oreste was still imploring Tipingee, holding his hands out to her. She could see Babette's jealous face behind him in the crowd. But it was Tipingee that Oreste wanted, not that ugly Babette. Tipingee rolled her eyes. "Oreste's feet are like two big yams," she told Belle and Mer. "If he steps on my toes, he might break them. Patrice now, he could dance. Lighter than breathing. You remember, Mer?"

Only with Patrice would she dance the kalenda. She wondered if he was making Christmas in the bush with the maroons? She wondered if he had a new woman now?

The music was sweet, oui. Mer looked down at Tipingee's feet and smiled; her toes were tapping to the music. Tipingee curled her rebellious toes under, but the music just went dancing along her spine, begging it to move and sway in time.

"Tipingee, soul," said Mer, "I think you want to dance. Your feet want to dance."

"Yes, go, Tipingee!" Belle said. "You're spry enough to keep out from under Oreste's feet if they mash you."

Belle and Mer laughed and pushed Tipingee into the centre of the dance. The music was sweet and Oreste was handsome, and she let them do it.

Oreste's face was glowing with sweat, his steps nimble. She knew she'd only been bad-mouthing him. She smiled, set her body just so, challenged Oreste with her eyes. And she began to dance.

He was good, this Oreste: the way he twisted and turned to

the music; the flourishes he made with his hands. He gave a little jump and Tipingee heard the crowd say, "Ah." She quirked her lips at him and matched him, move for move; made up some of her own into the bargain.

When the "Ah" came again, Tipingee thought it was for her, stamping out a rhythm with her feet, faster than hummingbird wings. But the music fell silent. "Hector, what's wrong with you?" she cried out, gesturing at him to continue. "Play, man!"

But Hector was staring past her, to the path. Everyone turned to look. Tipingee spun around. It was Father León striding by, black cassock dragging in the dust, putting backra magic on them all as he went; signing the cross and murmuring backra incantations at them in his Spanish-flavoured French. He was smiling, pleased with himself.

And beside him . . . "Patrice!" she shrieked, and ran to him. Patrice, her Patrice, her dancing man.

"Tipingee."

He embraced her. One of his wrists had rope tied around it. Father León was leading him by it, but Tipingee could see that the knot was deliberately loose enough that Patrice could slip it off if he wished. He'd come back of his own desire, then. Any runaway could do this; find someone to intercede for them, and return in the peace of Christmas time. On Christmas day, the masters would usually be lenient.

Patrice smelled of the green bush where he'd been living and of man sweat. His sweat. Tipingee felt her belly go soft with desiring. "Patrice."

"I'm home, Tipingee. Missed you too bad."

Yes, it's so his eyes used to crinkle when he smiled. So he would catch up his bottom lip between his teeth. More than a year she hadn't seen him. She sobbed into his neck, inhaling the smell of him as hard as she could.

"Let him go there, girl," said Father León. "Don't writhe on him in so heathenish a manner."

Tipingee drew away, her hand still on Patrice's shoulder. This day, Father's word would have to be law.

"Tipingee is my wife, Father," Patrice told him. And her Patrice grinned and winked at her.

His cheeks were hollow. What, did the maroons never feed him?

Father smiled a thin smile, tugged on the rope at Patrice's wrist. "Your wife? How quaint. Well, she must wait to perform her wifely duties until after we see what Simenon will do with you. Come along."

So along they went; Tipingee, Patrice, and Father León, with two or three of the small children running after them for a chance to get inside the great house. Little Ti-Bois was yelling and jumping with the excitement. Tipingee felt she could do the same; leap and kick like a young goat. Then she looked behind her. Hector had started playing his music again, looking a little sadly at Patrice. One who had got free had put the coffle back on his own neck. Some of the escaped did this, sometimes. Couldn't make treat with the maroons, and were starving, so they came back. Or couldn't live in the bush, so they came back to the torment they knew. Or missed their fellows too much. Patrice said he had come home for her. Tipingee could have wept with the joy of it, and the sadness.

Georgine with her heavy belly started trying to teach Pierre the dance steps. Pierre was jigging from side to side like a grasshopper. All red his face was, like the blans could get. His mouth was fixed in a shy smile. He looked embarrassed.

And there was Mer, just standing there on the edge of the circle, sad eyes staring after Tipingee. Tipingee beckoned for her to come, that half of her heart, but there she remained.

The other piece of Tipingee's heart was Patrice. A whole year she hadn't seen him, and now he had his hand in hers again. So Tipingee went with him this time. Mer must understand.

By the time they reached the walkway to the great house, they had become quite the procession; bunches of the Ginen came with them to see what would happen. Some were still singing the Christmas songs, carrying and drinking the portion of rum, distilled from their labours, that they got for this day. There were poor blans there too; the ones that Simenon employed. All come to see the fun. Even Mer had come, following along in the back of the crowd where she thought Tipingee wouldn't see her.

"Hey, Patrice," the book-keeper called out cheerfully. "Got tired of those jug handles you call ears, eh? Come to get them lopped off?" Then he and his compères laughed, slapped each other on the back. Tipingee held tight to Patrice's hand, the unshackled one. She glanced at him. He was biting his lips, but no other sign did he give that he had heard.

"Shush, fellow," Father León scolded the book-keeper. "Unseemly behaviour for our Lord's birthday."

"Yes, Father," the man muttered, tugging at his hat.

Patrice never said a word to the book-keeper. Tipingee knew why. If he responded, the book-keeper might imagine that a slave dared to make sport with him. Better they think you sullen than insolent. Heart aching with fretfulness, Tipingee squeezed Patrice's hand, but said nothing either. Too many blans around. She wasn't going to show them any weakness. By the Code Noir, Simenon could sever Patrice's ears for running away. He shouldn't have returned, shouldn't have risked the agony and disfigurement. Not for her. She jittered along beside him, vibrating with fear for him.

The gravel of the pathway felt harsh beneath Tipingee's bare feet, not like the moist earth of the canefields she was used to walking on. Rose bushes edged the path, open and panting in the late afternoon heat. That smell of flowers; that the world should have such sweetness in it! The only flowers in Tipingee's life were the scratchy yellow blossoms of her pumpkins. Butterflies and fat bees floated amongst Simenon's roses, gorging on nectar. The steaming Christmas air hummed with bees.

The great house loomed in its whiteness before them, like a large albino toad on the path. The verandah that wrapped around it looked cool and shady. Tipingee felt her heart beating warning. She'd never set foot on its steps before; never had business that gave her permission to be here. Suppose they made Simenon mad with their impertinence, accompanying Patrice like this? Suppose their master decided to punish them all? Only Father they had to intercede for them, and him a chancy saviour. She closed her eyes briefly and made up her mind to stay with Patrice, to brave Simenon's whips so that she might be with Patrice when his fate was decided.

Father led his flock gravely up the stairs. The only sounds were their feet thumping on the stone steps. *If there are gods still,* Tipingee prayed, *help us now.* She looked back. Yes, Mer was still there. Tipingee felt a little better. Not reassured completely, but a little more comforted.

"Do any of you heathens know 'Venez, Divin Messie'?" Father asked. By the look of disdain he directed at the whole bunch, it was clear that he included poor whites and blacks both in "heathen."

"Yes, Father," said a few voices.

"Good. Be ready to sing it, then. When I tell you, mind."

"Yes, Father."

He sighed, set his shoulders. He banged the knocker on the huge wooden door. It clunked like an axe biting into the chopping block. He knocked again, and favoured Patrice with a small, grim smile. "All will be well, Patrice." He sounded to Tipingee like a man trying to convince himself of what he was saying. He frowned at her, but she kept her hold on Patrice's hand. Patrice squeezed back. His palm was damp and slippery.

In a little while a young quarteronne, beach-sand-coloured, pushed the heavy wood doors open little bit and peered through. Her eyes took in Father León, his black prisoner, the woman with them, then got big as she saw the rest of the ill-matched crew shuffling its shod and bare feet on her master's verandah.

"Well, child?" Father said impatiently.

"Sorry, Father," she whispered. She bobbed her head, pushed the door open, and held it for them to pass through. As Tipingee made to get in the door, the girl blocked her way. She barely glanced at Tipingee, as one might at a stray dog scrabbling in a midden. "All of them, Father?" she said, looking to him as a sunflower would to the sun.

Chuh. Tipingee sucked her teeth in disgust. Little bit of girl forgot that part of her was African.

"Yes, girl," Father said impatiently. "Step aside."

A triumph, but it was like clay in Tipingee's mouth. She wanted to talk of it to Patrice, but Father would probably object. So she bit on her lips and stepped for the first time inside the great house where her daughter toiled every day, but where Tipingee had never been.

She heard Mer gasp, saw her look around her, the amazement on her face like one who'd died and gone to the land beneath the waves. The smith took his cap off, clutched it to his chest. He managed to make himself look smaller. Tears sprang to Tipingee's eyes. The smell inside the master's house; that smell, where did she know it from? Why did it make her want to weep? No weeping. Not here. She wondered would she see Marie-Claire. She thrust her chin higher and looked all around her at the high ceilings with their massive wooden beams, at the yards and yards of lace covering the long, tall windows. How many hours of toil to weave all that lace? Enough fabric to make dresses for her and Mer and Marie-Claire for the rest of their lives. White dresses. Or maybe the blans had machines to do that work for them. And an army of Ginen, doubtless, to work the machines. Wondering, Tipingee barely felt herself being nudged further into the foyer as the rest of the crowd piled in with them. She heard Mer behind, shushing the three small children.

Father gathered everyone around him into a little knot. "At my word, now," he said, "you begin to sing." Then he turned to the young quarteronne. "Lead us to Monsieur Simenon."

Looking doubtful, she turned. They started off after her. "Now," said Father, and except for the book-keeper and the smith, who had stepped back a bit from the crowd and were nudging each other and laughing, the group began a tattered chorus of "Venez, Divin Messie."

"Sauvez nos jours infortunés . . ."

They went deeper into the house. The Ginen's words began to falter as they gaped around, taking in the sights of Simenon's home. A narrow brown face peeked out of an open door. Marie-Claire! The child saw her father Patrice and made to run to him. A stern voice from inside the kitchen called her back. Marie-Claire watched them go, her face drawn with longing and worry. Tipingee ached for them all.

The group drew level with another open room. Tipingee looked in, to sounds of consternation. A gaggle of white women, swan-pale, odd, gaped back at them. The women were raising cut-crystal glasses, clear as water, to their narrow lips to drink cask-aged wine. No burning rum for them. Their delicate hands were gloved, white throats exposed. Their gracefully bustled behinds would put any African woman's high, round rump to shame. And their hair! Twisted, piled, and pinned. Tipingee found herself touching her own hair and flushing hot at the cane-rowed plaits that Marie-Claire had spent the evening doing for her. Hers looked nothing like the spider-web creations that were the hair of the backra women. She had been so proud of them, but now they felt like turds on her head.

The women kept staring. One of them started forward. "What . . ." She was slim as cane stalks, her bosom full and firm.

"My apologies, ladies, for disturbing your apéritif," said Father.

The book-keeper and the smith were red in the face from laughing, though they straightened up and dipped their heads when they saw the backra woman. "'Day, Mum," they mumbled. She never answered them.

Even the damned wench leading the group of them was biting her lips. Father scowled at them all and nodded to the white women. "Just some quick business with the master of the house, and we'll be on our way." The blan woman frowned, and withdrew back into the room. With one long, smooth hand she closed the door in their faces. But Tipingee could still hear the room of women laughing, their voices tinkling as though someone had thrown all the crystal glasses to the floor.

The group moved on, their singing only a lonely whine now: come, Divine One; come.

Ah! descendez, hâtez vos pas,
Sauvez les hommes du trépas,
Secourez-nous, ne tardez pas.
Venez, venez, venez.

And now they could hear the deep voices of men, drunken men. Father's lips were moving as he silently implored his white god. Tipingee clung to Patrice's hand, reached unhappily behind her for Mer's. She could have sobbed when she felt the dry rasp of Mer's palm against hers. She held on, held on to her loves.

An explosion of mirth came from that room of men; the deep, sure voices were full with assurance, with power. They spoke in arrogant France French, not the Saint Domingue French, and not the Kreyòl for the daily work of cutting cane and weeding and whispering to your fellows when the book-keeper was out of earshot. The sound of those voices struck Tipingee like shot; and not her only. The clump of pauvres blans and black slaves gathered in closer.

"The accursed man thinks that he can get sugar from beets," said one voice.

"He never does!" exclaimed another. "Why, what will we do then?"

Father took a deep breath, and led them into the room.

"Wai!" Patrice murmured under his breath. Tipingee understood his wonder. Even dreams were not so odd. Tipingee could never have dreamt the extravagance of the velvet and cord justaucorps jackets that corseted the figures of the nine or ten backras standing or sitting around the empty fireplace. Some of the men even wore black! So much money for strong black dye. Damask and linen shirts exploded forth like froth from under their gilets. They all wore white wigs, pigeon-winged or ponytailed, and small tricorne hats. A bevy of blans, as embroidered as their women. Ten backra men, all dressed as fine as any city ruler, but bleached as bodies pulled from weeks under the river. Tipingee's skin prickled. All heads had turned as Father had entered with his entourage. Which one was Simenon? She had never seen him.

"Ah," said a man from the armchair where he lounged, a glass of something deep red in his hand. Not blood, Tipingee remembered, but a kind of wine. "Father León, is it? And what a flock you have brought with you."

This must be their master. The other men smiled and laughed at his joke, slapping each other's shoulders. Simenon's demon's eyes of sky glittered. Father bowed his head slightly. "A good Christmas day to you, gentlemen. I was pleased to see some few of you in church this morning on this blessèd day of our Lord."

One of the men coughed. "Ah, yes. Indeed. Fine sermon, Father. Most uplifting." Another glanced sideways at one of his fellows. They both grinned.

Father seemed to stand taller. "If you came away uplifted, it was God's work, not mine. As I do God's work now, Seigneur Simenon."

Simenon only lifted an eyebrow. "As I suppose you must, since Mother Church so zealously commands it. What is that fellow you have brought with you, Father?"

Patrice tilted his chin up high and bit his lips together. So the

Ginen did rather than say words that would condemn them. Tipingee clutched her loves' hands tight.

Father put an arm around Patrice's shoulder. "This, Seigneur, is one Patrice, of your plantation, a runaway since last Christmas, he tells me."

"The devil you say!" Simenon leaned forward and looked hard at Patrice. "This is that Patrice? A year this wretch has had my men searching for him! Do you know how much I paid to find you, you brute? Eh? Do you?"

"No, sir," Patrice mumbled. He cast his eyes down.

"Seigneur," Father said, "Patrice regrets the mischief he has caused. But it is no more than must be expected when you allow the slaves in your charge to lack for Christian instruction."

Simenon glared at the priest, and now it was Father's turn to draw his chin up in the air. Father continued: "Patrice wishes to return to his labours, and he has bade me to make intercession for him on this most holy of days."

One of the blans made an angry noise. "The nerve of the devil, Simenon! He takes advantage of Christmas day to run away, and now he wants to take advantage of it again to return? You'll never let him, will you?"

"Hmm," was all that Simenon replied.

Gods, you gods, it was all going to go wrong. They were going to kill her Patrice, or maim him. Tipingee couldn't stop the two tears that rolled down her face. Mer touched her shoulder, gently.

A timid knock came from outside the door, and in came Marie-Claire, bearing a tray, silver, with the clear-water crystal on it; dishes, this time. Eh. These backra lived in little islands of heaven, a magical world that Tipingee had never before conceived.

"Ah," said a man in a deep grey justaucorps as he took one of the desserts from Marie-Claire, "Mango fool." Eager pink hands reached for the dishes.

Father frowned a little as he regarded the confection of spiced, puréed mangoes and sweetened milk. "Truly? I would call that 'Mango divinity.'"

Again that raised up eyebrow from Simenon. "Much of a muchness perhaps, eh Father? They sometimes say that the maddest fools have been touched by God." He leaned back in his chair, legs wide, and began to spoon the confection out of its dish. Tipingee watched yellow mango disappear into his maw as he ate of the good of his plantation. Simenon looked at Patrice as he chewed, considering. The Ginen huddled closer together. Marie-Claire kept darting glances over to her mother and Patrice, but the child needs must stay where she was, at service to the men, eyes bowed down.

Simenon ate the last spoonful of sweetness from his dish and let the spoon fall back into it with a ringing clatter. The tinkling echoed and swooped in Tipingee's head, round and round. Marie-Claire rushed to take the dish onto the silver tray. Simenon licked his lips. "What must I do with such a brazen runaway? Must make an example of him."

"Exactly," said one of the fine gentlemen in his turkey-buzzard suit of black. He gave Patrice a long look. "Set him to dance at the end of a whip. Teach him obedience." The others nodded, murmured, except one, who looked silently out the window at the butterflies dancing there, frowning.

"Christ forgave the sinners in the temple," Father León said bravely. Another blan clattered his spoon into his dish.

"I am not so holy, Father," growled Simenon. "There's no profit in it, and France clamours always for more sugar, more rum, more indigo, and taxes me past bearing. I cannot have compassion on a wretch who flees his labours to gallivant in the bush."

Tipingee shut her eyes tight and prayed for Aziri to deliver Patrice, prayed for miracles she feared would not happen. She could hear Mer behind her, whispering in her own tongue to

Lasirèn. They said the names of their gods together, and the chiming of spoons on crystal came a third time as a few more of the blans finished their desserts. *Venez, venez, venez.* Come. Save us.

The door creaked, the same note as the spoons on the glass. "Ah," said a high woman's voice with amusement in it. "It seems you brave fellows are having your own entertainment here." Master Simenon looked up, and the frown fell from his forehead as a salted slug falls from a leaf. He stood, smiling, and extended his hand. Marie-Claire, bustling about to collect the used ware, looked to see who had come in. Dismay creased her brow.

The collected crystal tinkled like the gossiping river, and to its music, a lady white as the moon was wafting towards Simenon, almost gliding in her beautiful lace-trimmed dress. She laughed gently, waved a languid lace fan before her face. With the light behind the vision of her, she seemed a thing of another world. The scent of sweet perfume came with her. The door whispered shut behind her, and in the faint breeze of it Tipingee thought she could just smell the sea. Tipingee closed her eyes. How strange a day this was! She opened them again, and finally recognised the lady; one of the backra women who had been in the first little room. But she was different now. Her eyes were too intent, as though they looked on more than men's eyes could see. And so odd, the way she moved! Like when Ti-Bois got piles of sticks and called them soldiers, and walked them with his hands to make them march.

The lady's gown rustled as she moved. She put her hand, white and slim as candles, into Simenon's own. Carefully, she said, "It is so dull in that parlour with the other women." She looked around again with those wide eyes; eyes drinking everything in as though for the first time. "Monsieur Simenon," she enquired, "what matter is at hand here?" She looked with a hungry curiosity from face to face. She fanned herself, gracefully.

"Please sit down, my dear," said Simenon. "You look a trifle overwarm. Do you feel well?"

One of the other backra men rushed to offer her his chair. "Oh, entirely well, Monsieur." She floated over to the chair, graceful now, as a manmzèl floats on the air, and folded herself and her wide skirts into the seat.

Simenon sat again, still smiling at her. He gestured at Patrice. "This fellow is a runaway. Can you imagine, my dear; a whole year of labour he has cost me! And now—"

"Now," interrupted Father León, "he has repented of his marronage and wishes to return."

The lady rapped her fan delightedly against the heel of her hand. "And you intercede for him, Father! On this holy day! How Christian of you."

Father bowed his head a little. "Thank you, my lady. Christian charity is my duty and my calling. I would instruct the blacks on this plantation in the ways of our Lord, for then I am sure that they would be less restless, but Seigneur Simenon claims that he cannot spare their time of a Sunday."

The lady turned wide eyes to Simenon; eyes blue as the shifting sea. "Is this true, my darling? Do your slaves work on Sundays as well?" She fanned herself, and the breeze from the fan made wisps of curls shift prettily about her face. Tipingee wondered at how that hair flowed like water. Backra women's hair was cornsilk fine.

Simenon looked uncomfortable. He grumbled, then: "Of course not, dearest. They have one day of rest each week. It is law," he admitted.

"Seigneur," said Father quietly, "it is also law that they should receive the word of our Lord. Please allow me to conduct chapel here on Sunday mornings. It will cost you nothing, I promise you, and will make your slaves more meek and ready to accept God's saving grace. A profit to yourself and to God."

Simenon didn't reply. He weighed Patrice out with his eyes; transparent demon eyes. Oh, you gods. When Tipi had been young, her mother telling her stories back home, back home where her name had been another name that she couldn't remember now, for that name had drowned in the salt sea of the Middle Passage; back home, listening to her mother's voice, could Tipingee ever have imagined that the monsters from the old tales were real? Yet here she was, living that nightmare tale, while a demon decided what to do with her beloved husband.

"What was it like?" Simenon asked Patrice.

"What, sir?" Tipingee could feel how still Patrice had gone. Was it a trap?

"You had a year in the bush," Simenon said softly. "You came and went as you pleased."

"Sorry, sir," said Patrice imploringly, but Simenon spoke over him.

"You transported yourself free as any wild beast in that bush for a whole year, mocking your master." And Master Simenon leaned closer, so close it seemed he might tumble from his arm-chair. "What was it like?" he whispered. "Was it glorious? No fretting about how many acres of cane harvested, or how many lazy wretches you need to buy to replace the ungrateful ones who've died on you? What was it like to be free? To dig in the soil with sticks for your food, or to hunt wild beasts of the bush for your meat?"

"Sir?" said Patrice uncertainly.

"Simenon, what ails you?" asked the turkey-buzzard man. He put his hand on the master's shoulder. Got it shrugged off for his pains. The backra who had been silent was smiling a little now.

"No juggling and juggling to make the books balance," Simenon said. "No weevils in the flour, eh? No accursed frock-coats plastered to your body in this hellish heat and no mildew in your wig! No wig, for that matter, eh? Eh? Come now, you can tell me! Was it not fine?" And the master laughed, regarded Patrice as though he might be a dear friend to sit and share palm wine and stories with.

The backra must be insane! Tipingee saw Patrice's eyes go wide. He opened his mouth to reply, but no words came out. It was the lady who laughed like the tinkling of bells. "Then you *will* grant him clemency, my dear! I thought you might!"

Simenon looked surprised, as did the men around him. He frowned at the lady, who reached a long white hand to him. "Oh, what a fine man I have picked for my fiancé!" she said.

And so Tipingee learned that their master was taking this woman into his house. Then Simenon was smiling again, grinning at his men friends and puffing himself up like the toad who has croaked and croaked and found him a wife. "All right, dearest," he said. "I will let him keep his ears. And yes, Father, you may have your nigger church."

Patrice would be all right. Tipi's body went cold with the relief of it. She marked the sudden drop of Patrice's shoulders from about his ears. Father sighed and made the sign of the crossroads on his chest. The backra men coughed and shuffled, but they said nothing to gainsay their friend.

"Oh . . ." gasped the lady. She sagged forward a little in her chair.

Simenon leaped to her side. "Élisabeth, are you well?" He touched her shoulder.

She straightened up again. "A little dizzy. It's nothing." She looked around her, dazed, at the backra milling around her. "But this is the men's parlour," she whispered. Her eyes were less bright now. She was no longer looking into another world. She fanned herself and slumped back in her chair, staring in confusion at Simenon.

She was not so beautiful, Tipingee could see now. That elaborate coiffure was plumped out with hair rats to make it look thicker. The powder that she had used to whiten her face ended in a line at her chin, and from beneath its pallour, two angry red bumps glared on her jaw. And she had a nervous manner of looking from face to face of the men in the parlour, as though waiting for them to tell her what to do.

"Girl," Simenon said to Marie-Claire, "bring us more wine. The port. And hop quick, now."

"Yes, Monsieur." Marie-Claire curtseyed with the tray still in her hands, and left quickly, still casting that look of fear at the backra woman. Did she fear the woman, or the spirit that had come riding in her? Tipingee would have to ask Marie-Claire about that later.

Simenon waved a dismissing hand at Father León and the clustered Ginen. "Go on now. Out of my sight, and let me enjoy the rest of my Christmas day."

Relief washed over Tipingee: at last they could leave that evil place. Soon Patrice would be back in her bed. Soon she could find Mer alone and ask, *who was it who had come as Patrice's saviour, hiding in the white woman's head? What ancestor, what spirit?*

They were almost out of the men's parlour when Simenon called out, "Wait."

Now it was Patrice with his eyes closed. Tipingee could see how his body trembled. Father turned back to the plantation owner. "Yes, Seigneur?"

"Thomas," Simenon said to the book-keeper, ignoring the priest, "see that our runaway there gets five lashes tomorrow."

Patrice made a small sound. Tipingee put her forehead to his shoulder; held the length of his arm tight against her breast.

The book-keeper grinned. "Yes, sir!"

"Just a kiss of the whip, mind," Simenon told him; "a reminder that he must not cross me. But don't hurt him much. I want him fit for work."

Tipingee could not be another minute in this house. Furious, she dragged Patrice and Mer towards the door. As they walked through it, she heard one of the backra men say, "They mean to raise another balloon into the air tomorrow, on the beach. This ballooning science is all the rage in Paris now, they say."

So many rooms, and all those corridors. She didn't know if she could find the way out. But they were leaving. The rest would follow her.

As they pushed through the door, Tipingee heard Patrice say to Simenon, "Thank you, sir; thank you. God bless you."

She knew he meant the god of the blans. *Yes, Master Léonard Simenon*, she thought. *Let your god bless you as He blesses us.*

Most times, I live in Jeanne, and learn her life. Sometimes, I dream. That is what it is called: dreaming. There are times when ginger-coloured Jeanne's mind holds me loosely, and my consciousness travels; to where, I am not sure.

Rare, to have rain in dry December. At first Patrice had welcomed the cool sprinkle of the passing shower on his whip-burned shoulders as he weeded the ratoon fields of young cane. Thomas had followed orders and the whipping had been over almost before Patrice could gasp from the pain; but his back was still sore, and the rain felt cool on the bruised skin.

So long he hadn't had to bend every day over sugar cane, feeling the ache like iron in his curved spine; the hot sun crisping his skin; the palm of his hand that grasped the machète stinging as its blisters burst. His back would be raw tomorrow from sunburn, so the rain was a blessing. He threw back his head and took sweet, clean water from the sky into his mouth. Rain trickled through his hair and down his naked body, washing the sweat away. Patrice tossed a clump of weeds into the sack tied around his shoulder and advanced, doing his best to keep up with the rest of the gang. So long his arms hadn't burned from digging, digging, digging in the earth or cutting down the razor-leaved cane from sunup till sundown. He blinked rain out of his eyes and pulled up a wet clump of weeds. He shook the earthworms out of it back into the soil.

A small snail with a cream-and-beige-coloured shell fell from the clump onto his hand. Come out to keep from drowning in the downpour. Ignoring that the rest of the Ginen were moving on ahead of him, Patrice held the snail by the tip of its shell and regarded it. In a little while the grey, glistening mass of it wormed its way out of the shell again, trembling. It pushed out eyestalks, tried to see where it was. Patrice put it into his palm and it sucked itself inside again, alarmed. He reached into a patch of young cane that had already been weeded and put it down there, out of the way of trampling feet.

The drizzle had stopped. Patrice caught up to the rest and set about weeding again. The book-keeper hadn't noticed him stop, for he was in the shed, sheltering from the downpour. The sun was back out now, but probably the book-keeper was enjoying a quiet smoke of his pipe.

The cloudburst had been cooling, but now Patrice was shivering and wet, his feet slipping in mud, worms, and damp leaves. His back felt clawed. It burned.

A flock of gaulin birds, garde-boeufs, descended on the field and started snapping up the frogs and worms flushed out by the rain and the weeding. The bright white birds fluttered and danced amongst the Ginen, mud people. Beside Patrice, Oreste misstepped and shouted as he fell heavily. Patrice, light-foot Patrice, barely danced out of the way of Oreste's machète as it swung wide. The book-keeper came running from the shed to see what the commotion was. He was fastening his fly. Slouching behind him was Phibba, pulling down her flour bag dress. She was knuckling at her eyes, her face sad. Patrice helped Oreste up, and back they went to weeding again. Phibba found her machète and bag and took up her place in the gang once more.

In the bush, in the accompong the maroon runaways had made, the hard labour Patrice did was to put food in his own mouth, a roof over his own head. Madness, it had been madness to come back. Sometimes he wondered why he had listened to Makandal. The Ginen could never win freedom here, on backra's soil. Why was he here? His baby was going to be born soon now, up there in the bush. That was where he could be free. Here he would bend his back long days into nights, and in between times of dodging the backra's whip, he would try to be a husband to Tipingee again. Try to avoid Mer's anger. And always, always there was an image in his mind of other hands digging cassava beside their hut in the bush, of other twitching hips, of young breasts hard and round as oranges, and a bright, trilling laugh. His Curaçao, his unborn baby's mother.

A gaulin bird stepped boldly into his path. "Away!" he said, shooing it with his hands. The bird fluttered up into the air, awkwardly, and landed on his shoulder. He made to brush it off. Some of the Ginen laughed and pointed. The book-keeper grinned, indulgent for the moment.

"It's me," whispered the bird, clacking out words its beak wasn't shaped to make. Makandal. His flight was clumsy because one wingtip had been clipped.

"What do you want?" Patrice hissed resentfully. The bird's clammy toes dug painfully into his sore back. It smelt of raw meat; worms and lizards. Patrice felt his stomach roll.

"Meeting tonight. In the old cabin by the river. Come in darkness. No torch."

It leapt off him, flew on its graceless way. It had shat on his shoulder. Patrice bent the burning iron of his back to weeding again and tried to remember the scent of Curaçao's body; the feel of her skin warm beside him in the night.

"Ow! Mama, don't pull so hard!" Marie-Claire put her hand to her head.

"Laisse, Marie-Claire," Tipingee told her. "Move your fingers so I can finish cane-rowing your hair."

Marie-Claire pouted, but she let her mother resume. Pretty soon Tipingee said to her, "Never mind the pain. You will look so pretty."

So my mother had said to me when the women came to cut out my sex in my eleventh year, back home in Dahomey. Ai, Lasirèn; that was pain. But my mama was right. So smooth and pretty the bouboun looked when it was healed, and I got presents, beautiful presents. I was a woman finally, and I would soon have a strong, wealthy husband. After a while I didn't mind that it was hard to piss now. When I came to this new world and had to tend to women of other nations and women born here in hell

96

who hadn't been trimmed, so ugly I thought them down there! What man would want them?

I found the calabash Tipingee kept of coconut oil and brought it to her. "Here. For Marie-Claire's scalp." The child smiled at me. Patrice's face she has. A comely face in truth, Mama. I must admit that.

Wasn't long after I began tending to uncut women that I realised: it didn't hurt them to piss. And their blood could flow smooth out of their bodies when their courses came, not get trapped inside and fester. I didn't have to cut them open so their babies could come out. Me, I began to envy those frilly-lipped cunts. Some of those women talked about loving, about the sweet sensations they got sometimes. I don't think it's so strong for me. They cut that part out of me. Mind you, plenty of the time, most of we Ginen women don't have the spirit for loving. Don't get pregnant plenty neither; don't have our courses regular. The food here doesn't nourish us enough for our bodies to grow babies.

"Marie-Claire," I said to the girl, "your mama's making a beautiful design with your hair. You will be lovely as Master's roses."

Marie-Claire smiled again with her Patrice face. "Tipingee," I asked, "where is Patrice tonight?"

"Don't know." She flashed me a warning with her eyes not to say more about it. "The weeding is finished for the night and he say he will come back soon."

"But so long ago that was, Mama!" piped up Marie-Claire. She hadn't seen her mama's hurt, angry eyes. "I have to be back to the great house soon before they realise I'm not there."

"Stop twisting about like that, or your hair will plait crooked," Tipingee scolded her.

Two raw calabash gourds there were, sitting on the table, green and perfectly round. "Tipingee, you want me scrape these out for you?"

Her smile that she gave me made the smoking, stinking castor oil lamp seem brighter. "Yes, my sister," she said to me.

Oh, my heart. Are we only sisters again, then?

With my knife I sliced open the green balls of the calabashes and scraped out the pulp and seeds. A good bowl the big one would make. The smaller one a dipper, maybe. I tossed the seeds and pulp outside the door. Maybe another tree would grow from them. I carved patterns into the calabash rinds: leaping dolphins. Made my thoughts run again on Lasirèn's command to me. I must do what she says; must understand how to do what she says. What, I asked myself, is a sea doing in the minds of the Ginen? I put the thought away. Lasirèn will show me.

Why is Patrice back? After two years nearly? He tells Tipingee he's missed her, but it's not so he acts. His eyes don't follow the sway and strength of her as she plants the cane. He doesn't seek her out. She goes and looks for him when they have time together, but when she comes back to me, her face is long and sad. He barely touches her, seems to be pining. Who is Patrice pining for, that isn't here on Sacré Coeur plantation?

So many times I try to ask Tipingee, to make her see, but she only says I'm jealous. Mama, it's true? I'm only jealous? Is Tipingee really so happy to have Patrice back with her in this cabin of theirs?

I peered out the door. The moon was hanging over the top of the bay leaf tree. "Curfew time," I told Tipingee and Marie-Claire. Scarcely did they notice me leave, so busy they were, chattering about how well the pumpkins were doing in Tipingee's garden patch now that Patrice was here to help tote water to them too.

The frogs were singing loud this night, clamouring for mates. The mosquitoes were thronging in thick clouds after the rain. They sang in my ears and bit and bit, no matter how I slapped at my skin. So smoky Tipingee's shack had been, but smoke had kept the mosquitoes away.

This little game I sometimes play for myself, quiet nights like these: I stand still, hold my breath so I can hear the crash of the sea against the cliffs at the foot of the plantation. The sea sound so far away is the voice of my water mother. I stood that way this night and tried to hear her whispered words clear.

A twig cracked. The frogs went quiet. I stayed quiet; listened. Over there, by Belle's shack. Someone was walking over there in the dark. Maybe old Cuba, that tattle-tale, spying to see if we're all in our beds? But why had she no torch?

A thump came to my ears; a heel hitting earth. It's not her. Cuba's bones are twisted. She doesn't walk so sure as this person I was hearing.

I could see the shadows now. Two people, trying to slide through the dark like breeze through the trees. They moved quickly, quietly in the direction of the river. A man and a woman, maybe. Looking for a private place to love.

I shook my head, me, and hurried for my home. Hope they had rubbed plenty sitwonel leaf all over them, or tomorrow they would be begging me for aloe to soothe their bitten skin.

My cabin smelled of the cocoa butter I mixed with certain of the herb medicines, and of the castor oil that fuelled the lamps.

I came into it in darkness. No need to find the lamp and waste it by lighting it tonight, for I knew where everything was.

My heart was weeping. Always it wept here, but tonight I could almost feel it leaking tears. Ah, Tipingee.

I shook my palette out so any centipede or ouanga mischief would drop out. Then back on the ground I put it, and I lay to close my eyes little bit until the sun came up and it was back to slaving again.

But no sleep came. My mind was only running on Tipingee, Tipingee. When Patrice had lived here before, it was better. We knew our places then, all three of us. Had a balance. One person shifts, the other two shift little bit too to preserve it. For me and Patrice, Tipingee was the torch moving between us. Sometimes it was he getting the light, sometimes me. And sometimes we both make space for each other and get comfort from her warmth. But now? Where do I fit now? Tipingee only has eyes for her Patrice.

Sleep was running from me like grasshoppers flee the fields in front of the cane cutters. I tossed on my palette, flung my hand out. It touched the gourd beside my bed, the one I had made specially. I sat up and opened it in the dark. Felt for the glass inside it; the glass whale that Lasirèn had given me. Its smoothness against my fingers calmed my thoughts a little. I stood up, took it to the doorway and leaned outside, holding my gift from Lasirèn level with my eye until I found the moon. Ezili the moon shone on the little glass whale; light dancing in the bumps and curves of it and filling my eyes with beauty. I kissed my gift, touched it with my tongue the way I might lick Tipingee's hard coffee bean nipples. Oh you gods, are you taking Tipingee from me?

A fleck of salt sand that remained on the whale rubbed rough on my tongue. I swallowed the little piece of sand. I humbled myself and ate salt. The gods will do as they wish.

I brought the glass whale back inside my cabin. As I went to put it back inside its gourd, my hand brushed some of my other things inside, the only things I owned. A lock from my dead baby's hair, tied with a piece of thread I'd pulled from my dress. My iron needle for sewing wounds, rubbed in coconut oil to keep rust away and pushed through a piece of flour sack. And the afterbirth. The afterbirth from Georgine's dead baby, dried and wrapped in oilcloth. It's Tipingee's hands that had caught that afterbirth, that piece of strong science. It's she had dried it for me. She hated births, but she helped me with them for love, she said. Where was that love now?

All my meek acceptance of the gods' wishes had run from me. I unwrapped the thing from its oilcloth. Small and long and rough in my hands like a piece of jerky. I held it to my nose, took in the musty smell of the thing that Tipingee's hands had touched out of love for me. I wondered could I get some of that love back out from it. Some of Tipingee's love back for myself. I licked it. Didn't taste like much. Like a piece of dried meat. We didn't get plenty meat, we Ginen. I bit off a piece. Chewed. Was tough. Tasty. Thought on Tipingee and wished for her to love me again. Swallowed.

I put my glass whale between my breasts and fell to sleep, rocking my Lasirèn so, like I'd begged for her to rock me.

The old, rotting cabin by the river creaked in the dark as the Ginen snuck into it one by one to hear what Makandal had to tell them. Patrice sat in a corner, nursing the toes he'd stubbed as his feet were fumbling across the threshold. It smelled of crumbling wood in here, full of roaches and ants and millipedes. And more and more, it smelled of people as the place filled up. People muttered softly out of the blackness.

"Who is that?" came a deep woman's voice.

"Fleur, it's you?" responded another, light and high.

"Yes, Marie-Jeanne. Jacques finally dropped to sleep and I sneaked away."

Patrice closed his eyes. Didn't make any difference, were they open or closed: he still couldn't see. With the whispering voices and the way that people brushed up against him from time to time, he could imagine he had died, was sitting with the spirits in the land beneath the waters. He was afraid. If anyone caught them out of their cabins like this after evening curfew . . . he tried not to think on the stories the Ginen had told him about Milo's death.

Where was Makandal?

The mosquitoes, drawn by the warmth of so many bodies, were gathering, whining in hunger. Patrice was thankful he'd thought to smear his body with citronella.

A warm body thumped into him, cursed, fell over him.

"Sorry . . . !"

Patrice tried to catch the person as she fell. His hands touched a breast, a shoulder. That whipping scar was familiar; the one shaped like a leaf of cane. He was the one who'd rubbed Mer's healing aloe on it when it was new. "Tipingee?"

"Who . . . ? Patrice?"

It was her. She touched his face, sat down beside him. She was laughing a little. He'd forgotten that about Tipingee, how she could remember to laugh, even in this place. "So it's here you were coming to," she whispered. Her voice was teasing, but a little doubtful. "Thought maybe you were going to spend the night in someone else's cabin."

She could warm him simply by speaking, this woman. "No, Makandal told me today about the meeting."

"Makandal? Didn't you and he fall out?"

"No . . ." The words came out before he could think that they might be rash: "Just pretending so. That way the backra don't get suspicious. It's Makandal . . ." No, better not tell her that it was Makandal who had persuaded him to return. Let her continue to think he had missed her. And in truth he had, terribly. Just that more even than the sweetness of her he had longed to live his days and nights without fear, without pain, without the crushing sadness that was sometimes so great that the weight of it bore some of the Ginen to their deaths.

Someone came in bearing a lit lamp, the flickering shadows it cast dragging their features into a mask of horror. Everyone hissed at him to put it out.

"Stupid man," Tipingee whispered to Patrice. She snuck her warm, callused hand into his. "Suppose the book-keeper followed him here by that light? Or old Cuba? That woman never sleeps. Hector!" Tipingee hissed into the cabin.

"Yes?"

"Congo John there with you?"

"Here," rumbled Congo John.

"The two of you go and see if anybody followed that lamp-light to us."

The sound of bare feet hitting rotting floorboards and the noise of people shuffling aside to let the two men pass told them that Hector and Congo John had gone on their errand.

"What are they going to do if they find anybody?" Patrice asked Tipingee.

"I don't know," she told him. "Serious business this."

"They have their machètes," someone said. It was the deep-voiced woman, Fleur.

Machètes? But if anyone was found murdered, it would be hell to pay for the rest of them. "Where is Makandal, eh?" Patrice asked Fleur and Tipingee. He could feel perspiration trickling down his cheek. He squeezed Tipingee's hand and felt her squeeze back.

"My friends," boomed Makandal in the blackness of the cabin. Patrice jumped at the sudden loud sound. His whole body flushed cold with fright.

"Makandal?" someone asked.

The voice rumbled a deep, reassuring laugh. It's so a father might chuckle when his child did something amusing. "Yes, my friends; it's me."

"Show us, then."

"You doubt me?"

"No, sah, we don't doubt you," hissed one voice.

But another said, "We have to be sure. Could be a trick."

"True thing that," responded Makandal. "Who here has a lamp? Light it for me, please, brother. Let me show you my face one little moment." Makandal's voice still sounded amused. "Then you will have to out the light again. Can't make your master know we're here."

"Your" master, he said. As though he didn't have his master too. Patrice knew well the fatherlike tone Makandal was using now. All fine and good if you and he were agreeing, but just argue with him once, and that voice could suddenly go sharp and biting on you.

The door opened. Patrice shivered in the draft from it. Two people came in, were challenged by others. It was Hector and Congo John, come back. No one had raised the alarm, they said.

Patrice could hear someone striking in a tinder box. Must have taken it from Simenon's kitchen; none of the Ginen were given anything so useful. Finally the spunk lit and was transferred to a lamp, which was passed hand to hand through the crowd until Makandal could take it in his whole left hand. He held it up beside his face; circled it down below his chin then up around to the other side of his face, like the sun circling the earth. Shadows jittered on his features, making them change; angelic one minute, the very Christian devil the next. Patrice shuddered. Sometimes his friend disturbed him.

Makandal smiled. "Everybody see me good now?"

"Yes, Makandal."

He blew the lamp out, hid the shining earth of his gaze again. Patrice took a big sigh of relief. The light had made him nervous. He whispered to Tipingee, "He loves to have eyes on him, eh?"

"He is a leader," she answered. "He must act like one."

"Is that the voice of Patrice I hear, talking over me when I'm trying to speak?" asked Makandal.

"Yes, Patrice," Fleur scolded, "hush up your noise. The man wants to talk."

Patrice, quivering at how unfair the accusation was, said nothing, just remained quiet. They must keep up their pretense, he and his friend Makandal.

Makandal continued, "My brothers, my sisters, you honour me. Tonight you have sneaked out from your huts, your cabins. You sneaked out from those cages the backra built for we Ginen, just to come and hear my thoughts. So brave a thing you did.

"But it's so my Ginen people are. Brave, we Mandingue, we Ashanti, we Congo, we Ibo, we Allada people. You know those words, my friends?"

"Yes!" someone cried out. The others hissed at her to be quiet.

Makandal laughed. "Yes, I see that some of you remember. Remember what we are, remember our names. We Mandingue, we Ashanti, we Congo, we Ibo, we Allada people. We Mandingue, we Ashanti, we Congo, we Ibo, we Allada people. Say it with me, my brothers and sisters."

And the crowd echoed, quietly, "We Mandingue, we Ashanti, we Congo, we Ibo, we Allada people."

"Again." They said it again.

Patrice whispered the words, thought of his mother saying, "You are Ibo. Never forget." He'd never really known what the word meant. He'd been born in Saint Domingue.

But now he felt it, felt something making the word "Ibo" sing through him. "Ibo people," he muttered. "Ibo."

"Again," said Makandal. Patrice chanted again with the rest of the Ginen. He could feel his eyes getting wet. Beside him, Tipingee was rocking as she said the words.

"Again."

The hoarse whispers of the crowd grew intense. The words flew like darts through the air. *Mandingue. Ashanti. Congo. Ibo. Allada. Mandingue. Ashanti. Congo. Ibo. Allada.*

Again and again and again Makandal made them say it until it felt as though the whole hut was rocking with the words, would shake itself loose and fling itself into the air on the power of words.

Mandingue. Ashanti. Congo. Ibo. Allada. Mandingue. Ashanti. Congo. Ibo. Allada.

"Stop!" Makandal commanded. The crowd fell silent. Patrice gasped. He was back in himself again, his head buzzing with the names the Ginen were no longer calling. The names that would stay in his head now, always being murmured in his head. The words that would bubble their strength in his veins. Ibo, he was Ibo. And a man of the Ginen. An African.

"Yes," Makandal mused, so quiet that Patrice had to hold his breath to hear, "brave people, my Ginen people. So tell me then, brothers and sisters," he continued, a little bit louder, "why are we here? Eh?"

There was an uncomfortable silence. Makandal said, "Anybody can tell me why we're here, slaving till our deaths in this white devils' land?"

Someone mumbled in a puzzled voice, "But it's the backra, Makandal. It's they who captured us, brought us here."

"True thing that," Makandal's voice boomed out of darkness. "Bought us like goats. And here we find ourselves, breaking back every day. But why? Anybody tell me why we put up with it?"

Patrice couldn't keep quiet any longer. "But what you want us to do, man? Eh? Tipingee told me what Simenon did to Milo, how he blanched Milo dead, just for talking his mind. Just for talking, Makandal. And they have guns."

"Poison works," cackled Fleur.

"Poison." So many times Patrice had had this argument, he was fed up of it. "You give one backra belly running, they'll hang ten of us and import twenty more to replace the dead ones. So what good is all your poisoning doing, except making the backra more likely to take out their fear on us?"

Makandal cut through Patrice's speech. "Poison weakens. Poison brings fear. Poison can kill."

"We can't kill them all before they kill us, Makandal!"

Makandal laughed, a low, scorpion-like hissing in the blind dark of the hut. "It's there you're wrong, Patrice." He raised his voice a little. "If everybody follows what I say, we could get them all one time, and have Saint Domingue for us; for the Ginen!"

"What?" Patrice had heard Makandal's fantasies before, but this was madness.

"Yes, Makandal; tell us your plan!" said someone else. Sounded like Congo John. Many voices rumbled in agreement.

"Friends," Makandal said, "thank you for having faith enough to listen. Some people won't even grant me that."

Tipingee leaned forward and whispered in Patrice's ear: "You sure he's acting? Seems like he really doesn't like you any more."

Patrice felt the words stick him like a piquette flung into his heart. "Hush," he replied. "Don't make people hear you."

He disagreed with Makandal, yes; always had. But by speaking it publicly this way he was only doing what Makandal had asked. So many days he had voiced these same doubts to Makandal in the canefields and later in the bush after Patrice was gone on marronage, when Makandal would meet him by pretending to lose his master de Mézy's goats and having to go wandering away from de Mézy's plantation to find them. They would meet halfway in the bush, between maroon land and the backra's. They would sit with the goats prancing around them, and they would argue and argue about the best way to get freedom in this wicked new world. And though he knew that Makandal was only acting his part now, pretending not to get along with him any more so that there'd be one ally above suspicion, it still hurt Patrice to have Makandal bad-talk him so.

Makandal had been quiet a few seconds. He said, "Plenty of you here have been helping me already, yes?"

"Yes, Makandal."

"Been taking the physicks I give you and slipping them into the backra's food, his wine, his water."

"Yes, Makandal. Making him sick too bad." The person giggled. "And anybody who eats great house food."

"Yes. Same thing too at Belle Espoir; all through Limbé. Now I know what works best. Now I can spread my net wider to catch whitefish. My brothers and sisters, lean close; let me tell you."

Patrice heard everyone suck in a breath and hold it, quiet, so they could hear Makandal's plan. He couldn't help himself; he was doing it too.

"A woman from Belle Espoir showed me a thing a few weeks ago; how to use a sharpened straw to inject medicine into the blood of the body for healing."

"Wai! What a marvel!" murmured Fleur in surprise. Patrice felt Tipingee beside him go still with attention. Her fingers loosened their grasp on his hand a little.

"Yes, my friends," Makandal continued. "For healing. So I think to myself, 'If for healing, why not for harming?'"

"But Makandal," Tipingee called out, "you want us to walk around jooking straws into the blans? They will kill all of us dead for sure!"

"No, my sister. Not into the backra."

"Where then?"

"Into their water barrels."

The crowd erupted in hissing and whispering. The water barrels! Makandal wasn't the only one who'd been trying to poison his captors. To protect themselves, the white people had taken to importing pure water in sealed casks from France. They used it for everything; to drink, to cook with. If the Ginen could poison the backra's supply of water . . .

Patrice couldn't stand it any longer. He let go Tipingee's hand and stood up. "What nonsense are you chatting, Makandal? So we kill the backra on two plantations, maybe three. Then what? After the rest of them get done with us, won't be anybody left to carry out your big scheme."

The voice that came back at him in the night was oily, triumphant. Days afterwards Patrice would feel it sticking gloatingly on his skin. "My brother Patrice," Makandal chuckled, "thank you for showing the rest of us how we limit ourselves when we think only in small ways. You're right, you know. If we only make havoc on a few plantations, the white man will suppress us fast, and the rest of the Ginen still will be in bondage."

People in the crowd murmured doubtfully, agreeing. Patrice breathed hard, taking in the smells of the bodies packed around him. He felt his name must really be Chagrin. This was supposed to be only play-acting, this sparring between him and Makandal, but the jibes stung like real barbs. Tipingee put an arm around Patrice. Makandal continued, "But do my Ginen people all make their thoughts small? Eh?"

"No, Makandal," a woman responded in a whisper.

"What, only one of you? Do the rest of you all have narrow little thoughts, then?"

"No, Makandal!" More whispered voices this time.

"Tell me again."

"No, Makandal!" The chorus of voices had grown.

"Tell me like you mean it!"

This time, the murmured "no"s had the passion of a quiet thunder of voices: "NO, MAKANDAL!"

"Good. So. Those of you who want to be small people, tell me your names. Right now; speak up."

In the ringing silence Patrice could hear the frogs wooing over by the river and the chuckle of the river water. "Ah," said Makandal. "Seems like you all want to dream big dreams with me. You all dream of owning your own land to work, of having enough food to eat, of having children to ease your old age."

Patrice thought of the bush he'd left, where he had those things already. He wondered if Curaçao had birthed her baby yet. If she would ever forgive him for leaving, for abandoning the dream he had with her for a bigger dream; a vision that he and all his people could walk free in this land.

"Even Patrice must have big dreams," Makandal gloated, "for I don't hear him whining like the mosquito in our ears no more."

The crowd burst into muffled laughter. Someone slapped Patrice on the back and said, "Never mind, man. We know your heart's good, even if your spirit is sometimes craven."

"This is what we're going to do," Makandal said. Suddenly his voice was all business. "How many of you are going travelling to other plantations on backra business soon?"

"Me, Makandal," said a voice. "Going to be part of a troupe raiding the maroons."

Patrice's heart pattered when he heard this. How could he warn the maroons? But likely they already knew. Maroons had informants everywhere.

"Me, Makandal," said another. "Going to Belle Espoir to train some of the Ginen there how to mind the boilers. Their boiler man fell into a vat of hot syrup."

Still another voice said, "Couva is going away soon. She's in the stocks tonight. Simenon got tired of her always running away and he sold her to someone else."

"See how that man makes his own enemies?" Makandal said. "I will go and talk to her tonight. I will sit by her and keep the mosquitoes off her body, and rub her back that's aching with being bent into the stocks. And I think she'll be happy when she's sold away to carry some knowledge with her, of how to make the poison she's going to put in the water casks that come to the plantation they have sold her to."

"And the rest of us, Makandal?" Fleur called out. "The other ones who're going travelling?"

"I will teach you all how to make the poison. I will teach you all how to use the straws. You will tell the Ginen on the other plantations; the ones you can trust, mind. They will tell others. When we have Ginen on all the plantations prepared to blow poison into the backra's water, we will strike."

"But . . ." someone said doubtfully, "that's still not the whole country, Makandal. How will we get to all the plantations?"

The ripple of the invisible Makandal's laugh made the hairs rise on Patrice's arm. "But that's the beauty of it, my people. We can reach all the plantations, yes. Quick as flight we can do it."

The noises coming from the crowd sounded unsure, uncomfortable. "My Ginen doubt me?" asked Makandal.

Silence. No one wanted to be made an example of, the way Patrice had been.

"I see," Makandal said, still chuckling. "My Ginen are prudent, not hasty. Good thing that. Somebody bring me back that oil lamp there."

A young man stepped forward with the lamp.

"Light it for me, my brother," said Makandal.

The young man knelt, put the lamp down to have his hands free. A sound came of stones striking against each other, then a small flame flared in the sombre night.

"Hold it up to me, my friend," Makandal told him. "High, so everyone can see."

The young man stood up and did as Makandal asked. The lamp illuminated Makandal's smiling face. "Mark me good, now," he told them all. He looked around slowly, at the faces he likely couldn't see, but knew were there.

Then he was gone. People in the crowd cried out and gasped. It was Congo John who shouted, "Look! There so!"

A hummingbird hovered around the lamp, dipping a little to one side; favouring its clipped wing. The young man holding the lamp just gaped.

Patrice sighed. Makandal was going against his advice, was showing his business to everyone. The first time Makandal had showed him this ouanga, this changing into other beasts, Patrice's whole body had chilled with fright as Makandal became a hound before his eyes; the type of vicious, tattling hound that the whites would take to hunt runaway Ginen. He'd fled, Patrice had, with the dog after him, moving fast for all that it only had three and a half legs, and barking happily. Patrice had tripped on a root and fallen, and had nearly wet himself when the hound leapt at him. It changed back into a laughing Makandal as it landed. Makandal had giggled and shaken his friend's shoulders and hugged him, but it was weeks before Patrice had forgiven him for that trick.

The hummingbird turned into Makandal again. As his feet touched the floor, he said, "All you travelling people will help, but where you can't go, I can go. I can be beast or bird. I can run or fly, and carry my message anywhere on Saint Domingue. I will teach all the Ginen on all the plantations how to poison straws. We will do it all together. We will kill them all. We will watch the backra rolling on the ground as blood and bile runs from their bellies. We will kill them all. We will kill them all."

The crowd repeated the chant with him. Patrice felt the buzzing in his head again, the power of Makandal's words, of his dream. All you gods, could it work? Please say that it could work.

Patrice held on tight to Tipingee's hand and together they muttered, "We will kill them all. We will kill them all."

They were slipping singly out of the broke-down cabin, one every few minutes, so as not to alert the overseer. There—Patrice saw Tipingee go on her way. As she stepped outside, he heard how the frogs by the river stopped their croaking. It would be his turn next. He waited till the frogs had been singing again for a few minutes, then quietly got to his feet and went to the door. One or two voices softly wished him to go well.

The night air smelled sharply fresh after the close quarters of the cabin. Ezili's moon face was low in the sky; only couple-three hours of rest left before they would all be woken for work. Tipingee would be waiting for him in their cabin. He thought of her hard, warm thighs and moved as swiftly, silently as he could away from the river to where the ground became hard-packed earth with clumps of grass and the bay leaf trees wafted their spicy scent into the air. He touched the big sky-rock for luck as he passed. It was still warm with the previous day's sun.

A hand reached down from the top of the rock and grabbed him by the wrist. For a wonder, Patrice didn't shout with the fright. Furious, he grabbed the arm that held him and pulled hard. Makandal came tumbling off the rock, dragged Patrice to the ground with his weight, and lay there, giggling. Patrice wanted so badly to punch him. "What are you doing, man? Eh? If I had cried out, it would have given us all away!"

Makandal twisted up onto one elbow and grinned at Patrice. His eyes were bright, his face happy. "It's working, my friend! You see how they listen to me? They think it can work, too! Oh, Patrice, you are a good man to have by my side. Thank you, man! Thank you!"

He pushed himself to his feet. Patrice got up too, still furious. He headed back to his cabin. Makandal followed. "Just a few months now, man!" he said to Patrice. "We'll fix them up, all the blasted backra. All of them!"

"Shh, Maka. Keep your voice down."

"Yes. Yes. Must stay quiet." He turned to Patrice, his whole body quivering with excitement. "But you see now that I was right? See how the Ginen can make up their minds to move together?"

In the hut, Patrice had been caught up in the thrill of Makandal's dream, but in the chill morning air, he wasn't so sure any more. A horrible thought occurred to him: "Maka, suppose it works. Then what? They're going to send troops from France for us!"

Makandal laughed softly, butted him in the ribs with the stump where his hand used to be. He knew that Patrice hated that. "I thought about that already, man! When all the backra are gone, we will have their guns. And we'll have a whole island full of angry blacks; hundreds to every one backra that was ever here. We're rising up, Patrice! We can fight! We can fight, man!"

"And what about the free coloured? They're not going to want to give up their property and their slaves."

"If they don't, we count them as backra too. We treat them accordingly."

Patrice remained silent. He concentrated on walking over the bumpy ground without tripping in the dark. Maka had always been a man with strong visions. And he had a way of making them happen. When his hand had been taken off and the flesh above it had begun to fester, Patrice swore it was only Makandal's will that had made the rot draw back, made the arm heal. And now he didn't work the fields any more, for his stump made him useless for cutting cane. He had more freedom tending his goats than most of the enslaved Ginen. "And what about me, Maka?" he asked quietly. "That game you and me were playing in there? You made me feel like a fool, man! What that was good for?"

Makandal stopped. Turned to Patrice. Put his good hand on Patrice's shoulder. "My brother, my friend," he said. "You are my general. And I need to keep you safe. The whites must never suspect you. So even the Ginen can't know that you and me, we're plotting together. It's you who will carry word of my plan to the maroons, you know. Think, Patrice! An army of maroons, already fierce. Think what we could do!"

Patrice sighed. They were near his cabin. He kept walking, kept thinking. He heard Makandal's soft goodbye, and out of his eye saw the three-and-a-half-legged hound running off to where Couva would be twisted painfully into the stocks, her body cramping and twitching. You gods, let Makandal's plan work. Let the Ginen cease suffering.

WORD

I find my way fully into the world! It only takes a minute of Jeanne's inattention. Music is the key, it seems; flowing as rivers do, beating like the wash of her blood in her body. Jeanne is helping me too, unawares; by humming. She doesn't even know what the words of the tune mean. She just tries to say them as she has heard her grandmother hum them. That tune is how her grandmother entreats her gods. Jeanne is hoping that she might call on them too; ask them what her future holds if she stays with Charles. Will they marry? She prays and fears that they will. She has seen her mother's belly stretched out with child, the tearing that nearly killed her when a sickly baby girl ripped its way out of her aching womb. So far, Jeanne has been able to keep Charles entertained with tricks she learned on the docks at Nantes. He, gasping in her hands or her mouth, barely notices that they do not fuck. But if they marry, he might want an heir. And if they marry, Jeanne and her maman will never want for anything again. So, hoping yes, hoping no, she was humming to call her spirits. If not Charles, she wanted her own wealth.

It pulls at me, that music. The rhythms take Jeanne's thoughts, drown them for a time in their flood. And suddenly I am finally master of her body.

Oh, what a wondrous thing, to be dressed in flesh! I revel in the feel of it. I run my hands over our face, smear away the powder and paint and wipe them on the expensive silks of our dress. I pull in air with our lungs, sense the trail of blood through our veins.

I have Jeanne get to her feet. She never once protests. Her floating mind, caught by the rhythm, isn't aware that it is being swept away. Still we hum. That chant! Beat, beat. My feet move in time. I let her throat continue the song. Now there are words coming from her lips. I dance. My torso falls forward, catches and holds on the beat, parallel to the floor. Jerks upright again. My feet stamp out the rhythm. My arms make a flourish, a swaying, as Jeanne used to do on the stage. Am I pretty now? Pretty as Jeanne? Am I graceful as she is, unawares?

A pox on all this cloth! I catch at it, tear it away with our hands. By herself, Jeanne is not so strong as to shred heavy silks. I am. The gown pools in rags at my feet. The stays are next, and the pins that hold our hair.

Stamp. Sway. Jerk towards the floor. Then up. Again. Feel air on our flesh, cool and sweet as rain. The pounding of blood in our ears comes in waves, crashing against our senses. My hands reach for our breasts, ripe as plums. I hold them, weigh them in my palms, thrust them forth as offerings. To whom, to whom?

And suddenly, I am elsewhere. Not in that stuffy dark room with its walls that smell of cigar smoke and stale wine. Not in Jeanne. Not in any body. I look at my arms, hands. So pale that I see right through them to the ground beneath.

It is hot. I am outdoors, somewhere. The green swaying of trees around me, a dirt courtyard, a well in the middle of it. A mean little church beside it. And blacks everywhere. Some draw up water in buckets from the well. Some carry baskets heavy with fruit on their heads. They wear scrips and scraps of dirty clothing. I stop dancing and turn in a slow circle, to see it all.

A rainbow-peopled land, this is; not just African-borns in it. I see white faces peering out of carriages. And mulattos too, running shops, or strolling the streets with parasols to keep them from the baking sun. Some of them, their complexions are as fair as those of Jeanne's body. Some of the mulattos, they strut proudly as the whites do. All these people, all of them; their dress would be outlandish, antique to Jeanne. What is happening?

No matter. I dance, dance. I ignore the visions of people wafting past me, and I dance, like Jeanne does. I turn my head, I smile. I gesture, point a toe, extend a long, lovely foot. I had put on beauty as a hermit crab puts on a discarded shell.

"Maman," says a child's voice, "who's that lady?"

It is a small mahogany girl, knotted about in rags, who tugs at the hand of an African woman. The woman's face is frozen in a permanent attitude of suffering. Mathilde, they call her, though that had not always been her name. Knowledge is coming to me now, as it does. The woman holds on to her child as though she can protect it from the world's every ill. She cannot, and she knows it. Yet for all the drawn look on her face, her body stands straight and tall. She will be dead within the year, from an abscessed tooth.

The child—Griselde—and her mother stare at me, gap-lipped. Mathilde mutters, "the Lady."

And so I learn that some of them see me, those blacks and browns and whites. One or two more stop to point. Most others, squinting, do not see and pause to wonder at the fuss their fellows are causing. I have an audience now! I know what to do. Laughing, I commence to dancing again. More people gather, and more. The blacks among them draw my attention. Even lost in the steps of my stepping and tumping, I can still see them, those darkest ones. They walk with eyes shifting all the time, to see where there might be danger. They step lightly out of the way of the white and light brown ones, duck their heads, and murmur apologies. The lineaments of their faces sketch tales of woe. Why must they live so?

One of them steps forward; an old black woman in a torn hand-me-down dress. Her shoulders are scarred. She lacks one ear. Her breasts sit oddly plump on her chest; she has never suckled a child. It comes to me that in this place, slave women's wombs rarely quicken; their bodies are too lean from endless labour, and their masters are not compelled to keep them well-nourished.

The old woman holds a hand out to me. "Ezili," she whispers. Her face is transformed with joy.

Ah, but the rhythm. I sway and stamp before the door of their little church, offer the ripeness of my breasts to someone, to something, coiled powerfully in the depths of my awareness. "Ezili," that serpentine presence whispers, large as all the universe. "You are Ezili."

Who speaks? I care not, can care not. The sun on this body of mine melts the ice of Paris, calls forth the sea salt beneath the skin.

Thrilled to float free of Jeanne's head, to be but air, to wander, I let myself drift and disperse on the warm breezes of this place, leaving people pointing at where I have been. An elegant white man who has stepped down from his carriage is making some sign on his body, over and over again; pointing to his forehead, his chest, his left shoulder, his right. I neglect to know what he is doing. I am more interested in those black and brown bodies.

Eddying like swells in a river, curious, I float in the warm air, over streets and shops and churches, and slaves bent double in fields. I swim in time as in a stream. In seconds I float through days and weeks, see the rains come and go, the crops flourish and be felled, until something catches my interest strongly. I approach the heavy earth again, enter into the house through the very grain of its walls.

Some festivities here. And something important to the ones who entice me, the black and brown ones.

SLIDE

There is a sound like bells ringing. There is drumming in this place; the booming of the sea, and then the bell-like sound comes three times, and I must go to it. I imagine myself clothed in silks and linens; the proper raiment for garbing beauty—I've learned this from Jeanne. And what I imagine becomes so. I am wearing beautiful clothing, formed, as I am, from air.

I enter inside a lovely house, and find myself more curious than frustrated to be sucked into someone's head. I can walk and speak among them this way.

She welcomes me, this one. Even though she doesn't even know that I am here. Unlike Jeanne, she dreams of being taken out of herself. She has made a good marriage and her parents rejoice, but she is not so certain. The man seems genteel, but he has hairs growing from his nose and a sullen cast to his gaze after two glasses of wine. She fears the cruelty that husbands can freely visit upon wives. Wine has loosened her bonds on consciousness, and unawares, she has brought me into her. An unknowing part of her rejoices.

This is so different from being rat-trapped in Jeanne's skull! I still retain some of my power to see all about. And I can make this one do my bidding. I wave her fan about my lovely face, pale as the moon. This is how it will be with me; I understand now. Some humans will offer their heads to me, to take my seat inside. They will slip me inside them, and they will be glad to host me.

I hold her hand up before my face. Eh! Milky white, with blue veins crawling beneath the skin. Jeanne would give anything to be such as she.

Where is the matter I have come to see? I make her smile, bid some cheerful farewell to her fellows, those other white women, high-voiced and exquisitely gowned in their archaic dresses. I make her leave the well-appointed drawing room.

There; voices, men's. And a summoning. A tinkling as of bells; once, twice, thrice: come, come, come. They want me, in that place. I take her feet there, have her open the door.

And what a tableau before me! Ah; there is the business that they are about. That one, he is in danger. A luscious game. I step forward, thinking perhaps I might help him escape it.

All eyes turn to me. I am exquisite, and I know it. "Ah," I make her voice say. "It seems you brave fellows are having your own entertainment here."

"Please sit down, my dear," says Monsieur Léonard Simenon. "You look a trifle overwarm."

I make her pink mouth speak with my words, and I charm those brooding men with my voice, with my breath, salty as the sea, as jism.

It is I who save that black man; I, myself! And then I leap into bodiless space again, free of her, where I might move as I will. I am clumsy here, jerky as a baby discovering that it has command of its knees curled under its belly. Yet all space and time are mine, can I but learn the way of it!

I stamp out the steps of the dance—yet there is a rug beneath my feet again. Toss my head—and behold once more the sombre furnishings of Charles's apartments. Oh, oh; Jeanne is reeling me back in. I am back in her apartments, in her head.

He is watching; the Charles man. I glance at him with Jeanne's eyes, yet she does not perceive him. She is caught up still in her own dance. Charles's face, shocked, is even whiter than its usual pallour. His mouth gapes. Wonder makes his visage ugly, slack.

But I care nothing for that. I wish to be free! Jeanne and I thump with our heels, toss our torso towards the earth, thrust back with our hips. We shake our shoulders. And still I offer our breasts, promise their juices to someone, something, not him. Oh. Let me be free. Free from this body and its overwhelming senses. Rushing like torrents. Air burning in through my nose, harsh yet needful. The softness of our flesh beneath my fingers. And the swelling joy between my thighs as they quiver; oh, oh.

"Oh, Jeanne." Charles's voice, the shock of his body being pressed to mine, the heat of his kisses, drew Jeanne forth fully. If Jeanne hadn't woken then, hadn't dragged me back into her, think what I might have done! I could have danced for them all, those Saint Domingue people in that rich man's parlour, twirling my hips as Jeanne does. They would have asked me their questions, and I would have told them my answers. Warned that Patrice to 'ware his friends. Told that sad healer woman, that Mer, of a cure for poison. Told that Simenon man that sugar beets and angry slaves would be the death of his profit. I would have danced, and they would have worshipped me.

Screaming in frustration, I sink once more to the cage of Jeanne's brain.

"What?" said Jeanne, shoving Charles away. Still he tried to work his lips against her shoulders, her breasts. She kept him off. "It worked? They heard me?" She looked around her, to see if her grandmother's gods had rained wealth at her feet. Then she noticed the foamy mess of torn cloth on the ground. "What . . . Charles, what you did?"

"My God, Lemer! That dance; what was it?" He brushed a hand down her naked, wet stomach, pulled at her pantalettes.

His touch made her skin prickle in distaste. "You've never done anything like that on stage! So wonderfully lewd!"

"Don't touch me." She pulled away, repelled by his hand so hot on her body. "It's to dance alone." Had she been dancing, then? What dance? To what music? She frowned. "I mean . . . I don't quite know what I mean." She stumbled, sat plumb down on the floor. "Oh, I'm so tired. Charles, what happened? Why you ripped my clothes like this?"

"Why *did* you rip my clothes like this," he corrected her automatically. He squatted down, put himself level with her, and took her chin in his hand. She jerked away. He frowned, but didn't complain. "Jeanne," he said eagerly, "you must tell me. What was that dance? Can you perform some more of it for me?"

She felt heavy. Dragged down. Only wanted to sleep. It hadn't worked. Still more of this life for her. "I don't know about no dance, Charles. Please fetch a robe for me. And let me rest, just a little. Please?"

His face was slack with awe now. "You were like a very serpent, Jeanne. Twisting and turning . . ." He touched her shoulder, reverently, as though she were a statue from antiquity. "Such grace. Like a snake. So sinuous."

He rose to his feet, turned away. She knew that look. In a minute he'd be wandering the street with his notebook, muttering half-written verses to himself and scaring the passers-by. "Just bring me my robe first, chéri," she implored of his retreating back as he left the room. Then she sank down amongst the tatters of her garments. Oh you gods, just to sleep a little while. How could she have been dancing?

Just a taste Jeanne had given me; a sip. But now I am beginning to divine the way to have more of it. Give thanks that this Jeanne is a dancing girl. Perhaps there will be more chances to lose her in music, to set me free into the spherical world where I can learn all that is and was and is to come. Then together and separately, Jeanne and I can dance once more.

I am quiet some little while, ruminating on dark bodies clothed in rags. I think on the feel of silk on skin, how gloriously it slides across the flesh and makes one shiver. It is better to be richly attired. People regard you then. They pay attention to what you say. It is better to have a lace fan to wave gracefully in the air, so . . .

Jeanne's hand moves! She makes the motion of flourishing the fan I imagine. Her mind is elsewhere, dozing, and for a short time, I have command. I strain to do so again, but it is gone. I wish I could make her scream out my frustration. I cannot think, encased in this one small head. I cannot see!

SLIP

XXVIII—Le Serpent qui danse
(Charles Baudelaire 1821–1867)

The Snake That Dances

Que j'aime voir, chère indolente,
De ton corps si beau,
Comme une étoffe vacillante,
Miroiter la peau!

How I love to see, my dear lazy one,
 Along your beautiful body,
Like a fabric that shimmers,
 The glistening of your skin!

Sur ta chevelure profonde
Aux âcres parfums,
Mer odorante et vagabonde
Aux flots bleus et bruns,

In the depths of your hair
 With its biting odours,
Perfumed and errant sea
 With blue and brown swells,

Comme un navire qui s'éveille
Au vent du matin,
Mon âme rêveuse appareille
Pour un ciel lointain.

Like a ship that awakens
 In the morning wind,
My dreamy soul sets sail
 For a sky far away.

Tes yeux, où rien ne se révèle,
De doux ni d'amer,
Sont deux bijoux froids où se mêle
L'or avec le fer.

Your eyes, where nothing's revealed,
 Neither bitter nor sweet,
Are two cold jewels
 Where gold and iron meld.

À te voir marcher en cadence,
Belle d'abandon,

To see your rhythmic walk,
 Careless beauty,

On dirait un serpent qui danse
Au bout d'un bâton.

Sous le fardeau de ta paresse
Ta tête d'enfant
Se balance avec la mollesse
D'un jeune éléphant.

Et ton corps se penche et s'allonge
Comme un fin vaisseau
Qui roule bord sur bord et plonge
Ses vergues dans l'eau.

Comme un flot grossi par la fonte
Des glaciers grondants,
Quand l'eau de ta bouche remonte
Au bord de tes dents,

Je crois boire un vin de Bohême,
Amer et vainqueur,
Un ciel liquide qui parsème
D'étoiles mon cœur!

You'd think a snake was dancing
At the end of a fakir's stick.

Under the weight of your idleness
Your childlike head
Balances with the indolence
Of a baby elephant.

And your body stretches and inclines
Like a fine vessel
Which rolls from side to side
And thrusts its masts into the sea.

Like a wave built by the roar
Of melting glaciers,
When the foam of your mouth
Surges to the edge of your teeth,

I feel I'm drinking Bohemian wine,
Bitter and triumphant,
A liquid heaven that showers
Stars upon my heart!

RATTLE

CHAIN

Jeanne dreams, and I am pulled to other places. Dark faces surround me, swaying as the drums boom, as the asson rattle shakes. They demand my presence, they make the bells tinkle. If Jeanne lets me go free, I must answer the summons of the bells, the faces demanding my presence. Black faces that look like my own, only mine is white, bone-bleached. Why? I try to ask them, why? Why do I not look like you? Why am I at your beck? But they do not answer. I only find myself in other heads, as I am in the head of Ginger Jeanne. They summon me, and when I can, I go to them. And while I am speeding to them between the worlds, I know their lives. For a little space, I know.

I arrive, and the black faces sing,

Ezili, O!

I do not understand. Riding in their heads, I ask, why am I here? The faces reply, Mother, will he love me? Mother, what is to become of me? Tell us, tell us.

BREAK

Tell us, the black faces beg, and a remembering of my time in free space bubbles up out of me like waters, and I speak, speak through the mouth of the head I am in. I say, He loves you because you turn yams to money in the market. If you like your love practical, then he is the one for you. And to the other I say, do not ask your future, or you will forget to live in your present. Go home to your baby; she is sick.

Oh, I speak. I speak in many mouths, and even white men listen, for love of my grace and beauty. I speak.

WATER

Matant Mer, it's too hot!" wailed Ti-Bois. Standing in front of my cabin in the swelling dark, he was wincing and skinning up his face above the calabash of ginger tea I had just done boiling for him. "It's burning my mouth. I have to drink all?"

"Yes, petit." Poor little one. Never enough to eat, not the kind of food that would make him grow strong. His teeth were falling out his mouth from it. "You must drink all. You want the toothache to stop, don't it?"

"Yes, matant."

I stood up from weeding my manioc patch and went to check the calabash. The drink was a little hot, in truth. I blew in it and swirled it around to cool it some. "Try now."

He screwed up his little nose and mouth and bent to suck from the calabash again. He took two more sips, then: "I don't like the taste too much, matant!"

Pauvre petit. Only seven years old, and trying to be brave. "You want me to make it sweet for you?"

A big smile he gave me with his little black teeth. "Yes, matant!"

So I went inside and got the lump of sugar that I had thiefed from the curing house. "Don't tell anyone I gave you this. You promise?"

He opened his eyes wide and nodded at me, all serious. Sweet child. I broke off some of the sugar, put it in his calabash, and mixed it with my finger. "I'm going to watch you now, and make sure you drink it all. So your teeth will stop hurting."

I put the rest of the sugar away, then went and knelt again to my weeding, but kept my eye on the child. The small cane trash fire crackled. The sweet smoke smell of it blew all around. Long, dry cane leaves rushed up from the fire, glowing red, then crumbled to black ash.

My mind went running on other things while I weeded. I'm not the only one displeased to see Patrice. Makandal didn't like him any more, it seemed. Makandal's favour flows this way then that, like the tide. He and Patrice used to be compères, always whispering and joking together. Used to have Tipingee frantic that the overseer would notice, would punish them for conspiring. But something must have happened out there with the maroons. Makandal scowls now whenever Patrice walks by. He spits on the ground behind Patrice. And Patrice pretends he doesn't notice, for it's not safe to cross Makandal. He might put bad ouanga on you.

Mama, what I must do? Tipingee asked me yesterday to make Patrice a packet for his protection. Best protection might be if he ran away again. If he only crosses Makandal, I know Makandal will find a way to lay him below the earth. Mama, is only that I'm jealous why I want Patrice to go back away?

"Matant?"

Eh. I told Ti-Bois I was watching him, but here my mind was roaming. I came back to myself again. "Yes, child?"

"I'm finished." He held out the calabash for me.

"Good boy. Mouth feeling better?"

He gave me a big smile with his rotting baby teeth. "Yes, matant."

I sat back on my heels and regarded him. "You want to share some supper with me?"

He sucked in his lower lip and considered. "What you have to eat, matant?"

I had to laugh. "Little méchant; what do you have to say about it? Eh?"

He just grinned back at me, for he knew I wasn't really angry with him. Ti-Bois knew me well. "All right," I said. "I will boil manioc with coconut oil and some salted pig tail in it, and plantain that Georgine gave me."

His face lighted up. "Plantain! The sweet plantain, or the hard green one?"

"Ah, Ti-Bois. If I tell you what kind of plantain, that will decide you whether you're going to stay for dinner or not?"

"Yes, matant," he said, with a child's honesty. "I like the sweet one. It's soft. It doesn't hurt my mouth."

I rocked myself to my feet, tossed the last of the weeds into the fire. Gave Ti-Bois the two big manioc roots I had just done digging up. Oreste was passing by, a plaited coconut leaf hat on his head. He had three coconuts carrying.

"Honour, Oreste."

"Respect, matant Mer."

"Nice evening."

"Cool breeze," he agreed. "Honour, Ti-Bois."

"Respect," the little one replied, wriggling for pleasure that Oreste was talking to him like an adult.

"Do me a favour, Oreste?" I asked.

"Ahh?" he said, waiting to hear what it was.

"Tell Ti-Bois's mother that he is taking supper with me. I will bring him home safe."

"Yes, matant."

"Thank you. Take some manioc for your trouble, eh?" I gave him one of the long, thick roots. He touched his coconut leaf hat at me with it and set off, juggling manioc and coconuts.

Ti-Bois was only pulling at my skirt hem. "But matant, matant; you still never said; it's the sweet plantain or the green one you're cooking?"

To my knees I got, and hugged him. "Oh, my darling; the sweet one, of course. Of course I will give my friend Ti-Bois a treat."

And up and down he jumped, making a little song of "Sweet plantain! Sweet plantain!" I laughed to see him.

"Come now, Ti-Bois. Before you eat, you have to work." I went inside and got two calabash bowls, a big one for me and a small one for him. "Come with me to the river for water."

He ran along on his little legs beside me, cheeping at me

like the nighttime frogs. "Matant, you see the great house the other day?"

"Yes, petit."

"I never been in there before."

"Me neither."

"You see how fine it is inside? When I get big, I'm going to live in a grand house like that."

"May it be so," I said. "If the gods will it."

"And plenty big red flowers going to grow outside it."

"Roses, those were."

"I know. Marie-Claire told me about them long time since. And long time since? Long time, I never believed her, that anybody would grow plants that bear no food, just flowers, so matant?"

"Yes, petit."

"Long time? I sneaked inside the great house gates."

"What?" I stopped and grabbed his little arm. So thin in my hands. "You went inside Master's gates? Ti-Bois, you could have been in trouble!"

A little shrug he gave me, unconcerned. "Nobody saw me, matant. When I want, I could sneak about quiet-quiet, and nobody knows."

"Oh, child."

He shook my hand off and went on skipping down the path. "And matant, guess what?"

"What, Ti-Bois?"

He stopped and turned back to face me. Such a puzzled look he had on his face. "Marie-Claire was right! Only those big, red, smelly flowers. I even tried pulling one up to see if it had roots in the ground you could eat, but the thorns bit me."

"Ti-Bois, you must never do that again."

"Matant, I still didn't believe Marie-Claire. I broke off one of the flowers and I ate it."

I laughed so hard I nearly dropped my calabash. "Ti-Bois; you lie!"

He smiled, uncertain what amused me so. "No, matant, it's true. I ate the flower."

"You ate one of Master Simenon's roses?"

"It tasted . . . it tasted like the way the perfume smelt that that lady was wearing. That white lady with the fan."

The lady that the spirit had ridden into Simenon's parlour. The woman our master was going to marry. "What you think about that lady, Ti-Bois?"

"She's pretty too bad. When I live in the great house, I'm going to marry her."

I leaned down close and shook my finger at him. "You will *never* say that where a blan can hear you."

He clutched the calabash to his chest and stuck out his little bottom lip at me. "But I *want* to marry her, matant. She's so pretty."

"Ti-Bois, hear me. Some things you must keep in your own private mind. You know those kinds of things?"

He nodded. Of course he did. "Yes, matant."

"Well then," I said, leading him to the river again, "who you're going to marry is a private thing. You keep it quiet till the time comes." *Mama, pray you let him learn to govern his tongue. For his life.*

When we got to the river, there was Georgine in the evening sun, on her knees with her skirt knotted around her thighs, dipping her bucket. She heard our footsteps and looked back.

She just nodded at us, cool. She picked up her full calabash, balanced it on her head, and came closer. She stood, swaying her head a little with the movement of the water in the calabash. She never said nothing. Now that she'd got her boy child, there was no more dancing with us blacks, and she barely spoke to me.

"Respect, child," I greeted her; more respect than she was giving me. She threw me a look, but I was still "matant" Mer. She wouldn't dare say anything rude. Wouldn't dare to snub me like any other field black. "Honour," she muttered finally.

Ti-Bois just gaped at her. Shoved his toes into the dirt and let his arms hang by his sides. Clever child. The Ginen need to mind their words around the coloured.

On the sand-coloured skin of Georgine's arm I saw a mark. I said to her, "How is the baby?"

That made her smile; talk about her son. "Michel is well, matant! So fat and strong. Pierre says that if Michel makes a good carpenter, he will free him; and me too, matant!"

"I'm glad," I said. There's not just one mark on her arm. In the darkening evening, I could see three more, maybe four. Each one little bit smaller than the one before. "Ti-Bois, go and draw some water."

Eyes still full up big of Georgine, he took himself down to the water. With her burden on her head, Georgine had to swivel her whole body to watch him go.

"Go careful in the mud, child!" I called to him. "Don't fall."

"Yes, matant." He thought he was being careful, but he was running, that light-footed, toes-first run of a small child. He made me so glad to watch, Ti-Bois did.

Georgine turned back to me. She looked troubled. "Matant," she said, quietly. "I've been wanting to ask you . . ."

"What is it, Georgine?"

"It's about when I . . ."

"Yes?"

She looked down, muttered, "Sometimes I can't go, matant. Can't make kaka."

"Oh. An easy thing to fix, my dear. You must eat more fresh fruit and greens. Raw, mind. Grow some spinach in that garden of yours."

"I just eat the leaves? Raw, just so?"

"Yes. With something else you like, until you get used to the taste. You like fish?"

141

"Yes, matant."

"Eat the raw spinach with cooked fish then. And get your Pierre to beg fruit from Master's trees."

She sucked her lips together, looked doubtful. "Yes, matant. Only . . ."

"What, girl? I have to fetch water for dinner for me and Ti-Bois."

"I should eat the leaves from the fruit, too? Raw?"

I laughed. "No, Georgine. Eat the sweet parts of the fruit. And come to me later. I'll give you some senna pods to ease you tonight."

"Yes, matant." She looked happier now. "I'm going now. My husband's waiting." She put her calabash on her head. Yes. There, on the underside of her arm; a blue bruise. The thumbprint to match the finger marks.

"He doesn't like you to keep him waiting for his dinner."

A big smile she gave me, with a scaredy giggle. "No. So impatient, he. He works hard in the day, and comes home hungry. I must go."

She swayed off towards the hut she shared with Pierre. Eh. Wives need to learn their duties. That backra Pierre was being a good husband to Georgine. He wouldn't beat a wife who was diligent. Maybe she's being slack. But those bruises looked so bad against her coloured girl pale skin. "Georgine!" I called.

She turned back. "Yes, matant?"

"Tell Pierre I said that if he wants another child from you, he must stop handling you so rough. He could hurt your insides."

"Yes, matant. Thank you, matant."

That's better. Her voice sounded light and happy now. I went to dip my calabash beside Ti-Bois's.

ALEXANDRIA, EGYPT, 345 C.E.

I leaned back against the warm tile of the bath chair and let the attendant pour the hot water over me. "Shit, that's good, Drineh," I told her. I closed my eyes.

"Hmm," was all she said.

I heard her going back to the pool to dip more hot water. I settled further into the chair and spread my arms and legs, anticipating a flood of warm water. The pat-pat sound of bare feet on wet stone came back towards me. I barely had time to register that I was hearing more than two feet, when a bucketful of cold water splashed all over me. I leapt to my feet, howling, "Damn, Little Doe!"

Little Doe dropped the bucket and she and Drineh ran, giggling, to the destrictarium. Drineh held her hand over her mouth, and she and Doe draped their arms over each other's shoulders and laughed till they fell to their knees. The bitches. Eleni watched us all, shaking her head. "Oh," I said to Neferkare the Little Doe, "I'm gonna get you now."

I was already running towards them; before Doe could dart out of the way, I was on her.

"No!" she yelled, her face merry. She held out her hands to block me, and she danced and twitched away, but I tweaked her nipples and slapped her rump twice, hard. Her breasts and thighs jiggled as she tried to escape my hands.

Drineh got in on the game too; grabbed Doe's hands and helped me tumble her to the floor of the destrictarium. I straddled her waist. "See, even your friend's betrayed you!" I said. And I began to tickle.

143

It always worked. Doe wriggled and kicked like any fish, but Drineh held her legs, and I dug my fingers into her belly and tickled and tickled. She tried to pull my hands away, but I wouldn't let her. Pretty soon she was shrieking, squirming so hard that she nearly threw us both off. "No-o-o," she wailed, tears of laughter in her eyes. "Gods, Meri; stop now."

"What's my real name?" I asked her. I tickled harder.

"Agh! No! I'm going to piss myself!"

"Not on me, you don't. My name?" I could hear Eleni chuckling. I ran my fingertips along the bottom of Doe's belly. She shrieked again. "Fuck! All right! It's Thais! You're Thais!"

"And will you interrupt my bath again?" More tickling and tweaking.

"No! Get off, you young demon!"

I stopped my tormenting and looked down at her. Her face was red and her short black hair stood out everywhere, but she grinned up at me with no remorse at all. "You gonna let me up?" she said. "People will think you're having your wicked way with me."

I chuckled and stood up off her. "Only in your dreams."

"In my dreams," she told me, "you're named Meritet, not that stuck-up Greek name." She rolled to her feet.

"Yeah, yeah. You and your ancient Egyptians. My parents gave me a decent name."

A woman nearby had stopped scraping her own body clean to stare disapprovingly at us. We ignored her. Nosy housewife, with her sagging tits and slack belly, staring at the whores. Old mare. I bet she was almost thirty. I sneered at her.

"Drineh," I said, "can I have a real bath now, please?"

"Yes," said quiet Drineh. She stood up and rearranged her tunic. We walked back to the bath chairs. Drineh picked up the bucket on the way. I sat back in the chair again, but I kept my eyes on Neferkare this time. She plumped herself down on a bench and cocked one leg up. Eleni started covering the leg with sugar paste.

Drineh was on her way back with a full bucket balanced on her head. "Hey, Drineh," I said, "you go to the Theatre yesterday?"

She made a face. "No. Saalim kept the baths open even during the games. I had to work." She dumped hot water over my head.

I blew water out of my mouth and sat up straight. "Oh, Drineh; you should have seen him!"

Her face went lovely with longing. "Felix?"

"Well, yeah," I replied. "Who else?"

She forgot to be so quiet then. "You saw him?" she squealed, jumping up and down. "Oh, Gods, Thais!"

"Judah and his boyfriend snuck me in, right to the middle rows! I could see everything. Oh, Felix was so beautiful. All blond, and strong. That bull never stood a chance. By the end of the fight, *he* was chasing *it*."

"What style does he fight?"

"Secutor. You know, with the round helmet. Didyma—Cups, you know?—she bet me two drachmas that he'd fight in Thraex armour. Ha. She owes me."

PROPPING

PARIS, SPRING 1844

I knelt in Charles's favourite work chair, rested my chin on my hands clasped on the back of the chair, and regarded him with satisfaction. He was bent helplessly over his own table, the one with the odd kidney-shaped indentation so perfect for my intentions; secured by his wrists with my tightly knotted shawl, the paisley. That boring old frock-coat was thrown up over his head and his trousers were down around his ankles. His ass pale as moons shone against the dark wood of the desk. "Are you comfortable, Charles?" I asked him.

"You devil, you angel. What are you going to do?"

His voice came out as a moan, muffled by the wool covering his head. I climbed down from my perch and walked towards him. He twisted his head under the frock-coat, trying to follow my movements. "Today," I said, "I think I'll show you what it feels like to be a woman."

"I *shall* show you," he said.

I smacked his rear firmly, with my open hand. He jumped. "You," I told him, "are scarce in any position at *this* moment"—I smacked again, harder—"to be schooling my talk."

"My *speech*," the brute said, his voice thick with desire. I knelt and bit on one of his cheeks, not so hard as to bruise. He cried out and rubbed himself against the smooth wood of the desk.

"Speech. I'll lesson you in speech. You'll sing for me far better than any of your poet friends could." I stood, kicked his feet as far apart as the pants around his ankles would allow. I slapped his ass again, a stinging blow. He called out, arched his back to bring his nethers closer to me. "Yes," I said. "Do so." And with my index finger, I pressed hard against the tight opening of his rear. It opened just a little to me, then he stiffened.

"Ai! Jeanne, it hurts!"

I pressed forward no further, but left my finger where it was. "I warrant it does." I pushed in a little more. He whimpered. The sinews at the backs of his thighs sprang forth.

"Jeanne, please."

"Ah, you're beginning to hum the tune now, my pretty. Do you feel how you are?" I pressed a little. "How dry?" Hissing, he tried to move away from my finger, but I had him right up against the desk. "How tight? How unwilling?"

"What . . . what do you wish from me?" He was trying to close even tighter against my finger, to push me out. I did not allow it.

"Has a woman ever felt like this when you've entered her?"

"Ah, um, yes. But . . ."

"Yes what?" I pushed slowly past the first knuckle. Oh, but the noises he made were exquisite!

"God, God; what must I do?"

"You really want to know?"

"Yes! Anything! Only cease!"

I jerked my finger out of him, causing him to cry out high and sharp. "Poor dear," I said. I laid my hands on his rump again. He twitched. "I will show you how to prepare a woman—nay, even a man, should you come to that—so that they are eager and ready for your embrace."

"You won't hurt me any more?"

"No, no more. Only pleasure now. You have my word on it." I caressed and stroked the poor ass I'd just been tormenting. Presently, he relaxed and began sighing again for my touch. I squeezed and tapped, and sometimes gently bit. I extended my caresses up his back and down his legs. Soon he was rolling his hips and moaning. "Oh," I said to him, "how fetching you are!" I reached between his spread legs, tickled his balls. I took firm hold of his pecker. He ground it against my hand, against the desk.

"Ah, Jeanne. Please," he whispered. "Please."

I ran a finger up the cleft of his bottom. He strove to open wider to me. "Yes," I told him. "Do you see what I mean? Do you feel more willing?"

"Oh, God, yes."

"But there is one more thing needed." I tapped his bunghole, very gently. "You're still dry."

"How . . . ?"

"There are remedies for that." I reached over his head to where he kept the effects on his desk for styling his hair. He liked it shiny, did Charles. I opened the large bottle of macassar oil he kept, and sunk two of my fingers into it. When I greased his crack good with that oil, he near collapsed onto the desk, his legs trembling from the effort of holding them open despite the confining trousers. "I think you are ready, my dear," I told him.

"Jeanne. Please."

"Yes, that is the opening verse to the song I want you to sing." And with two fingers, deliciously slow, I entered him. By the first knuckle, he was sighing. By the second, he was moaning and pushing back against me. By the third, all he could say was, "Ah! Ah! Ah!" as he wrung his hips in circles. When I began to pump my fingers in and out, he made a growling noise. I felt the insides of him clenching and releasing on my fingers, beseechingly. Sweat had started forth on his back. For purchase, I placed one hand on his spine, above his bum, and commenced to fuck him for all I was worth. And oh, he sang so sweet. "Yes," I said to him. "This is my lesson. You must take some time with us, make us willing. Then it is pleasure for man and woman."

All he replied was "Fuck me," over and over, howling it till he spent.

"Jeanne, where are my cufflinks?"

Our rough games this afternoon had still left us time to dress for the evening. "Which ones?" I answered over my shoulder, never moving from the windowseat where I had moved the damask drapes aside that I might sit. I loved the warmth of these rooms of Charles's. The Hôtel Pimodan was a fine place, très soigné.

"You know well enough which ones, Lemer," he replied irritably. "The ruby, the new ones I was wearing this afternoon."

"Oh, yes. I put them down on your bed."

The red paper on the walls and ceiling with its black foliage made the room seem even warmer. Too many years in drafty single rooms shared with my mother and grandmother and scores of horrid rats. Charles had given us our own rooms elsewhere, me and Maman. Me, with my own apartments in the middle of the river Seine, on the Isle of Saint-Louis! A quaint little street called "La Femme Sans Tête." Maman had grumbled, "What kind of man is he? Respectable women shouldn't be installed on a street called the Headless Woman." But I noticed how her face softened when she ran her hands over the elegant furniture, and how proudly she held herself now when she went out into the streets in her new gowns. The Paris shopkeepers smirked at her dockside Nantes French, but they took her money quickly enough.

Charles was talking of having the window-glass in his own rooms frosted. Said the clouds rushing by distracted him from penning his verses. Better enjoy the view through the window while I could.

Paris was raining this spring evening. The muffled sounds and damp dripping for some reason soothed me. Being near water always had, though I loathed to be in it.

This night, Jeanne, the ginger-coloured woman, is entertaining with her lover in his apartment. Charles has just purchased thirteen lithographs of Delacroix's for an astonishing sum of money (I know what money is now, and I had

been correct in my first apprehension; in some ways, it *is* food).

"Jeanne, is there enough wine? The Rhenish?"

I don't live here, yet he still treats me as his chatelaine. "You told me last week that you'd had the man bring some round. If you've not drunk it all, it's still there."

His peevish sigh reached my ears even a room away. "Would you look please, dear Jeanne, and be sure?"

"Must I do everything?" I snapped back at him, but up I got from the windowseat and went to the cupboard with his wine and his precious books. My stays made me lazy to move. Puffing with shortness of breath, I peered up into the cupboard. Five tall flagons of the Rhenish, the unusual rosé kind that he prefers. Charles likes his pleasures odd. And if the drunkards ran through all the wine, we could go to the café. I smoothed down the beautiful crisp silks of my dress and took as full a breath as my costume would allow.

Charles has just bought Jeanne a new gown, with slippers and jewels to match. They were delivered today. He's asked her to dress in them all, will invite her to sit under the new lithographs. He will hand her into the chair with a soft, white, sweet-smelling hand, make sure to place her under the picture of Hamlet berating his mother Gertrude for her second marriage: *"In the rank sweat of an enseamed bed, stewed in corruption . . ."* Charles fancies corruption, and women in it. Tonight, he wants to show off all his possessions, to make his friend Nadar jealous for the prize he lost when he gave Jeanne up.

I found myself back to the windowseat. Tonight the whores in Nantes and Paris would have much custom. Rain made the men long for the comfort of warm arms. They would go to the taverns. Not the ones with the fancy flickering gas flames; the old-fashioned ones lit with reeking tallow. The women they found there—the ones with the wide, empty smiles and the garish dresses—they'd buy those women lots of cheap wine. So it used to be with my maman, not too long ago. After many glasses of some man's wine, she'd be as cheerful as he wanted. Would wake the next day with a devil of a headache and a man she didn't recognise in the bed beside her, not sure if she'd made him pay or not. And my ill grandmother would rebuke her from her bed, in her broken French that still carried the taint of Africa, after all these years. I miss Grandmaman.

The rain dripped like tears. The poor souls who couldn't afford carriages hunched and bustled through the muddy streets. So many dresses I had ruined in Paris mud. But tonight I was warm inside, watching soft rain fall beyond the window. In my dreams, water had a much more fearful aspect than the light grey drizzle outside.

I batter at Jeanne continually now, trying to get out of her head, to get to the place where my sight is whole, in the round. No use. I am still trapped. Poor Jeanne dreams almost nightly of my watery, salty birth in drowning water, chained. Four it took to call me forth: three women calling out for their gods, and a dead child whose blood would never run warm in its veins.

Jeanne wakes at night fighting at her bonds, choking. What is strange is that she used to have these dreams as a child, too. I catch her memories of them. Once, a sailor who had a few days at Nantes and was spending his pay playing shake the tart with her mother had told them both of his last trip from Africa, how the vessel had begun to ship water belowdecks. Their cargo had been hundreds of souls taken from Africa, bound for slavery in the islands. "Before we could mend the leak," **he said,** "fully two-thirds of the poor brutes had drowned." **He called them brutes; black men, children, and women who had been teachers patient or testy, ironsmiths careful or lazy, dyers, rulers good and bad, priests, guardians for their younger siblings, joyful dancers, fierce or timid lovers. Yet he did not think of himself as a brute, that man. I wonder why not.**

The sailor told of how their sea-swollen bodies had carried the imprints of their fellows' heels on their shoulders and heads, as they had climbed upon each other in order to reach precious air as the belowdecks flooded. Little Jeanne had woken up that night screaming. She'd been dreaming of monkeys, little black monkeys being nailed into toy boats by laughing, pink-cheeked lads in sailor suits, and being drowned.

Adult Jeanne never goes near the water of oceans, streams, or rivers. She doesn't know it, but it was that nightmare that drove her until she had found a way to make a living as an entertainer. She had been drowning in the port of Nantes, in the whorehouse that is her mother's occupation and her grandmother's. A similar nightmare is driving me. I feel myself sometimes twisting in a foul swamp, its smell clotted and rank. I fight to break free of the slime. It catches in my hair and pulls me down deeper. I need to be free of this woman and her blind life. I need to learn the world that is my birthright, to go from baby steps to sure ones, to fly.

For all the sweet warmth inside the apartment, I had the small, constant feeling that I wanted to get out, out. Didn't know what I wanted. Surely not out into that leaking wet in my beautiful new green silk? Tramping through the sticky ordure of Paris's mud streets; where would I go?

I wanted to be out, I wanted to go. Go down to the docks and stare at the greasy sea. Or not down; up. I wanted to rise into the air and fly free. I thought awhile on flying, then started to giggle at the ridiculous view the people down below me on the earth would have, of my hoopskirt and my gaping pantalettes. I would shock proper ladies. They would faint delicately into their gentlemen's arms.

"What is it, Jeanne?"

"Nothing."

"Nothing is what amuses you so?"

"Yes." I leaned my head against the window again and waited for Charles's friends to arrive, all pomp and bombast.

And now here came my Charles, dour again, even after all our play, smelling of scent. My skirt billowed out for metres, so he could not approach me directly; had to come from the side. He slipped his arms over my shoulders, pulled me to him. I leaned into his warmth, marked the pallour of his skin against mine. That excited him too. But I cared not for it. Oh, for the porcelain skin of a rich lady!

He reached down and squeezed my breasts. I felt my nipples swelling against the corsetting. I pulled back his cuffs. "What, no marks?"

He slapped my hand away and chuckled. "Hush. Naughty Jeanne."

"'Naughty' was not what you called me some hours since . . ."

"Shh . . ."

". . . when you were straining to break free of your bonds." I summoned the image of him as I seen him just a little while ago.

"Ah Jeanne, you devil." He kneaded my breasts harder, ran his thumbs cruelly over the place where he judged my nipples to be.

"Yes," I answered, adjusting my body so his hands touched in the right places, "you said all that, and more too." He had writhed and moaned, called me she-dog, called me goddess. And when I slicked two of my fingers with macassar oil and slid them up his nether passage, he'd howled and begged me not to stop, never to stop, to plumb him till he bled, if need be, but to continue.

I sighed and put my face up for a kiss. "Carefully now. Don't smear my powder." Of course he did, and I would have to do it over. But I would find a way to punish him for that. He would like that, beg as he might for surcease. "Laisse, chéri," I told him, putting his hot hands and mouth from me. "Nadar and the others will be here soon. You'll want me beautiful as roses for them."

"I would wish you bruised as rose petals," he breathed into my hair, "and smelling as musky. Then they would know what we've been about."

I leaned against him and inhaled his cologne.

This congress that they make so often, this mock-violence of limbs twisting around each other for purchase and bodies flailing toward and against—it raises a heat in the ginger woman, in the core of her. Ginger is hot in its roots, after all, with a beautiful, lush red flower above. And ginger has a bite, as she does. She loves Lise with a deep, helpless adoration. Charles she loves, when things are well between them, with a sly, mischievous air. When it is poorly with her and with him, her love is sullen, resentful. She must play the wanton for him, and withstand the way he belittles her to his friends. He mocks her speech to them, and her poor skills with a pen. He tells them that he endures her ignorance for the sake of her beauty. And she knows what a scandalous black feather she makes in the cap of this bohemian who revels in drawing shocked gazes from the burghers of his city. So yes, she loves, but her love is bought, and Charles must pay. Her love buys silks, watered as though they'd been retrieved from locked chests in sunken ships; gold, that streams and flows around her neck and wrists in chains of liquid light; jewels that trickle and tripple from her ears. She's covered in the stuff, she soaks in it and it buoys her up when Charles is cruel; is it any wonder we both dream of drowning?

This solid flux, this gold that is all wealth and bread to her; I want it too. It comes from ships. It smells of seas. I was born in brackish water, salty as tears. Jeanne cries often. We have salt in common.

I twist and tug at the ginger woman Jeanne, but though I make her restless and fractious, she does not release me.

That woman, that white woman from Saint Domingue a century ago who let me into her head; she wanted for no material thing. Perhaps if I help Jeanne to a happier life, a life of plenty, I can be freer in the prison of her.

I'm learning fast. Can't make Jeanne do what she doesn't want to, but sometimes I can prompt her, prod her. I can make her mind have visions. Tonight I will fill her dreaming nostrils with the sea again, push her to move beyond this place.

SORROW

When Tipingee got like this, I knew to stay out her way. She was swinging that machète at the cane as though it's Simenon's head she was chopping. Sugar stalks were flying everywhere, and barely did she chop one row but she stepped over it and on to the next. Patrice and Oreste loading the cane onto the wain carts were running to keep up with her.

Last night she was with Patrice, not me. Perhaps Patrice did something to vex her? Her eyes were hard like stones and her jaws looked like she was biting down hard.

What could I say to ease her? What was wrong?

There. She stopped for a while and uncrooked her spine; pressed her hands against it and leaned back. She was blowing air, panting from the labour. I chopped cane as fast as I might to catch up with her. But there came Patrice. He got to her before me and looked around. The book-keeper's eyes had wandered off the field. He was propped against a wain cart, scratching the ox's neck and staring off into the sky. Seeing the book-keeper inattentive, Patrice neglected to pick up the cane lying at Tipingee's feet. He reached a hand out to Tipingee, slow like when you try to quiet a mad dog. She turned her head to him. Her heaving deepened into sobs. She made as if to touch Patrice, then sunk to the ground. I didn't know when my feet carried me to her; I just knew that I was there, me and Patrice holding her as she wailed, "Marie-Claire, Marie-Claire."

"Hush, Tipingee," Patrice answered her back. She was crying for her child, her child. My skin bristled on my flesh to hear her.

"Something happened to Marie-Claire?" I asked her. She never answered me, just held on to us both like we were flotsam and she floating in a shipwrecked sea. I looked to Patrice for the answer.

"Hush, Tipingee, hush." He stroked her hair. He said to me, "Simenon is selling Marie-Claire away."

Tipingee's body shook harder at his words. Patrice said, "He's going to mate her to free-coloured Philomise."

Tipingee screamed, shouted Marie-Claire's name into the air. And finally the book-keeper did notice. Came rushing at us, roaring for us to get back to work. We held each other. The whip landed on Patrice's back, bit at my shoulder. We jerked and cried out, Patrice and me. A welt rose on my skin and I could see tears welling in Patrice's eyes from the pain of the whip. But Tipingee was protected in our arms. For a little space, backra couldn't get to her. "Sir," I said to the book-keeper. I hauled Tipingee to her feet. "Sorry, sir. She's just grieving. Master's selling her child away."

Book-keeper's face got a look. I didn't know what that look signified. "Huh," he said then. He lowered the whip. "I guess even a bitch may howl for her pups."

Tipingee threw her hands round my neck. "She's too young to breed, Mer; too young! And that man; you heard about that man!"

Yes, I remembered what Georgine had told us that day of her labour, about how Philomise would grope her, and mock her fear.

"Don't fret, Mother," said the book-keeper sympathetically. "Your child has black wench's blood. She'll come to like the mating soon enough."

Mama, must my ears hear this? Tipingee's body jerked at his words, but she only sobbed. Patrice's face hardened.

"Get back to work, you three," said the book-keeper. His voice was a little kind. "Mourn the whelp if you must, but do Simenon's work. I won't punish you if you keep working."

Patrice clambered to his feet, wincing from the whip cut he'd got. "Yes, sir." He picked up Tipingee's machète, and I knew the look on his face. I warned him with my eyes. If he only touched the book-keeper, it would be the hanging tree for him. "Don't make Tipingee lose another one that she loves," I said, low.

My whisper made Tipingee know something was happening. She looked to Patrice. Saw the rage in him. Gently went and took away her machète from his hand. Meekly, he gave it to her. "Doucement, Patrice," she said, gently. "I'm right here. I'm going back to work now, yes? You go, too." She sniffed back tears and bent to her work again.

"Marie-Claire's not ready for a husband," was all that Patrice replied. "Not that husband, anyway." His face was sad, so sad for his daughter, but he picked up the cane that Tipingee had cut and took it to the wain cart. His back was running blood. Maybe the book-keeper would let me see to him when we had our midday meal. I returned to my own chopping, and wondered, suppose I had just let Patrice do it? Sink the machète into the book-keeper's chest? Once the backra was fallen, plenty of the Ginen would have seen their chance one time, to head for the maroons in the bush.

And how many of them would even make it out of the cane field? Some of their own fellows would cut them down for the chance of reward from Simenon; some bettering of their stations. And the maroons don't trust easy. Even did any of the Ginen make it through the bush to them, they might make the maroons suspicious. A maroon kills you, you're just as dead as if a backra did it.

And did Patrice only do it, cut the book-keeper down, there would have been no more Patrice; Simenon would have made sure of that. Oh, you gods. "Mama," I whispered, "forgive so evil a wish." I looked about me to see where aloe was growing that I might salve Patrice's cuts and mine.

Master must have changed his mind about Philomise. Before this, he never wanted to sell Georgine to a free-coloured man. True, Marie-Claire is darker than Georgine. So perhaps Master thinks her a meet woman for a coloured man. It must be that.

BLOOD

I dream Jeanne's memories with her, of times before Charles:

PARIS, 1842

I've had a letter from my mother, brought to the concert hall door by a bashful sailor whose ship had just put into port from Nantes. As she brings the letter to me, Lisette says, "He was handsome, too. Stared at me like I was cake. I asked him his name as he was leaving, but he just blushed and scurried away." She handed me the envelope.

I took it. I knew it couldn't be good. Maman had to pay someone if she wanted a letter written. Lise sat on her bed and watched me. I opened it. The handwriting was awful. I had to hold it over the lamp to make the words out.

Oh, you gods. "My grandmother is dead," I told Lise. "Buried in a pauper's grave." The letter was dated a week ago.

Lise came and sat by me and took my hand. "Oh, my heart, I'm sorry," she said.

I looked away from her pitying face, up into the ceiling. I blinked, and again. "No matter. It was a hard life, and she was ill. She's happier so."

But I knew I lied. My grandmaman had had bitter times, yes, and sorrow and fear, but she had made the good times outweigh those. She had eaten life up, relished it like the marrow she sucked from chicken bones, days when we could afford meat for our supper. She talked about the streets of her girlhood, in Dahomey, and how fine her father would look, dressed up in his finest robe, waiting for his men friends to come and call, to share

164

palm wine and talk politics. She had made fast friends of the women she whored with; not a one of them but would share their last sou with her. She laughed often. I knew she didn't want to go from life. Even two years ago when I left Nantes, old Gilles was still coming to call on her regularly. Maybe he had been at her bedside when she died. I hadn't.

I stood and began pulling clothing on, anything. "I must tell Charles."

"Alas! And I cannot . . . in the inferno of your bed turn myself into Proserpine."

—Baudelaire, "Sed Non Satiata"

Brown, brown skin," he mumbled against my shoulders. "Dark as night." He licked the flesh, descending down my body with an "ah," and an "ah." I wanted to talk with him about my grandmaman, gone from me, but he wished to rut.

"Enough, Charles." I pushed him away. He was milking at my paps like a thirsty calf.

Nothing deterred, he peered up at me, grinning. His happy face between the pillows of my breasts looked so comical that I put my sorrow aside for a moment and laughed with him. "I do not do it well?" he asked.

I shook my head no.

"Show me how, then."

As though I had not showed him a thousand times, with a touch or a sigh or an arching of my back. My mother says that men do not like to be schooled in how to love. But then, this man is not like his fellows. "Very well." I made myself more comfortable on the pillows. "Shift. Lie beside me. You get on top of me, I can't breathe."

"*When* you get on top of me," he corrected. But he shifted off my ribs. I ignored the shame rising in me at my brutish tongue.

I circled the nipple closest him with my thumb and index finger. "Here," I said. "With your mouth."

He bent and started sucking, like he would suck the nipple right off. It popped up, but it gave me no pleasure.

"No! No. Lick. With your tongue. All around."

And so he did. Yes, he did. I lay back and closed my eyes; felt the skin wrinkle and the nipple swell. "Yes, like so. Do it more. Yes. Now, gently mind! With your teeth. Ah, yes. Cease with the teeth now."

He stopped. I opened my eyes. His face hovered over mine, pink lips wet, a disappointed look on his face that I had made him stop. I smiled. "With your fingers, Charles. Pull and tease it out."

And his face brightened again as he understood, and set about the motion that I liked. Yes, my poet man. Like that. "Firm at first," I said. "Then firmer still. Oh. Good. Like so, like so. Now do the other one. Yes."

He straddled my belly and licked and teased and tugged until I was transported, arching under his hands and mouth. I urged him on, on, and I could hear myself slipping into the gutter dockside French, but I never minded it, and he didn't mind it neither, for he never corrected me this time. Oh, it was glorious.

"Lemer," he whispered, while his hands worked at me.

"Yes?"

"Is this what you and Lisette do?"

I looked at him, wary. But his face was still open, curious. His top lip was curling that way it does when his blood was running hot. Always he wanted to know about me and Lisette. I knew what to give. I knew how to feed his hunger, never sate it.

"Is it?" he repeated.

I only smiled, deliberately mysterious.

He butted his face then against my belly; plunged his fingers scraping deep inside my cunt. I gasped and tried to remain open against the pain of it. "Oh, you whore," he said gleefully. "You damned, indolent, black slattern. So cold you are to me, and I love you the more for it. Do you wish that these were Lisette's fingers? Lisette's teeth that bite at your breasts? And where is she now? Have you devoured her as you have me? Is this how the women of Africa love? Slut? Is it?"

What did I know of what African women did? I closed my legs against his hand, tried to still it that way, but still he shoved at me. So I lay back and let him take his pleasure. The wallpaper was peeling in the corner there, by the ceiling. Must tell Charles to have someone fix it. And I must get some more money from him. My mother needed new boots.

PARIS, SEPTEMBER 1844

No! I cannot bear it! I will not!"

Charles crumpled up the letter from his maman and flung it. It bounced off the new painting, the Marie Magdalène he had just bought from Arondel.

"What is the matter, chéri?" I asked him. "What does she say?"

"She cannot!" He flounced to his writing desk. "Where is my paper, Jeanne? Quick, I need a pen!"

I fetched the pen from where he had left it beside the bed, and the ink. He snatched them from me, and huffing and whispering, set to composing a letter.

"Will you not tell me the matter?" I asked again, stroking the back of his neck.

He jerked his head away. "Laisse, Jeanne! This is more important than your wiles!"

Oh, how vile he could be. "Well, certainly your maman is always more important than me," I snapped back at him. "I shall take my leave, then."

I turned to go, but he grasped my hand and pulled me to him. "No, Jeanne, please. I am sorry." He stood and pulled me into his arms, clutching at me fiercely. "It is so horrible! Please stay with me. You must help me write a response to her."

He was truly upset, if he wished me to help him compose words upon a page. "What does she say?" I asked.

He cursed, threw himself back into the chair, and began to write once more. "They have taken my estate from me! Imagine the shame, Jeanne! They have given the management of it to some petit bourgeois named Ancelle, and he is to dole me out a pittance every month!"

Oh! That poxy woman! Just as I come into some easement in my life! I looked to the painting, wondered what it might fetch. Charles believed it was a Fédèrico, or a Taddeo. I didn't care, but the painting might bring a good profit, if he would sell it. If the dealer Arondel had told the truth. The last painting that Charles had bought from him turned out to be a daub by some unknown. And the one before that too. And still Charles trusted him. He was like that. "Tell her . . ."

"She cannot, she must not constrain my life this way!" He muttered, scribbling. "How will I hold my head up in the world? How will I have the presence of mind to write my poems, if every hour of every day is only shame and disgrace?"

And how will you maintain the apartment for my mother and me? I thought. Who will procure medicines and warm clothing for my maman? Must I return to the stage, and dodge Bourgoyne's embraces, and hope that another gentleman sees fit to request an arrangement with me? And if that doesn't work? I thought of the smelly, filthy docks of Nantes, the alleyways of Paris where the whores slunk about at night. My mother had managed to keep me from the sailors until I'd seen my first blood, but every time we didn't eat, or Grandmama coughed the whole night and wept from her rheumatism, no money for medicines, I'd known I owed them a living for my life, for my miserable life. I cannot bear to whore any more. A gentleman is my only hope. Oh you gods, please let Charles's family see reason. They cannot beggar us so!

"You tell them that you must be free to manage your own affairs," I said to him firmly. "You have a lady and her mother to maintain, and a reputation. You make them understand how it must be."

I need new walking shoes, Charles," I said to him. I stepped over some trash in the Paris streets, lifting my hem clear. "The heels of these are worn down." How could they not be? We only walked everywhere nowadays. Always my feet burned now like they used to after hours on the stage, prancing around in those pumps.

Charles, his arm linked in mine, pretended not to hear me. He was staring at a widow in her black weeds, kneeling and talking softly to her child. But I saw him press his lips together at my words. He knew that he wasn't providing for me as he should.

A lady, out for a Sunday stroll with her gentleman, gaped at me, the pale negress, from behind her parasol. I clutched Charles's arm tighter and pulled myself up tall, like I'd learned to do on the stage. Ethiope or not, I was as good as she.

That wretched man, that Ancelle who Charles's family had set to manage his money; not even an advance he would give Charles. Not a sou.

But I wouldn't complain. I would be sweet. Charles's family, they were decent people. Good, solid bourgeois. His maman loved him. She would help, when she saw how he was suffering. "Charles," I said. He scowled and hunched his shoulders together; expecting a scolding, likely. I said, "I'm going to go back to the theatre."

Still he didn't speak. We came to the shop where they sell those lovely sweet pastries. Almost I could taste one of them in my mouth, crumbly and buttery. But we just walked by, as we must. At the junction, we crossed the road, so as not to pass by the tailor's shop. Charles had left his overcoat there for mending, and had not the money to pay the bill. Surely his maman must send money soon.

"Bourgoyne has a place for you in the theatre?" Charles asked me finally. His tone was sullen.

"Yes," I said, breezily as I could. "A new comedy. A singing part, with a most delicious outfit! Pink. It suits me well. With white stripes."

He laughed at that, and seemed to cheer a little. "You'll be all in stripes, like a very strumpet. How daring!"

An urchin crouched in a doorway reached a grimy hand to us. Boy or girl, I couldn't tell. Charles looked at the child. Bit his lips. Reached his hand into his pocket. A brace of laughing women swept by us, between us and the child. In their wake, Charles took his hand from his pocket and moved us along. He was right to, I warrant. Little bit from now, we might need that money. And him laughing at my acting. My small joy that I could still dance tasted sour in my mouth now. "Charles," I hissed, softly, so the gentleman in his frock coat walking near us wouldn't hear. "Don't mock at me. I need to work for us both!"

He stopped walking. I stopped with him. He turned to face me. He looked sad, and sheepish. He tucked a lock of my hair back behind my ear. It never remained in place, my hair. Squirmed where it would, like snakes. "I'm sorry, Lemer," he said. "You're right. I shouldn't make fun of you. I should keep you clothed in silk, take you to all the best plays. You should be in the audience, not on the stage."

I hated to see him look so. I smiled. "You will do so once more," I said. "I believe you will."

He only looked at his boots. Then he took my arm again. "Come. Let us see if Nadar is at Cousinet's. Perhaps he will accept our company for supper tonight."

And pay for the pleasure too, I thought. We must give him his money's worth, then; Charles should be witty, I should be beautiful. Always I am an entertainer.

SING

Come on in, now. Good morning, Hector. Good morning, Tipingee. Come in and hear the word of our Lord." Father León stood at the door of his new nigger church, beaming at the curious few of us who wandered in on this wet Sunday morning. "Good morning, Auntie Mer," he said to me, all smiles. I nodded to him, didn't smile back.

We all shuffled in and stood just inside the doorway, unsure what to do next. Father bustled in after us. "This way," he said. "Come and sit before the altar."

We followed him, and sat on the brick floor. Cold, that floor. Could give us aches in our kidneys. I must tell people to bring something to sit on when they come to Father's church.

This new church of ours; it was the hollowed-out inside of the old curing house, the one our master had abandoned when the men had built him a bigger one. It was nearly empty, save for that table, that altar at one end with a statue on it. There was a white cloth on the table, embroidered with bright silks. The statue was a lady, robed in white and blue. Her eyes inclined to the skies. Begging, she was. As if imploring the gods, her family. I wondered what her pain was.

It stank sweet like death, this church. Old sugar had sweated into the very brick. Rainflies, their wings fallen off when the rain had come, had crawled inside the church to remain dry. The little brown lizards were running everywhere; feasting, fattening on rainflies. They warned each other off from their hunting grounds, bobbing their heads and puffing their throats out. A roach, fat as an almond fruit, ran over my leg. In the shadows I could see others, crawling up and down the walls. Must not be too happy to have their home disturbed. I must tell the Ginen in this church today to bathe in the sea or the river afterwards. Unclean, roaches were.

Father stood facing us, his back to his altar. He looked us over, and his smile froze. "Where are the rest of you? There are hundreds of you on this plantation, but there are scarce twenty here."

His voice echoed empty in the large, high room. No one answered him.

"Where are they, I say?"

"Slacking." This from old Cuba. So pleased with herself she looked. "Too lazy to obey Master's orders to come here, Father," she said to the priest. "I tried to roust plenty of them out, but they're lazy. Still in bed. I will name all their names to the overseer. A whipping will make them hop smart to church next week."

I didn't even look at her, just at the ground. Said, slowly, but loud: "Plenty people up and about already, working hard. Tending to their gardens. It's the only good food we have to eat, and our only day free from Master's work to see that our food grows well."

Then I stared full into her face, into the eyes I had saved when boiling sugar exploded into them five years ago. She met my gaze for a little bit, then had to look away. She kissed her teeth in disgust. "Lazy," she said. But it sounded weak now.

Father looked vexed. He sighed. "Of course, of course, you must see to your pumpkins and cassava. I didn't think of that."

"Have your church service later in the day, Father," I said.

"Yes," old Cuba butted in, trying to make herself look big in Father's eyes. "Have it evening time, after the sun goes down."

"No," I said. "Have it late morning, just before the midday meal." The Ginen had their own worship, late Saturday evenings. In the dark, in the depths of the plantation, where no backra would see. Some of them were still sleeping this early on

Sunday morning, tired from their visit with our gods. If Father made the service a little later in the day, more might come. But not Sunday evening. That was when we spent time doing what we wished. Our only time.

Father just looked back and forth between the two of us, his face still sour. "Sit down, everyone," he said. We did. He regarded us all, then sighed. "God has given you a good thought, old Mer," he told me. He spoke to all the Ginen gathered: "Everyone hear that? From now on, I'll ring the bell late morning. Understand? You'll come to me after you've tended to your gardens."

And finished serving our own gods. "Yes, Father," we told him.

RIP

PARIS, JUNE 30, 1845

Jeanne, will you deliver a letter for me?" asked Charles. He had dropped by my apartment to see me and Maman for the first time in near a fortnight.

"What?" I stuck my head out of Maman's bedroom door, still rubbing flour and cornmeal dough between my palms.

My mother, chopping turnips on the dresser, muttered, "So you're his errand-boy now."

Charles said nothing to her. He had sat himself to table in the living room. He smiled sweetly at me, said, "I need someone I can trust. Will you take a letter to Ancelle for me?" He held the sealed envelope. He wrinkled his nose. "What is that vile smell?"

Poxy man. I returned to Maman's room, began dropping flour dumplings into the pot. Over my shoulder, I called, "If the odour of salted pig tail offends your gentleman's nostrils so, perhaps you can find someone else to fetch and carry for you." We were filling the pot with the makings for soup. But we had no money for wood for the fire. So Maman had made friends with a small restaurant nearby, run by gypsies. I would take them the pot, and they would fill it with water and boil it for us until it was soup.

I heard the chair scrape. He came into the bedroom, grinning. "I was in error, my dear," he said. "If the pig's tail has passed through your hands, then the essence wafting from it must be the purest fragrance of life." He took Maman's hand away from her knife, kissed her wrist gallantly. She tried to look indignant, but she gave up and giggled. Just a few minutes ago, she'd been complaining to me for the hundredth time that she'd been better off when she lived in a whorehouse in Nantes that had a kitchen.

"Please, Jeanne," Charles said. "I will take you and Maman to dinner afterwards."

We had been eating salt pork and flour dumpling soup for two weeks now, me and Maman. My mouth watered at the thought of crêpes with cream sauce, of crisp asparagus in butter. I looked at him. Had his mother sent him money, then? "How can you . . . ?" It would be too coarse to finish the sentence, to ask about money.

He laughed and took a surprised Maman on a brief waltz through the small room. "Don't fret, lovely Lemer; I can, especially after you deliver my letter to that devil Ancelle."

Had he found a way to get his inheritance released to him, then? "Will things be better now, Charles?"

"So much better." He ceased twirling Maman, who twittered like a very girl and delivered a weak slap to his shoulder. He came and took my shoulders and gravely said, "After today, Jeanne, you and Maman shall want for nothing."

I was uneasy. His smile looked like the ones I painted onto my face to dance in the theatre. "And this miracle will come about if I deliver the letter?"

"Oh, yes." He broke from me restlessly. "Come, where shall we dine tonight? Maman, whose establishment would you like to grace with your beauty?"

Maman looked at the pot of chopped-up food, and at me. "Cousinet's," she said. Not the gypsies' restaurant for us tonight, then. "Deliver the letter, Jeanne," she told me. "Dress for dinner first."

Charles laughed, a surprising sound. He had laughed little these past few months. "I'll go on ahead and make reservations. Here's some money, Jeanne. Take a carriage."

I made Monsieur Ancelle nervous, I knew it. I didn't like to, for we depended on him so, but did I merely raise my kerchief to my face, he would start like the hen seeing the fox. He blushed and stammered in my presence, and dropped his pen, and spilled the ink. I lowered my eyes and stood still, trying to keep my shoulders from shaking with laughter. "I shall not keep you, Monsieur," I told him.

He leapt to his feet, stubbing his knee on the leg of his desk as he did so. "Will you not rest awhile? I have an urgent matter to attend to, but afterwards, I can read what Monsieur Baudelaire has written."

I smiled at him, and his pink wrinkled face went red as beets. "I regret I cannot wait that long," I said. "The carriage is waiting. Charles and Maman are expecting me for dinner." I could hear my own belly grumbling. Would the accursed man never let me leave?

One thing about this Ancelle, though; it didn't matter if my French wasn't just so. He was trying so hard not to stare at my bosom that he scarce noticed. I wondered if he was one of those men who dreamt in the night of brown skin moving against his. It made me feel quite tender towards him. I smiled at him. Desire makes us all babies again. "A pleasure to see you, Monsieur." I gave him my hand, and you would think an angel had of a sudden placed his fondest wish into his open palm. He blanched, then the tips of his ears went pink as the salted pork I'd just been chopping up with that same hand. He regarded it— my hand, I mean—for some seconds, then slowly bent and planted a most respectful buss in the air just above my wrist. How sweet. I squeezed his hand a little in return, and took my leave of him. A vision of asparagus in cream sauce drew me on. Almost I could smell it.

The waiter fairly threw the dish of soup in front of Maman. A green tongue of it washed over the lip and back into the bowl. He'd been sneering ever since Charles entered with the black lady and her blacker mother on his arm. Maman ignored him, used to such as him. She was as starved as I for good food. She snatched up her spoon and began eating as quickly as manners would allow.

Charles hadn't noticed. His colour was high and he seemed merry, agitated. He hadn't yet tasted his own soup. "Did Ancelle open the letter, Jeanne?" he asked me.

"He had some other matter. He said that he would see to yours presently."

"You didn't read it on the way there?"

He never would completely trust me. I met his eyes. "It was sealed, Charles. You said it was for Ancelle's eyes." I likely wouldn't have been able to make it all out, anyway. Such big words Charles always used.

He favoured me with a sudden, strange smile. "Yes, that's quite true. Good, then. Good." He drummed his spoon on the table, loud. A fat burgher and a fat burgher's wife at the table beside us stopped their meal to stare at Charles. I don't believe he even saw them. He said, "I was in the garden of the Tuileries three nights ago."

I put my spoon down. "You were? But there was some excitement there, wasn't there?"

He laughed. "Oh, yes. Excitement. There were more than fifty men, the papers say," he told us.

"Huh," was all Maman would reply.

"The gendarmes beat them out of the bushes in the gardens of the Tuileries palace, and before they could take them into custody, the mob set upon them. Stones, caning, blows. The gendarmes had to run for their lives. I saw it from where I was sitting, on a bench by the water. I had gone to watch them, those men. I sought them out in the dark, to see their bodies as they came together, to . . ."

People were staring at us. "Charles!"

He looked right through me. His eyes glistened with excitement. He shifted in his chair, fidgeted.

"And the men?" I asked. "What became of them?" The soup

was delicious. I took my time to inhale it, then sip it, to let it linger on my tongue.

Charles shrugged. "Some broken limbs, I'll warrant. I saw two of them helping one of their fellows away. He was bleeding from the scalp. They'll all be more careful where they play buggeranto next time."

Maman laughed heartily at that. Charles fell to eating his soup for a time, then grinned up at us. "Next morning I was walking by the gardens, and I saw a pair of breeches hanging from the gate. A prize claimed by one of the righteous mob, no doubt. Waiter, more wine here."

It was all sport to him. He strolled through the Paris streets, always looking, looking. Eating up what he saw. We were all just food for his eyes, for his pen. Fodder for making stories with.

So strange he was this evening! His cheeks were flaming as though they'd been rouged, and he couldn't seem to sit still for an instant. He put his spoon down again, and stared so deeply into my eyes that I became uncomfortable. His own were wet with tears. "You are beautiful, Jeanne," he said. "I will tell you that you are beautiful so long as I'm here to do it."

Chagrined, I broke his gaze, but he reached across the table and took my chin in his, so that I was forced to look at him. "And when I am no longer here," he told me, "I want you still to remember how you pleased my senses."

"Charles!" I hissed. "You embarrass me!"

He held my gaze. "You will not want. I have seen to it."

"Huh," said Maman quietly, shaking her head. She could pile more scorn into one "huh" than any sailor could cram into an hour of cursing.

Mortified at his public demonstration, I could only keep still, hoping that no one else in the restaurant had noticed, and look into his wild eyes. Finally he moved his hand away, but still he stared. The waiter bustled up, three plates balanced on his arms.

"Ah!" exclaimed Charles, too loud. "You are saved, Jeanne; here is our main course at last!"

The waiter glared at him and set each plate down.

"Have you brought the Laguiole for my steak, man?" Charles asked. Oh, how he was vexing us this evening!

"Of course, Monsieur," the waiter murmured. But Charles picked up the knife to inspect it.

"Yes, yes," he said. "Ingenious workmanship, these knives, eh, Jeanne?"

I shrugged.

"A good point on it," he said. "Sharp as a demon's tooth. And a keen edge, eh? And see how well the bolster fits the hand. Yes, this will do very nicely." Before the waiter could reply, Charles waved him away. I bent to my meal again, hoping we could have it finished before he did anything else outrageous. I kept my eye on him.

For his part, he only tasted a morsel here or there, chewed listlessly, put his fork down again. He gazed out the window. "A lovely night, isn't it?"

"Dark," said Maman, chewing. "It's night."

"Lovely," he replied, with a catch in his voice. He picked up the knife again, stared at it with a mournful look on his face. He turned that sorrowful gaze on me, whispered, "Goodbye, Jeanne," turned the knife and plunged it into his side.

Every moment was clear as though I saw it through glass. Maman flung her arm across my body, as though to protect me. I leapt to my feet, screaming, my eyes only for Charles and the horror of the knife sticking out of his side. He clutched at the tablecloth. The plates, the food, the jug of water, all slid into his lap and crashed to the floor. Charles made no sound, only gave a terrible grimace, and reached trembling hands to the knife handle as though to pull it out. But he never touched it. Lips pulled back from his teeth, he collapsed onto his chair, and thence to the floor. Other patrons of the restaurant were screaming by now. I heard chairs scraping back, and the voices of men shouting for calm, for someone to call the gendarmes, a doctor. "He's mad!" screamed a woman's voice.

The waiter was back at our table, his face white as cheese. He bent over Charles, who was curled up tight in the food that had fallen, his lips moving over and over with words I could not hear. The waiter touched Charles's side, and then did my paramour scream in pain. The waiter brought his hand away red, looked at it aghast, and wiped it on his apron. "A doctor," he murmured. "I'll fetch one." He threw himself to his feet and ran out the door.

Maman had her arms around me, was clasping me tight to her. She sobbed, so quiet. When last had I seen her cry? "The fool," she whispered.

I put her arms from around me, went to kneel by Charles. He took my hand, squeezed it. He was trembling, all the colour gone from his face. His head was pillowed on a slice of bread. A plate lay broken under his hip, a slab of steak amongst the shards. A ruby patch of wet glistened through Charles's jacket. It stained the handle of the knife that stuck out from him, shaking a little with each of his breaths. "Lemer," he said, "it hurts. It hurts."

D on't fret so, Georgine," said Pierre irritably. Softly he was speaking, but his voice carried in the still twilight air.

"It's curfew time," Georgine said, quietly. Her little boy wrapped his fists in her skirt. So big and strong he was, at fourteen months. It was good to see a child fat with health. "The book-keeper might catch me not in our hut."

"I am here," Pierre told her. "You need not mind Thomas if you have a white man with you." He swiped his hat off his head, then squatted himself down on the ground outside my hut. "Ask Mer your question, and then let us be off." His little boy ran to him. Pierre smiled and gave the child his hat to play with.

"I . . ." Georgine was only wringing her hands over and over in her apron. Fine linen, that apron. And there she stood, dumb as any cow.

"Speak up, girl. I must go and make my supper before it's time to be in bed."

"Yes, matant. I'm sorry. I'm being stupid."

And the addled child dipped me a curtsey! Eh. Like I was some white lady. It vexed me, and it pleased me, too. "No matter, child," I said. "Just tell me what you have to tell me."

She threw a nervous look Pierre's way. But he and the boy were chuckling, playing catch with the hat. The boy held out his two hands, too far apart, as children will, then laughed like bells when the hat fell through them. Curls he had on his head. Light brown curls. What a thing.

They had no mind for her, Pierre and her child. She turned back to me. "Matant, I . . . you . . . would you let me plait your hair for you sometimes?"

185

"What?" Insolent girl.

She looked chagrined. "I don't mean to be rude, it's just . . . I'm feeling so much better now since you gave me the medicine, and I see that Tipingee's not plaiting your hair any more, and I know that you like it nice."

I scowled and busied myself, picking up trash that had blown into my garden.

Distress was creasing Georgine's forehead. She pulled at the fingers of one hand with the other, to make the knuckles pop. "Don't be angry, matant. It's the only way I can think of to thank you." She darted a look at Pierre. He saw it, smiled encouragement at her. Threw the hat for his healthy boy child to catch.

I sighed, straightened. "You're right, Georgine. I would like someone to comb it and plait it for me." I remained staring away from her so my face wouldn't give itself away.

Georgine's son shrieked with laughter just then, and ran into Pierre's arms. Pierre laughed and held him close. It was full dark now. I couldn't tell the little sand-coloured boy any different from his blan father. My belly was griping for hunger. I worked my throat, then said, "Can you come on Sunday? After church?" So hard to be the one asking for aid instead of giving it.

"Yes, matant," she whispered. She smiled for the first time since she'd come. She reached her hand out to her boy.

"Maman!" he carolled, and ran happily to her.

"I would like that." I turned my back and bent to my fire again. But I could hear them quite well as they walked away; her and her son and her man, chattering and talking of the day they had passed.

And oh, what a gift she brought me when she returned that Sunday! Georgine can write! Her carpenter man has some of his letters, and he's been teaching them to his boy. Georgine looks on and pretends she doesn't understand, then she practises in secret, afterwards, writing the letters in the dirt and wiping them out immediately afterwards. She is teaching me this thing on Sundays, while her spry fingers twist my hair into spiralled cane rows on my head. Sometimes I hear myself laughing out loud for the pleasure of it. On Sundays, Georgine makes me beautiful, and we write together.

PARIS, AUGUST 1848

Mademoiselle Duval." Nadar bent over my hand to kiss it.

I dipped my head to him, smiled. "Monsieur Tournachon." He's the only one who would talk to me of this high-born salon crowd. The rest of that thought I wasn't refined enough for them. They could all go hang.

He sat beside me. "Is he better now?" He jerked his chin over to the bar, where Charles stood, spinning his stories for a crowd of Paris's finest.

I patted Nadar's hand back and smiled at him. "You're his friend. Has he not told you?"

He shrugged. "He's Baudelaire. He tells me what he wishes. Swears he is as fit as a horse and ready to scale mountains."

"He is better," I said, my tone careful. The letter to Ancelle had been a suicide note, deeding all his family's fortune to me.

"But is he well?"

When Ancelle read the letter, he had rushed to Charles's hotel, fearful for Charles's health. Not finding him there, he had come to the restaurant, only to discover that Charles had been taken to the hospital. He got in his carriage and met us there. I asked him how he knew where to look, and he told me that he knew it was Charles's favourite restaurant, since Charles had so many receipts from there. Ancelle didn't seem such a devil to me.

I said to Nadar, "The wound in Charles's side is almost healed. It hurts only a little any more. And what a to-do from his mother and stepfather when he left their house and came to me and Maman!" I laughed. "He said he would not stay another moment in their care, being lectured to. Wouldn't stay long with us, neither. He's back in apartments of his own now."

Nadar laughed a little, shook his head. "Yes, that doesn't surprise me. But how is his spirit? Is that healed?"

I sighed, leaned back against the couch. "Truly, Monsieur? His mind is as troubled as ever. These fits he has, this melancholy. It plagues him mightily. I know a lady would make him a drink that would strengthen his spirit, put iron in his back. But he says I'm too superstitious. He won't have it."

"You are good to him. And you? How are you, my dear Jeanne?"

"Comme ci, comme ça."

"Only so-so?" And Mr. Nadar, the photographer celebrated all over Paris, looked deep into my eyes, concern on his face. Over at the bar, Charles had just cadged a brandy from some other gentleman and was telling another merry story. They all laughed to hear him. He knew how to sing for his supper, my Charles.

"Lemer," said Nadar, "tell me. What is wrong?"

I had forgotten Nadar for the moment. "I am sorry, Monsieur. My mind was elsewhere."

His smile made friendly creases in his face. "Still daydreaming. You haven't changed, Jeanne. Are you happy?"

Happy? I didn't know what to answer. "It's just that Maman has the grippe again. I'm worried about her." I didn't say it aloud, but Charles didn't always have the money to pay for her medicine.

"Ah," replied Nadar. He understood. He knew how his friend Charles's life stood. "Will you allow me to call on your lovely maman?"

"Monsieur Nadar, thank you." Maman would have more medicine.

I took Nadar's hand, held it fast. I would have kissed it, but that was not seemly.

He stood, and touched my shoulder briefly. "I will come by tomorrow. But now I must go and speak to Châteaubourg, and berate him for having brought his terrified nephew to our salon of degenerates."

He nodded over by the bar. A sombre young man stood there, practically under Monsieur Châteaubourg's armpit. Loud and laughing, there too was my Charles, telling about his trip to Mauritius: "The ship's biscuits went right through me, Dumas. It was quite scandalous. I had to relieve myself two and three times every hour. My poor nether parts were so sore, I would lie on the deck with my arse to the sun to air it."

"You never did!" exclaimed younger Dumas. His father rolled his eyes in alarm and swigged his brandy.

"Oh, I did. The sailors eyed my bare white bum as though it were Turkish Delight!"

Dumas father and son laughed at this, but Châteaubourg's nephew opened his mouth in shock. Nadar shook his head and took his leave of me.

Sometimes I wondered about my choice to throw Nadar over for Charles all those years ago. But Nadar, he had barely noticed. Just continued cheerful and handed me over like a book he had read already and was giving to a friend. Too easy. Charles, he took note of me. Difficult as it was with him, when he looked at me, he *saw* me.

I was sweating under my petticoats. So hot, this summer was. Perhaps we wouldn't stay long. At home I could remove the confining clothing. I took my fan from my reticule, snapped it open, and waved it at my face. The movement caught the eye of that woman—what was her name? "Poppet," I think she called herself when she was at the salons. Over there whispering in the corner with her stuck-up friend with the gaudy hair. That one had taken "Cat" as a salon name. They looked at me, then looked away again. Not them to talk to a black-skinned woman. I fanned harder, put my chin in the air.

"Sst!"

Just the quietest hissing noise. I grinned. I knew who that was. Looked to my left, and sure enough, there was Lise, just come in on the arm of her newest beau. So adoringly he looked at her, he seemed to see no one else. Lise winked at me behind her fan, jerked her head in the direction of Poppet and Cat. Then I saw the sign her other hand was making, almost hidden in her skirts: the rude fig, thumb thrust amongst the four fingers. I almost laughed out loud. Yes, I thought; they are cunts, those women. Fuck them. That's what cunts are good for. I blew Lisette a kiss on my fan. Poppet and Cat smirked and turned their backs on us. Lise blushed, took her gentleman's arm again, and they breezed on into the café, where a waiter seated them at a table.

I wanted a drink. Charles had provided for himself, but I was thirsty. I gathered my skirts around me, stood, and walked over to him. He was talking to Monsieur Châteaubourg's shy young nephew: "Poe is astonishing," Charles said, "a visionary. You must read 'Mesmeric Revelation.'"

The young man replied, "I confess I don't read English. I tried to learn it at the Lycée, but I fear I was too dull." He blushed girlishly.

"No need!" Charles told him. "I have just last month published a translation of it! Here; you must have a copy!" And out from his pocket he took a copy of the translation and offered it to the gentleman.

"Why, no; I couldn't possibly . . ."

"You can and you shall," Charles blustered at him. "After all, you're a writer, yes? Plays, I think you told me?"

"Just small conceits, yes. He's good then, this Poe?"

"Charles," I interrupted, "my throat is parched. May I have a drink?"

Charles waved a hand in the air at me. "Not just yet, Lemer; can't you see that I'm talking?"

Oh, that man! I subsided for the moment.

"Take the translation, Monsieur . . . Verne, was it?"

"Yes. Jules Verne." The young man took the book. He thrust it into his own coat pocket, not even looking at it. "I'm indebted to you."

"Nonsense!"

"But . . ."

"If you feel that you must make it up to me, perhaps a glass of wine for the beautiful Jeanne here?"

Monsieur Verne glanced briefly at me, then went even redder. Was my powder running? Was my rouge still on? "Oh," he said. "Why yes, I suppose I could."

Despite the heat of the day, my body went even warmer. He didn't forget me, my Charles didn't. He never did. Not a sou to his name, but he'd bought me wine with the last of his copies of the translation.

"To whom do I owe the pleasure, Madame?" asked Monsieur Verne. A green one, he is. That's not a thing to ask a lady you meet at the salons.

Charles took my arm. "Before you stands Jeanne Duval, the most beautiful actress in the world. My mistress."

I thought that Monsieur Verne would perish right there. I laughed and tapped Charles with the fan. "Don't embarrass my saviour, Charles! At least, not before he brings me wine."

Monsieur Verne fairly stumbled in his eagerness to get away from us. He spoke with the waiter, and presently a glass of fine Merlot came my way. I took it from the tray, and looked to see where Monsieur Verne was so that I could tip my glass in thanks to him. But he and Châteaubourg had claimed their hats and were already leaving. Monsieur Verne had the Poe translation in his hand. So proud Charles was of that book. I wondered if Verne would even open it.

It happens more often now. While Jeanne sleeps at night or dozes in the day, I sometimes drift too. That bleary-eyed little cur that she has sometimes naps with her, furry legs twitching, in her lap. Always I am tethered in her consciousness like that cur, or a lurching toddler whose mother has tight hold of its hand, but I can sometimes get a little distance from her before I am leashed in again. I don't wish to be a child any longer. The aether world streams. Many flows, combining, separating, all stories of African people.

Did you bring the ginger?" I asked Ti-Bois.

"Yes, matant." He held out the sand-coloured twist of root to me.

"Eh. And you even washed it, I see."

"Yes, matant. And the flour bag strips, too."

"Clever boy. Hang the cloth out the window to dry for me."

Ti-Bois went to the window of the slave hospital and carefully draped the torn strips of coarse crocus bag cloth on the window ledge. Over beside one of the other beds, old Cuba was doing her Sunday good deed; praying quietly with the woman who lay there with her baby. Lockjaw, the baby had. Probably wouldn't live past tomorrow.

The new man acted like he didn't hear or see any of us, only lay chained where he was on his palette on the floor, staring up at the ceiling. The book-keeper had told me about him. Had sent me here to see to him. Mathieu, his name was.

Ti-Bois came and crouched beside the man, inspecting him. So curious this little boy always was. The man never returned his gaze. I moved the calabash of cornmeal mush aside, took my mortar and pestle from my bag and set it on the ground beside the calabash. I ground the ginger root up in the mortar. Ginger smell pricked my nose with its clean, sharp scent. "Bring the crocus bag now, Ti-Bois."

"Yes, matant." Back he came dancing with the strips, waving them in the air like flags. I smiled at him.

"Not too much noise, petit. People are sick here."

"Maman says they are just lazy."

A woman with a whip-torn back raised her head from her palette and just looked at him. She said a word in a language I didn't know. Her face told me it was a curse. She spat, then let her head sink to the pillow again.

"Ti-Bois, give me the cloth. Go and fan the flies from that auntie's back."

"But I want to see what you're doing!"

"You can look from over there. Go and give her some ease."

And the little devil kissed his teeth at me as he went to do what I told him! "Ti-Bois," I said, "come here."

He slunk back, not looking at me. "Yes, matant?" he mumbled.

"What is that noise you just made?"

He looked at the packed earth of the slave hospital floor. "Nothing, matant."

"Do children make rude noises to their elders?"

"No, matant."

"What did you say?"

"No, matant."

"Remember that, and keep your lips buttoned, unless you can speak with respect. Go and do what I told you."

His little face was like thunder as he went, but he didn't make a sound this time. He squatted beside the woman and began to fan the flies away. She scowled at him, but then she sighed and closed her eyes. I must wash her wound out again soon, or it might become maggoty.

I knelt beside the new man's palette and put the mortar full of ginger root mash on the ground beside me. "Mathieu," I said, "hold out your hand."

Nothing.

"Mathieu."

"Mamadou," he croaked. But still his eyes were to the ceiling.

So. A Muslim name. He must forget it now, in this land. Must learn to speak like the Ginen.

"Your name is Mathieu." I reached and took his swollen wrist. He stiffened at first, then with a sigh he let the arm go limp. I took it in my lap and began packing the ginger paste around the puffy wrist joint. I wrapped the cloth strips over the wrist, over the paste. Pretty soon, warmth would rise up all over the wrist;

195

ease the pain in it. I laid his arm over his breast. Not a sound he made, not a look he gave me. I took up the calabash of cornmeal mush I had got from the barracks where they seasoned the new prisoners to do hard labour. I scooped some onto my fingers. Tried to put them in his mouth. He turned his head aside. "Haram," he croaked out. *Forbidden.*

"Yes, I know," I told him. "It's salted pig tail they cook it with." To Muslims, pig is taboo, unclean. "But you need to eat, Mathieu." I tried to feed him again, but he kept his lips sealed from me. I put the bowl down, and gently took his bandaged wrist. "You see this swelling here?" I said. "It's because you're starving yourself."

He just sniffed, and still looked at the ceiling. Some of the new ones did send themselves back to Africa that way, by not eating. Their limbs shrank, and their faces, but their joints and bellies bloated up. If they were determined, they starved to death.

"Plenty of the Ginen find ways to die when they come here first, yes? When they're being seasoned to this life. The blans throw you in the barracks, feed you pork, and dried salted fish with worms in it, and dayclean to daylean, they work you, work you in the fields. Cutting cane—"

Mathieu leaned away from me and spat over the side of the bed. A disgusted look on his face, he. Why? Maybe he was understanding some of my words? Probably. He'd been with us two months already; plenty of time to start to learn Saint Domingue French. I kept on: "—cutting cane, weeding cane, breathing cane, cane, cane. If you straighten up from out of the cane, they beat you." He jerked little bit. I said, "If you sleep through the morning bell, they beat you."

There. His throat was working. Crafty devil did understand me, after all. I touched his shoulder. He flinched from the touch. "Mathieu," I said softly; "you're never going to see your family again. Maybe you had a wife, children. A father or mother. Never again. They have to live only in your head now."

His shoulders were shaking. I could glimpse the fat tears running down his face. Ti-Bois had crept over to see. I let him stay. "Maybe you were a farmer, with your own land. Or a scribe, or a teacher. Maybe you were a soldier. All done now. Now you work in the cane."

He sobbed, like a dying gasp.

"I know you miss your family, Mathieu," I said. "I know the work is so hard that you ache all the time. I know how the food is dry and tough in your mouth, and you're shamed to let people see you with only rags or maybe nothing to cover your skin. Naked like a child."

His sobs were coming loud and fast. I whispered, "And I know that you don't want to live this life no more. You feel to just die. I know the way that feels."

Mathieu turned on the palette and flung himself into my arms, wailing. Ti-Bois giggled. "Ti-Bois," I said, "go back over there and tend to the lady. You're doing a good job." He cut his eyes at me, little méchant, but he went.

I held on to Mathieu's weeping body. He was thin. This had always been a thin man, I could tell, but now with the way he was starving himself, he was only bones. He spoke through his tears, a language foreign to me. I knew the grieving in his voice, though; the mourning. On and on he went. I heard one familiar word: "Allah, Allah," over and over. Mathieu was calling on his god. I rocked him, thought a bit. When he got little more quiet, I took his face between my two hands. Such woe in his eyes. "Mamadou," I said, using his real name for the last time: "one thing that I can say to you that you will understand." I had known some Muslims in my African home. In church Arabic I told him: "No man should take a life, even his own. Only talk to Allah; he is merciful."

He snuffled, deep in his nose, and pouted like a child. His face collapsed into grief. And he bawled again. So loud he bawled.

"Matant," called the woman who was having her back fanned by Ti-Bois. "Pity, do. Tell that man to hush up his crying. People are trying to rest here."

"He will stop soon," I told her.

He pushed himself from me, took up the calabash of corn-meal mush and took some of it on two of his fingers. He gagged on the first mouthful, poor soul. Me, I gave thanks that I was not so foolish, to scorn what little meat the blans gave us. The gods understand. They tell me that even the Muslim book says so. If haram is the only food you have to keep you from death, then eat haram. God is merciful.

I watched Mathieu force himself to swallow. "Good, Mathieu," I said. "Try again. You must eat and be strong."

Patrice came crashing in through the doorway. "Mer! Come! Now!"

Mathieu looked up at Patrice, curious.

"What is it, Patrice?" I said. "Someone's sick? Where?"

"It's Marie-Claire!" His face was grey with panic. "Please, Mer; somebody poisoned her!"

Marie-Claire! I was to my feet before I knew it, packing up my things. "Where is she?" I asked Patrice.

Jittering, he; anxious to go. "At Tipi's. You ready?"

"Almost." Oh, Marie-Claire. "Ti-Bois," I called, "go to my garden and pick a big handful of mint leaves. You know mint?"

"Yes, matant." He started quick for the door. Mint might ease Marie-Claire's stomach a little.

"Bring them to Tipingee's hut! Don't stay to wash them this time! Gods, I'm coming, Patrice."

As we left, I glanced back at Mathieu. He put a lump of the cornmeal into his mouth. Made a face, he, then swallowed, hard, without chewing.

I scurried fast as I could. Patrice was impatient, I could tell, but he slowed his pace to match me. We rushed past the Ginen working in their gardens this Sunday, cooking on fires, or just sitting in the sun, enjoying the little few hours of no work.

"What happened, Patrice?"

"Nobody knows. She was visiting her mother, they were making supper. Marie-Claire was all the time saying she didn't feel so good."

"Didn't feel good how?"

"Her belly's paining her."

"She ate meat from the great house!"

"No. Tipi asked her. Marie-Claire knows better than that, Mer!"

"It's true," I said. "She knows." But what, then? "Is anybody vex with her, Patrice?"

"I don't know, Mer! Who could vex with Marie-Claire?"

She was about to be given to free Philomise, a rich coloured man. "Anybody envy her, maybe?" Mama, some jealous somebody put ouanga on Marie-Claire?

"Don't know, Mer. Don't know. Hurry."

Seemed like forever before we reached Tipi's hut. We crashed inside. Nimble little Ti-Bois had run faster than my legs could carry me. He was already there, standing by the window, clutching the mint tightly in his sweaty hands. And oh, gods, there was Marie-Claire, on the floor where she had fallen. It was worse than I thought. Tipi held her child's upper body in her arms. She was brushing and brushing the hair out of Marie-Claire's eyes. Tipingee looked up at me, her face wet. "Save her, Mer. This one can't go yet. Can't go and leave me yet. Please, Mer."

I bent down to them. Thank you, Mama; Marie-Claire was breathing. Fast and shallow, but breathing. Sweat, drops of it, standing forth on her forehead. But so cold her hands were! And her lips gone purplish. I looked at her fingertips. No blisters there. Maybe not something she touched, then. Maybe not. One sandal was still on one foot; the other lying beside it. Master Simenon gave his house slaves shoes. Marie-Claire told us it's because he didn't want them trekking dust over his carpets. "Patrice," I said, "pass me Marie-Claire's sandals there."

He eased the one off her foot, fetched the other one, handed them both to me. I looked at the shoes carefully, me. No holes jooked in the bottoms of them. Not a piquette she'd stepped on, then. Nothing she'd touched. I examined her clothes and her whole body, all of it, like she was a newborn. No ouanga tangled in her hair or sewn into her dress or apron. Nothing in her mouth. No scratches on her skin, not even a mosquito bite.

Her eyes were gone red. I must hurry. "It's something she ate," I told her parents.

"Can't be," Tipi said. She brought her voice down low. Plenty ears everywhere, and not all of them friendly. "She knows what to eat and what not to eat."

"Then it's something she doesn't know about," I insisted. "Maybe some new food for the great house, come from France on one of their ships. Something she ate, something she drank."

"Drank?" Patrice repeated. His voice sounded strange. I looked up at him. He threw a look for Tipi. Her eyes got big. She grabbed my arm.

"Mer," she said, "save her, Mer; it's the water. I think she drank great house water!"

"The water? That wouldn't harm her. Great house water is always clean. One whole well, just for them."

Tipingee got a guilty, shamed look. She gazed deep into her daughter's face, smoothed her cheek with one hand. "Not any more, Mer. It's Makandal. He's poisoning the wells and barrels the backra drink from. Is she going to die?"

"What? The water? Oh, you gods. That man is just a curse."

"That man loves the Ginen," Patrice said. "He's fighting for us."

I looked at him, astonished. Looked to Tipi. But she just nodded at Patrice's words and stroked her daughter's face, love and sorrow in her eyes. "Makandal is our weapon, Mer," Tipingee said. "Sometimes the machète slips in your hand and cuts you. It's not the machète at fault then, it's your carelessness."

Marie-Claire began to convulse in Tipingee's arms. With a small cry, Tipi held her tight, tried to keep her arms from thrashing. She got a blow from Marie-Claire's hand for her trouble. Patrice leapt to them and helped to hold down Marie-Claire's legs. He got them still, then smoothed her skirts down. Such a frightened look there was on his face.

"I have to purge her," I told them. "Ti-Bois, you must run fast, you hear?"

"Yes, matant," he said in a high, frightened voice. Marie-Claire bent her body into a bow. Tipi held her and started praying in her tongue.

She had swallowed the poison already. It was in her belly. Must drive it right on through her. She must shit. "You know aloe, Ti-Bois?"

"Yes."

"Good. Run back to my garden. Bring back two fat aloe leaves. And tell somebody to boil a pot of water and bring it here, to Tipingee's hut. You understand?"

"Yes, matant."

"Run, then! Go!"

He left, running fast on his little legs. Oh, Mama. Help me to heal this child.

"Mer, I have senna pods," Tipi said.

Yes, that would work to get the purging started. "Where?"

I found them in the calabash Tipi pointed out to me. Took three. No time to wait for hot water. I chewed the bitter brown pods into a paste. "Hold her good," I said to Tipi and Patrice. I pried Marie-Claire's jaws open and put the paste inside. Another convulsion took her. She bit me. I pulled my hand from her mouth and stroked her throat. "She must swallow," I told them. "It must go down inside her. And we have to give her a healing bath. We need a cauldron."

"Fleur has one," said Tipingee.

Yes, it's true. She would boil corn in it for all the Ginen on Christmas day.

Marie-Claire still hadn't swallowed the paste. She must swallow. "Hold her," I told them again. Then I pinched her nose shut and held her mouth closed with the other hand. Her chest started to heave. Then she swallowed, finally. I let her go so she could breathe. She lurched in our arms. We three held her. Slowly, the fit passed.

"I'll go and get the cauldron," Patrice said.

And here was Ti-Bois with the aloe, and his mother Doucette, her face anxious. They stepped into the little hut, and behind them came someone else. Makandal. Come from his marronage.

"I was flying over, and I saw the commotion. I came down and people told me what happened. How is she, Mer?" he asked. Grave, his face was. Hypocrite. Was him that did this.

"Get away from this house," I said to him. Then I had to ask, "Unless you know how to cure her?" The words were sour like gall in my mouth. Me, asking Makandal for help. But he was a powerful bokor, wise with herbs, and there lay Marie-Claire, her skin gone ashy. This wasn't a time for pride.

Makandal knelt by Marie-Claire. Tipi looked at him like he was her only hope. His face was stricken. "Has she vomited?" he asked.

"No," I replied.

He touched Tipi's shoulder. "I'm very sorry for this, mother. Marie-Claire knew not to drink the water from the great house well. Must have been an accident."

She knew? Everybody knew about this but me, it seems. "You're sitting there, flapping your lips," I said to Makandal, "but you're not saying; you can help her?"

He held out a handful of bush. I didn't recognise it. It chagrined me not to know it. "When I heard about Marie-Claire, I went and found some of this where it grows. Boil it," he said, "and make her drink the water from it. She will vomit out the poison."

If she came back to her senses enough to drink. If we got it into her in time. "You go and boil some water, then," I told him. "Quickly."

With her child still in her arms, Tipi reached up and got a pot off the table. She dumped out the peas that were in it, right onto the floor. The green pods scattered. She handed the pot to Makandal. "You know where the river is," she said.

He nodded and turned for the door.

"You still want the aloe, Mer?" asked Doucette.

"No!" said Makandal from the doorway. "That would only drive the poison through her body faster."

Ti-Bois, poor little Ti-Bois, started to cry. "What I must do with them, then?" He held the aloe leaves out to me, begging me to take them from him. "I don't want Marie-Claire to die."

Makandal got a look of sorrow. "Oh, petit," he said to Ti-Bois, "this is not your trouble. We are adults. We will try to help her to live." He turned again, and put the pot handle in his mouth. Through the doorway I saw him become a dog, bounding away to the river. I heard some of the Ginen exclaim when he changed. Tipi and me, we held Marie-Claire. And we just prayed. Up to Makandal now. Patrice and Fleur came back with the cauldron. Doucette jumped up to help them. They set it on the fire outside. Fleur and Patrice must have said what we needed to the other Ginen, for people began to come one-one with buckets of water. They were filling up the cauldron.

Then back came Makandal, a three-legged monkey running on its hinders, with Tipingee's pot in its hand. He turned to a man again and cotched the pot beside the fire next to the cauldron. Patrice looked at him. I couldn't hear what Patrice said, but Makandal reached and touched Patrice's arm, soft. Then he came back in and got his bush from me. Put it into the pot. Pretty soon, was steam rising from the pot. Marie-Claire was quiet little bit now. Too quiet. Tipi was quiet too. Not praying any more. Only tears streaming down her face. Only her eyes watching Makandal, pleading with Makandal.

He came back in the cabin. "How is she?"

"Still with us," I said.

"Mash'allah." *God be praised.* He found a calabash and poured some of his tea into it. Blew on it to cool it. He came over and crouched by us. "Hold her head up."

Me and Tipi, we did what he said.

"Mer, open her jaws for me."

"This must work, Makandal."

"I know. Help me, please. I only have the one hand to pour with."

I pried open Marie-Claire's jaws. So soft her breathing, so fast. Makandal poured, but it all just spilt out her unconscious mouth again.

"What can we do?" cried Tipingee. "It's too late!"

"No." I took the calabash from Makandal, took a mouthful of the hot tea. Acrid. Leaned over Marie-Claire, me. Made a seal between my mouth and hers, and spat the tea down her throat. She gulped. It went down. Thank you, Mama.

Makandal tilted the calabash to my mouth again. "Give her more." So I did that. After three times, the little bit of tea I had swallowed began to work on me. I had to go outside to vomit. Tipingee took a turn spitting the tea down her daughter's throat, but pretty soon it made her sick, too. So it was that when Marie-Claire vomited out a great gout of liquid threaded with blood and woke up, it's Makandal was holding her, begging her with his eyes to be well. We came back in the cabin, me and Tipi, and he had helped her to sit up. She was on her knees, spitting out the poison. He had his whole arm around her belly, massaging it.

And she was holding on to the stump of the half a right arm. Holding on like it was life. Marie-Claire coughed, spat a last time, and sat herself down. Kept a hand on Makandal's thigh, for balance. Not seemly that she should do so, but what was manners right now? More important to see to the girl's health. She looked good at Makandal, soul-deep. "What happened to me?"

He bowed his head. "It's my fault. You must have drank something, eaten something, that had great house water in it."

She whispered, "You saved me?"

I saw the tightness of her grip on his thigh, and how Makandal gazed long at her, and I knew that we had lost her, Tipi, Patrice, and me, for all that she would live now. But Tipi looked on the two of them, Marie-Claire and Makandal, and just smiled a grateful mother's smile.

Next day we woke up and saw goats from de Mézy's plantation wandering through our master's roses, feasting. Makandal was gone again. He had just left them. Gone for good now, people said. On grand marronage, hiding out with the maroons. Marie-Claire mourned little bit, but she was young, and her sadness passed. She would have plenty more sorrow in her life before life was done. Simenon sold her away to Philomise, the way he had planned. Tipi wept and wept, but there was nothing to do. Marie-Claire might be better off so. He might free her some day, her new man. And he was one of the rich free coloureds, they said. Born to his money. Richer than Simenon.

Soon after Makandal was gone, we started hearing the stories. A plantation burned further over by the Cap there. Another one where all the blans died one night; sat down to a dinner party, began to eat, and started from the table with blood running from their noses and mouths. Poison, they said. Black man's poison. Blans afraid to drink from their own wells. They started drinking only water from sealed barrels. But when they broached the barrels, most times that was poisoned too. Patrice told me how

Makandal did it; sharpened splinters with poison on them inserted between the staves of the barrels. The same splinters I used to heal, to protect our children from smallpox.

Makandal, Makandal; his name was spoken wherever a white died.

And now Patrice was whispering here and there amongst the Ginen, telling them we must stand up, must rise up. Saying there were more of us than there were blans in Master's household. Stupid man. More bullets in this whole land of Saint Domingue than all of we blacks.

Saturday, 27 March 1852

In the past, Mother, she had some qualities, *but she has lost them; and I, I see more clearly. TO LIVE WITH A BEING who has no gratitude for your efforts, who thwarts them with permanent malice and stupidity, who considers you her servant, and her property, and with whom it is impossible to exchange the least conversation on politics or on literature, a creature who* will not learn anything, *though you yourself have offered to give her lessons, a creature who DOES NOT RESPECT ME, who is not even interested in what I do, who would fling my manuscripts into the fire if it would bring more money than letting them be published . . .*

Every time your dreaming mind sets me free, I float into the spirit place, into that aether that birthed me. There I can perceive a little bit more clearly. There are currents there. There is movement. Helpless, I tumble and splash from one to the next. Each eddy into which I fall immerses me into another story, another person's head. The streams are stories of people; I can/will/did see them, taste them, smell them, hear and touch them. I can perceive where one man's telling tongue will take him if he follows that branch of the river, or this. Where another woman will find the tributary that leads her finally to love, or to ruin. When I fall into the aether, I can sometimes choose to ride on someone's shoulders like a head on a neck, like a rider on a horse. It is difficult for me yet. I am a toddler. But at least I am no longer crawling. My perceptions are diminished when I am astride a horse, but if my steed has welcomed me, I can borrow that person's body for a little time; borrow their understanding of how to make their limbs move, make their tongues talk. In a willing head, I can dance and sway like the rushing spirit waters. Can sing and laugh like bubbling currents. Can speak. Tell fortunes. Give advice.

And then Jeanne wakes, and yanks me back into her.

I want to always be free, to *choose* to be enhorsed, or to navigate the aether world! I cannot make Jeanne's body do my bidding, can only be carried along in the waters of her flesh.

When I perceive the many stories of the folk of Africa, I like the love stories best.

TIDE

As Jeanne nods off, the rhythms of her breathing—of her brackish, beating blood—wash me to other places; often to that Hayti land, that Saint Domingue where women, men, and children in all the polished wood colours of blackness dance at night around poles set in the ground. Sometimes I arrive in other times, and their clothing is different; frocks so spare, so brief that Jeanne would think them scandalous; fabric that stretches marvellously, but that never tears. Jeanne would find the glass in the windows of future Hayti impossibly thin and clear. She would marvel at the bulbs of light in the ceilings. For me, infant that I am, everything is so strange—telephones as well as petticoats—that nothing is more strange than any other thing, and I become accustomed to them quickly.

EBB

They dance in those places, those times; they sing, and the drummers pound, pound out the pulsebeats. Sometimes it is French they sing, or a kind of French, different in one century than another. Those dancing people call, they implore, and suddenly I am there. I have lurched into another head, another body; not Jeanne's, for she sleeps.

The other head's thoughts fall away, except for a kind of ecstasy of surrender, the hint of a whispered name. And I make the body dance, jerk, prance. I make it leap. It falls into the arms of the people around it, who hold it up. Their touch; oh, their touch of skin on this skin I have borrowed. Its eyes roll in its head. The other people cluster around and **implore me:** I dare not have another child lest I die of it; how can I keep my husband from me?

And: I want the woman who lives in the shack down by the river, how can I make her look on me?

I talk of pennyroyal for keeping man's seed from flowering. I speak of how kind attentions and sweet breath can lead another to love. They say, thank you, Mother, thank you. **They clothe me in fine gowns, give me money, put lace fans in my hands. In honour of me they cook sumptuous feasts and give to the poorer among them. They love me, and I am good for them. And I dance. Truly, though I am mother to none, I care for them all. And I dance.**

Each time, the aether shows me more stories. Seas, breathing deep in their waters, carrying ships on their backs. Whole histories, of people, of places. I see the fifty male wives, adorned in dresses, of the warrior queen Nzingha of N'gola. She and her sisters Kifunji and Mukumbu hold off for a time the Portuguese who want the riches of Nzingha's

212

country. I see a black beggar man in a land of snows, wearing a ship on his head for a hat, and for his bread telling tales of capture and adventure. I see the spring-fed lakes of new-borns' minds. I swim in them, and they are clear as air. I splash in joined tributaries of lives, watery webs that connect each one's story to each. Then Jeanne wakes again, and the leash draws tight once more.

BEAT

This sleeping night though, I do not dream the column of the peristyle, the centre pole by which I descend to walk amongst my supplicants. I do not dream the herky-jerky bodies as they tump and sway. Instead I am otherwhere, in a room of massive columns, painted in bright pictures. The beautiful pictures on the columns are echoed in the things that lie before me: lotuses standing gracefully tall; people seated, or singing, or kneeling, their foreheads touching the ground in front of me. I see tables full of food, of loaves of bread and pitchers of grain beer. The heat here is bright as the sun. There are women dancing, their linen dresses a weave so fine I can see their bouncing breasts and pumpkin-round asses and the shadows of their vulvas. They shake belled rattles, like many assons. What is this I am seeing? The dancing women call and bow and shake their bells. It is not any kind of French that they sing.

There is another here, in the aether with me! She is gracefully dressed, like the women, in transparent linen. She turns her head towards me, reaches out a hand. Her head is a cow's. I do not know how I do it, but I jerk myself back along the storystream, out of her reach. She is terrifying, and the women are singing for her. I know that if she responds to their song, the tree-trunk-thick columns would shake with the power of her. I want to creep back to witness. Who is she? Does she do it? Does she low her love in large words to the women who so honour her? I am about to know who she is, when Jeanne, unknowing, drags me back into her wakening head, and we both find ourselves still trapped in her living body.

But a whisper has followed me back from the aether. Hathor. A goddess of love, of elder Egypt.

She loves. She loves those people. Is she like me, then? Am I like her?

Jeanne, wake up!" Charles's hand on my shoulder sucked my dream out of my head. Sweet Choux-choux and Tatiana on my lap yipped at him for disturbing me.

"Jeanne," Charles said, "where is the cat?"

Was that gold I saw in my dreams? And music I heard? "Shh, Choux-choux," I said, petting my darlings. "Did nasty Charles frighten you?"

Charles took me by both shoulders. He was frowning. "Never mind those mangy mutts, Lemer; where is Mignonne?"

Beautiful, shameless women, dancing in gauze garments? So I had danced for Nadar in my private rooms when I was still at the theatre.

"Lemer? The cat?" Charles is sounding peevish now, and angry. Time to handle this.

"It snapped at me, chéri," I told him sweetly, so sweetly. Had there been a statue too? And perhaps an animal of some kind? "See, look where it scratched me." Nasty cat. Always peering at me like it knows my secrets.

"Have you locked her away, then? She will be frantic!"

"It kept stealing Tatiana's food. Poor baby was getting so thin."

"Where did you put her, Jeanne?"

I only looked at him, and stroked my babies. They licked my hand. Their breath was sour with the cheese I'd given them hours since; I could smell it. Perhaps it was a cow, that animal?

"My God! You've done away with her!"

"No! I only put her outside for a bit." Or maybe it was the statue, not an animal; had it had a calm, bovine head?

"Out of doors? You ran her away?"

"Oh, Charles. I'm sure the wretched thing will come back." I pulled back little bit in the bed and clutched Tatiana and Choux-

choux to me tighter, for Charles was red in the face. When he makes his lips thin like that, I must be wary. But he only said,

"When?"

"What?"

"When did you put Mignonne out into the street to die? Tell me, quickly!"

I pouted. "Not long. Before I fell to sleep. She won't die."

He glared at me and raced to the door, muttering, "Perhaps she's still in the doorway."

Serve him right for selling my jewellery. Now I didn't have nothing to buy medicine with for Maman. And she with the croup so bad. I settled back on the divan to try again to escape into sleep. Bells, had those been in my dream? Bells, and a pagan statue.

The door slammed and Charles was a flurry of black, at me before I even understood that he was there. Silent, so silent, this man of words. He seized me by the shoulders. Choux-choux growled and leapt at him. He swiped the little dog off the bed, and I screamed. My poor Choux-choux thumped when he hit the floor. Tatiana leapt down after him. They cowered, whimpering. Charles was shaking me so hard, I thought my neck would snap. I grabbed at his wrists to stop him. Strange; in moments like this, you forget that you can speak. Wordless, I wrenched his thumb up off my throat and bit. He hissed and threw me from him. The back of my head crashed into the corner of the divan, and I fell to the floor. My body was too hurt and stunned to speak then, even if I had wished to. Charles, he just stood over me, glowering. "She is gone," was what he said. "Thanks to you. She will be trampled in this city! Some street urchin will kill her and roast her for his dinner."

He turned and left again. My head hurt. My arms were numb with the shock and pain. I couldn't raise myself up for many a minute. Tatiana came and crouched by me, and licked my tears away. I lay till I was no longer shaking, then I dragged myself to my feet and began to dress. Going to my own apartments, me. Wouldn't let him find me here when he returned.

But next day, there he was outside my door. I had drowned hot chilies in rum, had been drinking that brew all night for the pain, but my head still ached. I opened the door a sliver only. There he stood, the beast, all solemn. In a breath of fire I whispered, "The dogs will bite you if you're not civil."

"My God," he whispered. "What have I done to you? Oh, Jeanne, I am so sorry."

Drums in my head; drums. "Then go away back again," I muttered, and closed the door very softly, so as not to jar my poor skull.

Thursday, 11 September 1856

Dear Mother,

My liaison, my liaison of fourteen years with Jeanne, is broken. I did all that was humanly possible to prevent the rupture. This tearing apart, this struggle, has lasted fifteen days. Jeanne replies imperturbably that nothing can be done with my character, and that anyhow I shall myself some day thank her for her resolution. There you see the gross bourgeois wisdom of women. For myself, I know that, whatever agreeable happening comes to me, joy, money or vanity, I shall always regret this woman. Lest my sorrow, whose cause you may not understand very easily, should appear too childish to you, I will confess that on that head, like a gambler, I had rested all my hopes; that woman was my sole distraction, my only pleasure, my one comrade, and despite all the interior torment of so tempestuous a relation, never had I envisaged the idea of an irreparable separation.

BREAK/

September 1857

What should I think when I see you flinching from my caresses, if not that you're thinking of that other woman, she whose black face and black soul have come between us? Upon my word, I feel humiliated and shamed. If I didn't have so much self respect, I would bury you in insults. I should like to see you suffer.

—Apollonie Sabatier in a letter to Baudelaire

1859, PARIS
MAISON MUNICIPALE DE SANTÉ

Prends garde! Careful there, Lemer. Here, take my arm."

"Thank you, chéri." I stood up slowly from the bed and rested awhile until the small cough passed. I tottered towards Charles, leaning on my cane. So feeble my legs were after the stroke. Too young for a stroke, me. The doctors said it was my illness brought me to it.

The nurse in her nun's white smiled with all her rotten teeth to encourage me. "That's it, dearie. You'll have clean fresh sheets when you come back."

"Yes, Sister," I mumbled from my half-ruined mouth. "Thank you, Sister."

So sweet she smiled at me, and started pulling the bedclothes off the musty bed. Eh. I was a better actress, in my day. All her pleasantry was for Charles's benefit, so the fine gentleman would be impressed. When he wasn't visiting me, the damned nurses took their sweet time to come and see to me, no matter how I called.

The weak and twisted right side of my body dragged. Charles looked at me, then pulled a kerchief out of his pocket. He dabbed at the right corner of my mouth. I felt to perish from shame. The lax right side dribbled sometimes, and I couldn't feel it. Angry, I jerked my head away, but that made the little phthisic cat-cough start up again.

"All is well, Lemer," he told me, gently as to any baby. He put the damp kerchief away and bent his arm so that I might hang on to it. He had to pull my right arm into his; I couldn't make it move. "I hate being this way!" I said to him, trying not to let my mouth spit.

"Shh. You are beautiful. Come, let me promenade you to the world."

Despite my despair, I giggled at his silliness. He kissed my cheek. The right one. I felt only a ghost of a kiss. Slowly, he walked me outside and down the steps of the nursing home.

Paris was changing. Prefect Hausmann was making this city a vision of France's future, a sparkling jewel. I leaned my head against Charles's shoulder and marvelled at being able to see clearly in the street so long after dark. Wondrous, how the streetlamps had a glow around them. The gas flames would flicker and burn all night and never go out. Who could ever have conceived of such a thing? As the carriages went by, the horses' hooves made wet clomping noises in the damp. Paved streets in Paris, imagine it! Of good, strong wood, no less. No more ruining one's dress from carriage wheels splashing stinking mud. Yet my cane broke the crust on a pile of dung, releasing its smell of rotting grass. When the streets used to be hard-packed earth, the dung from the horses was soon mashed into it by the feet of passers-by. Now it falls from their rears and sits there, waiting to foul a gentleman's shoe or a fine lady's skirts.

"How are Tati and Choux-choux?" Charles asked. He had that look and that wheedling voice you get when you humour a child.

"My dogs? Lise is looking after them for me. She likes them." He never had.

I could see my body reflected in the glass windows that so many establishments had bought with grants from Hausmann's administration. Cane strike, heel strike, drag the useless leg.

I looked in the window of Boutique Vernon, where Charles had bought me that cunning blue silk gown. I looked old. I tried to draw myself up tall, to smile. The frozen side of my face wrenched the smile into a grimace. I could feel the tears start down, warm on my left cheek, cold on my insensible right one.

"I am become a monster," I whispered with my slushy mouth to Charles. "Take me back."

"Shh, shh. Sois tranquille, Lemer," he said. "You will get better. You will be the beauty of Paris once more. Here, just one step. Then another. Yes, like that, Lemer. The walking will make you strong. Come."

And cane strike, heel strike, drag, off he led me down the boulevard.

"I have almost enough for a new book of poems," he said to me.

"Huh." Taking the chance to speak, I said, "Rude ones like the last ones? You going to make the law fine you again?"

His face set hard. "No. I'll be careful. They won't even let me speak of the case, can you imagine it? Threatened to sue me again if I did." Then he frowned a little. "But the Belgians want to publish *Les Fleurs du mal* there." He gave a wry, bitter laugh. "The Belgians are the crassest of bourgeois, but they do not take a man to task for showing the world at its most ugly."

"Hmm."

We walked little more, then he said, "I'm translating some more works of Poe's."

"Hmm," I murmured again, half-hearing. No longer a true liaison between me and Charles, not for years now, but he had sworn to me that he didn't wish me to go a day without money. Begged me not to go out into the slippery streets without a companion to take my arm. He can be kind. Better for us to be apart, though. We claw at each other when we remain too close.

Look how the lamplight shines off his balding head. So many years with him. I had watched every single one of those hairs fall. Almost a marriage I'd made; almost-white me. Best I could hope for. I think I did well. I think Grandmaman would be proud of me. Nearly I could hear her voice in my head. *Only pity, girl, is that you let him fuck you. It's that fucking has made you sick. He gave you his disease along with his money. Your maman never taught you the other tricks to satisfy a man?*

Never mind. Cane strike, heel strike, drag. The damp Paris air was making my cough worse. "Charles?"

"Hmm?"

"I want to leave the sanatorium. They don't treat me well."

He glanced at me. "Likely you just vex them by not taking your medicines properly."

"They keep one set of sheets for me only."

"What?"

"I am a negress, Charles. When they wash the sheets, I lie on the bare mattress until the linen is dry and I may have it again. They make me make my own bed."

He frowned and thought a little bit. "You need to leave there. I will see to it."

Eh. So easy? "Where will I go?"

He sighed. "I am taking an apartment in Neuilly. You can stay with me."

"Oh."

Yes, take us there. I like the branch of that story, where its forks will lead. Say yes, Jeanne.

Back living with Charles again? I can almost hear my grand-mother speaking her mind. She would tell me to go, to let the man from the monied family look after me.

Was probably him had given me the pox, never mind I'd rarely let him swive me. All my tricks for avoiding sickness, and still Charles had gotten around them. I thought of the sores on my cunny, this sickness that had come on me, and the anger started to rise like bile in me again. I looked in a window at the reflection of my crippled body, shuffling like a crab's. I pulled my arm from Charles's own, and stumbled as it came free. I couldn't get the cane under me in time.

"Oh!" Charles caught me about the waist and steadied me. "Take care, Lemer!" he said, all concern in his voice. Poxy bastard. Careful to set the cane against the pavement first this time, I jerked myself out of his grasp.

"I'm going back to the sanatorium now," I said, and set off before he could say anything. Cane strike, heel strike, drag. I blocked the ugly sound from my mind. Boring old Neuilly. Joël had been a few days in Paris, before he lost too badly at cards and went back to Nantes. He had visited me once in my apartments, before I got sick. Nantes was far from Neuilly, but perhaps Joël would come if I asked. I ignored the sombre, balding man who was holding so tight to my upper arm lest I fall.

At least we'd spawned no brats, me and Charles.

"I want us to be at peace in Neuilly, Jeanne. I need the quiet in order to write."

I only sighed.

He took my arm again, his face suddenly joyful. "Don't you think it will be well, Lemer? To live together again? As brother and sister this time? I will have you near, and know that you are looked after."

I grunted. Near to Charles again, every day. The truth was, a contrary part of me was glad. I leaned on his arm and stumped my way back to the sanatorium with him.

RATTLE

I am not your withered, dead grandmaman! Can you not hear me? It is my voice, not hers. You are withering like her too. You are drowning in the brine that's filling your lungs, when I had other plans for you. But yes, at least no whelps. Bad enough you have *me* ensnared so. I don't want to share with another passenger inside your body. When I travel on my leash to other places, I see what breeding leads to. Mothers, fathers, generations fret about their children's welfare. Look at how your paramour's mother sorrows for her child.

Enough! I want to dance, Jeanne, not drag like this, spitting up sputum from a weakened chest. Can you feel the rhythm of your swollen heart, how it misses beats betimes now? The pattern is patter is pat is tern is torn is broken-ken-ken. I don't want to stumble. I want to be able to feel it when skin touches mine. I want us beautiful again. Only when you sleep and let the tether slip can I be free from your drowning for a little while. I want so much more for you!

And there's a thing I don't know. When you die, what will happen to me? Will I be liberated to dance forever with those other Africans, to tell them always of how to be beautiful, how to be loved? Or will I suffocate with you in the liquor of your lungs?

Monsieur! Monsieur Baudelaire! Forgive me, I do not mean to intrude on your perambulations. I only wished; oh—your shoes! Such a state they're . . . I am sorry, Monsieur. Pardon, pardon.

"I? You don't remember me, then. But I remember you. I can't thank you enough. Your Mr. Poe, your translation—oh, Monsieur, how you changed my life that night! Verne. I am Jules Verne.

"But my manners are unforgiveable. It is cold. Here; let's go to a restaurant. There's a fine one only two more streets over, service à la russe. Will you—will you come with me? May I buy you a glass of wine?

"A meal? Why, of course, yes. Certainly. I . . . Certainly.

"Sir, you are shivering! At the cleaners, you say? You left your overcoat with them in this weather? What a sturdy constitution you must have, my dear Baudelaire. Here we are. Oh, sit, please do! I am so pleased to see you again!

"Where do I begin? In my folly, I almost didn't read that work of Poe that you so generously gave me. Put it aside in my apartments, and might have never picked it up again, except a chance boredom one night . . .

"And oh, my dear sir; when I did—I cannot tell you! I cannot explain. That man, that Poe; what a mind, what a vision! Here, waiter. Bring us a bottle of Merlot. Will that do, my dear sir? Yes, of course, whatever you wish. The fish? And the steak? Oh, by all means, by all means.

"But isn't he just a marvel, Mr. Baudelaire? Such fantasms I see when I read his work. Such . . . oh, I cannot describe it!

"Yes, I bought your other translations, too. But I haven't told you, you know, the most wonderful part!

"I began that very night. What I had been writing, those little plays, I saw the flaws in them, the lack of vision. That very night, I tell you, I took up my pen. Ah, here's dinner. No, please. Go ahead without me. I took my meal just a little while ago.

"Monsieur, I have written novels. Perhaps you've heard of them? *Five Weeks in a Balloon* and *Voyage to the Centre of the Earth*? I was lucky enough to get them published right away. Jules Hetzel picked them up. I have even written about our marvellous Mr. Poe!

"How are they doing? My dear sir, the publisher had to print more copies! He has contracted me to write him a novel each year! And I owe it all to you, and to Mr. Poe. Oh, it's shown my father, I can tell you that! Cut me out of his will, he had, when I didn't become a lawyer. Now he's had to eat his words.

"Dessert? Why, yes. What would you like? Waiter, please accommodate my friend here.

"And how goes your translation work, Mr. Baudelaire? Yes, good, good. I look forward to it. What? Poems? I didn't know that you were a writer, too! As well as a translator? Why, that's splendid!"

ALEXANDRIA, EGYPT, 345 C.E.

Meritet," Nefer called. Her voice echoed in the cool dark of the baths.

"Yeah?"

"I'm worried about Cups."

"How come?"

"Is Felix fighting again tomorrow?" Drineh asked me.

"No, it was only a two-day show. He went back to Rome today."

"Shit. It's my day off tomorrow."

"So, about Cups?" said Neferkare loudly from where she sat. "She's whelping again."

The housewife gasped. Eleni smoothed linen strips of honey and lime paste onto Nefer's calves, then yanked a strip off. Neferkare winced. She inspected the newly hairless place on her legs and smiled at Eleni. "Looks good," she said.

Eleni told us, "Cups thinks it was that accountant, the one with the twisted leg. Says he didn't pull out in time."

She ripped another strip away. Nefer hissed, but only said, "I keep telling her that I know this woman who makes crocodile dung balls like the ancients did."

"Phew!" replied Eleni. "What for? More of your old time sorcery?"

"You mix the dung with acacia paste and sour milk. Then you make it into balls, and—" Nefer mimed putting something up into her snatch.

"No!" Eleni yelped. "What's that do?"

The housewife was towelling herself off now. She pretended

not to be listening, but if she'd had donkey's ears, they would have swivelled towards the sound of Nefer's voice.

"Don't listen to her, Eleni," I said. "Nefer's always going on about how our ancestors did everything better."

"But crocodile dung?"

"It keeps you from getting pregnant!" Nefer insisted. This time the housewife didn't even try to pretend she wasn't taking in every single word. Heh. Maybe by tomorrow she'd have her own supply of dung ball suppositories.

I wrinkled my nose. "I don't blame Cups for ignoring you, Nefer. That's disgusting. I never heard of anything like it." I turned back to Drineh. "And Drineh, guess what else happened at the games?" I said.

But she was looking thoughtful. "I guess I know how they'd work, though," she said. "The dung balls, I mean. I bet the smell keeps the men away."

The housewife looked horrified. Eleni cackled. Drineh tittered, her hand to her mouth to hide her teeth. Ground down to nubs they were, from chewing cheap sandy-floured bread. Nefer laughed out loud, all smoky. "True, that," she chuckled. "No fucking, no babies."

"You want more water, Thais?" Drineh asked me.

"Yeah. More on my hair," I told her. "I want it washed good today." I pulled my long black hair up from the nape of my neck and leaned forward. Drineh poured. The water sluiced gloriously over my scalp. I'd left my blonde whore's wig in one of the bath's lockers. With any luck, someone would steal the itchy thing.

"I'll rub the olive oil through it, after," she said.

I nodded. I closed my eyes, enjoying the wash of water over my body. I started figuring in my head. I'd entertained four men this morning, and Nefer and I were dancing at a party tonight. So I'd made good money in tips already today, and I'd been promised more in payment for tonight, plus any tips I made there. Soon I'd have enough to have my sistrum restrung; three of the bells had fallen right off. I didn't really like dancing at parties; all the men feeling you up when they could get you alone. But Tausiris liked the extra money it brought in. He sweared he'd free me when I was thirty. "You'll be too old for the work then," he'd told me. "You can find yourself a nice husband." Fifteen more years of fucking six men a day and dancing for them at night! Would any man want me when my womb had fallen out from all that jumping up and down?

"Meritet?" Nefer called to me again in her sand-scoured voice.

"Yes, O sweet Little Doe?" I replied. I didn't know which was funnier, the old-fashioned Egyptian name that Nefer insisted on using, or her whore name. All the girls teased our aging Little Doe. Too many years of sour wine and smoky inns had roughened her voice till she brayed more like a goat than a doe when she cried out during fucking. This time she ignored my jibe, though.

"I'm really worried about Cups," she told me. "Two children she has already, and Tausiris charging her extra for room and board for them. How will she manage with a third?"

"Sometimes they die unborn," Drineh pointed out.

"And maybe that'll kill her when it starts to rot in her belly," Nefer said. "Don't wish that on her!"

"Well," Eleni murmured, "there's always . . . you know." She nodded towards the back of the baths, where the drains were. The bones of many newborn babies littered those drains.

"No, not that," I said quickly. Nasty Roman habit, that. I could just hear my Nubian mother: *Why can't they just give them to someone who wants them? Like we're doing with you.* Yes, Tausiris had wanted me, all right. He'd known my full lips and high southern behind would fetch him a good price with the sailors. "There are other ways," I told my friends. Me, I drank lots of pennyroyal tea and stuck a wax cup up there before I fucked, but it was too late for Cups to do any of that; the accountant's seed was already growing in her. "If Cups has a healthy child, there's plenty of us to help her look after it, and sometimes she can draw money from the pot to pay Tausiris with, just like she does now."

"Yes," Nefer replied, sounding a little more hopeful. "Maybe it'll go like that."

All the whores at Tausiris's place relied on the pot. We all put in a few coins every time we made something, and every month a different one of us got the whole amount that was in the pot. Nefer often bought eye paint and expensive honey for her legs with hers, but I knew that she always salted half of her pot money away. She only had three years to go to freedom, did Nefer. She wanted to start her own dance school, teach the young girls the "ancient ways" that she was always on about. Her and her blessèd Hathor. Only one temple still left to her, and the Christians had broken all the images of her face. What good was a dead goddess to us?

Cups usually spent her pot money on her children. Little Helena was smart, and Cups paid for her to take lessons with a scribe; maybe she'd get to be some fine lady's secretary when she grew up, instead of just another whore. Me, I tried to save, but I didn't have any grand plans for my life when I was free again. Mostly all of my money went to buying kif to smoke.

Drineh stood and unknotted her tunic where she'd tied it up round her knees to keep it out of the damp. She reached a hand to me. "Time to go and scrape," she said. She helped me out of the bath and we joined Nefer and Eleni in the destrictarium. The housewife slyly inspected my body. I drew myself up tall. I knew that naked I looked just as good as her; better. The housewife wrapped her towel around her and scurried out of there, her thighs jiggling in her rush to be away.

Eleni watched her go, then kept sugaring and plucking Nefer's legs. "I gotta hurry, friend," she said. "Wouldn't be surprised if that one went and tattled to Boss that we're working for free. Hey, Drineh; keep an eye out for the old turd, will you?"

Drineh sighed. "Okay." She rubbed me down with some olive oil—third pressing, I could smell how cheap it was—and then began to scrape me clean with a strigil. My skin was tingling nicely. Nefer was yipping and making little hissing noises as Eleni got on with plucking her legs smooth. So vain about those legs, Neferkare was. When the men asked her why a hangdug old goat like her was called Little Doe, she'd tell them it was because of her strong, slim legs. They were, too. Looked real nice on her.

"Pretty Pearl in there?" bellowed a voice from outside. I frowned. It was Beshotep, Tausiris's fat steward. Running errands for his master again. "Thais?" he said, using my real name.

"I'm here," I shouted back. "What's doing?"

The little pig stuck his head right into the destrictarium. Wanted an eyeful of us. That's all he ever got. And he took it too; stared me and Nefer up and down good and long before he said, "Tausiris says come. Customer at the tavern's asking for you."

I sighed. "I'm on break. He knows that." Nefer rolled her eyes at me. Tausiris could drive us hard when he had a mind to.

"What's that to me? Tausiris says that Antoniou always pays right away and I'm to fetch you." He frowned at me, crinkling his stubbly bald head. "You better come now, or both of us will be in trouble."

I ignored that. "Oh, it's Antoniou who wants me, is it?" An easy customer, if Tausiris would let me deal with him my way. "How long's he been in the tavern?"

"Just came in now."

"Okay. Go on back. I'll be just behind you."

"But . . ."

"Tell Antoniou that I was all wet from my bath," I said, "and that I stopped to get dry and changed into a nice clean tunic. Tell him I'll be right along."

"And will you?" Beshotep asked. "I don't want to get whipped for you."

"Yeah, yeah. I'll be there. And listen," I said. "Tell Antoniou I'll be all oiled and nice for him when I get there, all right? And give him some of that Black Corinth wine while he's waiting, okay?" Antoniou loved that wine.

Beshotep looked doubtful. He opened his mouth. Quickly I said, "It'll be on me. Tell Tausiris to charge it to me. Just let me finish my bath, please, honey?" I wheedled.

"All right," said Beshotep, looking like he trusted my word about as much as he trusted the rains. "Just don't be long," he told me, "or I'll make sure that you get a whipping. You girls are always trying to shirk." It was close and damp in the bath house. He used a corner of his wine-stained kilt to wipe the sweat from his forehead and left.

"You girls are always trying to shirk," Nefer imitated him. "Like to see him spend most of his days with his legs spread."

"Never mind," I said. "Drineh, rub me down well with that sweet oil. Antoniou likes the slippery feeling."

She giggled. "Maybe I should collect your oil scrapings," she said quietly, "and sell them to him."

The high ceiling sang my laughter back to me. "Yes," I said, "I bet he'd pay for it too, like a rich woman buying gladiators' used oil. I'm an athlete after all, aren't I?"

Drineh looked at me. I could see the question in her eyes.

"Yes, I am." I raised my voice and made it echo in the high-ceilinged room. "I'm the brave and fearsome Pretty Pearl; oxen-eyed as Hera; champion at making the beast with two backs! I could make you rich, Drineh!"

Nefer and Eleni snorted at that. Drineh just shook her head and set about wielding her strigil on my body again. I leaned back to enjoy the pampering and a few more moments of peace before I got back to work. "You know what I'm going to do when it's my turn next to draw drachmas from the pot?" I asked Drineh.

"No; what?"

"I'm going to buy a pallia from the market. One with a fringe."

NEUILLY, FRANCE

No. I don't have enough, Joël." Leaning on my cane I stumped over to the fire, took the poker and began stoking it. Joël followed me.

"It's not so much money, Lemer. Get it from your poet man, why don't you?"

I shooed Tati off the armchair by the fire. She looked scoldingly after me, went and lay near the fender. She'd become lean since Choux-choux died. She missed her friend. I sat down, slowly, using my cane the while. "Joël, did you hear what I said at all? I don't have enough, and I'm not going to ask Charles. It's your debt; you find work and pay it."

He scowled at me. "Find work? I moved all the way here to Neuilly to look after you, but I must work my black ass to the bone while you and your white man lounge off in this grand apartment and feed each other bon-bons?"

I straightened. It hurt. I used my cane to drag the stool close to me. With both hands I lifted my lame leg up onto it. Madame Charlotte, my healer woman, said that would help the blood not to settle in my foot and poison it. "Joël," I said, mouthing the words carefully around the numb side of my mouth, "how often must I tell you? Charles is not rich."

He grinned then, came and sat at my feet, heedless of the fine wool pants he was wearing. It's my money paid for those pants. "Jeanne, I don't mean to fret you. But it's you who asked me to come."

Only the truth to that. So long I hadn't seen him. And Charles always gone nowadays, lecturing.

241

"You and me always looked out for each other, didn't we?" said Joël. "You're going to put me aside now that you have a fine lover?" He put his head in my lap.

I stroked the strong bones of his jaw. Plunged my fingers into his thick black hair. "Sweet as cream you can be," I said, "when you want to be."

"Mm," he murmured, ignoring me. "Just a few little francs I need, and Caillou won't be coming to the door day and night demanding his money, and I'll find work and pay you back next week."

"Even if you get work, you'll only gamble your pay away again." I took my handkerchief from my sleeve and dabbed at my mouth. That numb side dribbled sometimes.

"Lemer, don't be so harsh with me." He turned his head into the fork of my thighs and inhaled deeply. "You always smell so good; do you know that?"

What a way that man could always make me juice up fast. I laughed and shoved his head away. "Forward man."

He sat back on his hands and looked up at me with that devilish smile. "But you like me so, don't you?"

I frowned. "It's wrong, Joël."

"How do you know? You don't even know if your mother was telling the truth."

"You're my brother." *Perhaps.* Half brother, and not even raised by my mother. I'd been fifteen before I met him, before I even learned of him. Up until then I'd thought Maman only had one other child, the stillborn one that she almost died from.

So damp I was with longing for Joël. "Get away from me, before Charles finds you like this and challenges you to a duel."

Joël leapt to his feet, mimed sword-play. "Oh, yes; my blade against his Lordship's sharp wit!" He jumped and leapt about in a mock fight. My cane clattered to the floor. I had to hold my sides with laughing.

"Oh, Joël, stop. You're so silly!"

242

Now he mimed being Charles, mincing about and flapping a handkerchief in a free hand. I nearly pissed myself to see him playing the dandy. He grinned at me and pretended to be routed. "Oh, please, sir!" he squeaked. "Not the nib! Anything but the nib!" He cowered from the deadly quill of an invisible Charles. My head hurt, I was laughing that hard.

A low cough came from the doorway. Charles stood there, scowling. Quickly, Joël and I composed ourselves to look more seemly. Joël picked up my cane and handed it to me.

"Lemer," Charles said, "has there been a letter from my mother?"

Before I could answer, Joël leapt to the doorway, took Charles's hand and shook it vigorously. "My eminent sir," he said, "how are you this fine day? Are you well?"

Charles looked confused. "My head hurts, frightfully. And I'm vomiting again. Uh, and you?"

"Oh, brilliantly good, brother-in-law. As ever. I laugh at my troubles and spit in the eye of God."

Charles had already turned away. "I am pleased to hear it," he muttered. "Lemer? Did the mail come?"

"Yes." I creaked to my feet, got over to the cabinet. I took the key from my bosom. Almost I could feel Joël's keen gaze on it. I opened the door, took Charles's mail out, and handed it to him. He flipped through the envelopes and picked one.

"Why didn't you tell me there was a letter from the publisher?"

"Couldn't make out the handwriting."

He shook his head. "Jeanne. You really should work on your reading, you know. I keep telling you that I will teach you to be better at it." He tore the envelope open.

"Never you mind me. I manage. I can write a shopping list."

I glanced at Joël. He was pouting, like he used to do when we were young. His shamed face. Couldn't read a word, Joël couldn't. I asked Charles, "What do they say?"

He was smiling. "It's a bank note. Payment for my poems."

At that, Joël stepped forward. "Ah, Mr. Baudelaire, sir . . ."

"Hush, Joël," I said. "I'll see to it."

Charles looked from Joël to me. "See to what? What is it?"

"Nothing," I said. I patted my mouth with the kerchief. "It's nothing."

But Joël wouldn't remain quiet. "I was asking the loan of a few sous, sir."

"Joël!"

"Don't fret yourself, Jeanne," said Joël. "This is between us men."

Charles frowned at him. "You want me to give you money?"

"A loan, sir; only a loan. I, uh; I have a bill come due."

"You want me to pay your bills for you?"

Joël's face got angry. He stepped a little closer to Charles. "It's not as though you'll miss it, you being a gentleman and all. Only for a few days."

Charles stood taller. "Are you mad? Are you insane?"

Joël put a big hand on Charles's shoulder. Charles brushed it off. Oh, please don't let them fight. "I," Joël replied, "am not mad. Sir. I am the brother of the lady you're keeping in debauchery in your house. I have come here to make this house seem respectable. You owe her, and you owe me."

Charles was laughing, low and nasty. "Really." He sat on the stool I had got up from. "Respectable. From debauchery." He grinned up at Joël, a sharp-toothed smile. "I'll have you know that I take care of Jeanne. I give her all I can, and more. It is my obligation, gladly undertaken, but it ends with her." And now he was serious again. "Pay your own debts, Monsieur."

Joël stood there, his fists clenched. They were the size of turnips. He glared at Charles. Then he turned to the door. "Later, Jeanne," he growled. He left.

Charles just sat there, calm like a statue, reading his blasted letter from Mummy. "Did you have to shame him so?" I said.

"*I* shame him? That man is shame walking on two legs." He looked up from his letter. "Why is he here, Jeanne?"

I could feel my face flushing. "He is my brother." I wiped my mouth. "He looks after me when you are away."

"Your brother, is he? Why did I never hear of him before I brought you to Neuilly? Why does he spend all his time with you in your room?"

"He tells me stories, keeps me entertained. It is so dull here."

"Helping to look after you, is he? Does he pay any of your bills?"

I looked at the floor.

"Does he? Does he pay for the noxious potions you have Laetitia buy for you from that hideous old witch woman?"

"That old woman was a friend of my mother's."

"Never mind that. Is Joël giving you money for his upkeep?"

"No."

"None, Jeanne?"

"No. He's not working any more."

"When did he stop?"

"When I met him again, when he came to Paris. Before I got sick and went into the sanatorium."

Charles came and took my chin. Cold, his hand was. I looked up into his face. He was aging, my Charles. Headaches all the time, and those fits of malaise he had, where he could do nothing but lie abed. The clap can make you so. Perhaps the same would happen to me.

"Jeanne," he said softly, "are you supporting that man with the money I give you?"

"He is my brother." I reached up and patted my damp mouth dry. He let my chin go, pity on his face. Used to be he would look at me with longing.

"He's using you," he said. "An old, sick woman. He's despicable."

I am not old! "He loves me, Charles. Yes, he has his faults. Do you love me, Charles? You used to."

"I can't afford to keep both him and you." He had busied himself with his letters again.

Sadness pinned me where I sat. He hadn't answered me. "I know. I will ask him to leave us and return to Nantes."

I must ask Laetitia to get another physic from the herb woman for me. One to make Charles love me again.

DRINK

So much I had longed for this. Dreamt about it nights. Saw it days in my mind's eye. Feared that I was too ugly now for him to want me. I looked up at Joël; dared to face what I saw in his eyes.

Kindness. Desire? He grazed his thumb over my lips, and I felt my nipples point hard at him; *you, you.*

Yes, just so, my Jeanne. We are made to be loved, you and I.

Joël's eyes looked on me as they had done when I was whole. Grateful, wanting, I opened my ruined mouth and took his thumb in. It tasted of salt, of molasses and tobacco. I sucked on it.

"Yes," he murmured. "Do that."

The numb side of my face, never quite recovered, couldn't hold. Mouth water began to leak from the corner of my lip. Ashamed, I made to pull away.

"No," he said, "Stay."

Listen to him, Lemer.

With his free fingers, Joël wiped the moisture from my chin. "I like it, the wetness. Fifteen when I met you, remember? And you still sucking on your thumb at night like any baby. Suck, Lemer."

I groaned, licked the length of his thumb, took it deep down my throat. He put his index finger into my mouth beside the thumb. Then the middle finger, then the ring one. He was stretching my mouth, and I longing for more.

"Go on," he said. "Make them wetter."

I pulled away, rubbed my face against his shirt, leaving a trail of damp there. I pressed against him, anxious to feel his body on mine. He was hard inside his pants. I began to unbutton and unbutton the endless buttons of the damned house dress. Little whimpering noises I was making. My own moisture making the cleft between my thighs damp. The sores had been gone from my cunny some weeks now. I thanked the heavens I was better down there. I got the dress open, dropped it to the floor. I sucked again on his fingers, opening my mouth wide and taking them deep into my throat.

He brushed his other hand over one of my breasts. I gasped, mouth water-slick around his fingers. He slid that free hand down my belly, found the opening in my pantalettes and spread it. I leaned on his shoulder for support. Spraddled my legs for him. I could smell my own heat rising up from me.

He took his fingers from my mouth, leaving it lonely, but as he held the pantalettes open with one hand, he pushed the wet fingers of the other, slow and insistent, into me through the opening. I could feel every inch enter. I nearly screamed for the pleasure of it. "Joël," I begged.

"Yes. Yes, Lemer."

Yes, Lemer. Just so. Feel how you flow, and I with you.

My lame leg was aching with the effort of holding me upright, but what did I care for that? I started riding his fingers, reached for his hard prick. He breathed out, hard. I put my wet mouth up for a kiss.

A low cry came from the doorway. With my clumsy leg, I had to lean on Joël to turn and look. Charles stood there. I tried to leap away from Joël, and the leg finally collapsed me. I tumbled to the floor, heavy. And just lay there, looking to the doorway. Charles.

White, his face was. Bloodless. Tatiana slipped in the door behind him and came and jumped into my lap. I held her, stroked her thick fur. Charles hadn't moved. Joël just smiled at him and held himself tall. He put his fingers into his mouth and licked them clean of my juices, still looking at Charles. Like a man struck blind, Charles turned, stumbled into the doorframe, then left.

"Go and get him, Joël! Tell him . . ."

"Tell him what, Lemer?" He looked down upon me. "He's seen all he needs to know. I'm sorry. We should have been more careful." But the look on him was triumph, not sorrow. And I felt it too. I smiled at him. My love for Charles was gone these long years. I should leave my life with him, too. Go with Joël. He would get work as a stevedore. I would mend the torn knees of his serge work pants. Charles and I could be friends, not a man and his mistress locked in a demented affair.

Play out the game first, Jeanne.

A knocking came at the front door, loud. Charles? Asking permission to enter his own residence? Tati leapt down from me and ran, yipping, towards the front door. "Help me up, Joël. If it's him, it should be me who answers the door. He might temper his behaviour if it's me."

Joël drew me to my feet and helped me button my dress back up.

Ah. It begins. Will you have the wit to see what I am doing for you? At least I can give your mind peace.

I should have been more frightened. What was Charles going to do to us? But I was calm, so calm. "Hand me my cane," I said to Joël. He gave it me, and I stumped to the doorway. He was still knocking, getting louder this time. I opened the door.

A black man stood there. A wiry little slip of a man with a foolish grin on his face, there in our doorway in Neuilly. He wore baggy work clothing and an old cloth cap. How the neighbours must be staring. This house was become a regular nigger carnival.

"Yes?" I said, frowning. Where was Charles?

"Pardon, Lady," he said. His voice rumbled low; odd in that small body. "Is this where . . . I mean to say . . . Joël told me that I could find him here?"

"Moustique!" Joël came behind me, his hand on my shoulder. "Come on in, man!"

I backed clumsily away from the door to let the little black-amoor in. He grinned at Joël, bobbed his head to me. I didn't give him my hand. "Who is this, Joël?"

He clapped the man's hand in between the two of his, and chuckled. "It's only Moustique, the most disreputable lout in all of France! So glad to see you, Mous!"

Moustique grinned back, put a hand on Joël's shoulder. "Man," he said. "What are you doing in this little country town? Begging your pardon, ma'am." He glanced at me, bobbed his head, then turned his smile on Joël again. "The train took hours to get me here! And then a lumpy carriage, with this great talkative turnip of a man driving, you should have heard him! Why are you all the way out here, Joël? Were we in Nantes so dull that you had to leave?"

Joël smiled. He reached for my hand. I limped over to take his. "I'm looking after my sister here," he told Moustique. "Have to make sure that her lover keeps her well."

"Joël!" I said. "Mind your manners!"

"Oh, don't worry, Lemer. Moustique and me been friends for so long. I can talk frank when he's around."

"Joël, you're embarrassing your beautiful sister. Come; you don't offer a thirsty man something to drink?"

So. He was well-spoken, for what he was. "Well, Monsieur Moustique," I began, but Joël interrupted, laughing:

"Monsieur! You don't have to 'monsieur' him; he's just old Moustique!"

"Ah, to you I am. But the lady can be told my given name." He bowed in my direction, playing courtly. "Madame Lemer, my mother was pleased to name me 'Achille' at my birth. My friends only call me 'Moustique' because I'm of small stature, like the brave mosquito. But so honoured I'd be to hear my real name come from your lips."

Why, the smooth-tongued charmer! I found myself smiling and inclining my head to him, like I was some grand lady. Joël just stood there, hang-mouthed. Despite my doubts at having one of Joël's wastrel friends come to visit, I told him, "Please join us in the parlour, Monsieur Achille. Let us all take a beverage there together, yes?" I escorted them in and fetched a bottle of Charles's favourite Rhenish wine. Achille's face brightened when he saw it.

"The gentleman of this house has a fine palate, I see." He rose and took the bottle and glasses from me. Out from his back pocket he fetched a corkscrew! Was the man ready for drink at any hour, then? He used it to pull the cork from the bottle, so deft. He poured little bit into one glass, which he presented to Joël. Confused, Joël put the glass to his mouth. "No, my friend," Achille said to him. "Smell it first."

Joël took a cautious sniff.

"Is it well?"

"Smells like wine, like that posh wine Baudelaire's always drinking."

"Now taste one little sip of it."

Joël obeyed.

"The taste is to your liking? The bouquet fills your nose? The scent is pleasing?"

Joël shrugged. "I suppose so."

Achille smiled. "Monsieur approves, then, and we can all drink."

He poured for all of us. The wine flowed into the glasses with scarcely a sound; smooth like the running river. Achille twisted the bottle as he poured, so that not a drop fell that he didn't want to fall. I was purely astonished. He presented me and Joël with our glasses. He had done this before.

"Are you someone's servant, then?" I asked. Why was he dressed so poorly, if he worked in some rich house?

"Moustique's a cook," Joël informed me.

Achille sat back down. "A chef, if you please. All the gentry in Nantes crave to have food prepared by these hands." He cracked his knuckles. "And I crave to play some cards, Joël. Where do you go for entertainment in this town?"

"Now you're speaking my language!" Joël laughed and slammed his wine glass down onto the table, so hard I feared he'd snap the stem. "Drink up, Mous; there's a place I want to take you to."

And there it was. For all his fine ways, Achille was just another layabout like my brother, gambling away his earnings and spending any left on the whores in the jook houses. I sipped my wine to hide my disappointment. "Monsieur Achille," I said, "how are things in Nantes?"

He smiled at me. He had fine features. "Well, some of us are still black, you know."

Joël chuckled at that.

Achille leaned towards me, his face eager. "But have you heard of the new wonder that is come to Nantes?"

I shook my head.

"A giraffe! From Africa!"

"A what?" I said. "What is that?"

"Oh, Madame Lemer; the most astonishing animal. From the place they took our forefathers from. Imagine a deer. Yes?"

253

"Yes, I can picture it."

"Now, imagine a deer the height of, oh, a two-storey building."

"It's a giant deer?"

"In a way; but I'm not done yet. Imagine its legs, long and sleek, yet thick and strong enough to bear a body the size of a house. Now, imagine that the animal's neck is also long."

"Long?"

"Moustique, what nonsense are you feeding us?" laughed Joël.

"No, it's true! A long neck; long enough that the beast could stick its head to the top of the church spire I saw yonder as I was coming to you!"

"No!" I said. "You lie!"

"I speak only the truth, as my mother taught me. Now, give it a head like a horse's."

I shook my head and drank more wine. "Nothing that looks like that could live. Its head would break its neck. Joël, tell him."

"Mous, stop telling tales."

"You must come with me to Nantes, then, and see it. And there's more than that, you know? Its hide is tan, and covered all over in brown spots, like the leopard."

Joël got to his feet, laughing. "Oh, now you've gone too far." He took Achille's sleeve. "Come. Let's go."

He pulled Achille out of the house, with the little man calling over his shoulder, "It was a gift! Really! From some Egyptian pasha to the English King George! It's living in the botanical gardens in Nantes! People visit it every Sunday!"

I followed them to the door, chuckling. I scarce noticed my dragging foot. Outside, Achille turned and took my hand. "Fabric printed like the giraffe's spots is the height of Paris fashion nowadays." I laughed and waved him away. He kissed my hand. "I'm telling the God's truth, Madame. All the fine folk are wearing it." He turned to my brother. Laughing, Joël put his arm around Achille's shoulder and they headed off down the road.

As I was about to go back in, I saw him coming. Charles. His head was down. His bald patch gleamed rosy-peach from the setting sun. His hands were stuck in his pockets, his face like storm clouds. He wouldn't look at me.

Hold fast, Lemer. The moves of the dance are happening yet. Step this way now.

I stood and waited for him. I had to face him. I owed him that.

Step lightly.

His face was closed to me. He shoved past me into the house without looking at me once. I followed. "Charles, I'm sorry."

He went to our room. He closed the door in my face. "Charles!"

I could hear him bustling about inside. Could hear things falling, closet doors opening.

Step that way now. Now, twist.

"I'll send him away, Charles!" I called through the door. Nothing. The door opened. He was standing there, carrying a valise. He dared a glance at me. His eyes dampened with tears. He looked at the floor. Sniffed.

"I'll let you know where I've gone," he mumbled, "in the event that you need anything. Don't contact me otherwise."

"But Charles, please!"

He waved me away. "No. Don't. Don't touch me. I'll keep providing for you, but don't touch me. Don't see me. I'm going now."

He did.

Yes, finished now.

I heard him shut the front door, oh, so gently. I sat in the near-est chair. I couldn't even cry. Charles, my man of words, gone, and only Joël left to me. But Charles wouldn't beggar me, he'd promised. He always kept his word. And there I would be with Joël, love of my heart, of my body. Should I be glad?

1 January 1861

My dear mother, I have now been living here (Rue Louis-Philippe, Neuilly) for a fortnight, and, as usual, I'm very unhappy. Understand that in a moral sense, not a physical one.

I have returned to my old idea of installing myself permanently at Honfleur, except for one week each month (for I have to go to Paris regularly on business) and then I should be able to pay my debts as I incurred them. Because, for reasons I may explain to you, I probably won't return to Neuilly.

I need more than this, Lemer."

I counted the last franc note into Joël's hand. "It's all I have."

He scowled. "Get him to send you more, then."

"Joël, he sends what he can. His mother holds the purse-strings, you know."

He said nothing, but he thumped the wall as he strode out. Big hands, Joël had. Heavy hands. He slammed the door.

17 March 1861

Dear mother; I confess that the woman was beautiful, and my indulgence therefore perhaps suspect. But last January something frightfully monstrous happened; it made me quite ill. I don't wish to talk about it. It would tear my heart out.

What have I done for seventeen years, but forgive? Yet if one yields to Jeanne, here's the danger: the following month, the following week, she comes back requesting more money, and so on forever.

A few days ago, Malassis told me that Jeanne had come to ask him to buy some books and drawings. Malassis is not a dealer. He prints new books. There are hundreds of dealers of old books in Paris. I rather suspect that she picked Malassis to hurt me, to wound my pride. It is all one to me, if she chooses to sell the souvenirs which every man leaves with a woman with whom he has lived for years.

SAW

Suddenly, an impulse of my will moves me. That is the only way I can describe it. A pulse, the way muscles feel when I am embodied. For the first time, I go, in a direction I choose! I flex my desirous will again, stronger this time. And I go, I go. I push through the clinging fog, I dive deeper into it. I swim and swim and swim, and reach a point where I can swim no more. The flow is stilled here. It's stagnant. It coats me, and I feel filthy and sick. I turn and swim out of it, back into the rushing ectoplasm. I revel in the cleanness of it. I move in another direction. Move in time that is no time, until I flop into another stagnant pool. Again I clamber out of it and go another way. This time I am beached, left gasping in a nameless, foetid horror of a place where there is no sustaining aether. There is nothing. It is undescribable. I twist and flap until I drop down into the mists again, gasping, thankful. What is wrong here? I do not know. I do not know how to understand. I swim slowly this time, thinking.

JIZZ

ALEXANDRIA, EGYPT, 345 C.E.

I scurried back to the tavern to go and see to my customer Antoniou. A busy day in Alexandria today, so close to the big Rose Festival. When I got to the market, I had to push my way through the crowds. Plenty of people had come into town for the festival. Me and Nefer already had three nights of dancing lined up. I'd be able to get a new tunic, too, to go with my sandals. And some perfume.

A donkey passed me in the opposite direction, headed for Canopic Way. It was weighed down with packs, and it was being pulled by a Nubian man, his feet dusty to the ankles from the road. He nodded to me. I dipped my chin at him. His deep brown skin and crinkly hair reminded me of my mother. Maybe with the money she got from selling me, she and my father had bought some land. Maybe there had been enough left over for her to get new combs for her hair. I remember that the old combs had lost some of their teeth. I remember.

Someone is fucking the body I'm in. This is not Jeanne! Have I traded one cage for another? I try not to despair. There are ways to travel forth from my horse's head, and I am learning them. Perhaps this body will not be a trap for me, as Jeanne's is. I wriggle with joy at life, at another adventure. The wriggling brings a sigh from behind me. Hipbones slam against this person's asscheeks, a pleasantly numbing percussion. A cock pumps in and out of . . . ah. This new body is a woman's too. She's on her knees on a stone bed, gripping the head of it for purchase. The man inside her is muttering a mixture of Greek and heavily accented Latin. He smells of the sea. She, this new she, smells of olive oil. Her body is slippery with it.

It is dry here, and hot. That man, he feels good in us. She is distracted, and so she leaves me able to direct our movements. I spread our knees further, arch our back. Whisper to him to encourage him. The language in which our body whispers is Greek, a Greek from an older time of this Earth. She is dark-skinned, this beauty, and ruddy, like copper. Her head tells me that she lives in great Alexandria, and her name is Thais. Or something else. Or something else again, but she doesn't think about her second and third names much. Three names. She's another three-twist, this one. A braided girl, sister to the three who birthed me. No salt-pucker of bitterness in her, though. Perhaps this will be interesting.

JAZZ

The man behind us—the sailor Antoniou, Thais's head tells me—clasps me tight around our belly and pulls us closer. Against Thais's back I feel the curled tangle of sweaty hair on his chest. He whispers hoarsely in Thais's ear, "Pearl. Pretty Pearl." Ah, that is her third name. The one she tells to people who pay her to fuck, or to dance. Antoniou says, "Dance for me now. Dance on my prick."

And so we do. I help Thais to shake and buck and leap. I spread our knees more and push our behind back at him and jiggle till he howls. Our cunt clenches happily. Ah, glorious to be in a fit, strong body again. He holds us tight, shoves deep, so deep into us, judders like a hooked fish before he pants once more, hard, and collapses upon our back, whispering grateful allelujahs to the Christian God.

Antoniou had already paid Tausiris to fuck me, but still he left a few drachmas on my bed. I counted them. Enough to buy some sweets from Claudia in the market! She made the best halwah. I squatted, and with two fingers, reached deep up into my cunt.

He was a good man, Antoniou. As I cleaned myself up, I could hear his deep, hearty voice out in the bar. Always telling stories from his travels. He'd been to Syria, he said, where Drineh's grandparents came from, and even to Karakum, where the people have their heads in their bellies and their speech is only "Oomph! Oomph!" Me, I never went anywhere. Just boring old Alexandria.

Ah. There it was. I pulled out the wad of lambswool, damp with Antoniou's spunk and my juices. And something more, too; crumbs of wax. Shit! With all that shoving, Antoniou must have broken the pessary! I pushed my fingers inside of me again and bore down, the way that Nefer had taught me to do. I could feel small, softening lumps of wax inside me. I swept them out as best as I might. "Beshotep!" I called. I heard a resentful rumble in response from the direction of the kitchen. "Bring me water for washing with! Fast!"

I didn't want a brat, to be mewing at me all the time, and me never getting to go to the theatre, or hang around the market with Drineh and Judah. I didn't want to be like Cups. I started jumping up and down, landing hard as I could. Nefer told me once that that would shake the man's seed out.

"A new dance, I see," came Judah's amused voice from the doorway. "Not graceful, but it definitely has vigour."

I ignored him, and took three more jumps for good measure. "Just give me the damned water. The cup broke."

269

He got serious then, and hurried into the room with the jug. He handed it to me, then turned his back while I squatted again and washed myself inside and out. "Will you be all right?" he asked in his soft voice.

"Dunno."

"Who was it?"

"Antoniou."

He made a knowing sound. "Yes, that one's dick could plunge in deep as your liver."

"Fine for you to be appreciating his charms. You don't have to worry about getting babies."

"You should take him in the ass, like I do."

I sighed. "Yes, I do that for the others. But Antoniou's special. He's nice to me."

"So nice that he'd take you and your child in?"

I stood. Water trickled down my legs. "No, I guess not." I found my shift and pulled it on over my head. "You can turn around now, Judah."

He came and embraced me. "It'll be all right," he said.

I held his slim body tight to me, taking comfort in the warmth of him. "Yes, I guess. I'll take Antoniou's tip and buy a charm with it tomorrow."

"Better take some of his spunk with you, too. They'll probably want to put that into the charm." Judah sat on the bed, flicking his curly blond hair off his shoulder with one hand. He pulled his knees in together and tucked his feet under. Even when he was serious, he never forgot to show off how pretty he was. "Whose turn is it to draw money from the pot this month?" he asked me.

I pulled my hair back into a knot and dragged the wig on over it. "Cups. Damn, this thing is hot."

He looked disappointed. "Not me? You're sure?"

"I think so." I bent to knot my sandals. "You were two turns ago. It's Cups, then me—I'm going to get a new pallia—then Nefer, then you. Why?"

270

He just looked down, mouth pursed. "No reason."

I sat beside him and took his hand. "I thought you said I was like your sister, Judah."

He sighed. "Yes."

"Well, you can tell me then, can't you? Brothers and sisters should trust each other."

He looked at me, blushing. "I wanted to buy Gallio Velius a present, that's all."

"Hoho!" I shoved his shoulder. "I knew it! He's really caught your eye, hasn't he?"

He looked down at his knees. "He's all right." Then he took my hands. Grinning, he squeezed them. "He says I'm beautiful! He says I'm his favourite boy! Can you believe it?"

I chuckled. "Well, he's right; you are lovely." And Judah might even remain his favourite boy, too. Until Velius made a good marriage. Then he'd stop coming to the taverns, and Judah's heart would be broken again.

From a menu of questions that supplicants could ask the gods at the busy temple of Serapis in Oxyrynchus, Egypt, 3rd Century C.E.:

72. *Shall I receive the allowance?*
73. *Shall I be reconciled with my child?*
74. *Is the absent one alive?*
75. *Shall I become a councilman?*
76. *Shall I be sold?*
77. *Shall I profit from the affair?*
78. *Shall I remain where I am going?*

. . . Well, then the sail went over, almost took my head off, it did, and this great wave washed over the ship. It tore me off the rowing bench I was clinging to and started to suck me over the side." Antoniou waved his arms in the air as he was talking. The mug in his hand reached the end of its chain and stopped him short. The dregs of his beer splashed over the side onto his shoulder and the floor. He frowned and drained the mug.

"What'd you do then?" asked Didyma. Little Helena was sitting in her lap, with Judah beside them. Judah and Helena played cat's cradle with some string.

"I?" Antoniou roared. "I nearly drowned, that's what I did." Judah snorted.

Helena looked up from her game at him. "You're not drowned," she said in her clear child's voice. A bunch of men at the bar laughed.

So did Antoniou. He knocked his mug against the counter to let Tausiris know he wanted more, then let it go clanging toward the floor. "True enough, you little flea. You want to know what happened?"

She nodded at him. Behind the bar, Tausiris came over, pulled Antoniou's mug up by the chain, and refilled it. It was going to be packed in the tavern tonight, with Rose Festival customers. Judah and Didyma would be busy.

"As I was going over the side," Antoniou said, "I groped about with my hands for something to hold me. Like this I groped." He swept his hands about his body, his eyes clenched tight. "And I caught something! Well, it caught me."

"What was it?" I asked.

Antoniou smiled at me. "Our net. Huge thing, our net was. Got my hands tangled tight in it. Nearly broke my wrist. Got my

273

whole body tangled in the damned thing, in fact. It caught me like some great hairy fish and held me fast."

Helena giggled.

"And the water rushing over me, and no air in my lungs. But I held on to that net for dear life, and prayed to Mother Mary to save me."

"Meri?" I asked. "Your mother's name is Meri?"

Antoniou chuckled at me and patted my knee. "Not my mother. The holy mother of our Lord Jesus." He made the Christian sign; forehead, chest, and shoulders.

"Then what happened?" Helena asked him. Her cat's cradle string dangled from her fingers, unheeded. Judah was rapt, too, just waiting to hear the rest of the story.

Antoniou squatted down before her. "Then, little flea, Mother Mary heard my prayers, and sent a crab the size of a man to save me."

Helena's eyes grew large. Judah got a big smile on his face.

"The crab swam through the rushing wave, and with its claws it snipped a hole in that net. Then it reached in and drew me out to freedom. By then, the wave was leaving the ship. The crab stood me upright on my feet, saluted me with one of its front claws, and said, 'God bless you, Antoniou.' Then it leapt back into its sea home and swam away. I got on my knees and thanked Jesu that I am a righteous man."

Didyma laughed. "Gods, Antoniou; what a tongue you have for telling tales with!" She slid Helena down off her lap. "Come, Helena. Bed for you. Tausiris, I'll be back in a moment."

"Be quick, Cups," he said. "Customers starting to come in."

Helena complained that she wanted to stay and hear more stories, but her mother took her by the hand and led her to bed. A man came to the bar and talked low to Tausiris, who nodded and signalled to Judah. They went off to Judah's room. He was dressed nicely, that man.

It wasn't time yet for me and Little Doe to leave for the party. I wanted to hear more stories too. "Where are you going after this, Antoniou?" I asked.

He settled back on his stool, took a swig of his beer. A rib-thin stray dog slunk into the bar and began licking the place on the floor where Antoniou'd spilled his beer. Antoniou waved some flies away from his face and said, "Next? Next, the captain says we're taking a load of wheat to Joppa. In a few weeks. It's going to the Roman garrison in Capitolina."

"Aelia Capitolina?" He gets to go everywhere. "Have you been there before?"

He grinned at me. "I have. Ah, girl, it's glorious there. There's that new Christian temple, you know? The one that Constantine built? Magnificent. All covered in gold, floor to ceiling, with a thousand priests saying a thousand prayers to Jesu, sunup and sundown, and a huge statue to his mother, painted in every colour of the rainbow."

"A statue to the goddess Meritet?"

"Mary, girl. Mary. Don't say it in that heathen way."

I tried to imagine a statue to someone with the same name as me, but a goddess, a virgin goddess and her dead son. "What else is it like over there?"

He came and sat beside me, put his arm around me. I cuddled up against him. He said, "The winds blow cool in the evenings, and you can sit outside your house and watch the hills gleaming gold against the blue dusk sky. I'd like to take you to see it. Some day, if you can pay the captain's fare, let me know. I'll take you travelling, chick."

"Oh . . ." I turned to ask him to tell me more, but Little Doe came in from her room. She was all got up in her dancing clothes, carrying a basket of rose petals. "Meri, aren't you dressed yet? Go and put on your things, or we'll be late!"

"Shit." I stood up, kissed Antoniou on the cheek. "Sorry, love. Gotta run!"

It was a good night at the party, a rich man's Rose Festival feast. Doe and I sang and shook our sistra, and I danced. I did the goddess Nut move where I balance on my hands and feet, bent in a bow above the ground, then turn with my back arched so that my breasts stick up into the sky; they always like that. Then we tossed rose petals all over the floor. They liked that, too. It was a good month, that one. Men who come for the Rose Festival spend a lot of money. Between whoring and dancing, Doe and I did well in those weeks.

"You're not kicking your heels up high enough after the turn," Little Doe said to me. It was late at night. We were walking home after a party, a rich lady's birthday celebration. "And you should hold your hand like this." She tried to demonstrate. I was busy counting my tips. "Meri, are you listening to me?"

"Say 'Thais.' Yeah, I hear you." I knotted the money into a corner of my pallia. My feet hurt. Some drunken woman, dripping jewellery, had stepped on my toe when she tried to imitate me. Romans couldn't dance worth a damn.

It was late. I drooped all the way back to the tavern. But when we got back, it was still jumping in there. Packed to the walls with drunken men. The place reeked of that camel sweat that Tausiris calls beer. He and Beshotep were pouring as fast as they could, and Cups and Judah were waiting tables, when they weren't taking customers to their rooms to fuck. There were three men waiting for whores. Little Doe and I threw our stuff in our rooms and got to work. The sun was eating the moon in the blueing sky before Tausiris let us all stop. Cups was crying a little as she took herself to bed, and cradling her jaw where Tausiris had backhanded her for serving someone too slowly.

Fuck, I thought my feet were going to fall right *off*, and my arms were shaking from lifting all those heavy mugs of beer.

I went into Judah's room to say good night; good morning, really. And we'd be back at it in a few hours. He was sitting on his bed in only his tunic, his head thrown back, rubbing his feet. He was nearly asleep, sitting up.

"Here," I told him. "Let me." I started rubbing my thumbs along the bottoms of his feet.

"Oh," he breathed. "Thank you."

"I'm so tired, it feels like there's sand in my eyes."

"I don't want to think about it." He lay back and closed his eyes. He clapped at a mosquito that was whining in front of his face, then threw one arm over his eyes to keep out the brightening day.

"This is our life," I told him.

He lifted his arm a little, peered out at me from below it. "Cheerful as a peacock song, you are."

"We'll work till Tausiris decides to release us . . ."

". . . *if* he decides to release us."

"Then we'll find husbands who'll work us some more."

Judah giggled. "Not me. I'll *be* a husband. Have a pretty, rich wife, lots of slaves to fetch and carry for me."

"You want a wife?"

"Well, yes; what else? That's what you do, Thais; you marry and you get a family, and you look after them and they look after you."

"Yeah, I know." I felt so sad and weary all of a sudden.

Judah chuckled. "And you leave your lovely family at home when you go and wrestle with the boys in the gymnasium."

"Well, you will. I'll be the one left at home with the brats. But before all that respectability?"

"We do this," he said. "Be slaves. Take tips, take bribes, make friends in high places if we can, save our money." He shrugged and covered his eyes again. I started rubbing his other foot.

"And we live in Alexandria until we die."

"What's wrong with Alexandria?"

"It's boring!"

"What's the matter with you, Thais?" he asked gently.

Suddenly, I was close to tears. "I want to go places!" I told him. "I want to go and see my grandmother in Nubia. I only met her one time, when I was a baby. I want to see Aelia Capitolina," I said, surprising myself. Till that moment, I hadn't really known it.

There is a whispering in the space between times. No, not just one whispering; many. There is an eddy in the aether, swirling around Aelia Capitolina. Some of the whispering is strongest there. I want to see what's there, but in Thais's head, I am rarely free to travel as I like. But she can take me in her body to Aelia Capitolina. Yes, child, let us go there.

"And I bet you want to go to the heavens, too, and drink nectar with the gods." He was nearly asleep before he finished the sentence.

"Judah!" I said, shaking him. "We could do it!"

"What? Wha . . . Min's prick, Thais, let me alone."

"No, really! I just remembered what day this is! We could go to Aelia Capitolina! Today! With Antoniou!"

Judah was awake now. "He'd take us?"

"He told me he'd take me, if I could pay the fare." He'd been speaking honey to please me, but no matter. "I earned enough money these past few weeks for the both of us! Come with me, Judah? Aelia Capitolina is so grand!"

Judah sat up. "I have an uncle who owns a farm just outside Capitolina."

"So it's set, then! Let's go!"

It's not like we had much to pack. I wore my best sandals and my favourite dress, so that was fine. Threw my pallia on over the top. Put my dancing dress and my sistrum into my bag, 'cause you never know.

"I don't know how I let you talk me into this," said Judah, slouching into my room. He was knuckling at his eyes.

"Shh!" I said. "Beshotep will be up any minute to start the fire. We have to be gone before they find out."

Judah lay on my bed, put his head on his bag, and closed his eyes.

"Just don't fall asleep," I told him.

"Okay," he said, through another yawn.

I packed my doll, the rag one that Papa had made for me so many years ago. I'd brought it with me when I came to work at Tausiris's. Ages now since I would fall asleep cuddling it, but I didn't want to leave it behind. I used to imagine that it smelt a little like Papa; of goats and honey.

That was it. I straightened up and looked around my little room. Wouldn't look any different without me in it. I shook Judah's shoulder and put my hand to his mouth to remind him to be quiet. He sat up with a sigh and glared at me like I'd trod on shit and was making a bad smell, but he got up and stumbled out of the tavern behind me. As we snuck out the front door, I could hear Beshotep just stirring in his room. He was sleeping in late, that one; the sun was almost up. I hurried along quickly, and reached my hand behind me so that Judah would take it. He didn't. I looked behind; he wasn't there. Oh, you gods! Had he abandoned me, then?

But no, there he was, sly as a cat, coming back out of Tausiris's at a run. He was grinning all over his face and he had a stoppered clay jar under each arm. He caught up with me and pushed one at me. "Here! Now, let's move it!"

I scampered. Didn't say a word to him until we were around a corner or two. Then I slowed a little. "What's in them?"

He chuckled and pulled the stopper out of his. "Food, you fool!" He pulled out a handful of olives, stuffed some into my mouth and the rest into his.

The olives were wonderful; briny and chewy. I'd forgotten how long it had been since my last meal. I ate them, pushing the pits into one cheek with my tongue as I did. "What's in the other one?" I opened the jar I was carrying and stuck my nose into it. The honey smell of dried dates filled my nostrils. "Oh, Judah; you're a genius!" I fed him some of them, took some myself, and re-sealed the jar. We would be in *so* much trouble when we got back. Tausiris had a heavy whip hand with his slaves when we angered him.

Antoniou had said that his captain's ship would be leaving just after sunrise. We didn't have much time. We hurried along the sea road, spitting pits at each other.

I could hear the docks before we came upon them. Men shouting, seabirds cawing, the braying of donkeys. I could smell what it was like down there, too; the reek of still sea water and rotting seaweed. Cups liked to come and watch the ships being loaded and unloaded and flirt with the brawny men. Me, I preferred to go and hang about the market. Lots of boys my age there, and pretty things to buy, when I had money.

Judah and I turned down the last stretch of the sea road. We could see the fat, gaudy trading ships now, bobbing in the water.

Bright as a star come down to earth, the huge lighthouse on Pharos island towered over the whole scene. Cups said it was mirrors they used to catch the light of the sun. I didn't like it. Hurt my eyes to look at it.

Lines of donkeys waited on the shore, laden with jars and sacks and led by their masters. There were men taking goods onto and off the ships. They wore only cloths tied around their loins so that they were unencumbered in their labours. Half the time the cloths came unknotted anyway. They covered nothing. Judah grinned. "I love watching strong men work," he said.

There was a book-keeper at each pile of goods being brought onshore, keeping a tally on papyrus. I even saw one woman book-keeper. She must work for some fine lady who had no husband. Maybe little Helena would get work like that when she grew up.

"How're we going to know which ship is Antoniou's?" Judah asked.

I hadn't thought of that. "I don't know," I said. They were all so big, the ships, and each had lots of men scurrying all over them. I'd only imagined Antoniou standing there alone on the dock, welcoming me with a hug and maybe some of those sesame sweetmeats he always carried. I was worried now. Perhaps he'd already gone?

I led Judah right down to the docks, dodging donkeys, men staggering with heavy burdens, and the stray dogs that always sniffed about the docks, hoping to snatch a meal. I looked around, clutching at the money knotted into a corner of my pallia. It was all just confusion to me. Please, I thought to no one in particular, don't let the ship be gone already.

Judah walked up to a massive man who had just let a heavy sack fall to the ground beside a pile of goods. "Hey," Judah said, "do you know a sailor named Antoniou? A Greek?"

The man straightened up, sighing, his hands at the small of his back. He stretched, then in a deep, raspy voice, he said, "Whose ship's he work on?"

"We don't know," I told him. "He's Greek, and he's a Christian, and he's got an accent, and he's got black curly hair all over him."

The man gave a rumbling chuckle. "Look around you, girl. Could be any Greek on any ship, and there's plenty of them, Greeks and ships both."

It was true. The harbour was full of ships. And my description fit a score of the sailors I could see all around me.

"And I swear, half of them are called Antoniou," he said. "Look, I gotta get back to work. See that ship over there?" He pointed.

"The green one with all the jars loaded up on it?" Judah asked.

"Yeah. That's Daidalos's. He hires plenty Greeks, 'cause they're his countrymen and they speak the same language. Go and ask there. Hurry, though. They're about to put out to sea."

We rushed over to the ship, with people shouting at us the whole time because we were getting in their way. We looked up, up, up at it. So big! I bet even the old pyramids weren't so big. There was a man down on the ground, unravelling the rope that would set the ship free. "Hey!" Judah shouted. The man ignored him. Judah ran up to him and touched his shoulder. "Wait."

The man looked up. He had one weepy, sore eye. "We're off. What d'you want?"

"Does Antoniou work on this ship?" I asked.

"Yeah. Antoniou from Syria, and Antoniou with the lame leg, and Antoniou the foreigner, and little Antoniou. Which one you want?"

Desperately, I said, "He's a Christian, and he's about so tall, and he has a wife back home."

The man shrugged. "Who doesn't?" He turned to his job again.

"He likes to tell stories," Judah told him. "Great whoppers of stories."

The man stopped and squinted up at us in the sunlight. "Does he wave his arms about when he talks?"

"Yes," Judah and I said together.

"Does he like boys and women?"

"Yes!"

"Does he have a scar on the back of his neck? About so long?" The man held his thumb and finger apart. I didn't know if Antoniou had a scar.

"Yes, he does!" said Judah. "I've seen the back of his neck plenty times."

"That's little Antoniou, then. Yeah, he's here. You going aboard? You got money?"

I grabbed Judah's hand and pulled him to the gangplank. "Yes! Yes!" I said. "We can pay! We're going to Aelia Capitolina!"

"Sure," the man muttered, and kept on about his job. I didn't pay him any more attention. We ran up the gangplank. He came up behind us, and they began to pull it up. The sailors on the deck, a ragtag bunch, stared at us curiously. I didn't care. We were going to Aelia Capitolina.

"Anybody seen little Antoniou?" I asked.

ROCK

Judah held my stomach while I was sick over the side of the ship. I spat and spat to get the sour taste out of my mouth. "Gods, Judah. I just want the world to keep still again, just for a little!"

"I know," he murmured.

"Antoniou said we'd stop feeling sick soon!"

"I did," Judah replied.

"Yeah, well, that's no help to me. Oh, shit . . ." Another gout of upchuck heaved up from my belly. If I never tasted salted dried fish again, I would get down on my knees and thank every god I knew. And my head hurt, and my breasts. I hated sailing.

"I have to go, Thais," Judah told me. "It's my watch."

I just waved him away, too busy being sick. We'd only been four days on the water, but he was turning into quite the sailor, Judah was. Had to. The ship was out to sea before I'd discovered my mistake. How was I to know that I didn't have enough money to cover our fares? How was I to know that we'd have to pay for food and drink? Our dates and olives had run out pretty quickly, but not before we had the runs and were sick to death of the sight of them. So, Judah was working as a sailor, and I was paying my way in the manner I knew best: as a whore. I didn't even get to see Antoniou all that much! He was busy, busy, all the time busy. Not like when he came to see us at the tavern. Always climbing some damned mast, or mending some damned rope. Just like bloody Judah, who was loving it that he got to spend time with the sailors. Giving his loving away for free, he was, since he was earning his money in other ways. He said the sailors were all beautiful, even the ones with scars or damaged limbs.

The fucking ship wasn't even going straight to Aelia Capitolina. How was I to know that Capitolina wasn't a port city?

I stared out to sea. My belly hurt. Time for my courses soon, I guess. Looking at the horizon was the only thing that kept the dizziness from coming over me. Antoniou let me and Judah share his tent out on the deck, but I preferred to sleep right out in the open, uncovered, though it was cold sometimes. I didn't feel so ill when I could get the wind in my face. When I had to go into one of the sailors' tents to service them, they'd learned that they'd best do their business quickly, else I'd be spewing all over their beds. And they'd better not touch my breasts. Gods, but they hurt!

I had thought Antoniou would come out and sleep with me, nights, but he said it was too cold and he didn't like getting sprayed with sea spume all night. "Get enough of that during the day," he told me.

I just wanted to be in Aelia Capitolina, or Joppa, or wherever the fuck we were going, on solid ground. We were nearly there, Antoniou told me. Another night. Please, let it only be another night.

I went looking for some wine to wash the taste of vomit from my mouth. The galley guard liked me; he'd sneak me some.

That whispering; it's like many voices, speaking, but I don't quite make them out. I almost can. When Thais sleeps and I am set free, I travel to that between place and I strain to hear. Sometimes I think I can see shadows moving too, but it may be just clouds. I catch a glimpse that could be that Hathor lady. I can swim the betweenplace better now, and I always avoid the streams where I can taste/see/sense Hathor. She makes me think about what *I* mean, and she frightens me. Sometimes it's Jeanne I taste in the flow, her story being, was, and will-being. That taste satisfies me. It is something that I helped to weave, something ultimately strong, despite tears and broken threads. Sometimes it is Mer, and Georgine, and Tipingee. And not just women. Patrice is in my storystream too. And Georgine's little boy.

There is more besides; half-sensed forms, half-heard voices. I feel like human babies must, straining to make their limbs and senses work, without knowing quite what they do. Like them, I feel like crying, like squeezing out that salt water of which I am so, so weary. These bodies that entrap me—they are nothing but brine bound about by flesh.

We will be in Aelia Capitolina soon. Perhaps there are answers there. I try to soothe the Thais girl's stomach, but her body keeps rejecting food. I am dizzy when I am within her. I try to make her sleep, often. It's easy. She is very tired these days.

Who's there, whispering? What are you saying? What are you? Are you speaking to me? What are you trying to tell me?

SAINT DOMINGUE

I think I understand what Father is trying to tell us. A test, a trial. The Ginen are being tested by their gods. Tempered. And our reward, if we are true to them, is that they will take us to them. Mami Wata, is it so? Can I dare to believe that it is so?

My legs won't work right," Judah laughed.

"Me neither." We held each other as we walked down the gangplank into Joppa. Sea legs, the sailors had told us. Said we would have gotten used to walking on the rolling deck, and we would stumble on dry land.

"Move it, children!" growled Claudius behind us. The men needed to offload their cargo onto the donkey carts waiting to take the wheat to the Roman Legion. Maybe we could hitch a ride that way to Capitolina.

Antoniou wasn't coming. He was still on the ship somewhere. He'd kissed me goodbye, but I could tell that his thoughts were somewhere else. Judah'd heard that Antoniou had a favourite brothel in this port. Probably he'd head there right away. I'd thought he really wanted my company. I was so stupid.

Our feet hit the sands of Joppa. I wanted to lie down right there and hug the unmoving earth, I was so grateful. But there was no time. The bustle of the port jostled us, and I almost got separated from Judah. We grabbed on to each other's hands and held on tight.

"I'm hungry," I said to him. He looked surprised. I hadn't been hungry much at all since the nausea started.

"Don't look at me like that. It's because we're not moving for once, thank the gods. Let's go and buy some lunch. I have money." This time, I knew it wouldn't go far, but I had more than Judah did, cause I'd been too sick to spend my earnings on food.

Judah looked around. "Okay, let's eat. I've been here once before, a few years ago, as they took us to be sold into slavery." He gazed at the streets around him to get his bearings. "This way. After that, we can see about begging a ride."

"All right."

Judah led us off down one of the streets. He thought he remembered a market there. On the way, I stared at people till I thought my eyes would leap out of my head! I was used to Jews; there were plenty in Alexandria, the men with their fringed shawls, but here there were so many of them! "Everybody talks funny," I whispered to Judah. "They're all speaking Hebrew. Sounds like gargling."

"Thais, we're the ones who talk funny here." He heaved his bag higher up onto his shoulder.

"What do you mean? We talk normal."

He just shook his head and didn't explain. We bought some bread from a vendor and some garum paste to dip it in. Must have been a long time since I'd eaten a full meal. It was delicious.

The soldiers did let us ride with them to the garrison. More fucking to pay our passage, sometimes right there in the carts amongst the sacks of grain. Judah complained the whole way there. "I hate Roman soldiers," he whispered to me one night when we'd gone off a little way to piss. "They're the ones who destroyed my city. You know what Aelia Capitolina used to be called before Rome got its hands on it, don't you?"

"No, what?" I found a smooth rock, rubbed it clean against my tunic, and used it to dab my nethers dry. It was warm from the day's sun. I tossed it away.

"It was Jerusalem," Judah said.

"Yeah? I've heard that name somewhere."

Judah shook himself off and smoothed his linen kilt back down. "It existed for thousands of years before Rome sacked it." He fussed with his pleats until they were perfect. Seven days of travel, and I looked like shit. Judah was as perfect as a Festival rose.

I stood up and sighed. "Time to go to work," I told him. I was with a skinny balding man tonight. He had bad breath. Judah and I picked our way back to the camp in the dark. Hoped I could keep down the dinner we'd eaten. I still wasn't quite recovered from the sea trip.

That other place, that rancid, stagnant place in the aether. It draws me towards it. There are other places I can go in the spherical world, but they all end up there, at the blockage. I cannot get by it. Its taste is foul. It reeks of grief and horror. I gather my forces—I am much more able now—and throw myself at it, hoping to break through. Instead I land in it, and it is vile; corruption creeping into every sense. Spitting, gagging, I fight myself free, but I am back where I started. This cancer, it blocks my freeflowing world. Forces it to move in only one direction. I must, must clear it.

When I start to be dragged down into human time as I have been before, start to feel the weight of bones and flesh again, it makes me as bitter as poor Jeanne is for so much of her life. Is it back to Thais, then? She my only means of travel as she plods her single-visioned way to Capitolina? Must I be sunk forever in her puking flesh, drown in her? What will become of me? And what is wrong with my flowing world of stories? I scream anger into the careless ocean of aether, but there's no reply.

Aelia Capitolina was all hills. The donkeys trudged along a road that went up and up. They clambered up it, uncomplaining, to the soldiers' garrison. We stopped in front of its gates.

"You two are off here," said one of the soldiers, jerking his chin in the direction of the path that led back to the city.

I didn't remember his name. He was the one in charge. He liked me to suck him. "Can't we come in?" I asked. Judah rolled his eyes at me. He just wanted to get away from them. But I wanted a bath.

The soldier just laughed at me. "What, and let the Centurion know we had two whores with us the whole way back? We'd be polishing his armour till our arms fell off."

The others chuckled with him. "Off you get, chicks," one of them said, shooing us off the cart.

We clambered down. I heard my tunic tear on a nail as I went. It was my favourite tunic, too. But I hardly cared any more. At least I still had my doll.

"Can you at least tell us the way to the Christian church?" I heard Judah asking. "The big one?"

I didn't wait to hear the directions. I was off down the hill already, looking for somewhere to puke. It was so bloody hot in this city! I spat out my breakfast, then went back to the path. Judah was on it, kicking stones as he went. He looked happier, now he was away from the soldiers.

"I think we should just find someone to take us to my uncle's place," Judah said. He stooped to pick up a rock, and heaved it down the path. It bounced away over red dirt.

"No, I want to go to the church first," I told him.

Yes, child. Take me to the whispering.

He looked at me. "You're sure? You don't look so good, Thais. My uncle would look after us. We could rest a few days, then come back."

It sounded good. It'd make sense to get settled somewhere first. But . . . "the Church of the Holy Sepulchre first," I said.

"Okay," he said. We continued on down.

"Thais, listen; when we get to my uncle's place, we have to be on our best behaviour, right?"

My head ached.

"Thais? Did you hear me?"

"Yes, I did," I said, rubbing my forehead. It was starting to pound. "Your uncle's an old fart, is he?"

"I guess. He's just very, you know, orthodox. You won't be able to wear any of your fancy clothes around the farm, and you'll have to help with the chores, and observe Sabbath."

"Gods, that sounds dreary. I might as well be back in the tavern in Alexandria."

"But he's a good man, though. And my young cousins are so sweet. Lila, Tamar, and Farah. Only they're probably not so young any more. It's been seven years since I've seen them. I was only a boy then myself. And Thais?"

"Yes?" My belly felt like a dogfight was going on inside it.

"We can't talk about me liking to go with men, okay?"

"Why not?"

"Uncle thinks it's a filthy Greek habit."

I chuckled at that, despite how ill I felt. "Shows how much he knows."

"He thinks I'm the manager of Tausiris's tavern. Thinks I should come and live with him and work on the farm once Tausiris frees me."

I made a noise of disgust. I tried to imagine Judah up to his knees in mud behind a plough. I laughed, but that made my belly hurt more. My bag felt heavy, and the sound of my sistrum chiming every time it banged against my hip was making me dizzy. I kept walking. "Judah?"

"Yes?"

"You're a Jew, right?"

"Yes. Why?"

"Well, how come you don't wear the fringed shawl, like the men do here?"

He didn't answer for a little while. Then he shrugged and said, "I don't observe the Sabbath either, unless I'm here visiting my uncle. I was born Jewish, but I just feel more Greek, you know?"

"I think I know. Me, I feel both Nubian and Greek." Judah's uncle would probably throw several fits if he knew that Judah'd been wearing weights on the skin of his dick to reverse his circumcision; said that he was tired of the men at the gym staring at him and knowing he was Jewish, not Greek. "I'm thirsty, Judah."

He smiled at me. "One of the soldiers gave me a skin of wine," he said, "in gratitude for this little trick I taught him."

"You have wine? Give me some!" I hadn't even noticed the skin slung over his shoulder. I felt better already.

He handed me the skin. I stopped, put my head back, and held the skin up to my head. Sweet red wine poured into my mouth. I swallowed the first wonderful mouthful, then gagged. Spilled wine all down the front of my tunic. "Fuck," I said to Judah, "what's wrong with it? He's given you sour wine!"

"Here, let me taste it." He took a small, cautious mouthful, lowered the skin, and frowned at me. "It's just fine, Thais. Not the best wine in the world, but it'll do."

"You're mad," I told him, continuing down the path. "It tastes like camel's piss."

"Pretty Pearl," he said from behind me, "sometimes I don't know what to do with you."

"Just get me to the Church of the Sepulchre." I thought of all Antoniou had said about it, how marvellous it was. I wanted to see a marvellous thing.

We were finally in the city. We stopped every little while so that Judah could ask directions. A woman was staring at me. I glared her down, then nudged Judah. "What's up with her?"

"They don't get many Nubians here," he said. "You look strange to them."

"That's silly! Only my mother is Nubian! My dad's a Greek!" What a backwards place this was! But Judah found us a stall that sold bread with honey, and once I'd eaten, the world looked much brighter. I recognised some of the food in the market; olives and dates and barley, and I heard a few people speaking Meroitic and Greek, and saw some more Roman troops. But still, it wasn't the same as Alexandria. "It's so dusty here, Judah. Why aren't the streets paved?"

He tousled my hair. "It's not like Alexandria everywhere, Thais."

Well, I knew that. What did he think I was, a child? "Oh, look at that." A woman was walking by, wearing a beautiful yellow pallia. "That's so pretty. Wonder where she got it?"

Judah smiled at me through his fifth piece of bread and honey. "It's good to see you bright-eyed again. Hey, you think we can afford some of those dates? They're stuffed with pistachios."

"No, we can't. Come on, let's go." I didn't tell him, but I didn't actually feel so good any more. My belly was hurting, low down. Probably from the food. I had eaten so fast. He asked directions in Hebrew from the vendor. The answer really did sound like water tumbling over sharp rocks.

"He says it's a long way," Judah said. "We can walk, but it'd be better to rent a donkey."

"Oh," I said, thinking of my hard-earned money. Wonder

where a whore went to work in this town? "Let's see how much a donkey costs first."

We asked around until we found the stall of a man who would let us ride his donkey and lead us to the church. Judah found out the price. I hated not being able to talk to anybody. "Tell him that's too much, Judah."

The man shrugged. Judah didn't need to translate that. Well, maybe a stroll would help ease my aching belly. At least my breasts didn't hurt any more. "Let's walk," I said. Gods, it was hot! And the market smells were making me queasy. I'd gotten used to the constant sea breeze on the ship, and the roar of the waves. And even on the trip to the garrison, we'd been in the open for most of the ride. Here, it was all people jabbering. We got directions from the man with the donkey, and set off. Hilly and dry, this land. Pretty soon, my feet were powdered to the calves with dust.

"Is it much further?" I was sweaty and hot, and my head and my belly were pounding.

Judah shaded his eyes and looked up at the sun. "Another hour or so, I think. The vendor said it would be close to sundown before we got there."

Damn. Walking wasn't helping. It felt like I was going to be sick again. Last time I buy any food from that stall!

It felt like my courses were coming, too. About time. They should have come while we were on the ship.

"You all right, Pretty Pearl? You're sweating all over." Judah was looking at me, worried.

"It's okay. My head hurts a little, that's all."

"Do you want to sit for a while?"

"No, let's keep going." If we weren't going to even get to the church until sundown, we'd have to spend the night at an inn or something. Which means we'd have to pay for it. I wondered whether we had enough money. "Come on, walk faster."

He did, but it was me who kept slowing us down. I stopped

twice to be sick by the side of the road. The dust, red dust; it got in everything; my hair, my nose, my eyes. My throat stung with the sour taste of being sick, and my belly cramps were coming in waves now.

"You are sick, aren't you?" said Judah. "Shit."

"No. Yes. Let's just go to the church. They'll look after me there, won't they?"

"I don't know." He sounded scared. "Your skin's gone a funny colour; all grey."

"It's the dust," I muttered. I hated Capitolina.

It felt like hours before we got to the church. A long, long time of walking. I don't remember the journey too clearly any more, just that I hurt and Judah kept asking me if I wanted to stop.

But I am determined that we keep going. Something is wrong with this Thais. Something has grown in her that is making her sick. If she dies, if her dying throws me out of her as Jeanne's did, who knows where I'll be tossed to? Then maybe I won't get to find out what that susurrus is in the aether. I nudge Thais to keep walking. She's strong and young, and she wants to see Aelia Capitolina badly too. So she keeps on for my sake, for hers.

We were finally at the Church of the Sepulchre. It was near dark. People had come out to sit in the atrium around the church, to get some of the cool breezes of evening. Children were running around playing, old men gathered talking. No women—they'd be home preparing food. Judah was muttering about finding something to eat, but my belly was too painful to feel hunger. My head was pounding so hard I could barely hear the shouts of the children and the old men's arguments. I was holding on to Judah's arm for support, and I didn't care how people stared.

It was beautiful, the church, just like Antoniou had said. It was huge. They had lit the lamps, and it was outlined in flickering light. It rose up into the sky, piercing the dusk. I'd never seen

299

anything like it in Alexandria. "It looks cool inside," I whispered to Judah. It hurt my head to talk. I cried out and held my belly, curled myself around it.

"Thais! What is it?" asked Judah. He crouched down around me, my friend did. He was so good to me. There were snakes writhing knots in my gut; crocodiles fighting in there.

"Judah," I said, "I think I'm dying."

"No, no, you'll be okay." I think he was crying. His voice sounded like it. "Come. Come inside the church. We'll find somewhere for you to lie down."

He almost had to carry me in. I could barely walk. There must have been people gawping at us, but I couldn't help from crying out with the pain. Judah dragged me up the steps. As though she were far away, I heard an old woman's voice saying, "Is she your wife? What's wrong with her?"

"I don't know!" Judah wailed. "She's been sick all day!"

We were finally inside. Lamps everywhere. It was almost as bright as day. There were knives in my belly, tearing their way free. I let myself fall from Judah's hands to the stone floor. It was warm from the day's sun, not cool. I couldn't care. I knotted myself around my belly and cried on the gods to stop the pain.

"Stop it, young lady, this instant! You can't speak the name of your pagan gods in here!" It was a woman's voice, a different one than before. Younger.

"Shush, Ruth," said the old woman. "She's in pain. She doesn't know what she's saying."

"Isis!" I begged. I could only think of Little Doe telling me how Isis helped women. I needed help. "Please!"

"Isis," said the old voice, "love goddess of Egypt and Nubia. A temple to Venus used to be right where we're standing now."

"Well, it's God's home now," the younger voice said grimly. "Praise be, Jesu has triumphed over their pagan witch."

I didn't give a damn for their chatter. I was rolling on the floor now, Judah imploring me to be well, to get better, not to die.

Something tore loose in my belly and I screamed. I felt hot liquid rush from between my legs.

"Oh!" exclaimed the old woman. The young one called on Mother Mary. The old woman knelt painfully beside me. She took my shoulder and tried to stretch me out. I cursed her and curled up again.

"Child," she said, "you're bleeding. Is it time for your courses?"

"I think so. Oh, it hurts."

"Does it always come upon you like this?"

"No!" I rocked with the pain. Felt another gush from my cunt. Judah was sobbing, kneeling beside me too. He stroked my hair.

"When did you last bleed?" the woman asked.

"She must leave, Kandace," came the voice of the young one. "She's defiling this holy space." I ignored her. When did I last bleed? Through rolling pain, I cast my mind back. Not on the ship. Not during the Rose Festival . . .

"If she's ill, as Christians we must minister to her," said the old woman.

I grabbed her hand. "I haven't bled in weeks and weeks," I told her. "More than a month."

"Then I think that you are losing a child. That's what's wrong. Look at all that blood. You were pregnant."

"Well, she isn't any longer," said the young woman's voice, "and she's making a mess. And she needs a doctor," she said. That part sounded like an afterthought to me. "Help me get her to my cell."

When they picked me up, the pain crashed over me, the worst yet. I know I screamed again. Then I knew nothing.

Saint Mary of Egypt

Mary came to Alexandria in Egypt at the age of twelve to pursue a life of prostitution, not because of need, but to gratify her insatiable physical desires. Some years later, she decided to embark on a pilgrimage to Jerusalem on the occasion of the Feast of the Exaltation of the Holy Cross. She had no intention of completing the Pilgrimage; rather, she hoped that the trip would provide her with many opportunities to gratify her lust. She left Alexandria by ship, and paid for her passage by committing numerous lewd acts with the sailors. Once she had arrived in Jerusalem, she persisted in her wanton ways. On the Feast of the Exaltation of the Holy Cross, she joined the throngs of the faithful making their way to the church, in hopes of drawing even more souls into sin. But as she attempted to enter the church, she was stopped at the door by some invisible force. Thrice she tried to enter in, and thrice was prevented. She took herself to a corner of the churchyard to ponder, and was suddenly seized with remorse for her venal life. She began to cry bitter tears and beat at her breast, exclaiming at her own sin. Then she noticed a statue of the Blessed Virgin Mary, mother of our Lord, in a sconce above the place where she was standing. Abandoning pride, Mary of Egypt prostrated herself before the image of the Virgin and beseeched her help in entering the church.

—Adapted from various Catholic texts about the life of Saint Mary of Egypt, the "dusky" saint

I tear loose from Thais, as the little dot of cells tears away from her too. I'm tumbling, no control. That would have been a child, that thing growing in Thais. As I am a child in this spirit world. I don't learn fast enough. It didn't learn fast enough how to stick in Thais's belly.

I spin about and try to see the pattern in the mist, but all I can do is be tossed. And suddenly there are voices, voices as I spin in the nothing. A face spins past me, there and gone. There's someone here! What is happening? I keep tossing, whipping around. See the face once again. A woman. Big, with gentle eyes.

"Sister," says a voice from inside this nowhere place. The shock of it divides my sight like rivers branch. There is another face, and another, all whizzing by me too fast to see. They gaze at me, curious. There are more of them, then? It's too much to understand. I am fragmenting, dissipating, like mist when the sun strikes it. The whispers I've been hearing are theirs.

What is happening? I want to understand. I look with spirit's eyes into the swirling aether.

"Sister," it comes again. A woman.

"Who's there?"

The mists begin to curdle, to take shape. I am slowing now. They are the one slowing me. I can only bob in the flow, watch them appear. One is a biscuit-brown beauty, wreathed in pink mists that hide and reveal her, like so much lace. She lazily waves a cut-work fan, smiles at me. One is bent under the weight of her sorrows. Her earth-brown hands are knotted as roots and her eyes are sad, but her back is strong. Hands on hips, she waits calmly for whatever comes. The third comes surging at me on a vast gout of the aether. She is large beyond my imagining. Each breast is a mountain and her laugh is the crashing surf. She is the cool brown of rich riverbank mud. Her powerful tail sweeps like a crocodile's.

"Welcome, sister," say the three voices, whispering painfully loud. No, not three only. For each woman has echoes of herself, all around her. Some are small, some large. All look like her. And with my growing perceptions, I can see that each echo has its own echoes, and each echo's echo its own, branching and dividing endlessly.

"What are you?" I say to them.

"Your tormentor. Your saviour," they tell me. Time is only water in a bowl to them. I can see how they swirl it. They are here and elsewhere, acting in the world and in the aether, they and their echoes, even as they are speaking to me. They are a sour slave woman who knows hope is dead, holding a baby's head as its mother pushes it out of her womb. They are a vain girl with soft, black hair, dancing on a Greek sailor's prick. They are a ginger-haired woman, drunk on smoke and sex and staring into a pot of piss. And more than these, and more. I am dumbfounded.

"That's the broad view," says the sorrowing one. "Look at us. Look closer."

The gargantuan fish woman is one of her smaller echoes now, and I am closer to them all. Closer. I can see into the fractals of their eyes. My own face gazes back at me from those infinite reflections, and it is all their faces.

They are me.

"Frèda," the coquette names herself, toying with misty pink lace that looks strong enough to strangle.

"Lasirèn," bubbles the sea woman in Pidgin, cradling whole continents on her bosom.

"Danto," weeps the sad one, mourning for her losses. Her hard fists flex in anger. In her name I perceive echoes: Danto,

D'hanto, D'hantor, D'hathor. Some few of the Haytian slaves were North African, and a small memory of Hathor's love still clings to them.

They are me, these women. They are the ones who taught me to see; *I* taught me to see. They, we, are the ones healing the Ginen story, fighting to destroy that cancerous trade in shiploads of African bodies that ever demands to be fed more sugar, more rum, more Nubian gold.

The slave Thais would have borne a girl, to be raised in a whorehouse as another slave girl. Another African body borne away on the waves.

"Je-Wouj," I name myself to my sisters, myself. I hear my echoes, all our echoes, say it with me. I am Ezili Red-eye, the termagant enraged, with the power of millennia of Ginen hopes, lives, loves. "*We can lance that chancre,*" we say. I can direct my own pulse now. I see how to do it. I, we, rise, flow out of ebb, tread the wet roads of tears, of blood, of salt, break like waves into our infinite selves, and dash into battle.

Beat Break/ Beat
Break/
Beat!
One-

        . . .↓
        Drop

Blues sister
       soul
Throwing W
      O
        R
          D
           S
Sharp
    as vinegar to the tongue

I slip into the head of a white woman, through the brine that wets her eyes. Coiffed and perfumed as Ezili Frèda, light-skinned Power of love and romance, I say in a voice like tinkling bells to the preening man beside me, "Then you *will* grant him clemency, my dear! I thought you might!"

And a man goes free, to help plot a revolution.

I climb into a bus alongside a tired working woman whose feet hurt. She finds a seat at the front, where her kind are not supposed to sit, and lowers herself into it with a sigh. Her kind are the black workers, the black poor. They are the ones who use the buses. The woman is arrested when she refuses to give up her seat to a white passenger. In the quiet protest that follows Rosa Parks's simple act of refusal, black people bring the city's bus system to a halt for over a year by refusing to use public transit. Ezili Danto can bear much pain, but sometimes she holds fast, refuses to be moved. The city outlaws segregation of public buses.

Tossing bitter water
With a shake of head, a twitch
of eye.
Slide slip, tongue slip
RATTLECHAINBREAKWATER
Break, waters break
Slip spill
Gush

As my mother whale self, I swim in real seas that surround Saint Domingue. I swim down a cove, where I appear to a sad Mer fishing from a rock and tell her, "The sea roads. They're drying up." I tell her that she must find a way to fix it. Years later, she will think she has failed me, but I act in the world through such as her. Her every act of love, of healing, strikes a blow to the evil we fight.

Propping sorrow
Chin on palm, balanced on elbow
Tottering
Spit
Split
Blood singing
Salt
Roads ringing with the rush
Rip tide, ebb tide, flow
Beat
BREAK/_{beat}
RATTLE
DRINK
Salt
SUCK
Salt
Dance
Dance
Dance

I almost didn't feel it. Was weeding the fields, shuffling along with the others, pulling up every plant that wasn't a cane stalk. A good day, for all that I was tired. Tipingee had come to see me the night before, and I still had the smell of her in my nose, and the clouds were keeping the sun from beating down on us too plenty. As I crouched and plucked, I found myself humming a tune my mother had taught me. The meaning of the words had left me long time since, but the little song was still there. Cool day, a skin-memory of Tipi's hands on my body in the night, and my mother's voice in my head. A good day.

It's only chance that the little glass whale bounced against my calf when it fell. Lasirèn's token. Since the time when she had given it to me, I had tied it up into a knot in the hem of my dress, so it was always with me. It was tight, that knot, and I checked it every morning. But it came loose that day, and the glass whale fell out. Was just this small touch against my calf, and when I looked to see if a centipede or a lizard had jumped on me, out of the edge of my eye I saw the whale burying itself in the damp soil. Even then, I wasn't sure what it was; little piece of thing disappeared too fast. Something made me feel my hem, then look at where the knot gaped open.

Wai, my Lasirèn! I dropped to my knees one time and started digging in the dirt. Had to find it fast before the book-keeper saw that I wasn't working. Stones I pulled up, and twigs, and slimy slugs. My heart was only pounding, pounding. Some of the Ginen were looking at me now, but they knew better than to stop working. The line of weed-pullers swept past me. I had to find it!

I pushed both hands into the rank earth, deep as they would go. Felt my fingers bruising; didn't care. Earthworms shrank, frightened, as I pulled them up out of the ground; I paid them no mind. I sifted the soil through my hands; nothing. Moved over a little and dug again. As I broke apart the clods of earth, the sun glinted off a bright something buried in them. It was my whale. I stood up and took my place in the line again. My fingers were trembling so much I could barely re-tie the knot. A few of the Ginen looked at me, curious, but nobody said nothing. I bent to my weeding again. Plucked and plucked until my hands stopped shaking and my chest wasn't pounding.

It's Lasirèn who made this happen. I'd been ignoring her. She sent me to do her work, and I'd been fretting instead about my own business; about Tipi, and Patrice, and whether I was to be alone now. Lasirèn would cast me away unless I did what she asked of me.

I kept my fingers weeding, set my mind working. That night by the sea, she had said to find out why her sea roads are blocked. How, though?

But though I worried at the problem till daylean that evening, no answer came to me. I tromped back to my hut and scarce noticed the other Ginen doing the same; my mind was only running on how to clear Lasirèn's roads of power so that she and the gods might use them to set us free.

In my hut, by the light of the oil lamp, I crumbled dried mint leaves into pig fat from one of my calabashes. I laved my hands in the cool grease that smelled sweet of mint; into the cracks in my fingertips and my dry hand-backs. Then I rubbed my aching feet with the ointment, dirty as my foot bottoms were. A soothing thing. Mint makes your eyes see clear, too, if you drink a tea made from it. Calms the stomach and clears the brain.

As hundreds of light-skinned free women, I defy the blan law that tells us that coloured women must go barefoot. We march through the streets of Port-au-Prince, heads tall, hips swaying, our biscuit and tan beauty searing the eye and mak-

ing the white men sweat. We chant, "nou led, nou là:" *we're ugly but we're here.* We chant it loudly, knowing that white men moan at nights in their wives' beds, and soil the sheets with their spunk, thinking on our "ugliness." Onto our bare feet we have knotted jewels, our jewels, for we are rich women. As we march, every one of us a Frèda, if only for that day, our feet sparkle in the Port-au-Prince sun with diamonds, emeralds, pearls. We are ugly, and we're here.

My eyes didn't want to stay open. I was on my palette and asleep before the stars came out.

I fight as another three-twist; fierce, libidinous Queen Nzingha of Matamba and her two sisters, with their harem of beautiful men. Together, we three, imbued with Ezili Je-Wouj, lead our army and our country and keep the thieving Portuguese slavers at bay for forty years until Nzingha's death at age eighty-one. Our kingdom is finally overrun then, but while we were fighting, our blows hit home.

And then I was awake again, on the floor of my hut. What woke me? I looked at the lamp on the floor beside the bed. It was just beginning to gutter. Only asleep a little while, then. Half the night left. Stupid Mer, to fall asleep with the lamp burning.

Ezili's griffonne moon-face was shining full this night. Another month gone by. It's her light had woke me, filling my little window and making a path into my hut. I looked in that glowing path, and almost I didn't feel surprised to see the glass whale lying in the dead middle of it. It's not me who had taken it out from the knot of my skirt. "Mama," I whispered, "what you want me to do?"

The golden bar of light was a road, pointing. I knew where it was leading. The Ginen had been whispering about it all during the day, quiet, behind the book-keeper's back.

I stood up, blew out the lamp, reclaimed the whale by the light of the moon, and tied it into my skirt hem yet again. "Make it stay there this time," I said to the lwa my mother. "I'm going."

I stepped outside my door and looked around. I could hear old Papa Kofi snoring from in his hut. And there was still a lamp-flicker of light in the window from Zelda's. But no one abroad to see me break curfew. I wouldn't be the only one this night, neither.

And yes; there was the moon path, going towards the dark corner of the plantation. The blans would be asleep in their great house by now. Tonight, the Ginen were going to sing and celebrate off in the trees where the backra couldn't see nor hear. Usually I never went to the dancing, but the moon was telling me that I would learn something there.

But I would go to the river first. "Just to wash, Mama," I said. "Just to feel my body clean." I slipped off into the darkness, walking quiet.

One summer New York night, a group of men who love men and women who love women hang about the front of a nightclub, harassed and kicked out by the police. Inside, the police arrest five women with men's bodies and one mannish woman. As they try to leave with their prisoners, a Puerto Rican woman with a man's body throws her high-heeled pump; the first missile of resistance. A tall, black drag queen breaks his bonds and flees free. Another six-foot black vision in sequins and glitter throws himself into the attack led by queers, faggots, transvestites, and street youth, into the victory they will call Stonewall. Black Madonna, Sylvia Rivera, and Marsha P. Johnson all teach us Ezilis more about beauty, defiance, and resistance.

By the riverbank, it was dark as blue indigo cloth. I soaked my feet in the cleansing water and scooped up more of it into my hands. I washed the rank canefield sweat from me. Cool air on my damp skin made it prickle. Made my nipples hard. I wished if I could swim in the river, put my whole body in, but I had other business this night. Mama, your waters are a blessing. I untied the rag covering my hair and tied it round my waist to keep it safe. I bent low over the tumbling water, and took the risk. Dipped my whole head in, praying that Lasirèn wouldn't take my head and pull me down forever into the water with her. She didn't. My feet stayed planted firm on the riverbed. I thought my thanks at her and scrubbed my hair and scalp. A blessing. When I pulled my hair out from the stream, a little silvery fish was struggling in it. I laughed. "Yes, Mother of Fishes. I'm minding what you tell me." I freed the fish and let it dive back into its home. Did it swim with Lasirèn in her waters, hiding in her krinkly hair? My hair was dripping water all over me. I squeezed it out, as much as I could. Tied it back up. And went looking for the moon path.

There it was. I was far enough from the slave cabins. No one to see me but people going the same way as me. I stepped into the moonlight and followed it; followed until I could hear a soft thumping. Followed until the noise was drums. Followed till I could hear the Ginen laughing and talking. Pushed through a stand of clove trees to the clearing.

Eh. There was Patrice, using a coconut leaf rib broom to sweep the clearing. Tipi started when she saw me. Jumped like my own heart in my breast when my eyes looked on her. How long she'd been coming to the dancing? And she never asked me once to come with her? No. She would go with Patrice instead, then come to Jesus church with me on Sunday mornings, as Simenon had ordered us all to do. And there was Fleur, squatting beside a big pot of food on a fire, stirring it and laughing. With her wood spoon, she dipped out some of what was inside. Gave it to Hector to taste. He smacked his lips, a thoughtful look on his face. Then he reached to scoop a whole handful from the pot. Fleur gave him a good shove and he fell on his behind in the dirt. Both she and he were laughing, laughing. The Ginen, laughing. Even Mathieu was there, his body not so wasted now he wasn't trying to starve himself dead any more. Some of us called him Mamadou when the blans weren't around.

Mamadou was digging a small, deep hole. A long, bare tree trunk stretched on the ground beside him. He looked up, wiped his brow. Saw me. Smiled and beckoned with his chin that I should join them. I took two full steps into this magic place. Tipi smiled to see me, and Patrice too.

"Rum, matant?" Oreste held out a calabash. I took it and put it to my lips. The smell was strong. Raw white rum. "Devil's drink," the blans called it. I smiled around the curve of the hard calabash rind in my mouth. So tonight, I'm a devil.

I took a swallow. It caught in my throat, hit my chest like a blow. I coughed. Could feel my eyes tearing up. I gave the calabash back to Oreste. "No more." He grinned at me and put the calabash to his head. By fire flame, I watched his throat work. I think he drank every drop. He went from me, over to the drummers, and took his place.

A shadow stood up from the shadows where the trees were. Made me jump. "Honour, Mer." He came over to me.

"Respect, Makandal." Eh. Thought he was up in the bush with his maroons. "What are you doing here?"

"Come to dance," he said. "To sing. I miss the kalenda. And you? You come to join us?"

"Yes," I said, "to dance." There was more meaning to his question than that, but I would find out all that in a little bit.

He leaned close to me and looked hard in my eyes. "You mean, you've seen sense finally?"

Half a truth would maybe quiet him. "The Lady told me I must come here to learn sense," I said. I pointed up to the moon. With every word from me, I smelt the spirit of the rum coming back out of my mouth. Strong.

Makandal whispered, "They still talk to you, then? The woman gods of the rivers and the sea; of the moon?"

Eh. Still this hard-ears man hadn't learned. "Yes, for I serve them."

"Yes, so well you serve. Help the Ginen endure, help them accept."

I shrugged. "How are we going to do otherwise?" But my belly turned in me, in defiance of my own words. I hated to live this life in Saint Domingue.

Makandal leaned in closer to me. "We can fight, Mer. We are plenty, and the blans are few. The gods will help us."

Is it so? When Mama couldn't even make her power felt here in this land? "I'm not sure they will help, Makandal. Not sure they can."

He just laughed. "It's all right, Mer. I've found who I serve."

"Sometimes I fear that you serve only yourself."

He kissed his teeth, irritated, but before he could say anything, Oreste called out, "Makandal! We going to start now?"

Makandal turned his head. "Yes, brother! Soon come!"

He looked back at me. "If your spirits sent you here, Mer, I'm glad of it. They're here to witness how I fight for them too. Fight for the Ginen." He walked towards the fire.

The flames on Makandal's face made him look like a thing born in fire. Tempered. It's truth he was speaking to me just now. Makandal wanted to clear us a path to freedom too, just like I wanted to do. We should chop that clear road together. I saw another familiar figure in the flickering dark. Eh! Marie-Claire! I went and stood by her. She smiled and took my hand.

Plenty listening ears all around us. I didn't want to talk her business too loud. "How you came all this way, child? Where's your husband?"

"He won't miss me tonight, matant. He drank the draft I gave him, and he's sleeping deep and hard. A horse brought me here. A beautiful lame horse, with half its right front leg missing."

314

The helpless look of love on her face made me shiver. And there was Makandal, over by the drummers, gazing back at her like she was his life. Oh, Mama! This is what you brought me here to witness?

Oreste brought his hands down on his drum, once, hard, then started up a new rhythm. The other drummers followed. Something different to this drumming now. Makandal, he was dancing, tumpa and tumpa to the drums. No kalenda this. What was he doing? People swaying. Somebody singing now, a hoarse old voice. Bella?

The words. The words. It's like I almost remembered them. Remembered a hand warm on my shoulder, and me small. Standing wrapped in beautiful cloth, such bright colours. Me looking up into a face; my mother's face. Her smooth skin, like clay. I have more wrinkles now than my mother did. Her eyes, how they gleamed when she smiled. The coils and coils of her braided hair.

Makandal stamped the ground, leapt into the air. Landed and spun around, low. Marie-Claire cried out, "Ye-kê-kê-kê-kê-kê-kê!" Made me start. Didn't know that little bit of girl had so much voice in her. Joy on her face, in the swinging of her body. And Makandal jerking one way, the next way. Matching her. He didn't even know that he did it, so deeply his spirit called to hers. So Mother Sea reflected the clouds in the sky. So the wood took the shape of the axe head that bit it. Not good.

Then he stopped, sudden, like somebody had transfixed him with a machète. I gasped. But no, there was no one near him. No blade sticking out of him. Almost he fell, but two men rushed from the crowd and caught him. They held him upright. His eyes were only whites. Drunk he looked, bad drunk, and a mad grin on his face. He looked around him like he was seeing something else; not this clearing, not these people. "Papa Oguuu!" Someone shouted.

What was this? I took Marie-Claire's hand in mine and held tight. "Don't worry, matant," she whispered. "He's all right. The ancestor is on his head now, is all."

A lwa? No, no! Makandal isn't supposed to do this; he's not a priest, not a real one, for all he claims to be! Only the true priests of Africa should take the gods into their heads. Not for us Ginen to do! "We must stop him!" I hissed at Marie-Claire.

"No, no, matant," she said. The Ginen all around us were all dancing, singing, calling out. Surrounded by them I was, by pressing bodies. No way to move. "It's right, matant. Papa Ogu began to come to Makandal little bit ago. Ogu will free us." She smiled and patted my hand.

The blacksmith ancestor will free us? The warmaker? Mama, is it this you want me to see? I stood and stared at dancing Makandal. My stomach churned in me, sick.

DOWN

Makandal huffed like a racing horse. He staggered. Marie-Claire screamed and tried to run to him, but the bodies around us prevented her. Makandal caught himself. Stood up straight. His eyes, his eyes; rolled back in his head till all I could see was the whites. What was his soul looking on? He smiled, a terrible smile. His lips skinned back hard from his bared teeth. "Oh," said Marie-Claire. She looked happy. "He's all right now."

"My Ginen, are you here?" called Makandal. Wasn't his voice that. Was deeper than his and rough. He spread his arms, the whole one and the half. When the moon caught it just right, I could see his missing right hand. Was that a machète it was clutching; one with an iron blade? But I could see right through it, and sometimes it wasn't there. "Are you here to fight for your freedom?" Makandal shouted.

"Yes, Ogu!" the crowd shouted back.

Oh, you gods. Not so loud. Too much noise they're making.

I look in the streaming possibilities, spy the forked and branching channels of Makandal's flow. A strong man, with vision. A fierce and necessary man. He can burn Saint Domingue clean and free like brush fire clears the bush for planting. But what is he doing here tonight? It was folly to come! He should bide his time, let his generals do his work. He can rout the slavekeepers, if only he keeps himself safe! But there he is, on backra land, doing the dance, the call for me. I can help him. I will be able to go into his head. I will make him go back to the bush, to safety. Now . . .

"Back away, back away, watery one, cunted one. This horse is mine, not for you. He's mine.

What? What is that on Makandal's head? What are you?

"I tell you, he's not for you, O fish. He fights for me. With iron. With steel. With fire. Back away."

People were holding him, but Makandal's body threw itself one way then another. He roared. Marie-Claire squeezed my hand tighter. "What's wrong?" she muttered. "It's never been so for him."

Leave him to me! It's me he's calling! He should not be here!

"He doesn't care for his own skin, for his safety. He cares for the Ginen more than himself. He's my child. That's our way, him and me. Souls of war, forged in conflagration. Swim away, water child, moon child. Go. LEAVE US!"

He pushes me. That thing in Makandal's head pushes me out. And I'm floating in the nothing, the rushing nothing between being in one body and another. It's tossing me like waves. Nothing I can do. He handled me, *pushed* me into the river!

SEE

For a time I simply float, gulping in the waters, trying to comprehend that there is another power; this Ogu. Yet another! Not a fractal reflection of me, but something else, new. Male. I cannot fathom it. It is too deep. I am working so hard to take it all in, and here is yet another thing.

I scan the branching echoes of the Ginen mind. They are supposed to be mine, those waters. Mine to travel, to mind. The springs of them feed rivers which flow into seas, which dash themselves dry, beached on the chancre.

The cancer that blocks the waters' flows still hunkers there in my vision, bloating. As soon as I chop some away, more grows back. Time has no past or future for me, just an eternal now. But like a human, I am now trapped in "had been." I thought I had learned my task. I had met myselves, had learned that I must fracture in order to fight. And I was fighting well. *Am* fighting well. But now, here is another, fighting me, and he is a Power too.

Well, water puts out fire. I gather my swells and eddies, suck in tsunamis, leave off chopping at the greedy chancre, and charge to spit oceans in the eye of that other, that him.

Joël would likely be gone most of the night. So dark in here. Must buy some lamp oil. I'd kept a few sous back from him.

Tapping the walls with my cane in the blackness, I dragged myself to the parlour, got the rum out of the cabinet. Looked on the windowsill. Yes, there were some raw eggs left. I'd been boiling them in a little pot I held over the lamp flame. Joël and I had been eating them with hard tack and cheese, but the cheese was done. We ate the last mouldy rind yesterday.

I made a little crack in one of the eggs and sniffed. Not spoiled yet. Praise be. I was hungry as the devil, and no one to see to me. I'd let Laetitia go long since, to find someone who could pay for her services.

I broke the egg into the rum. Beat it with a fork, watched the rum go creamy-yellow. Threw the fork onto the counter with the other dirty things. The falling fork broke a green, smelly crust off a fancy plate. The whole room reeked of rotted food. I had no heart to fetch water to wash the dishes in. Icy, the water from the well was. It made my hands burn. I needed a bath, but I couldn't be bothered. The whole world seemed dull and dark and cold.

The mice had been nibbling at the sugar loaf again. Little black mouse-droppings lay like raisins all around it in a circle, and I could see the marks of their teeth in the cone of hard sugar. I scraped a handful of sugar off it. Grandmaman had liked this drink sweet. I mixed in the sugar, used a knife to chivvy slivers off some nutmeg that Achille had brought. I kept a piece of nutmeg in the corner of my mouth all the time now, like my juju woman said. Made me less nauseated.

The sweet, sharp scent of the punch soothed me. I took the glass to my bedroom. Got awkwardly under the covers. Cold, my God, so cold. No money for more wood. Eh. Should have burned Charles's mildewed old books and papers, instead of trying to sell them. Would have got more good from them that way.

I put the glass to my head. It tasted creamy, and the rum bit nicely, and the nutmeg smell was a comfort. Grandmaman used to say that the egg strengthened the blood. I needed strong blood now. I was getting headaches plenty, like Charles. I sucked and sucked carefully from the glass and tried not to spill any from the side of my ruined mouth. I drank until there was no more. I pulled myself from under the covers and went and made another one. Then a third. There were no more eggs after that. Didn't know what Joël and I would have for breakfast. Didn't care. I didn't finish that third drink. I remember leaning over to set it on the nightstand, and the room tilting at an angle. Don't know when I slept.

Look, over the treetops," roared Makandal in someone else's voice. He pointed the machète with his ghostly hand, his hand that extended into the other world. We looked where he pointed. Smoke! Red sky! It was coming from the great house. Oh, my mother; the Ginen had set it on fire! Marie-Claire yodelled her triumph cry, and the rest of the Ginen joined her. Mama; should I be glad?

I suck at him with whirlpools, yet he only laughs. He steams my substance away to nothing. I roar at him with waters; he roars at me with flames, and I flinch from the heat. I try to drown him, but he engulfs me. I battle with him for Makandal, but I can't get into Makandal, no matter how I push. The other one riding him is stronger.

People would burn over there, white people and the brown slaves of Master's house. Mama! Tell me! What to do?

But there is another pull. A person is calling me. No drums, no dance, but she calls. And then there I am, in her head. Mer, this one is. I float in the streaming story of her, and I know her. Good, I have a body now. I can act in the world.

I felt the world going away from me. I staggered. Eh. So odd it felt. Like being a visitor in my own body. Like I was watching myself. Noise all around me, and fire, and drumming. People dancing and crying. Makandal dancing. The dirt crumbling beneath my feet. The smoky scent of burning wood, the musk-sweat of the Ginen all around me. My feet began to stamp, my body to twirl. Marie-Claire let go of my hand. Her eyes were big.

The other Ginen backed away. Could hear, me; voices whispering, "Mer? Who's that? Matant?"

Twirled and stamped, me, till I broke free of the crowd. I rushed like tidal waters to where Makandal stood, grinning his berserker grin. "Ogu!" My voice crashed, the way the breakers smash against the cliffs. Salt sea that I was smelling?

Makandal turned, looked at me. "Yes, wife?"

Wife? I am no wife to you!

"Go back to the bush," I heard myself say.

There is a smile that certain fighters get in the thick of battle. Ogu rides them, and they know their cause to be righteous, and they fear nothing. See nothing but the fight. Feel no pain. And they smile, smile. Skin their lips back from their teeth like they've already drawn back their blades to deal you their death blow. And they are not there behind their eyes. That was the smile that Makandal turned on me now. "I belong here," he said. "By the fire. With iron in my hands. Stay out of my way, old woman."

He is like me, Makandal's rider. So we are not alone in our land of aether, Hathor and I. Ogu, they call this one. I call him usurper. Outrage fills me, but no time, no time! This battle is happening in the mortal world of time, and time is flowing away, like water poured on desert sands. Ogu is pitched for battle. Makandal wouldn't listen to Mer my horse, but in the many flowing strands of the Ginen's story, I could see a thing I could do. Mer could warn the slaves in the great house of the fire. She could protect those my people. And she could mislead the whites, send them away from this bush meeting. She could take me to them, and I could beguile them as I had before. I could speak to them through

a white woman's body. I turn Mer's body to run, tumble, flow through the bush to the great house, to save, to save.

I turned to run; there were Ginen in the great house, sleeping. "Stop her!" Makandal shouted. I heard the rifle shot, but I wasn't hit. I took two more steps, but screaming stopped me. I turned. Marie-Claire lay on the ground, her chest covered in blood. It was Patrice screaming Marie-Claire's name over and over again. Hector was the one with the gun. He looked so stricken, it was as though he'd shot himself, not sweet Marie-Claire who'd thrown herself in the way to protect me.

Makandal looked at her, griefstruck, then staggered. Stood again. He pointed at me. "She was going to warn the blancs! Hold her!"

Ginen bodies grabbed me, dragged me to the ground. I landed so hard, all the breath was pushed out of me. They had shot Marie-Claire. *Tipi,* I thought, *I'm sorry.*

Ginen hands turned me over on my back. I tried to make the air come back in my body. Ogu was standing over me in Makandal's body. He grinned his terrible grin. "Hold her good there," he said. He knelt by my side. "Going to talk our business, Mer?"

I tried to tell him no, but I couldn't speak, just listen to the singing in my nose as my chest tried to suck air.

"That tongue won't wag any more," he told me. "You. Hold her head. You. Open her mouth."

He reached his good hand into my mouth and took hold of my tongue. His hand tasted of ashes and rum. Mama, no! Mama! I struggled, but too many held me. He drew out my tongue until it stuck from my mouth, slimy in his hand, but still he held it.

What will you do to this body? No!

Too much egg punch, and made with the last of our eggs, too. In the morning I woke to the drums banging in my head. Oh, my soul. Too much rum. I ventured a hand out from beneath my warm covers. The glass was on the night table, overturned. The drink that had spilled out of it was frozen.

I needed to piss. I clambered out of bed, shivering. Thought I would swoon with the pain from my head. Did my business on top of the piss ice already in the chamber pot. Filled up the chamber pot. Must go and empty it.

My head spinned when I stood up. Thought I would vomit. I tried not to let my mind run on the three raw eggs I had drunk.

I clattered out into the living room. My head, my head. And suddenly, there it was again, like that time before. Something struck me down with a great blow. A light exploded behind my eyes.

BLOW

Ogu in Makandal's body used his good hand to draw my tongue out from my mouth. Then, smiling, he used the arm that was not there and sliced the spirit machète across my tongue.

Pain exploded like light in my head. I tried to scream, but with no air in my chest, it came out a gurgle.

With that axe slash, the river, the mighty rolling river that is one Ginen story crashes full tilt into a dam. Its waters boil and boil, angry; and go nowhere. That story is stopped dead in its bed. The pain of it throws me back in time, back into living Jeanne.

Another lightflash of agony felled me. I saw the chamber pot flying from my hands, the yellow piss leaping out in a curve from it. Everything was happening slowly. Felt my knees hit the carpet.

And then nothing.

HOLE

Pain. Pain; so bad I thought I would vomit. I begged Mama to let me faint. So bad that my flailing threw off the Ginen holding me. They went to pin me down again, but Ogu motioned them back. Pain. I rolled on the ground. I could breathe again, but when I cried out, no sound came. I reached to touch my tongue. It was there. I tried to say, *What did you do*, but no words came.

And Ogu only smiled. "Your tongue will never talk Ginen business again," he said.

The roaring dammed waters grew quiet and stagnant. Home for mosquitoes and cholera. Pushed out of Mer's head, of Jeanne's, in shock, insensible, I floated.

I hoped I'd never go back to that sanatorium. I didn't remember the nuns taking me there. Didn't remember anything after I'd fallen to the floor, unconscious. Joël found me that morning, got a doctor to see to me. Had Charles pay for it. It was Charles had given the money to take me to the sanatorium. But two weeks of the nuns' disdain of my black body was enough for a lifetime. I was glad to be going home.

It was dark when I got back to Neuilly from Paris. The money Charles had sent was enough for the train, but I had to walk the rest of the way. So cold! By the time I made it to the front door, my hands were fair frozen. It took likely ten minutes before I could breathe enough warmth into them that they would grasp the key so I could turn it in the lock.

No lamps lit in the house. Maybe Joël was truly gone, then. I stepped inside. Had to be careful not to bump into the furniture. So *cold* it was in here! But here I was now, arrived on the other side of the room, yet my cane had hit nothing. Didn't strike the table, like it usually does, nor the armchair. Why did my cane make a sound so hollow when it tapped? I turned to look back the way I had walked. Slack as an old woman's mouth when she sleeps, the front door creaked open. It gave me light from the streetlamps to see by.

Oh, you gods. The room was empty. Not a stick of furniture. All gone. "Joël," I whispered. "How you could do me so?"

A small, snuffling noise came from the depths of the apartment. Then a whimper. Tati, my Tatiana limped out, not so much flesh on her as on a rat. She looked, and when she saw it was really me, wagged her precious tail. Ran haltingly over and begged to be taken up. She was nothing but hair and bones in my hands. I kissed her. "Oh, my little girl, I'm so sorry. When last did you eat?"

She just licked my face. The salt from my skin was all the comfort I could give her, for I had no food.

Mother of memories, mistress of mistresses,
O thou, my pleasure, thou, all my desire,
Thou shalt recall the beauty of caresses,
The charm of evenings by the gentle fire,
Mother of memories, mistress of mistresses!
                              —From "The Balcony," by Charles Baudelaire

Not even a bed that bastard Joël had left me; not even a quilt. In my room, my clothes were all tumbled out onto the floor. He had tossed them out of the dresser, then taken the dresser. He would get plenty money for Charles's furniture.

I wadded up as much of the clothes as I could carry in the weak arm and the strong one. Went back to the living room. Tati followed me.

One half-burnt log had been left in the fireplace. I found matches. Stuffed the clothes into the fireplace, and put the log on top. My gowns took the flame right quickly. They spat, throwing off beautiful sparks of blue and gold. Damned log took forever to catch, though, and the dresses burnt to ashes very soon. I was trembling from the cold before the log began to glow. I threw more gowns on top of it. I took another gown, the warm silk one with the pink stripes that Charles had made fun of. I had made the customers cheer when I danced in that gown. I pulled it on over my dress, not caring how I looked. I made myself a bed of gowns on the floor. Tati climbed into it and looked at me, her eyes shining. Not a morsel I had to give her, yet she loved me still. It made me weep. Clumsy, I got into our bed. I curled up beside her, drew my coat over us both and closed my eyes, praying for the room to heat up soon.

As Gypsy Mary knelt and prayed in supplication at the foot of the statue of the Virgin, she felt a presence come upon her. She swooned and fell insensible to the ground. She heard the voice of the Virgin Mary, forgiving her sins and telling her that she could enter the church. Gypsy Mary stood, and this time was able to pass within the church without any difficulty. Inside, she adored the Holy Cross and kissed the floor of the church. She then returned to the statue of the Virgin.

—Adapted from various Catholic texts about the life
of Saint Mary of Egypt, the "dusky" saint

Thais?"

"Ah?" I responded.

Judah scrunched back a little further into the cave, where there was some shade. I was sitting just inside the cave mouth. Red rock and dirt as far as the eye could see. Away at the horizon, low down, light shimmered on the ground. I'd learned that though it looked like water, it wasn't. No sense in walking towards it, hoping for a drink. It only disappeared. I wasn't thirsty, anyway.

It was peaceful out here. I had left my bed in some nun's cell that was attached to the Church of the Sepulchre, and just walked, away from people. Well, not Judah. I let him follow me. We went for hours, past the river Jordan, out into the desert where it was quiet. I guess it was hot out here. I couldn't seem to feel it. "What were you saying, Judah?"

"I just want to know . . ."

I touched my belly, rubbed it. The baby had been growing in there. "Well? What do you want to know?"

"Gods," he said, "I hope there aren't any more scorpions in here." He shuddered and pulled his knees up to his chin. "That last one was the size of a donkey, I swear. How much longer are we going to stay here, Thais?"

I wonder if it would have been a boy or a girl.

"Thais?"

I wonder if it would have looked like Antoniou, or like me.

"Pretty Pearl?"

Maybe like both of us. Brown, but not so brown as me, and with big, black eyes, and a mass of thick, soft hair like spun wool—the best kind of wool—and lips like pomegranates.

"We could still go to my uncle's place," Judah said. "There's a man in town who says he'll take us there, for a fee. We could bed a few soldiers and earn the money that way."

"Hmm."

"Or maybe I could work the soldiers by myself, you know? Maybe you're still not feeling well."

I think it would have been a girl. I'm sure of it, as if someone had whispered it in my ear. I could have named her Meritet, like Little Doe's always calling me.

"Or maybe we could go home, Thais? To Alexandria, I mean?"

"Meritet."

"What?"

"Call me Meritet."

"Meritet?" he said.

"Yes?" I patted my belly. I'd never even felt a swelling there. Nothing to warn me. There'd been too much noise around me, and I couldn't hear.

I looked at Judah. Looked like someone had dipped their finger in the river and traced a line down each of his cheeks in the dirt that covered them. It got everywhere, this Capitolina dust. "Why are you crying?" I asked him. "Why are you looking at me like that?"

"Nothing." His face was so sad. He crawled past me out of the cave. He stood. "I'll go and get us some more water."

The river wasn't so close. We'd really come a long way out of the city. I looked at the sun. "You won't be back until sundown." I crawled to the back of the cave, where we'd stored our stuff. I could tell that my knees were grating on stones, but I just couldn't feel it. I found the amphora, the one that had held the olives we'd stolen from Tausirus, those weeks ago. I went back to the mouth of the cave and handed the amphora to Judah. "See if you can get some beans, too, okay? The green ones, still in the pods."

He sighed. "Don't you want anything else, Thais?"

"Meritet."

"Okay, you're Meritet. You sure you only want beans? That's all you've eaten since we came here."

"That's all I want."

I heard him trudging off over the desert, but I didn't pay much attention. They told me at the church that I was full, and now I'm empty. But if the baby's gone, why do I still feel like someone's living in me?

There were tiny pebbles embedded in my knees, because I'd crawled on them. Some of them were ringed in blood. I scrubbed the pebbles away, sucked at the red smears left on my thumb.

I didn't like going to the river, anyway. I'd look at that running water and I'd feel the blood come running out of me again, the wet, rushing blood that had carried my unborn baby away.

Full. I was so full. I lay back on the narrow rag of carpet that Judah had found for the floor of the cave. I closed my eyes. It was quiet here, and dry. No rushing.

Gypsy Mary knelt once more at the feet of the Virgin, and prayed for guidance. Our Lady appeared to her again, and told her to cross the river Jordan and go eastward. This she did the following day.

—Adapted from various Catholic texts about the life of Saint Mary of Egypt, the "dusky" saint

Gods," Patrice whispered. "I don't want to see this." Father had set up his altar outside, here where they were going to burn Makandal, right in Cap Haïtien's square. He was standing over the altar, mumbling. Me, I was praying, praying, for the burning not to happen. Makandal was half djinn. I was praying for him to use his power. Why hadn't he gotten away from them?

There were blans milling around. White men sweating in dark wool. They whispered together, then talked in loud voices, in France French. They looked angry, frightened. So did the Ginen. The book-keeper was supervising two of our men as they beat a pole into the ground. They had no choice, those two. They were going to kill one of us. Kill the man who'd helped them fight for freedom. What had I helped my Ginen fight for?

Little Ti-Bois stood by, watching, his mouth open. Mama, I'm sorry. I hadn't fought, hadn't cleared your roads to freedom for your people. I got no answer from her. Shamed, needing comfort, I reached for the glass whale knotted into my skirt. Just held the knot in my hand.

I feel Mer's hand tighten around the knot of me. Glass me. No body, no colour. I didn't help her that night when Ogu cut her. I can't help them, any of them. I am no use. I will leave her limbs under her own control.

Patrice kept stepping a little way forward, a little way back. His feet wanted to pace and pace, I could see it. Tipingee took his hand to still him. He glanced at the backras standing over us with guns, and he held quiet. Let his arms hang long at his side. Tipingee held one hand to her neck and closed her eyes for a little bit. I saw her other hand go even tighter around Patrice's own. There were roads in Saint Domingue lined with African heads on poles. The blans wouldn't call it war, but they were killing us. Every day more of us. Hundreds by each sunset, we heard. The Ginen in the great house told us. They heard it from our master, who spoke freely with his friend in front of them, for he thought the Ginen too stupid to understand the France French. Master Simenon was sickly a lot nowadays, and his woman too. Marie-Claire was no longer there to season their food with Makandal's poison, but another cook had taken over the task.

Patrice was rocking little bit from side to side now, frantic for his friend. Hold still, Patrice. Hold still, and keep your head.

I stood where I was, just a silent nègre woman. My tongue wouldn't speak since Ogu took my voice from me. Tipingee had more lines on her face now. But Marie-Claire had lived. They had sent her home to her brown man, and he was having her tended. She was healing. Hope somebody watching her knew to bathe her wound every day with hot water, to give her garlic tea to drink.

There stood the hut that held Makandal. No windows on it. Must be hot as the Christian Hell in there. Bolts on the door. But no chains could hold Makandal. Why he hadn't escaped?

I prayed to the Lady on Father's altar. So many gods. Must ask them all for help.

The Ginen from the great house stood a little way off, dressed in the master's and mistress's cast-off clothes. So fine, those clothes looked. Clean. There was Georgine, her little boy twisting in her arms, bored. Pierre stood with them.

The men were finished putting up the pole. Two blans broke away from the rest, motioned to one of the other blans with a gun to follow them. They went to Makandal's prison hut. They drew the bolts back and opened the door. All the Ginen drew as near as we dared. Did a goat run free from that cage, or a cat? Did a bird fly out of it?

No. The three blans went in, and presently they came back out of them. Two of them had Makandal, bound, between them. Tipi gasped. Belle and Hector began to cry. Because Makandal had no right wrist to bear the shackles, they had shackled the left, then wound the chains completely around him, trapping his arms against his body. How many days he had stayed like that? How had he made water, said his prayers?

Makandal stumbled. The blans held him up. He blinked in the sun. From the state of his britches, I could see that he had had to piss and shit right there where he lay, in his clothes. Like being on the ships again. I couldn't bear seeing this, but I must watch. Makandal, come away from them!

His face was bruised, one eye puffy. He looked about, peered into the crowd. "Marie-Claire?" he shouted, hoarse.

"She lives, Makandal!" Patrice shouted to his friend. "She's well!"

Makandal nodded, smiled. Some of his teeth were broken.

One of the backra men with the guns stepped up to Patrice, threatened him with the butt end of it. "Shut up," he said.

Patrice looked down. "Sorry, sir." The man went back to his post.

Makandal's executioners, they led him to the pole in the ground. They stood him up against it. Someone brought more chain. They wouldn't use rope, for rope might burn up and set him free. Chain they could recover from the flames and use again. They began to wind the chain around Makandal and the pole both. The pole we raise up when we worship, the poteau-mitan, is the ladder for the gods. This is not what the centre pole is for.

Ogu, why don't you free your son? Mother, why is this happening? You gods? Where are you?

The blans finished tying Makandal to the pole. Their man kept his rifle trained on Makandal, though. They had him, but they feared him still. Now the book-keeper had the two Ginen men bring the firewood and pile it around Makandal's feet. One of them murmured to Makandal, touched his shoulder. For that, the man got hit with the butt end of the rifle. He reeled away, went to get more firewood. Patrice made a small sound in his throat. Not even that I could do. Oh, let me not see this.

The Ginen men finished piling up the wood and came back to join us. Tears ran down both their faces. And still Makandal didn't make his move. What drama was he planning?

"Ginen!" Makandal shouted. The man with the gun threatened him, but Makandal only looked upon him. "Let me speak," he said. The words came mushy out of his broken mouth. The man lowered his gun.

"Are you hearing me?" Makandal shouted again.

"Yes, Makandal!" we said. Even me, I said it, though no sound came out. Let them shoot us all, all for speaking, but we replied to Makandal.

"I will come back!" he said. "I won't leave you!"

He had a plan, then. Thank you, gods. Still we cried, sucking salt through our noses, but some of us were smiling now as we wept.

One of the blan executioners took a tinder box from his pocket. He bent to the kindling and worked until a flame caught. The man stepped away, grinning. He pointed at the flames, at Makandal. "There's your rebel now!" he shouted. Tipi reached a hand to me. Then Patrice did. I went and stood with them, holding their hands, but facing out from them so that I could see Makandal. I had to bear witness.

Makandal looked down at the flames. They weren't touching him yet. He tried to shift his feet away, but the chains held him too tight.

So many black people I had seen die in pain, quickly or slowly, since I came to this place. But oh, you gods; burning takes a long time. The burning one screams until he has no more voice, but still he tries to scream. His skin, his flesh, sizzles and blackens. It smells like pork roasting. He tries and tries to pull free of the fire. His clothes, his hair, go up in flames and finally hide his ruined face. All this we watched, the Ginen. Even some of the blans watching—Simenon's wife, the other women, and some of the men—were weeping by the time it was done, by the time the column of fire that had been Makandal gave one last, terrible shout. The pole holding him snapped right in half. So horrible a noise it made. The burning thing that had been a man collapsed into the embers. When it fell, a wail went up amongst the Ginen. Then Fleur shouted, "Look! There he goes!" She pointed into the air, her face alive with joy. "See? A manmzèl!"

We rushed forward. Some of them could see it, see the manmzèl buzzing in the air, heading for the sky. They laughed and held each other, they danced. I could not see it. I did see one thing, though. I saw the door to Makandal's prison creak open as the wind blew by it. I saw inside. I saw the pan on the floor, that he had had to eat from with his arms bound, crouching on the ground like a dog. Some food was still in that pan. A length of salted pig tail, curled pink around itself, and a flat, ashy chunk of dried salt fish. Nothing else looked like that. They hadn't even cooked it, had just given him the pickled meat to eat. All this time, they had been feeding him salt, subduing the djinn part of him. Without the djinn, he couldn't change.

Did he eat the food? Or did he starve himself and fly free one last time? Mama, what just happened here?

Belle was leaping and prancing, shouting Makandal's name over and over. Ti-Bois just stood and shook, snot bubbling from his nose. His mother was kneeling beside him. "It's all right, petit," she was saying. "He felt some pain, but he's all right now. He is." Ti-Bois didn't look so sure. I wasn't sure either. The smell of burnt flesh was still in my nose. In my head, I could still hear him screaming in agony. I wanted to believe that Makandal flew away, but my wishes can't fly freely so. They're rooted to the ground like me, who eats salt.

It was the knocking at the door that woke me next morning. The fireplace was cold, full of grey ash. I could see metal clasps lying in it, and scorched buttons. In the air I could taste the reek of burnt cloth; the dyes, the sizing. I sat up. Tati licked my face. Her breath was foul. It hurt to move.

The knocking came, louder. Charles? Come to save me? I clambered to my feet, fell onto the lame knee, got up again. Charles? I stumbled towards the front room. "I'm coming! Wait just a little!" The knocking stopped, and I feared he'd gone away again. "Charles?"

I heard the door open before I got there. He came in. Oh, God; reprieve from this horror. I felt the tears of joy start to come. Tati flew ahead of me, barking. Then I heard the little whimpers she gave when she was happy and being stroked by a friend she hadn't seen in a long time. Charles, bless you for coming for us. I stepped into the front room.

There in my home stood Moustique, the gambler. Joël's friend. He straightened up from patting my dog. He was smiling, the blackguard.

"What, come for the rest of my things to hock?" I shouted. I flew at him as best I might, and struck him in the chest with my fist. His look of dismay pleased me. But my weak arm betrayed me; it was only a glancing blow. "Get out! Get out! You and Joël! Damn you both!"

I beat at him with both hands. Tati leapt around us, barking for joy at the game. I got Moustique across his cheek with my nails. Ah, there! A line of red sprang up on his face. I reached to give him another, but he took my wrists in his. Small as he was, it took him a little fight to get control of me.

"Lemer, stand off!" he said, holding my wrists away from him. "I'm not here with Joël!"

Come by himself to rob me, had he? I kicked his shins. With the good foot, unfortunately. The weak one wouldn't hold me, and I toppled. I knotted my hands in his lapels, so Moustique tumbled with me. I landed hard on him, heard the air get knocked out of him. Good. Bastard. I commenced to slapping him again. Tati joyfully took a corner of my frock in her teeth, started growling and pulling at it.

"Lemer, please!" Moustique tried to fasten my hands again, but I pulled away from him.

"You are the blackest type of African!" I shouted. "Preying on a poor, sick woman! You and my brother!"

He was holding his hand to his injured face, watching me to see if I would fly at him again. "I sent him to jail for you," he said.

"What?"

"I have just sent my friend to jail for thieving from you. He wouldn't bring the things back. I told him I would do this if he didn't. It was wrong of him to treat you so. I told him. He laughed. I had to keep my word." His eyes glistened wet.

"You . . . I . . ." I fell silent.

He sat up. "I came to tell you. The officers are returning all your furniture. Today. It will be years before Joël is free. He'll come out hating me, if he survives. I'm very sorry for all of it. I am sorry, Lemer."

And then he did cry, this grown man. For the thing he'd done. For his friend betrayed. For me. Just quiet tears, rolling down. Tati went and licked his face. "Phew," Moustique said; "you smell like carrion, dog. Here." He pulled something out of his pocket, wrapped in bloodstained newspaper. He unwrapped it. A meaty neckbone, raw. "Lamb," he said to me. He put it on the floor and Tati leapt upon it. My stomach gurgled with hunger.

351

With the back of his hand, Moustique wiped his tears away. He stood and then reached out to help me up. I got to my feet, and finally beheld him well. His coat was thrown on over his chef's whites. He was wearing an apron under the coat. The apron was all stained, dark red, down the front. I pointed to the stain. "What happened? Did you kill the lamb yourself, then?"

He looked down at himself and smiled. "Oh. I spilt wine, making a beef Bourguignon. I heard you were coming home from the hospital. Didn't want you to arrive and see this." He waved about the empty room with his hand. "I rushed to get here to tell you that you would have your things back. Forgot to change. It's nothing."

Oh, you gods. Not nothing. Not nothing at all. My mind threw me back to another place. *A bed, and me and Lise in it. And a vision in a pot of piss.* A man in a red-stained apron, standing in an empty room, twisting his hat in his hands. Just so Moustique had been doing when I saw him standing in my apartment just now. And a woman's arm, coming at him. And her in a pink-striped gown. I looked down at the extra gown I'd pulled on for warmth, its gaudy silk stripes spilling off my shoulder to show the drab dress underneath. "Heaven strike me dead," I murmured. "It was you Lise and I saw."

Moustique took a step to me, took my hand in his; gently this time. "Jeanne? Are you all right?"

I just looked at him. Hadn't been able to make out his features well that night he appeared in our piss pot. "What will you do now?" I asked.

"Me? What will *you* do, you mean. You are ill, Lemer."

"True enough. Been ill before." I didn't know what I would do. My features were too ravaged, my body too broken to dance any more.

"You can't stay here, with no one to look out for you. Your poet man says he can't help you any more. He's beggared. I'm working in Paris now, Jeanne. The pay is good, and they give me an apartment. Come and stay with me. Or in another apartment, if you prefer. Only come. Will you?"

Sometimes my grandmother would divine with cowrie shells. She would throw them to the ground. Sometimes she would look how they'd fallen, some open side up, some down, and she'd smile at the pattern they made. In my mind, I heard cowrie shells fall into a pleasing pattern. "Yes, Moustique. I will come."

His smile lit the day. "Good," was all he said on the matter, though. "And will you come with me right now for breakfast?"

You're dancing well, my Jeanne. Dancing in the groove I've laid for you, dancing a new story to your life. And if you can still dance, how dare I stop?

Moustique—Achille—was doing better than well in Paris. Has his own restaurant now. So long as he stays in the kitchen and cooks, the rich folk who come there to eat never know that the place is run by a black man's hands. Or a mulatresse's. They think I am but a maid, some white man's byblow given a position out of guilt.

I read much better now. I have had lots of practice, keeping the books for Chez Achille. And we eat well, Achille and I. Tatiana, too. She is fat and her coat is glossy. My health is sometimes fragile, but when I must take to my bed, Achille cares me well, whispers stories to me in the evenings. My hair has thinned, and sometimes for days, I am weak, weak. But Charlotte says that many people with the clap in their blood live long. Pray the gods I may be one of those. She says I cannot pass it to Achille, that it has taken root these many years in my body and wants no other host. I cried when she told me that. I could embrace my love and not fear to make him ill.

Achille kisses my balding scalp. Tells me he loves me. I have taken to wearing bright scarves on my head. I tie them in the tignon styles that my grandmother wore, and I hold my aching head high when I walk in the streets. Sometimes I have flour on my chin instead of powdered chalk. Sometimes I have ink on my hands instead of gloves, but I am a woman of property, and I am loved.

I think of Charles sometimes. The thought no longer makes my heart curdle in my chest. I hope that he is well.

"Daydreaming again, Jeanne?" Moustique sat on the bed beside me. He leaned over and nibbled my bare shoulder. The heat from his naked body warmed me. I nuzzled my face into his neck, smelling him. Sometimes I think that I take my lovers in through the nose. Lise had smelled warm and salty, like hot soup on a cold day. Charles had had a faint fragrance of fresh jism about him, except when he was in the depths of malaise. Then he smelt a little sour, like an ill baby, and you'd want to dandle him and feed him sugar water to soothe him. And Moustique? He smelled of clean sweat. Always made me want to make him sweat more. Today his scent was mixed with that of bread, fresh from the oven. He had been making pastries. The odour of vanilla and rosewater rose off his dark skin.

"You smell like a girl, all cheap perfume," I joked, saying the words carefully with my half-numb mouth.

He laughed and lay back on the bed. "And what would my lady like to do with her maidservant?" he asked.

I eyed the lean, hairless length of him. I smiled. My smile is only half of one these years past, but it doesn't frighten Achille. I reached for my dress that was lying on the bed; pulled it to me with my withered hand, then tossed it to him with my good one. "Put it on."

The tip of his prick jumped. A friendly delight came over his face. "Put it on you, or on me, chérie?" he asked, his voice gone rough.

Ah, we both know what we want from this game. "You're the one being girlish, wearing scent. Put it on you."

He leapt eagerly from the bed, his excitement evident. No one seeing the bulge he made in my frock would think him a girl. But we had found a solution for that, he and I. Sometimes we would bind that poking flesh up against his belly, then put my pantaloons on him. He could still feel me stroke him through the cloth. Sometimes he loved it better so, to pull up the dress he was wearing, to see the frilly underclothes beneath it.

He had the dress on now. He stood before me, posing for me, his chest out, his waist drawn in. "You are beautiful," I said.

"Such a beautiful girl." My cunny was getting warm. "But so dusky, that skin. Bring me the face paint," I ordered my lovely rude maid. "We will make you even more comely."

"Yes, Mistress," he whispered, and walked, hips swaying, to the dressing table. I sat and watched him, feeling like the happy old rouée I had become.

RIFF

Can vows and perfumes, kisses infinite,
Be reborn from the gulf we cannot sound;
And rise to heaven suns once again made bright
After being plunged in deep seas and profound?
Ah, vows and perfumes, kisses infinite!

—From "The Balcony," by Charles Baudelaire

So, he is dead." We had finished serving the noon meal at Chez Achille, and it was quiet now, only a few customers.

"Yes," Lise said. "I saw it in the paper this morning. In his mother's house, they say."

"She took him in when he got too sick, then? Huh. At least the old bitch did right by him in the end."

"Will you go to the funeral?" asked Lise. She sipped the coffee I had just poured for her. She closed her eyes and sighed. "Oh, perfect. Just bitter enough. Where does Moustique find this nectar?"

"Joël sends the beans specially, from his plantation in Haiti. Up in the mountains." That had been Achille's gift to Joël once Joël was out of prison; the money to set himself up wherever he wished. Joël had picked Haiti, and his letters to Moustique were friendly, if cool.

"Will you go? To the funeral, I mean?"

I considered. "It would make a lovely scandal, wouldn't it? The poet's cast-off black mistress, weeping aged crocodile tears at his graveside."

Lise grinned. "It would."

"But we are busy here that evening. A large family celebration."

Lise looked into my eyes, touched my hand gently. "You've changed, Lemer."

"Have I?"

"Do you miss me?"

"Sometimes I do."

"Will you sit with me a moment?"

I took a seat on the edge of one of the chairs. Can't have the patrons thinking I'm swift to take my ease. I put the heavy carafe of coffee down. Lise picked up her cup again, took a sip. She frowned. "Monsieur Shephard has asked for my hand."

361

I smiled broadly as I could. "Oh, Lise! So wonderful!"

Her lips bowed up a little at their ends. "Yes, I suppose it is. It's what we dreamed of, you and I. Fine men and fine fortunes."

"And no nigger babies for you." The words fell heedless from my ruined mouth. Her English beau was from their gentry, a wheaten-haired banker's son.

Lise blushed. "I was stupid that day, Lemer. I am sorry."

"I know, my dear." Our friendship was deep enough to hold hurt and joy both. I rubbed my leg, the one that dragged a little. Pins and needles in it today.

She bit her lips, looked at me. "I have something to ask of you. A big thing."

A wedding cake? A love spell from my juju woman? "What, sweet?"

"It's Stéphanie."

"Your daughter? Is she ill?"

Lise looked stricken. "Henry won't take her in when we marry. Says his family won't stand for the scandal." She put down the cup and seized both my hands in hers. "Oh, Jeanne, if she were with you, I'd know she still had a mother!"

I just sat. No words would come. A child to foster. I, who had never wanted children. Stéphanie was seven now; plump and merry as a young Lise. "I . . ." I looked at my Lise, my girl. She was no longer a girl. She hadn't had a part in the theatre for two years now. This man Shephard was solid, sensible, she said.

Stéphanie came and stayed with us sometimes. She upset our house, me and Moustique. She painted her cheeks blood-red with my rouge, put on my dresses and my fine shoes, then got flour all over them in the kitchen, making "dolls" with the dough that Moustique gave her. The cooks tripped over her, and gave her stomachaches from feeding her too many sweets. Her loud laughter disrupted our guests' meals. We laughed a lot with her when she was here.

"She can stay with us," I said, before I could change my mind. I knew Achille would love to have her live here.

Lise gave a cry and leapt to her feet. She took me in her arms, scandalising the genteel man and woman at the nearby table. "Jeanne, thank you," she murmured into my ear. "Henry will send you money for her upkeep. He promised he would. Stéphanie loves you and Achille, she's told me. You'll be so good for her!"

I just held my girl in my arms for the final time.

Mama Jeanne?"

"Hmm?" I handed Stéphanie the basket so that I could pick up my cane. Ten days I'd been abed this time, insensible. I was still a little weak, but I needed an outing. To the market for greens would do. "What is it, Stéphanie?"

She held the door open for me, and we stepped out into the spring day. Paris stank of dog shit, melting in the spring sun. "Why are boys so stupid?" she asked.

I laughed. "What has Richard done now?" Our sommelier's son was fourteen to Stéphanie's twelve.

She flounced along beside me, pouting and swinging the basket. "He keeps sneaking up on me and pinching my arm. I'm all bruised! Look!" She pushed up the sleeve of her frock to show me. I supposed that faint blush on her peach-fuzz arm might have come from a pinch.

"He likes you, Stéphanie."

She sucked her teeth in the African way. She had learned that from Moustique and me. "Richard is a dolt," she said.

"Hmm," I responded. "Have you told your maman about him?"

She frowned, so like Lise. When Stéphanie first came to us, it had been months of anger and tears for Lise having left her. She still wouldn't talk about Lise much, but I know she kept every letter from her mother in a scented box under her bed, tied about with a green ribbon. "Maman only wants to know if I'm doing my lessons," she said.

"Yes." Truth to tell, I wasn't paying much mind to her right then. That walk, that hat; I knew that man.

"Stéphanie," I said, fumbling in my purse. "Here's some money. Go and get us some pommes Pont-Neuf from that vendor across the street."

She looked at me, confused. She'd never seen me eat from the vendors. She didn't know there had been a time that was most of what I ate. But she went.

The man I had seen was approaching me now, on the same side of the street. Some of his hair had gone grey, but he still walked spry. He hadn't seen me yet. I was used to acting on the stage. It was an easy thing to slump a little lower over my cane, to limp a little more. An easy thing to let my drooping mouth go even slacker. To scowl. I was wearing an old, faded dress and run-down shoes; just good for tromping through the mess of the market. But Nadar wouldn't know that. He would only see a beggar.

I limped towards him, my eyes hooded, muttering. I saw him start. Now he knew me. Knew that the ailing, bedraggled old witch with her head tied in a black woman's tignon was Jeanne Duval, named Lemer, sometimes called Prosper. I heard him gasp. I made shift not to notice my previous lover, the famous photographer. I hobbled by. I was in the life I wanted now. His world of salons and manners held no flavour for me any more. I walked on.

"Mama Jeanne!" shouted Stéphanie, running back across the road. She held out a newspaper cone filled with steaming chunks of fried potato to me.

I straightened tall, and smiled at her. "Thank you, child," I said, and took the food from her.

A few months later, she dies a happy woman, Jeanne does. At first when I got trapped in her body, I set her on the path of joy out of curiosity, but now I find that I am glad I could be of service. As she leaves the world of flesh, the fading chant of sorrow that comes is one bittersweet woman's wet death rattle. Jeanne's lungs have been sopping as sponges, and her heart has finally galloped its last. She's been gasping and gasping for days before this, and me unable to get out of her as the brine bubbled out of her mouth.

As Jeanne's awareness melts, like foam dissolves back into the sea, I wish I could melt with her. Mer, speechless. Makandal, captured; I am being no help to the Ginen.

But no, I'm lifting, soaring free of the swamp of Jeanne's syphilitic body. I am in my spirit body again! When I look at the skin of my forearms, it is still ghostly pale. The images that people make of me, that they dance to when I am not there, they are pale too. Those people know that I am a being without a body. I have no colour.

But I am free! I'm soaring, soaring. It's like dancing, like singing, this flight. Through and through the clouds until even they dry up and burn away with the heat of my passing. I fly even faster, to make more heat. I will have no more dampness about me, no more water, no more salt tears or piss or blood; no more flesh. The dry warmth that gathers about me is all I will have from now on. I soar on, fleeing the world I have failed.

Allelujah!" wailed old Cuba. "God be praised, Father!" She got to her feet. She tossed her hands in the air, tilted her head to the sky, eyes clenched shut. The Ginen congregation stopped its ragged singing of the hymn and turned to stare at her. "Allelujah!" she cried again, shaking her head back and forth. Beside Tipingee, Mer's shoulders shook with silent laughter. Father León, what a look he gave Cuba! Such behaviour in his church. But of course the old woman couldn't see him with her eyes closed. Tipingee grinned at Mer, sat cross-legged and waited to see what would happen next.

"Cuba," Father said, "compose yourself. That is not the way to behave in the house of our Lord!" Beside Tipingee, Fleur gave a low chuckle in her throat.

"But I feel it, Father!" Cuba told him. "I feel the spirit of our Lord." Still she kept her face turned to the sky, ignoring the world around her. She began to rock from side to side. Grinning, Oreste began to clap out a beat, to belt out the hymn in his sweet, piercing voice like a bell. Pretty soon, the other Ginen joined in. Mer clapped her hands too. So nice to see some pleasure on her face. It had been long. Mer had never been one to trust too much in good feelings. Now she had almost no reason to give thanks.

Some of the Ginen leapt up to dance. Yes. That felt like real joy, like real thanks to the gods. Tipingee began to sing along.

"No!" Father León shouted. "Stop, all of you!" He hustled out from behind his altar, Bible in hand. He ran over to Cuba where she stood barefoot on the cold ground. Shook her shoulder. She opened her eyes and looked at him, like she was waking from a dream. She brought her hands down to her sides. "Stop this!" he bellowed at the Ginen. Everyone stopped.

"Yes, that's better," Father said. Grave, he was. He straightened up and looked over all of his congregation. He shook his head. "Sometimes, God forgive me," he said in his outlandish Spanish accent, "I fear that they may be right who say that the African is as base as the monkeys in the trees, that he will never learn to truly love God."

No one said anything.

"What am I to do with you?" he asked.

"Sorry, Father," a man's voice mumbled.

Father looked out over the crowd, his mouth set hard. "I will start again," he said. "Cuba, you will say nothing for the rest of the service. Do you comprehend?"

Cuba looked down at the ground, then nodded, sullenly.

"Good. The rest of you, you will make the responses as I have taught you, and nothing else."

"Yes, Father."

"You will sing the hymn with grace and dignity, like good Christians. You will not clap your hands or drum, and by God, you will not dance."

"Yes, Father."

"Lord have mercy on us all." Shaking his head, he returned behind his altar and resumed the nonsense words of the service.

Tipingee sighed. She had wanted to water her pumpkin patch before the sun got too harsh. Sunlight on wet leaves would burn them. Her pumpkins would have to wait until this evening. She locked eyes with Mer, and was pleased to see her friend still laughing her quiet laugh. The simple amusement in Mer's eyes filled Tipingee's heart up, made her smile too. "Amen," she said at the end of the prayer. Mer looked at her, smiled back, then turned to look at the statue of the Virgin on Father's makeshift altar.

We had waited and waited to see if Makandal would return, but he didn't. My voice came back little bit. It's hoarse and low.

Hurts to use it too much, so I choose my words careful. Georgine is still teaching me my letters. My hands, so impatient with sewing, have finally found a use for it, other than closing up wounds. Georgine brings me scraps of cloth, bits of thread that our mistress gives her. There are wonderful colours some-times, and soft silks. I piece them together into squares. I whis-per to Georgine the words I want to embroider on them, and she writes them in the dust for me. With my needle and Mistress's threads, I copy the shapes onto the squares of cloth.

I give a light-skinned slave the courage to offer a gift of beauty and knowledge to a sad, powerful black woman. The bond between Georgine and Mer grows over the years, and the younger teaches the older to write words which she embroiders in flowing thread on banners which fly over Ginen celebrations, singing a song of freedom as they snap in the breeze.

With the thread, I paint pictures on the cloths: Lasirèn, Ezili, Ogu, Kouzin Aka. All the lwas. And the Lady too; Mother Mary. I paint her with thread onto bright flags. Because from all those Sunday mornings in Father's nigger church, I've come to under-stand something: I know who that Lady is. She's beautiful, the Lady. That much the blans understand. Father burns incense for her, for he knows she likes the sweet perfume of it. I must listen with more attention after this to what Father tells us of his gods. Maybe it's not all nonsense after all. One day in his church, when I looked at the Lady's pale face, I understood something, a small something. They had it wrong, the blans. Seems they get every-thing wrong. The Lady's gown should be pink and white, not blue and white. And her baby is a girl, not a boy.

She's pale, the Lady; a sang-melé. Pale and white, since she comes from the other world beneath the waters. That makes sense. Father calls her "Mary," but I know her real name. Ah, my Ezili Frèda, to see you in this place!

When the Ginen go in the nights to pray, to plan, Tipi and I take the cloths with us. We hang them in the trees. The breeze makes them flutter. They are our prayers, the prayers of the Ginen.

"I want to go back, Tipingee," whispered Patrice in the dark. We were sitting outside Tipi's and Patrice's cabin, talking by the light of one smelly lamp, slapping the mosquitoes as they landed on our skin. The night was burning hot, so we sat outside to get some little cool breeze. Plenty of time to scurry inside if we heard the book-keeper coming to make sure we kept curfew.

"You want to go back where, Patrice?" Tipingee asked.

Patrice put his chin on his knees. "To the bush," he said.

Tipingee turned to look at him. "What, back on marronage?"

"Yes."

"Back away from me?" she said, her voice quiet.

He tap-tap-tapped his palm against the ground, gently, like someone who wanted to hit harder but was preventing himself. "No, Tipi. Not away from you." I heard the pain in his voice. "Away from this place. Makandal's gone. More Ginen getting killed every day. We can't win against the backra. Why should I stay? You would come with me, Tipingee? Eh? I know the way. I could get us there safe."

Me, I held still and listened to my heart leap in my chest. Tipi, maybe gone from me. I waited to hear if they remembered me beside them. A lizard scurried by my toes. Hard to see in the dark. I think it had all its four feet, though.

"What is the bush like?" Tipingee asked Patrice. "How do you go there?"

He blew out air, looked up to the sky. "It's hard. When you're trying to reach it, you move fast, through the day, through the night. You climb up hills, down them. You have to cut through bush. The leaves have thorns sometimes, and sometimes the branches spring back at you and slice your skin. Flies follow your sweat by day, and mosquitoes follow your blood by night. They torment you. You can hear them whining in your ears, but you don't see them, only feel them when they bite. Pretty soon, you're covered all over in bumps and you're scratching them all the time. And you're hungry. Your food runs out quickly, and your water. If you don't find a stream, if you didn't bring anything to catch rain water in, you might die of thirst.

"Sometimes you come upon a cliff, and at the bottom of it, you see the sea, and the Cap over there. If that happens, it means you were going in circles, and you have to start over again. You try not to stop to sleep. When you can't go any more without sleep, you try to find a tree you can climb, so if the blans come after you with dogs, the dogs can't smell you out. You sleep in the tree, and every minute you wake up, frightened you're going to fall. I fell out of a tree once, still sleeping. Thought I had died when my body hit the ground. Thought a backra had shot me. During the day, you run, run. Sometimes you have to sneak into plantations to steal food. Dig up yams, cassava. Steal from other Ginen. Better to steal from them, 'cause sometimes if they catch you, they won't talk. They'll just watch you go. But you never know if they're going to keep quiet, or if they'll tell the blans and next thing you know, the dogs are after you. You eat the food raw, for the smoke from a fire might draw the blans to you. Your belly aches. You get the runs.

"Then you get there. You get to the deep bush. And it's *bush*. Dark like the devil inside there. Hot. You hear the crickets singing, and all the trees look same-same. No paths. You don't know where you're going, you just walk, and climb the endless hills. Don't know how to find food. More mosquitoes bite you. If night comes on you before the maroons find you, you don't know where to sleep. Wherever you lie down, you can feel things crawling over you in the dark. Hear things flying past your face. Bats, spirits, you don't know. And still you're hungry, and thirsty. When the maroons find you, you're so glad you just drop down on your knees. Then they put their guns to your head and ask you what you're doing there, if you've come to betray them to the blans."

"That's how it is?" said Tipi.

"There's more. You go with them, and your feet are sore from walking, and you don't know what's going to happen. It's more bush and bush and bush, and then you hear a parrot call. One of the maroon men calls back and you jump, for he sounds just like a parrot too. They make you turn a corner with them and push through some vines, and you're there. In a compound. An accompong. Like the Ashanti just come off the ships talk about. Black people walking everywhere, going about the business they *want* to be about. Smiling. There are children, Tipi! Not like here.

"The first few mornings, you wake up before the sun. You wake up at the time when the book-keeper would ring the bell. Your heart's pounding, 'cause you think you're late to go to the fields. And maybe you go to the fields, yes, but it's fields made by black people. It's food growing for black people to eat. No whips. When you get tired, you stop and go to the river for water.

"Few more days, and you realise you're walking different. Your back is straighter. You feel tall, tall. You're tired when you settle down to sleep at night, just like here on the plantation, but you fall asleep thinking of all the things your labour will bring for you. Not for your master. For you. That's what it's like."

"Oh . . ." Tipingee said. I nodded. I understood why Patrice wanted to go back.

"I told you I have another woman there, Tipi."

"Yes."

"She's young. She's strong. She would share the wives' work, and she would mind what you said. You would have no master, no mistress. Would be you giving the orders this time. I think I have a child there, too. You will come with me, Tipi?"

"Can Mer come too?"

"What?" Patrice sat up and looked at me like I suddenly just appeared there in front of him.

"Can Mer come with us, I said." Tipi looked at me. She hadn't forgotten I was beside them. "Do you want to go to the bush, Mer? With me and Patrice?"

I looked at this woman, my heart, my sister. By the lamplight, I could see her face glowing with the dream of a place where the Ginen could come home to themselves again. Could we ever get far enough to be free of the blans? Tipi, I want to go with you.

"No," I whispered. "I can't come."

"Why?" she cried out. She leapt to her feet. Patrice whispered for her to shush. She lowered her voice. I shut my eyes against the pain in it when she said, "Mer, you won't come with me? You won't come and live free with me?"

"Ti-Bois," I told her, my heart breaking, "he's getting big now. A few more years and his voice will deepen. He's learning healing well from me. Georgine has another baby coming. And Belle's hand is starting to heal. If I leave, would be no one to put compresses on it. And you know Hector has a sickness of the spirit. Days in the field, he works beside me and tells me how sad he feels all the time, how sleepy. I listen to him, Tipi. I think it helps him. When I can steal it off Master's trees without anyone seeing, I give Hector kowosol leaf tea at night. Won't make him happy, but he sips it, and looks into my eyes while he drinks, like a child gazes trusting at his mother's face. The tea helps him to sleep. I need to stay, Tipi."

She said nothing, only walked off into the darkness. I heard her footsteps, then they faded and there were only the crickets fiddling in the bushes. Beside me, Patrice sighed. I said to him, "You want me to come with you and Tipi?"

He sighed again. Considered. Replied, "If you come, I will treat you with honour. Like I do here."

It was truth. He was always respectful to me. And thoughtful to Tipingee. A younger wife would mean less work. But Patrice didn't say he *wanted* me to be there in the bush with them. I didn't remark on it. We sat together by the guttering lamp and waited for Tipingee to return with her answer.

With a final, grunting push, the woman squeezed the baby out from her. "It's a girl," said Tipingee. The child began to wail.

"How does she look?" I asked from where I sat on a stool beside the woman's palette. They had told us the woman's name, but I didn't remember. Mind getting dim nowadays.

"She looks strong," Tipingee replied, with a laugh in her voice. "She's wriggling so much, it's hard to hold her."

"Let me hold her," the child's mother said. Her voice sounded frightened.

"Don't worry." I leaned down and patted her arm. "Tipingee won't drop her. You know how many babies she's delivered with me? She's my hands and eyes now." Ah, Tipingee. A hard choice you made, staying with me in bondage instead of going to the bush and to freedom with Patrice. And every day I give thanks that you are here with me.

"I'm just washing her," Tipingee told us. The child's cries let me know when Tipingee sponged her with a wet cloth. "Here she is."

My darkened eyes saw Tipingee as a shadow, smelling sweet of rosewater, that came and knelt by the woman's side. "Oh . . ." the woman said.

"Let her take your nipple. It will comfort her. She's just made a hard journey."

She's got a harder journey coming, poor little slave girl, I thought, but I did not say it. There was no need.

Marie-Claire's husband had grown even richer than before. He had bought me and Tipi both now that we were too old to labour in the fields, and brought us to live with them here, not far from Cap Français. He had gentled little bit as he got older.

We were his, but he treated his wife's mother and her companion with what respect he could muster for slave women. For the first time in our lives, we had some ease. Tipi and I still ministered to the slaves on the nearby plantations, though. I felt sad when I thought of how I had failed Mami Wata. I had not discovered what she wished me to do. But I had taught Ti-Bois about her; what her favourite foods are, and colours. How to sing the songs that honour her. Ti-Bois is a man now, they tell me. Perhaps he will find a way to clear the spirit roads for Mami Wata.

The little girl was making strong sucking sounds. Mama, pray you that this one lives. No lockjaw or smallpox. "What will you call your child, mother?" I asked.

The woman's voice was soft, tired. "Dédée," she told us.

"Dédée Bazile," said Tipingee. This was Bazile's plantation, and his slaves took his name.

"Yes," the woman answered.

Dédée Bazile, they will call you Défilée when you and I march with the Haitian soldiers of the revolution, urging them to keep moving. They will call you mad after your brothers are massacred and grief makes you wild. They will call you sane again when you collect the torn pieces of the body of the black Emperor Dessalines who made the flag of the land he called Ayiti, as the original Taino inhabitants had named it. Dédée Bazile, they will obey you when you demand that Dessalines be buried. I call you Défilée Danto. Sister.

I wondered what would happen to people like us. There were more stories every day of slaves planning to rise up. Even the free coloureds, they were meeting and plotting how to get out from under blan laws which forbade them from voting, told their women how to dress. I think Makandal was right. There is a time to fight, fierce as a cornered dog, for your freedom. But I have not the heart for it. It is ugly in this world, and when the killing starts, the same stick will beat the black dog and the white. Mama, I pray I will be coming to you soon.

Forty days and forty nights,
Inna de wilderness.

—Jamaican folk song

There was a whispering, a whispering. Just inside my head. I could almost hear the words clearly. Sitting on a red desert rock, I pulled my spine up straighter. Judah, bless him, knew not to bother me when I got like this. I could hear him where he lay in the cave, keeping still in the heat of the day. I could hear his breathing. Could hear the scurrying of a scorpion behind that bit of scrub over there. Could hear my heart slushing in my chest.

I hadn't eaten in many days, nor drunk water, neither. When I did, the sound of the food moving in my belly and the shit moving through my gut were so loud that I couldn't hear anything else. So I took no food, no water. I needed to hear, to listen. What were they saying?

What are they saying? I strain to hear, to see. This young Meritet who holds me in her is learning to listen, and I along with her.

My womb had gone silent, too, I think. I hadn't bled again. I listened for it, coiled tight as a nut in my belly. Silence. Judah's body gurgled and grumbled in its sleep, noisy at its work of turning beans to shit, water to piss, air to breath. How could he stand all the noise? How could he sleep through it? How could he hear the whispering, if all that was in his ears was his own body's rumblings?

I quieted even my breathing and I listened, hard and deep. There came a voice, not spoken:

Blighted rock everywhere, and not a bit of shade. God of gods, which way is the fucking road?

Clearly, I was now listening so hard I could hear thoughts. That was not me, calling on some other man's god, nor Judah neither. I opened my eyes. There was the sound of feet scrunching on gravel, of a staff hitting rock. Lizards scurrying out of the way. My wide open ears heard the man thinking his own name. I stood, quickly, and scrabbled down to the foot of the rock, where I couldn't be seen from the direction he was approaching. "Zosimus," I called out.

"Wha . . . ?" came the deep voice. "Who calls my name?"

Judah was awake. I heard his eyelids blinking, tick, tick. "Judah," I whispered, "stay hidden." He rose to a crouch, but stayed inside the cave as I asked.

"Father Zosimus," I shouted again, "please stand off, for I am not dressed." My one good tunic had fallen apart. In the day's heat it was no matter. In the chill of night, I stayed warm inside the cave, under the rugs that Judah had brought there.

"Who is there?" said Zosimus. His feet were moving closer. A Christian monk like he would be horrified at my woman's naked flesh.

"Stand off, I said, for I am naked."

He gasped and stopped moving. There was a great bird, soaring high above us, hunting. I could hear the lazy flap of its wings. Zosimus's thoughts were all, *What's there? Who's that? Is she pretty?* Judah was mostly thinking, *What now?* These past weeks had been hard on poor Judah.

"Do you need assistance, my dear woman?" called the monk. I could hear that he meant it, too, would offer aid if I needed it. Even though a fragment of his mind was whispering words he strived to ignore, of bouncing breasts and bellies. A good man. Suddenly, I wanted to talk to him.

"Only throw me your cloak," I said, "that I might be covered." Judah, protective, made to come out of the cave and reveal himself, but I motioned him back. I stood behind my rock and waited. In these few short minutes, my hearing had grown even more keen. There was a snake, a day's walk away, winding across the sand from one rock to the shade of another. Far above me, the hawk saw a tiny mouse down on the ground. The bird snapped its wings shut and dove for the kill. The hopping mouse that was its prey ran some little way, its feet making a loud pat-a-tat in my ears. It only squeaked once when it was caught. The hawk fed, with wet, tearing sounds. My belly pulled about itself even tighter.

Zosimus was panting with the heat as he undid his cloak. Presently, he threw it up over the rock. It landed almost in my hands. "Thank you, Father," I said. The cloak was simple undyed homespun, the colour of my skin when I had been long out of the sun. It smelt sweaty. I heard the scritch, scritch of fleas clambering through its fibres. I tied it around my neck and gathered it about my body. "You may come and see me now," I told Zosimus. I sat in the shadow of the rock.

I could feel the eager curiosity that pulled him around the curve of the rock, and the disappointment when he spied me. He found me thin, the flesh of my face wasted. That surprised me. Had it been so long that I hadn't eaten? And Judah was always after me to drink water. I did sometimes, didn't I? Did I look so different from the beautiful girl who had entered the desert?

"Your name, girl?" said Zosimus. He was a big man, with a massive, hooking nose and a frizzy head of copper hair and beard. The beard was lighter in colour, as it often is with men, the hair of their chins being younger than that of the tops of their heads. His eyes were like the Nile at the point where it meets the sea: a vibrant brown with green moving in them. Judah was thinking that Zosimus would be handsome if he cleaned himself up a little. Judah was also thinking of lamb chops. His belly rumbled so loud that I expected Zosimus to hear it. He didn't, and he didn't hear the hawk take wing again, its belly full with meat. Maybe it had a baby in a nest somewhere. Maybe it would spit some of that food up to feed its child. My breasts no longer ached. Their milk had dried up.

"My name is Meritet," I said to Zosimus. "Will you sit with me?"

He did, lowering himself and his bags to the ground with a sigh. He had a rotting tooth. I could smell it. He had decided that I was a desert whore, one of those raving Christians who mortifies the flesh—and keeps it on her bones—by offering her body for money (muttering prayers to Jesus the while) to men passing through the desert. Let him think what he would. It was fun to listen to it.

"Do you need anything, child?" he asked me.

"Would you listen with me?" I replied.

"What? Listen to you?" He looked confused.

I shrugged. "All right. That'll do too."

Making more noise than the crashing seas, Judah had settled himself back down onto one of the rugs. He was dozing, his mind telling itself stories.

"Do you want me to hear your confession?" asked Zosimus. "Is that it?"

"What's a confession?" It was itchy under the smelly cloak.

"You're not a Christian, are you?" he said. Now he was thinking about people burning up in fires. I don't know why. It wasn't that hot here in the shade.

"No, I'm not much of anything, come to that," I said. "Nefer-kare wanted me to worship Hathor, and my mother worships Isis, and my father, well, I guess Bacchus. He likes a good cup of wine, Daddy does. At least he did the last time I saw him."

Zosimus looked pityingly at me. "Poor child, what has happened to you? Will you come back with me to the city?"

"No, I don't want to go back yet. It's quiet out here. You can hear the rocks breathe. Can't you hear them?"

"Rocks don't have life, Meritet."

"Don't they? How do you know? They expand when the sun is on them, I can hear it. And all through the night, when it's cool, they get smaller and smaller. And then big again during the day. That's like what our chests do when we breathe, isn't it? Only slower."

"The rocks get smaller?" He shaded his eyes and looked up at the big rock that was sheltering us. "What do you mean? This rock—it shrinks at night until it's a pebble?"

He wasn't very smart, this one. I put my hands up to my hair, which had wound itself into thick, tight locks. Each one cast out tendrils and tried to trap its neighbours. I was forever keeping them apart. With my hands, I separated some of the locks of hair, tearing them away from their sisters. "They don't shrink enough that you'd notice, Zosimus. Just a tiny little bit. I hear them creak as they do it. My ribs creak like that when they let air in and out of my lungs. Do you hear that? Do you hear your ribs creak?"

He gave a bemused little laugh. "I hear my belly rumble when I'm hungry," he said. "And if I've been running hard, or if I'm very frightened, I can sometimes hear my heart hammering in my chest. Feel it, is more like it. But no, I don't hear my ribs creak, except that time I was wrestling with my big brother when I was a child, and he sat on my chest. Thought he would crush me."

His chuckling made lines spring up on his tanned face. I liked that. He pulled a leather bottle from around his neck and offered it to me. "Would you like some water?"

I shook my head. "No. It makes too much noise inside me when I drink it."

He frowned. "You asked me what a confession is. It's when you tell a man of God your sins."

"Why would I do that?"

"So that he can implore God to forgive you."

"Why wouldn't I go to the temple and ask the gods myself?"

He unstoppered his bottle and drank from it. The swallowing sounded like rocks banging together. He wiped his mouth with the back of his hand and looked at me. "Well, there's no temple around here, is there?"

"No, I guess you're right. I went to the Church of the Sepulchre a little while ago, but I didn't ask the gods anything."

He looked shocked. "There is only one God at the Church of the Sepulchre; the true God of the Christians!"

He was a lot older than me. Before this, a man like him would have cowed me. But now, I had been a mother, if only for a little while. "Zosimus, that church is built over the tomb of your Jesus, right?"

"Yes, praise his name." He made the Christian sign on his chest. I made it with him, out of respect.

"And your God lives there too?"

"Well, yes, I suppose he does," he replied doubtfully.

"And I saw a statue to the virgin Meri there as well."

"Mary," he said, correcting my pronounciation. "Yes, the image of Christ's mother is also there in the church."

"So, that's three gods: Jesus, his father who has no name, and his mother Mary."

Zosimus gasped and traced the Christian cross in the air between us. "Child, you blaspheme! Mary is not a god!"

"But Jesus is, and your God is?"

"Ah, yes."

"So that's still two!"

He sighed. "They are two aspects of the same thing."

"Like Isis and Hathor," I said.

"Oh, God preserve me. Not like Isis and Hathor. Those are false gods, and base, being women."

He was making no sense. I decided to try talking about something else. "Father, I work in a tavern in Alexandria."

"So you *are* a prostitute, then. How sad."

383

I shrugged. "I'm a slave."

"You've run away from your master? Child, that is a sin."

"I'll go back soon. But listen. I came here, and I went to the church, and I thought it would be so wonderful, but I didn't like Capitolina, and when I tried to go into the church, I got sick, right there at the door."

He looked at me as though I were a leper. "You couldn't enter the house of our Lord," he whispered, "because you debauch your body with men."

I didn't know what he meant. "I fell right at the feet of the statue of that Meri woman, and I started bleeding, bleeding. Then I heard a woman's voice, and she told me . . ."

But Zosimus had leapt to his feet, a look of reverence on his face. "Our Holy Mother spoke to you?"

"No, not then, but after the bleeding stopped, and I was lying in a bed they gave me there, I kept thinking I could hear whispering. But it was too noisy in Capitolina."

He nodded slowly, signalled me to continue. I don't think he was really hearing me.

"I left the church and went down to the river, but I still couldn't hear clearly. I crossed the river, and I came here. And I've been sitting here being quiet, so quiet. I can almost make out the words. Can you hear them, Zosimus? Can you tell me what she is saying?"

"Meritet," he said, but his gaze on me looked right through me. "When last did you eat?"

"Oh, I don't eat any more. Except some beans sometimes."

"And you don't drink," he said, staring at the water bottle in his hand that I had refused. "How long have you been out here?"

"I don't know. Months and months, maybe. I'm not paying attention. I don't get my woman's blood any more, so I can't tell." Under a big stone beside the cave, buried to her nose in the cool sand, a frog shifted, waiting for the night.

"Our mother Mary talks to you, and you've been out here for years, and you neither eat nor drink," said Zosimus. He threw himself to his knees. That must have hurt. He bowed his head down to the sand. "Holy Lady," he muttered into his chest, "please bless me."

Clearly, he wasn't going to be any help. "Oh, just get behind me, Zosimus," I said irritably. "Over there, where I can't see you."

He turned his face up to me, blinking like a slow and stupid snake. I waved him away. "Go, I said. A little further off. And try to keep quiet for a while. I need to think."

He went! That big old man, he did what I told him to! I'd have to try that on Tausiris when I got back.

But I did need to think. Judah was quiet again, sleeping. Zosimus's raspy breathing and ragged heartbeat distracted me for a while, but soon they settled into a rhythm, like the beats that Nefer would play when we danced. I closed my eyes and settled deep within myself, hunting for the whispering. The words were coming clearer.

"Are you ready to hear me now?" said the voice from within. It seemed I could hear the water running deep beneath the desert sands, could hear the fluttering flames of the sun.

"Yes, I think so," I replied.

The words were coming clearer. "I'm ready to hear you now," I said to the whispering voices. I settled in the flowing aetheric, and calmly paid attention.

First, an egg rolled to my feet, sealed and perfect. I tried to pick it up. It weighed as much as the universe. I let it be, rolling in a tight circle around its smaller end. Lightning cracked and thunder roared, delivering two people to stand in front of me. A woman and a man. They looked like my

cousins, and they too had more echoes than I cared to number.

Voices, millions of them echoing, telling me what I had done. I strained to hear, to make myself sit so lightly on the sand that my body wouldn't rasp against it and drown out their words.

My/I sisters were all there too, of course. An old man, a peasant man, came limping on a crutch. He wore a battered hat on his head. He smiled at the company gathered, and they welcomed him in, patting his back and greeting him like a cousin.

I had been a good friend to Neferkare Little Doe, and to Drineh and Cups and Judah. I had loved my mother and my father. I had desired to see some of the world, and I had done it. And what else, I asked them? Light, so light I made myself, to hear them better.

A man stepped out of a ship, which had borne him on the belly of my Lasirèn self. A giant snake traced its infinity sign path in the aether as it approached. As they saw it, all the women, even me/we, went to our knees, our breasts in our hands, and made reverence.

I had carried that child in the blood of my belly, like a ship on the sea. I had made it a home, even though I hadn't known it was there. Is there more? I couldn't feel my body on the sand, so hard I was listening.

A power of disease oozed towards us, in the leaking sores of smallpox. He could ravage worlds.

The child wasn't built well, couldn't live, so its spirit went back between the worlds. There will be other children in the world. Not my fault! My soul leapt with joy.

A thickly muscled man with a mad smile came running heavily into the circle. His selves brandished an axe; a machète; a sword. I matched his grin. *"Husband,"* I greeted him.
He laughed. *"Wife. You know us now?"*

I knew it now. I had done no wrong. My name is Meritet, and I had been pregnant, and I was no longer. I could think that now, and be at peace with it.

"I know you,"* I tell him. One of his echoes is Makandal, hale and still full of fight. I smile at him/them. *"I don't fight this fight alone, do I? I can be water and anger and beauty and love, but there is also iron and fire, warfare and thunder and storm."
***"And sickness,"* says the smallpox one.**
***"And family,"* says our cousin in his battered hat.**
***"And death, and change,"* says one I didn't see before, for he never keeps still.**
"There's healing, and mothering, and age."
***"And youth,"* say a pair of beautiful twin children, brown arms about each other.**
***"There's infinity,"* hiss the snake and the egg.**
We are all here, all the powers of the Ginen lives for all the centuries that they have been in existence, and we all fight. We change when change is needed. We are a little different in each place that the Ginen have come to rest, and any one of is already many powers. No cancer can fell us all, no blight cover us completely.

I shouted out loud with the joy of it. Zosimus exclaimed in fear. Judah woke, banged his head on the cave ceiling as he sat up to run to me. I laughed. I was light. "I still have my doll with me," I told them. They were in front of me now, gazing up at me, thunderstruck. "I have the doll Daddy made," I said.

Zosimus stared at Judah crouching there, Judah's tawny bush of hair and beard, the fuzz that had covered his thin body since he hadn't been eating so well. The many hairs glowed in the sun. "A lion," Zosimus whimpered, and backed away.

I ignored him. "The first few nights here," I told them, "I clutched it to me when I slept. But it's not my baby. I never even wanted a baby. I'll bury it tonight. I'm grown now. It's time to let it go."

"Meri," said Judah quietly, as you would to calm a wild beast, "you're floating."

I was. Sitting on the air like on a pillow. Wonderful. Zosimus made the sign of the cross again, and started praying for all he was worth. "Mary, Mother Mary, bless me," he was saying. He was looking right at me. The silly man was praying to me.

It was nice up here. I could see so far!

But Judah looked frightened. So I climbed down from the air, went and stood beside him. He reached out and touched my shoulder, my hair. "Oh, don't look at me like that," I said. "I'm better now. Want to go find this uncle of yours I keep hearing about?"

Judah made a small sound in his throat. His face had changed too, in our time in the desert. He looked older. Slowly, his eyes began to see *me,* not the crazy girl who floated. "You do?" he asked. "You really want to go? Now?"

"Yes, I do. It's boring here." I was already in the cave, rolling up the rugs. I threw Judah's clothes out to him. "Come on, let's leave." I found my doll, hugged her to me, then tucked her under my arm. I'd bury her tonight, wherever we were. I stepped back outside. Judah was still standing there. I could hear Zosimus paternostering away somewhere off to my right. Judah was still looking at me like he didn't quite know me. "Thank you," I said to him quietly. "I've been just sitting here moping all this time, and you've been really kind and patient."

"How're we going to pay our way to Uncle Lev's?" he asked.

"The way we know best, Judah. On our backs."

He laughed then, and some of the old Judah came back into his face. He picked up one rug. I got the other, tucked my doll into it. He said, "We'll have to clean ourselves up first, though. We look awful."

"We can wash in the Jordan. That'll be good enough."

Mary of Egypt lived alone there in the desert for forty years, eating only herbs and green beans. One day a monk, a holy man named Zosimus who had come to pass the month of Lent in the desert, heard Mary of Egypt call out to him by his name. She begged him to lend her his cloak so that she might cover her nakedness and accept a blessing from him. She told Zosimus the story of her previous dissolute life, and they prayed and conversed together. She had received no teaching in the scriptures, yet through prayer and fasting had been able to hear the word of the Lord. She begged Zosimus to meet her at the river Jordan the following year and administer to her the Blessed Sacrament.

Zosimus returned to the monastery, and a year later, came back to the river Jordan bearing a small portion of the undefiled Body and precious Blood of the Lord Jesus Christ. When he arrived at the spot that he and Mary had chosen, she appeared on the opposite bank of the river. She made the sign of the cross upon her body, and thereupon walked upon the waters to meet Zosimus on the other side. He gave her Holy Communion. She raised her hands towards the heavens and thanked God for her salvation. She asked Zosimus to come to her again in a year's time, to the spot where he had first found her, where she would be in whatever condition God ordained.

Zosimus went away again. When he returned a year later to the spot where he had first found Mary of Egypt, he discovered her corpse, guarded by a lion, and miraculously uncorrupted. Scratched into the ground beside her was a note that she had died on the same night a year before that Zosimus had given her communion. The note requested that he bury her body in the desert.

With the help of the lion, Zosimus dug a grave. He buried the body of Mary and prayed for her soul. He returned to his monastery to tell for the first time the wondrous tale of Mary of Egypt.

—Adapted from various Catholic texts about the life
of Saint Mary of Egypt, the "dusky" saint,
patron saint of sailors and prostitutes

Zosimus gave us some of his drinking water for the trek. My keen hearing was fading, but I could hear the great huge stories he was inventing to tell about me and Judah when he got back to the monastery. Me, a pious Christian saint, repentant of her wanton ways, expiring as she achieved the pinnacle of her holiness. Judah, a fierce lion guarding my miraculous unrotting corpse. Zosimus was as bad as Antoniou. When Judah and I set off towards Capitolina, Zosimus was still kneeling in the sand, staring at us.

I hoped we'd get there quickly. Damn, I was hungry.

Acknowledgements

They say that it takes a village to raise a child. Sometimes it feels as though it takes a village to make a book. In the years during which I've been writing this novel, a veritable colloquium of friends, colleagues, and strangers have provided me with critique, historical references, research, information, shelter, food, money when I had none, and introductions to people who could help me. I cannot thank them enough for their immense generosity and the incredible gift of their time, which more than ever, I recognise as precious. To the names I've remembered and—mea culpa—the ones I have not, boundless gratitude and thanks to you all, including: Ibi Aanu, Patrick Barnard, Shelley Bates, Isobel Bedingfield, Judith Berman, Jihane Billacois, Jayme Blaschke, Jennifer Busick, Richard Butner, Rich Bynum, Susan Casper, Ted Chiang, Austin Cooke, Myriam Chancy, Candas Jane Dorsey, Gardner Dozois, Andy Duncan, Sudharshan Duraiyappah, Suzette Haden Elgin, Carol Emshwiller, Karen Joy Fowler, Robert Frazier, Greg Frost, David Findlay, John Garrigus, Gayle Gibson, Molly Gloss, Lyn Green, Peter Halasz, Rebecca Handcock, Liz Henry, Russ Howe, Peter Hudson (who may well have gotten me started by sending me an article that got me thinking), Ethan Joella, Jim Kelly, Judith Kerman, John Kessel, Ellen Klages, Sarah Leslie, Jonathan Lethem, Jaime Levine, Kelly Link, Donald Maass, Nancy Mayer, Nathalie Mège, Farah Mendlesohn, Betsy Mitchell (who first said "yes"), Nadine Mondestin, James Morrow (O, long-suffering soul!), Kathy Morrow, Pamela

Mordecai, Bruce Myer, Marie-José N'zengou-Tayo (respé!), Roland Ottewell, Kevin Quashie, Renée Raduechel, Juan Rodríguez, Kris Kathryn Rusch, Penina Sacks, Ita Sadu, Jason Schmetzer, Les Shelton, Delia Sherman, Midori Snyder, Maryvonne Ssossé, Jennifer Stevenson, Bruce Sterling, Pat York, Ryan Williams, Walter Jon Williams, Betty Wilson, Marlene Ziobrowski, the students, faculty and staff of the Writing Popular Fiction program at Seton Hill University, the incredible knowledge bank of the folks on the listservs of fem-sf, the Writers' Union of Canada, and the "research" and "ask-the-expert" boards of sff.net. Blessings and thanks too to the institutions that preserve history, among them: the Toronto Public Library system, with its Reference Library and its Black History/West Indian collections, and the Royal Ontario Museum. I want to particularly thank writers Joan Dayan (*Haiti, History and the Gods*), Ron Eglash (*African Fractals*), F. W. J. Hemmings (*Baudelaire the Damned: A Biography*), and the late Angela Carter ("The Black Venus") for their inspiring words, and John Garrigus, whose translation of the words of Moreau de Saint-Méry ended up not being used. Much appreciation to the many lives, from the oldest ancestors to the youngest, whose stories gave me the material with which to make this story. I've done you justice as best I could. I beg your understanding. And, as ever, much love and respect to my mother Freda and my brother Keïta, always steadfast in their enthusiasm and encouragement.